LORD DISMISS US

Other Phoenix Fiction titles from Chicago

A Use of Riches by J. I. M. Stewart
The Department by Gerald Warner Brace
Bright Day by J. B. Priestley
The Good Companions by J. B. Priestley
Angel Pavement by J. B. Priestley
The Survival of the Fittest by Pamela Hansford Johnson
In the Time of Greenbloom by Gabriel Fielding
Solomon's Folly by Leslie Croxford
The Last, Long Journey by Roger Cleeve

Michael Campbell

LORD DISMISS US

The University of Chicago Press
Chicago and London

THE UNIVERSITY OF CHICAGO PRESS, CHICAGO 60637
THE UNIVERSITY OF CHICAGO PRESS, LTD., LONDON

Library of Congress Catalog in Publication Data

Campbell, Michael, 1924–
    Lord dismiss us.

    (Phoenix fiction series)
    Reprint. Originally published: New York: Putnam,
1968.
    I. Title.   II. Series.
PR6053.A4883L6   1984   823'.914   83-18173
ISBN 0-226-09244-5 (pbk.)

LORD DISMISS US

CHAPTER ONE

"Ah, hah! You pampered Asiatic jades!"

Eric Ashley flung wide the door of the classroom and struck a Tamburlaine attitude, throwing his gown back over one shoulder and cracking an imaginary whip. He adopted a sneering expression, with his eyes fixed upon two boys in the front row. The veins at either side of his impressive forehead throbbed.

"You are twenty-five minutes late," said Carleton. "As usual."

"And you won't bluff us by shouting," added Johns. "This is costing our parents money."

"Pampered wenches."

The pose remained, but his eyes had moved over the room. "Where is Master Steele? Or did he go forth into the big rude world?"

"He didn't," said Carleton. "He's been out looking for you. As usual. We can't be bothered. It's too boring. Anyhow, he came back and said you hadn't slept in your room. The Pedant's taking Latin next door, and he told him to go off and tell the new Head. We decided you hadn't an idea when the term began and were probably off in Rome or somewhere."

"Knowing your predilections," said Johns.

There was silence. He stared at Johns, and for a moment they were afraid that the subject had become too tender.

"And how does the creature know whether my room has been slept in or not slept in?"

"Matron let him in," said Carleton, and all ten of them laughed.

Ashley ran his fingers through his straight blond hair, breathing through tight nostrils. "Into my boudoir?"

"Yes. Through the dispensary."

7

"There is no such entry, you servant girl."

"Of course there is. Didn't you know?" said Johns.

Ashley picked up the book with which they all had been supplied, saw that it was *Phèdre,* and said fiercely, *"C'est Venus toute entière a sa proie attachée."*

"I hope that has no relevance," Carleton remarked.

"Witty fellow," said Ashley, moving over to the window which looked out onto herbaceous borders and lawns and upon the low house opposite. In the relaxed atmosphere of the end of the last term, someone had affixed to its pink-tiled roof an enormous notice—PEDANT'S PALACE—referring to the distinguished housemaster who lived there. Ashley's gaze was abstracted, but even so he registered mild surprise that the notice remained in place. He then observed Steele walking along the path between the borders. "Ah, hah, Judas *s'approche.*"

"Are you speaking of the senior prefect?" said Johns.

"I hope you're not seeing visions again," said Carleton.

"Did you return that book, you pale, puerile Protestant?"

"What book?"

"The account, by that good fellow and saint, the Abbé Duval, of the smiling vision of St. Catherine of Compostela, twice seen by him in the foliage of a plane tree at Châlons-sur-Marne."

"Of course I did. Ages ago. I didn't believe a word of it."

"That's enough. *Ça suffit.*"

"Are you going to teach us French now?" inquired Johns.

Steele entered. He was the senior prefect. He intended to make a career of the army.

"Oh, sir, you're here."

"Our time is short for idle gossip. Where have you been, child?"

"Well, sir, you weren't—"

"Sit down, Steele, dear boy. You have worked hard for the public good, and must be weary. Tell us about your odyssey. Did you have the great fortune to encounter our new headmaster?"

"Not just now, but—"

"Hélas!" Ashley made a gesture with an open hand in the manner of the Comédie Française.

"I knocked on the study door, but there was no answer."

"Ahh. What mystery have we here?"

"Have *you* met him, sir?" The question came from the back.

"No, my dear Petty. I have not. I returned this morning from Assisi. From Assisi, Carleton."

"How was St. Francis?"

Ashley stared him in the eye and breathed, but could not resist a smile. It was startling when it happened—a transformation. A smile of great charm. An aging troubled spirit became a good-looking fair-haired young man of twenty-four.

Carleton, encouraged, and pleased, as they all were, added, "That explains the empty boudoir, anyhow."

But Ashley had moved toward him, taking the gown from off his shoulder, and was striking Carleton with the end of it and saying, "You are an impertinent child."

Carleton caught it.

"Let go."

"I won't."

"Let go, Carleton."

They were pulling at the gown.

Ashley flushed.

"Let go, Carleton."

"No."

Ashley turned scarlet, and the two veins stood out, and he shouted, "I shall have you *whipped,* sir!"

Carleton let go.

Ashley moved away and returned to the window. He was recovering. He swept his gown over his shoulder, Roman style, and looked out, with his eyes wrinkled up against the light. He seemed, again, far older than his years. He sniffed, and tweaked his nose with two fingers.

"What exactly happened to the Horrors?" asked Johns.

"When a man devotes his life to Herodotus, he deserves a better name," said Ashley.

"He was supposed to be devoting his life to *us,*" said Carleton.

"So he did. So he did. The dear sweet old man."

"We hardly ever saw him," Johns pointed out.

"He was ever present. Someday even *you* will understand, Johns."

"We know he died on vacation, but how?" asked Carleton.

"Are you Agatha Christie's favorite nephew, sir? Is it im-

9

portant, damn you? His heart gave up. He had one, poor man. He had one."

They sat watching his cheekbones agitating, in profile. Carleton especially could see that there was much there, but like the others, he ascribed it to an adult world. It was remote, and beyond reach. Nevertheless, sympathy and curiosity drew from him a remark that *was* daring: "He once said you were brilliant."

A little spasm went over Ashley's profile. He continued to gaze through the window. Then he turned slowly and looked at Carleton with an empty expression. "To who?"

"To all of us."

Ashley examined them all, but they did not feel that he was seeing them. "Pah!" he said, and turned and picked up a piece of new chalk from his desk. He wrote on the blackboard the word "The," and the class roared it out in unison as he did so. Again they loudly declaimed the words, one by one, as he wrote them ornately in a circle: "The birde has flowne."

Then, they cheered as he hurled the chalk at the back wall and swept out of the room.

A tinny bell was ringing for the eleven o'clock break, and the classrooms were emptying into the long sunny corridor, down which steamed Jimmy Rich, looking like the people's choice. His teeth were smiling and flashing. His black hair, parted down the middle, swooped up in waves. He had a dimple in his square chin. He should have been wearing a gown for class, but he was not. His sports coat was flaming orange and purple. His shoes of burnished gold clacked loudly on the red-tiled corridor. The boys were scattering before the wave of his approach. They were asking him if there was to be cricket that afternoon, but he was laughing them off.

"Now then, lads. Now then, lads. Stand away now. Eric!"

Ashley, who was walking between the herbaceous borders, with boys rushing past him, halted and looked around in perplexity, closing his eyes a little because he had short sight.

"Well, me bold Eric. And where have *you* been?" asked Rich, placing a large hand on Ashley's shoulder and unwittingly moving him along at a faster pace than before.

10

Ashley felt the indignity, yet it was both odd and pleasing that this being from another world evidently sensed something human in himself.

"We are buffoons again," he said.

"Cheer up," said Rich, releasing him. "The first day's the worst."

"Or are we?" said Ashley. "How can we know the dancer from the dance?" It was an open question from his beloved Yeats.

"Do *you* know you were supposed to be here yesterday, me lad?"

Rich had captained Ireland at rugby. A great hooker. Protestantism had compelled him to teach the game at an English public school.

"I was not apprised of that," said Ashley.

Rich laughed, and shouted after a passerby, who had leaped over one of the borders, "Off the grass, boy!"

There were imitations behind them of "Off the grass, me boy!"

"Your cheerfulness makes me feel ill," Ashley murmured.

"You can thank Nancy for that."

Ashley glanced at his companion. It was so rare—such openness, such proud and childlike love. "I understand your good Matron has been admitting people to my boudoir."

"Ha, ha, haah!" Rich's laugh was an explosion. His large but remarkably liquid frame quivered. "Don't tell that to Crabtree. He gave us half an hour each on morals yesterday."

"You mistake my meaning," said Ashley. "Ah, no. No, no. The Matron, too?"

"Joker," said Rich. "No, not Nancy, God love her."

Ashley found it strange that Rich was a good ten years older than himself—and the Matron older still. Rich had arrived last term, and this late romance had bloomed slowly, under daily scrutiny by two hundred boys and a staff of twenty-odd, though less so by the latter, because a games master was a person slightly out of line.

"Anyhow, you've missed nothing. He told us to tell you he wants to see you at half eleven."

"Indeed."

A vine as old as the school formed an arch. They had passed under it and were walking between more borders. There was an ancient mulberry in the center of a lawn, which had just been cut, to greet those returning, by a septuagenarian named Gregory. And there were two old pear trees against a reddish wall.

It was properly civilized, Ashley thought, and antique, but it smelled of captivity. It was not a university garden.

The hoped-for Cambridge lectureship had gone to a well-known English poet. He had visited Assisi to see the Giottos again and to talk with his good friend Father Paolo Mancini.

"You're an odd lad, Eric. You haven't even asked me what he's like."

The buildings ahead were taller and gray. The bright class-rooms and Pedant's Palace were the new buildings, and these the old. Boys rushed past toward the dining hall, where milk and biscuits were being served. Ashley did not see them. He saw an elderly gentle man, by name Greville Wilks, translator of the complete and final Herodotus, one who strangely resembled his late dear father.

"It seemed of small import," he said.

"What! Are you kidding? There'll be changes all right. You'll see."

"Classic situation," said Ashley. "Dear Mother of Christ."

Rich was confused, also a little embarrassed, being an Irish Protestant.

A narrow gate led away into the Quad.

"*Au revoir*," Ashley said, with a slight bow.

"Don't be late now, or you *will* be in for it."

"Have no fear."

Ashley went through the gateway and, once in the Quad, was reminded that this elegant forum for a young and dangerously live community was dominated by a memorial to the dead. The mown lawn and bank mounted to a stone cross, set against the trees of the distant wood.

He suffered a clouding of the spirit, a sense of absolute futility.

But it passed. The day was as sunny as Italy, and he was curious to see his bedsitting-room, his partial home, particularly since it must contain a door that he had not yet spotted.

CHAPTER TWO

"According to my informant, Mr. Ashley was seen walking up the drive at ten fifteen," said Mrs. Crabtree. She was standing in front of the grandiose fireplace in the Head's study, with her eyes on the ceiling and her hands behind her back.

Her husband sat at his desk at right angles to one of the two fine windows. This was their first public school; but they had already run two prep schools, and he knew that she never entered his study without information. Where it came from, he seldom knew. It was usually valuable and frequently alarming.

"His luggage consisted of a briefcase."

"Oh?"

It seemed to him a very modern word, though it came from the Latin. She was always surprising.

"It must have given him little time to attend to the sixth form," she added.

Philip Crabtree pulled down the corners of his mouth. His lips were almost purple, with the lower one protruding, and his face was rubicund. His hair was sandy, turning gray, and it had been cut high above the ears, to show that there was going to be no malingering.

"We intend to put a stop to that sort of thing, if it exists," he said.

"You are going to be busy."

Her eyes came down from the ceiling and, after some little dips of her chin, settled on the floor.

He knew these budgerigar-like dips; they indicated extra relish. Something shocking was probably on the way.

"How do you mean?" he murmured.

"One has heard things," she said.

He had a disturbing suspicion that she meant brand-new

13

things. But he said, "Old Wilks had been here too long, Cecilia. There has been slackness—both in the classroom and in the field. Maybe other things besides. But that is why we have been appointed. The school is small, but well placed on the list. It is our job to set it to rights, and I am confident we shall."

She had meant brand-new things, but she decided to postpone her news.

They were on a high hill in Buckinghamshire. The Head's House was Georgian and pink and formed the center of the façade. The windows gave onto a long grass slope, the cricket field, a small lake, trees, and, farther off, the village of Marston.

"The setting is noble," he said, glancing at the view. "We must see that the spirit matches it."

"I should have thought that was the province of our chaplain," she said.

The chaplain was the Reverend Cyril Starr, and all that Crabtree had encountered to date was a sphinxlike appearance and a perturbing smile at any reference to higher things. He had placed a question mark against his name on the list, also a *B*. He was one of fourteen bachelors.

"I was speaking of the school spirit. There is a greater challenge even than bringing Weatherhill up to the mark. They say that the system is finished, out-of-date, and worse besides. I intend to prove them wrong."

She did not look at him but heard him with respect. Determination was his outstanding gift. Unprepossessing, puritanical, humble in the presence of titled folk, and the possessor of a second-class degree in history, he had nevertheless brought two prep schools out of near collapse into the house-full category in double-quick time. Herself the possessor of an astonishing first in classics, she had sensed his fortitude and his ambition, and married him for it. She had hopes of a major school.

"Steele will be a tower of strength," said the Head.

"I am informed," said Mrs. Crabtree, "that Steele only holds his position through the refusal of Master Carleton—now the second prefect."

For a moment she feared an apoplexy.

"Are you telling me that Carleton refused the offer of the senior prefectship?"

"I understand he expressed a disinterest in the running of

14

the school. There was also some vague excuse of work. And I'm told he received the secret support of two housemasters." She waited and looked at the floor. "Dr. Rowles and Mr. Milner."

Mr. Milner was the Pedant. Dr. Rowles had been assistant headmaster through four reigns and most of his forty-seven years at Weatherhill, and a question mark had been placed against his name.

"I'll have a word with Carleton," said Crabtree, who could scarcely speak. "If Ashley doesn't look smart, I'll have to send a boy for him."

"Might I stay for the interview?"

He looked up in surprise, and could see no alternative. "If you wish."

"I am interested in our Mr. Ashley."

He did not dare wonder why. His eyes strayed to the school magazines.

"One can see here the way the wind's been blowing," he said, tapping at them with a knuckle.

Mrs. Crabtree had marked certain entries to bring this point to his attention.

He pulled down his mouth as he read again the news from boys recently departed. She had made a cross with a red pencil against their names.

"P. L. Graham—I have been working as a clerk on the Midland region of British Railways at Crewe, but six months ago I received promotion to a better position at Paddington Goods Station."

Incredible. And there were more.

"H. J. Huggett—Being posted to Bournemouth I was fortunate in being provided with an Austin Mini. My work entails visiting our shops in the Hampshire area which boasts 47 branches. Bournemouth is a very pleasant seaside resort which I can firmly recommend to anyone in search of an uncluttered holiday with ample variety."

There was even a case of possible unbalance.

"M. L. Ivor—My rank is captain, but I do not use it in private life. Next month I shall be on holiday in the Isle of Man which will be the fifth country I have visited—Ulster and Eire, England and Wales, and now the Isle of Man!"

15

But the Head's features relaxed, and he nodded with satisfaction as he turned to an earlier copy of the magazine and read the entry from an old boy who had left Weatherhill twelve years ago. Mrs. Crabtree had used a *blue* pencil and made a tick.

"I have started up rugby among the Africans, and we trounced some European teams in our very first season. These fellows score tries at tremendous speeds. My African house-boy I have had since the old Chimvu days brought large crowds to their feet simply ripping through the field. It is one of the conditions *in or near* my house that the chap must be prepared to learn rugby."

"This is the spirit we shall recapture," said Crabtree, tapping the paper. "We may not be colonizers anymore. But we can be leaders. It is *not* the function of a public school to produce underdogs."

His wife felt a thrill, mingling pleasure and disgust.

Ashley knocked and entered.

The room disconcerted and then distressed him. The Old Man's library—his leather-bound volumes, even the shelves—had gone and had been replaced by pale gray wallpaper. There was a new green carpet. A cold wind had blown through, dispelling the pipe smoke of decades. The Old Man's portrait was changed into the self-consciously authoritarian profile of the rosy gentleman who sat at the desk in his chair. Before the painting a wide-hipped but by no means heavy lady in crossword-puzzle tweed scrutinized the wall above Ashley's head.

"Come in, come in, Mr. Ashley. I'd like you to meet my wife."

A small cold white hand came from behind her back. Ashley could scarcely feel it.

"Headmaster has granted permission for my presence," she said, over his head.

Shy and determined, he thought, a troublesome combination. In spite of the hint of mockery, her words were pretentious.

"I see."

"Well, let's get on, shall we?"

"Let's try."

Ashley didn't mean to say it audibly. But the sense of shock hadn't left him. They were impostors in this room.

Apart from a slight pursing of the lips, Mr. Crabtree might not have heard. "Please take a seat."

Mrs. Crabtree was now looking at the floor; this meant that she had made a quick scrutiny in passing. She had seen a young squire in a brown tailored glen-check suit, with elegant handmade shoes.

"I've been glancing through examination results, Ashley— I'll call you Ashley, if you don't mind; I prefer to be called Headmaster, it makes things simpler for all concerned—in English and French, that is, among the senior boys, and I find, well, the most extraordinary variations. Some of the marks . . . Carleton's here, for instance, in this scholarship of his . . . are outstanding. While others . . . a considerable number . . . seem to come terrible croppers."

"We all have our favorites," said Mrs. Crabtree. "I have been a teacher myself."

"That is *not* what I was suggesting, my dear."

"I should hope not, Headmaster," said Ashley.

"I apologize for misunderstanding," said Mrs. Crabtree.

Ashley had noted her photograph as a young woman in a silver frame on the desk: intelligent, quite a beauty, but remote. A graduate in something. Chin up. A strangely period photograph, although her hair was exactly as now, held by a hairpin above each temple and waving up into a clump over her ears. The eyes were beautiful—large and sad.

"What I imagined, Ashley, was that the more advanced teaching comes more easily to you."

"Some learn. Some don't."

"But, uh, my dear fellow, that is the point. At Weatherhill we want *everyone* to learn."

"You want the impossible."

"Now listen to *me*, Ashley—"

The door opened, and a girl in jeans posed against the wall on which had once hung a charming moth-eaten tapestry. It was gone. She looked sulky. She had her mother's brown eyes. She said, "Miss Bull won't give me lettuce for the rabbits."

"Oh, really!" exclaimed her father. "Leave this room at once. You are *not* to interrupt me in this way."

"I'll speak to her shortly, Lucretia," said Mrs. Crabtree.

17

"They're hungry," said the girl, calmly leaving the room but shutting the door hard.

"My daughter, Lucretia. She's fourteen, I regret to say," remarked Mrs. Crabtree.

"Now listen to me, Ashley—"

"Regret?"

"It is not quite the place. I fear for her virginity."

"Ashley! Will you kindly listen to me?"

"Very well."

"This is the main reason why I wanted to see you people. It's quite clear to me that standards have been allowed to slip for many years. My predecessor was far too old. He should have retired long ago—"

"I disagree."

"I will not tolerate interruption! You may or may not know, there have been two new appointments to our Board of Governors, coincident with my own as headmaster. Lord Mountheath and Sir Charles Pike are absolutely behind me in the need to bring back the public school spirit to Weatherhill."

"I've never been quite clear what that means," said Ashley.

"That is only too evident. One of the things it means, Ashley, is that the whole team scores good marks, for the honor of the school. And if this means that on your part you give less attention to individuals like Carleton and more to the general good, then so be it."

"It's a wonder the Labor Party doesn't approve."

"Kindly allow me to speak. And if it means that Carleton must forgo special attention for the general good, then so be it. A boy who refuses to be senior prefect has obviously something else that is more important for him to learn than French."

"The school spirit?"

"Exactly. He must learn that he is a member of a team. I intend to have everybody at Weatherhill joining in and pulling together."

"You should have no trouble about that."

Mrs. Crabtree looked quickly at Ashley, glanced at her husband, and returned to the ceiling.

"You think not?" said the Head in complete surprise.

"A great many are addicted to it already, I understand."

"I don't follow you, Ashley. That is far from my information.

I am speaking of corporate pride. We must regard ourselves as members one of another."

"That's pretty well what I meant."

"A school is like a ship. I may be the captain, but we must all sail her together."

"Heave ho, me hearties," said Ashley.

There was a scarlet, amazed silence from the Head. A faint pink came over his wife's cheeks. She needed a shave, Ashley noticed. He himself was trembling.

She was the first to recover.

"Mr. Ashley would seem to be amusing himself at our expense, Headmaster," she said.

Crabtree, already alight, heard the familiar relish in her voice and exploded. "Any more of this from you, Ashley, and I shall go to the board and request your resignation. I will not stand for it! I have now told you your obligations. You had better fulfill them."

"One is not compelled to listen to cant," said Ashley. "You must excuse me. I have to introduce Milton to some small boys."

So saying, he rose and walked out of the room.

Mrs. Crabtree was again the first to recover.

"We shall have to watch our Mr. Ashley," she said with several dips of the chin.

No reply was forthcoming or necessary.

CHAPTER THREE

 Unimpressed by the new appointment and uninterested in rumors of change, the Reverend Cyril Starr sent out word that all Starlings would be welcome for tea from four o'clock on.

He did not call them Starlings. But he had been here for twenty-three years, and he knew well that this was what they were contemptuously known as by those who were not among the chosen. It amused him mildly, as did almost everything else.

The chaplain had the most luxurious appointments of any member of the staff, and the only ones that were in the Head's House. They were at the top, on the second floor. There was an unfortunate proximity to those in command. Hitherto this had given him little concern, but he was not happy about the new arrivals, both of whom he already disliked. (The daughter was disliked as a matter of course, young girls being hors de question.)

All afternoon a trail of Starlings came past the oaken chest that had reputedly belonged to Lady Jane Grey, into the rear of the main hall, and up the fine staircase. Mud came with them. Mrs. Crabtree intercepted three, complained about the mud, asked each where he was going, and received a disturbingly direct answer.

She also intercepted Philomena Maguire, an Irish witch whose height was six foot two under a mop of black hair which covered her eyes. She could look out, but nobody could look in. It was an unintentional but ingenious arrangement. Philomena was carrying a large silver tray, loaded with cakes, cups and saucers of priceless china, and an exquisite silver teapot. The same question was put to her, and she looked out through her hair at this peculiar woman and replied, "It's the chaplain's tea. I always do it, miss."

"Mrs.," said Mrs. Crabtree.

"Mrs.," said Philomena.

Mrs. Crabtree shivered. This girl was one of a terrifying company of black-clothed, occasionally white-aproned harridans who inhabited the dark stony basement cellars and were known as the domestic staff. Shrieks were heard constantly from below. But it was not what Mrs. Crabtree at first feared. In addition to belonging to the untouchable lower orders, they were hideous beyond even adolescent desire and banished *in toto* under the name "skivvy," and in turn the boys were to them a weird joke, vaguely regarded as the upper class.

Down in those dank places great steaming caldrons were heaved about by practiced bony biceps, and black-clothed armpits exuded astonishing odors. Fortunately between Mrs. Crabtree and them there was a lady housekeeper, fittingly named Miss Bull. But Mrs. Crabtree's was the superior command, and she could not entirely escape contact.

"By the way, miss—" said Philomena.

"Mrs.," said Mrs. Crabtree.

"Mrs. then," said Philomena. "Has the chaplain told you about his food?"

"His food?"

"Yeh. He gets these pains in the tum—stomach, poor soul. And he has to have special food brought up. I bring it. Miss Bull does the orderin'."

"I'm sorry to hear it."

"Ah, that's all right. It's just it seems the school food wouldn't do him at all. He has to have smoked salmon and cold duck and that sort of thing. Special like. D'yeah know what I mean?"

"Yes, I think I do."

"Righto. I just thought I'd tell you."

Philomena went upstairs.

The chaplain was sitting in his black habit and silver-buckled shoes in a great oaken chair by the fire, and the Starlings tended to sprawl about the floor. He liked them looking up at him. They were the chosen for reasons incomprehensible to the more average members of the school. To them the Starlings were the ugliest, dirtiest, slackest, stupidest, and smelliest boys on display. Terrible slackers, they were. Most of them did farming, which had lately become a legitimate alternative to games. Several of them had almost continuous ailments to similar effect. Two of them, perhaps the weirdest of all, doted upon a falcon which they kept in a cage up in the woods.

But there was a clue to their charm in the pictures on the chaplain's walls. Above the mantelpiece was a reproduction of an enormous Academy painting, showing five boys, freckled, pimpled, and with flaming ginger hair, leaping naked out of a rowing boat into brilliant blue water. The chaplain considered them angelically hideous. And there were other paintings of beggarly boys, of the Spanish school, who were hideously angelic. (The three naked figurines were Greek and of less complex appeal.)

Mrs. Crabtree had looked in here out of curiosity, before the chaplain's return, noted the adornments, and suffered a fluttering of the heart, which for a moment she feared was going to turn into an out-and-out attack. It was one of the brand-new things which she had been going to tell her husband. The chaplain had been attending a retreat in the Hebrides. She had looked up the place, studied the qualifications of those present, and come to the conclusion that the proceedings would be very high indeed. She herself was a clergyman's daughter and similarly inclined.

Because an undeniable odor arose from the Starlings—partly farmyard and pigs, and partly pure Starling—the chaplain burned cedarwood in the fire, which was lit all summer by Philomena Maguire, who was in love with him. He even took a second precaution. Always in his hand, and sniffed at every now and then in the manner of Cardinal Wolsey, was an orange. He went through roughly a dozen a term.

The Starlings looked up at the chaplain in fascination. He was an astonishing sight. His head was absurdly impressive: a livid white face with a vast forehead and a thin smooth covering of inky black hair. The central parting was white and faultless. Black eyes twinkled and mocked. The mouth was a wide slit above a square jaw, and it could smile with an infinity of sarcasm and worldliness. Centuries ago he might have been some terrible leader of the Church, and he looked especially right for the Inquisition. Now he was chaplain at Weatherhill School, Bucks.

"Our friend Robert is evidently partial to chocolate cake," said the chaplain, with his eyes wickedly twinkling.

It was one of several unique features of the chaplain's salon that the Starlings were called by their Christian names. This often confused the Starlings, who were not sure what they were. But they all could tell that Robert was really Hastings, the spiky-haired, filthy-necked, much-stained boy sprawling beside the plate of chocolate cake. The chaplain saw him as a charming elder brother to Huckleberry Finn and was delighted to detect a faint blush.

"Yes, steady on, Hastings, you greedy hog."

The chaplain was mildly amused and gratified that they addressed one another in their quaintly rough way as if he were not there or rather as if he and they were friends and equals.

But a sudden waft of hog, or something, came from the speaker, who was seated beside his extravagantly buckled shoes, and at once he brought the orange to his nose. His nails were manicured, and he wore a huge blue ring.

"Not so *violent*, Philip," he said, placing his free hand on the boy's unexpectedly sticky head. "Ugh!" he exclaimed, and he made a face of the most elaborate disgust. They all laughed, but the disgust was in great part genuine. He put the orange in his skirted lap and took a large handkerchief of exquisite lacework out of his pocket and wiped his hand with care.

"Philip has his own brand of frankincense," he said. "It's called Frankenstein."

The laughter came thinly. He did not notice. He knew that he had a special gift for making the sorts of jest that schoolboys enjoy.

"I have to raise a matter of extreme seriousness. And then we may continue with our festivities."

Everyone stopped chewing.

"The summer term is, as you know, the time for confirmation. I believe I espy five of you who will be preparing for this profound experience. Let us have hands up, shall we?"

The five, who included Robert and Philip, put up their hands. One of them had been told by his parents to say that he was having nothing to do with it, but *they* were not sitting here on the floor in this room.

"I believe that's what they nowadays term bingo," said the chaplain, and there was laughter, but of a near-hysterical kind. "Profound experience" had come out most awesomely in his deep Shakespearean voice.

"I shall be preparing you privately," he said, and the five paled, and the fifth began to think that his parents had been right. "But I take this opportunity of reminding you that you will be expected to attain a state of grace. There will be abnegations." He relented. He smiled wickedly. "A little less cake for Robert?" There were titters of release. "A little less Frankenstein for Philip?" There was laughter.

"I shall not insist upon it, but I would like to point out that it will be very much easier for you if you decide to make confession."

There was a hush—a sense of excitement, and embarrass-ment, and guilt.

"I will be available at all times to hear your confessions," said the chaplain.

Several of those present had confessed in former years and would incidentally be Starlings until they left. Of the five, the fifth decided that his parents had been right, and the four wondered what they had done to confess or, with such short time at their disposal, what they could do so that they would have something to confess.

They could think of only one thing.

But could they confess it?

Or could he possibly mean smoking? Which was an indulgence a bit like cake or hair oil. Or had that been a joke?

Was smoking, or was it not, connected with a state of grace?

Everybody sat in pain—those who knew and those who didn't.

"And now let us hear of your holiday escapades," said the chaplain, smiling. "Has Charles been bird-watching again?"

So they continued with their festivities. Stupefying in the heat, and in any case being almost uniquely limited conversationalists, they talked with difficulty. Philomena had pulled the green satin curtains on both windows, to exclude the sunshine which the chaplain found so painful. The coal fire and the cedarwood blazed. The tropical air was perfumed. There was an atmosphere of exotic dalliance that had always made an irresistible contrast to life in the farmyard. And there was safety.

They sat secure from all beatings and raggings and the verbal abuse to which they were continually subjected, absolutely safe, and a little sick on a very rare species of China tea.

The chaplain himself well understood these attractions. The truth was that, in addition to the pleasure of dirty necks and imagined dirty knees, this assembly was a blow struck against the rest—the unspeakable games players and takers of cold showers. The chaplain had suffered too, if only verbally. It was mutual shelter. It was languorous disdain. The flag of No Surrender flew from the top of the Head's own house.

So he sat, smiling and at peace, and was mildly amused as a fetching young ragamuffin, Humphrey Watson-Wyatt, haltingly regaled them with some perfectly gruesome details of a fortnight spent with his golfing parents at Gleneagles.

CHAPTER FOUR

Tea parties were also being held on this first strange day by Mr. Dotterel, who was known as Dotty and taught mathematics, and Mr. De Vere Clinton, who was known as the Beard and taught art. Both had premises in the new buildings.

The company at Mr. Dotterel's was rugged and none too brainy. They all smoked, though not in his presence, and several of them had achieved the most daring of all forbidden activities—a visit to a public house in Marston.

The company at Mr. De Vere Clinton's was artistic. Hair was long. Sports coats were colorful. Trousers were kept up with pink tweed belts. Sandals were worn, and vivid socks.

At both receptions, behavior and discourse were of a much freer nature than those which prevailed at the chaplain's assembly. Both Dotty and the Beard tended to put arms around their young visitors. And both showed an appreciation of ribaldry and could join in to uproarious effect.

Also, the subject under discussion by each group this afternoon was identical. There were nine new boys this term, and it was important to decide on their potential.

This sorry collection had come a day early and wandered about together, suffering from homesickness and mutual disinterest, and this morning had come under close observation as to their sex appeal and possible willingness to make themselves available. Unknown to each, his one hope of being gently treated was centered on his claims of being a "bijou," a quaint term of whose origin even Dr. Rowles—who was known as Roly and occasionally, on account of his tendency to call a spade a spade, as Arsehole Rowles—had declared himself ignorant, even though he had been assistant headmaster through four reigns and nearly forty-seven years.

The annoying fact was that both assemblies agreed that there were only two potential jewels in the whole bunch and that it was one of the worst bags in years.

Of the two, Dotty's group gave the major vote to Allen, who was well built and dark, and the Beard's favored Fitzmaurice, who was slim, fair, and an Honorable.

At least three of the remaining seven were agreed to be very likely Starlings, than which no one could say worse.

The majority was not invited to tea. The Junior House messed about and became reacquainted. There was an uproar of chasing between desks, slamming the lids, Ping-Pong, and argument in the Big Schoolroom, alongside the Quad. The attraction of a sunny day for decaying adults was meaningless to them. It was dark and cool in there, and clouds of dust could be seen in rays coming through the windows.

Everyone went into the Junior House and became fags for the first year. Then they went into one of three houses, named after former masters, Priestley, Sheldon, and Pryor, which were presided over by Roly, the Pedant, and the Cod. The Junior House was more or less controlled by Mr. Wall, who was older, gentler, and more vague than Mr. Chips.

Up from the war memorial, on the Chapel Square, through a beautiful wood, and on top of a grass hill, was an ancient swimming pool, whose cement had turned green. It was crowded. Boys walking the still higher hills, could hear the shouts and splashes from below. These were the lovers, though some were merely smokers. Up on these heights there were vast clumps of gorse bushes, whose scent would be a nostalgic memory in the future, mingled in many cases with the oddly exciting smell of the first cigarette, inhaled through the nose. They gave ideal protection to the amorous—and to the smokers.

The lovers walked slowly in pairs, lingering and shy, and nervously happy; nothing to be said except "I missed you." This was unthinkable in the holidays. It belonged here.

Of course, some went too far. It was thought shocking that Henderson, who was a prefect, and Finch Minor should be seen walking through the Quad in their bathing trunks and on up into the wood, with Finch Minor, who had only been here for two terms, carrying a bearskin rug.

26

Carleton changed in his dormitory. Jimmy Rich had decided that there would be no cricket, but boys were invited to come to the nets and exhibit their prowess. As a result of the year's departures there were five vacant places on the first eleven.

This was Carleton's last term, and it was going to be marvelous. He had gained his entrance to Oxford. His decision, by which he had surprised even himself, not to be senior prefect would now pay off in freedom and pleasure. It was a point well understood by his housemaster, Dr. Rowles, who had not objected. Having himself spent a lifetime as second-in-command, he was secretly pleased to see so intelligent a boy in a similar position, leaving the captaincy to that crashing bore Steele. Everybody knew about it, including Steele, who was too flattered and thick-skinned to care, and in a distant way it gave a little unfamiliar luster to Dr. Rowles' own position.

"Changing in dorm," as distinct from the changing room, was a prefect's privilege. This one was the largest in Roly's House, which lay adjacent to the Big Schoolroom, and it was a chilly and impressive place, with oak beams up in the vault and square wooden pillars that relieved the monotony of wardrobes and thirty beds under dark blue blankets. The keeping of order was shared by Johns, another prefect, who slept in a distant corner.

It was exciting to be back in one's whites after a whole year: a fresh open shirt, the soft feel of his dark blue blazer, the immaculately pressed longs with a white-flannel smell. He was careful to arrange the points of his shirt collar outside the blazer. The badge on his top pocket sported colors for all games. He put on his blue peaked cap and looked at himself in the little mirror that hung inside the wardrobe. He felt dashing.

His white boots made a satisfying crunch of studs across the wooden floor. Dr. Rowles' study and bedroom were off the stone landing outside the dormitory. As Carleton went down the stone staircase, he saw his housemaster coming out of the Big Schoolroom. There was bedlam behind him, and he had his hands over both ears. Dr. Rowles—who was a doctor of philosophy—could not stand noise or burning toast.

"Oh, *please* have a game of Ping-Pong, sir."

"Ah, clear off, Harris. Not now. That voice of yours goes right through my head. Ah . . . Carleton!"

"Hello, sir. I didn't see you last night. How are—"

"You're looking fit. Listen here"—Dr. Rowles lowered his voice conspiratorially, took Carleton's elbow in a strong grip, and turned him back to the stairs—"that extraordinary bird, Gower, is on the prowl again."

He spoke with a critical relish similar to Mrs. Crabtree's, but with more wonder in it.

"Already?" said Carleton.

"I've just encountered him in his most unlikely base of operations—the washroom—and booted him up the arse."

The Doctor went ahead, into his study. He sat at the desk at which he spent nights working at mathematical problems under a green lampshade. The abstract joy of higher mathematics provided an essential and God-given relaxation from the continuous study of humankind at its most curious. Sometimes he would leave off and invite Carleton or Johns to come in his dressing gown for a cup of tea out of a white mug, with biscuits from a tin. It was fun, sitting there, with the others all asleep next door in bed. They would discuss the novels of E. M. Forster. (The Doctor quoted Ashley's opinions, with respect.) And the literary criticism of Virginia Woolf, which Dr. Rowles considered good, but of the second class.

Rowles was small and strong, with a huge head and pale blue humorous eyes that wrinkled in amusement or opened wide in wonder. He appeared in a new thick tweed sports coat almost every term—luxurious and original in color, though never as gaudy as Jimmy Rich's—and he ceaselessly brought his brown spongy-soled long-lasting shoes to an amazing polish. He exuded a strong clean tweedy smell. He was always washing his hands, and since he kept his shoepolish on a bench in the washroom, it was not surprising that, for one reason or the other, he had met Gower.

"He's an extra*ordinary* bird," he said.

He was sitting with his powerful fleshy hairy hands folded comfortably in his lap. (His large watch was buried in a black jungle on his wrist.) But he now turned to the desk, picked up his tobacco pouch, and lit his pipe in great clouds. Carleton feared that he was in for a session. He was dying to get to the nets.

Everyone at Weatherhill was an extraordinary—or, at the

least, a curious—bird to Dr. Rowles—even Steele, who was a curious bird simply because he *was* so crashing a bore. It was the interest and the distance that resulted that had maintained him securely in the position of housemaster for so very long. These qualities also assured stability in times of crisis, of which he had known, and privately enjoyed, a great many.

Rowles met the new creatures with a puzzled amusement and said good-bye to the old without much regret. They came, and subsequently, one presumed, the Lord dismissed them with His blessing. There was not much difference between them when they came, and not much more when they departed. They were all birds of a feather and all curious. The supply was inexhaustible. It was an agreeable occupation. The only drawback was the teaching. He was a poor and impatient explainer to the simpleminded and as he had once sadly remarked to Carleton, he should really have had to concern himself with the sixth form only at a school academically superior to this.

Another trouble, of which he was unaware, was that in his detachment and out of the necessity to find the boys at least curious the Doctor tended to exaggerate their characteristics under one convenient and inaccurate label. Carleton had long ago become the Cynic. No denial was permitted. It had annoyed and hurt and would not be forgotten.

But in the case of Gower, Dr. Rowles' summing-up was perfectly accurate. Gower was certainly an extraordinary bird.

Gower belonged to no group and was never invited to tea. He worked alone. His occupation was kleptomania, and though he had been here for only one term, the pickings had been considerable. The corridor of lockers containing overcoats alongside the washroom and the wardrobes in the two downstairs dormitories to which it led satisfied his unlikely passion. But he had also made baffling sorties right into the common room —also off this corridor—which was shared by Carleton, Johns, and the two other prefects of Priestley House, and cake, canned pineapple, and other treasured objects had gone, with Gower, out the door or window.

This was known only to Rowles and his four prefects, and known only by circumstantial evidence. Gower had not yet been seen at work or found in possession. The boy was a master hand—and equally so at producing hay fever, impetigo, and many stranger conditions which excused him from games and left him free to carry on his occupation. Rowles and Carleton, who was head of the house, had given up long afternoons to depositing the bait and posting themselves behind doors, but to no avail.

And it was not merely that Gower had declined to act. Frequently the bait was gone!

He was a sallow-skinned boy with slanting eyes and a dark neck, and he had the largest organ that anyone had ever seen. It was a truncheon. And it was the object of savage mockery and unexpressed admiration in about equal shares. Whether or not it made him steal canned pineapple was a matter for the analysts. But it did not appear to worry him—to the contrary.

The horrible fact was that Gower had several times smilingly acceded to the request, from junior associates in the upper dormitory, to exhibit his extension. There were cries of "Gosh!" and "Ugh!"—again in equal shares—as it spread away across the room.

Gower's smile was half-fear and half-taunting. Being plain, idle, unwashed, and above all nonconformist, he was open to destruction. Hence the fear. But he knew himself to be indestructible and moreover, to have a secret advantage in his occupation. Hence the taunting. The combination could not have been more dangerous: it infuriated others and also encouraged them to action.

He was, for example, beaten harder because of the smile, which he wore throughout that operation. He also customarily wore an exercise book inside his trousers, which helped the smile. But even when this was removed, the smile remained. And it was still there when he left the room.

The simple fact was that as long as Gower knew that he held their provisions and pocket money in the palm of his hand, he could smile at them all.

In studying his case, there was the question of the home background. But Dr. Rowles had possessed neither the evidence nor the inclination to investigate this. All he knew, with wry amusement and even a little wondering relish, was that Gower's father was a High Court judge.

Dr. Rowles avoided parents. The mothers were the worst,

and women he could scarcely bear to address in any case. They were an extraordinary breed. He was compelled to speak to them only on Weatherhill Day (June 28), when they came in hats made of artificial cherries and feathers, and he moved in horrified wonderment among them. But the fathers, in the parental sphere, were almost as bad. The way they both regarded the extraordinary birds they had hatched filled the Doctor with an amazed distaste. They had no comprehension whatsoever of the nature or potential of the creature they had fostered.

Their invariable attitude was an affection that made him wince and a pride of creation that was blind as a bat, being frequently directed toward idle little liars. It was in part excused in his mind by the fact that the creatures could not possibly show their true natures at all in the holidays. Because nobody could be as blind as that.

It was the Doctor's absolute assumption that the creatures lived, strove, learned, revealed themselves, and developed here.

At home they merely existed.

Seated at his desk at this very moment, he was struck by the thought that he was disrupting Carleton's natural progress, and he said abruptly, "Look here. You were on the way to your cricket. You carry on. We'll deal with this matter another time."

Carleton wondered if he should protest his interest. They had otherwise labored upstairs for nothing. But he said, "Righto, sir. Thanks."

He moved to the door.

"You heard . . . by the way, Carleton . . . the Cambridge people turned down the unfortunate Ashley."

"Oh. No, sir. I didn't. That's too bad."

"You're sympathy is characteristically overwhelming."

"I *was* sympathetic," said Carleton, beginning to bridle.

"I don't like it myself, but it's none of my business. He's a very curious bird."

This was tantalizing.

"How do you mean, you don't like it, sir?"

Rowles puffed his pipe, blew out smoke, and clearly decided not to say something. "It's no matter. Far be it from me to expose myself to your cynicism, Carleton."

"I'm *not* cynical."

"Ah, come off it, Carleton! By the way, have you made the acquaintance of our newcomers?"

"No, sir."

"He'll want to see all you prefects."

"They say he's a tough nut," said Carleton.

Rowles opened his mouth like a fish in exaggerated surprise and, flushing a little, made a high soprano noise, "Tee-hee!"

Carleton wished he hadn't dared it. Dr. Rowles would pass it on gleefully to his confrere, the Pedant, and they would commune over Carleton's "cynicism."

"Well, isn't he, sir?"

"Oh, come now, don't ask me, my dear fellow," said the Doctor, swiveling on his chair toward the desk and, through a cloud of smoke, bending over some problem he had set himself in an exercise book.

Cautious to the last, thought Carleton, going out.

CHAPTER FIVE

His housemaster's assumption about mere existence in the holidays was much to the point in the case of Carleton. It was true that he had reaped all the benefits of a cultivated background. But at home he knew no one of his own age. T. P. Carleton (Terence Philip) had lived a virginal, sinless, essentially solitary life for just eighteen years. It would have been beyond belief to youths born in less exceptional circumstances, but it seemed entirely normal to him. He was shy about answering the telephone in anyone's presence, had smoked several cigarettes in the lavatory, and had recently taken to drinking a glass of beer openly at home.

The same was true of many of his associates.

Carleton was good-looking and intelligent. He had not learned humility or unselfishness. He had brown hair and brown eyes set far apart. He was an only child, in the sense that he had a sister who was ten years older, and married, and gone. His mother adored him, and his father was extremely proud of his batting averages. They lived only fifteen miles from the school, his father being a gentleman farmer of literary tastes, and his mother a poetess of repute.

"Is there no friend you'd like to bring home?" they would ask, until they learned better.

There was none, and it was not so strange. In this immature society, friends were really first made at the university. At school there was love, and there were other people good at cricket, too. But friendship demands a development of the persona in two people; and this was rare.

He had some community of interest and humor with Johns, with whom he was joint editor of the school magazine. (Carleton had vague hopes of being a writer, and he had returned from the holidays with a short story which he intended to submit to Ashley, if he could nerve himself to do so. Johns wrote satirical poems of great promise.) But Johns despised games. His father would not care for that. Also, he was ugly; this would be embarrassing and would reflect on Carleton. He is asked to pick one companion from the whole school, and he comes home with this beaky-nosed fellow! Is this the best he can do? Is our boy not popular?

This assumed reaction by his parents was nonsense. But looks were terribly important at Weatherhill.

Carleton had maintained this strict partition in reverse as well. That is to say, his parents had never been permitted to come to the school—not on Weatherhill Day or to the end-of-term summer musicals, in which he had twice taken a leading role, or even to the chapel on Sunday nights.

They could collect him on the four permitted Sundays, provided that they stayed in the car. Once his father had come wandering through the place against this ruling, and after some moments of horror Carleton had felt an unexpected sense of pride. He looked more interesting and distinguished than most of the other fathers. The barrier erected by his own caution had been broken for him, and there was release. Still, it must not happen again.

On the two main days when parents exhibited themselves,

Carleton's ban was not merely provoked by the dangers inherent in such an exhibition. On his account there was also the danger of upsetting the picture of perfection so zealously maintained at home. The old boys might bowl him out for a duck. And heaven alone knew what the end-of-term show looked like from out front! Was he really acting? Or was it a laughably pathetic children's charade? He would not dream of risking it.

He went downstairs, along the corridor where Gower operated, and into the prefects' common room, to collect his bat, which stood in a corner among their four canes. Johns was stretched out on the faded ottoman, engrossed in some book about his passion, the cinema.

"Gosh, how you can lie in here on a day like this beats me!"

Johns did not answer.

Carleton registered the fact that only after the holidays did one see what an appallingly shabby and smelly little room it really was. There was a gas cooker on an old cupboard, on which the toast was frequently allowed to burn. They would sit and eat it, with jam, at the square table which nearly filled the room. This was covered, not with a tablecloth but with an old rug, which hung down to the floor. One of the other two, Rogers or Pryde had stuck a cutout on the wall, of a naked cutie with blown-up breasts. Carleton considered it hideous and—whichever was responsible—falsely boastful.

Carleton and Johns found the other two alien. It was mutual. No one ever said so, but they knew it. Rogers and Pryde could give six strokes with relish. They could strike fear into fags and apparently relished this, too. Carleton and Johns could not manage either of these things. Johns was entirely satisfied with this fact. But Carleton felt that it was a lack in him as a prefect, especially as he was head of the house.

He collected his bat and, wanting to be friendly, said, "What is it you're reading?"

"A new tome about the magic screen, given me as a compensation for returning to prison."

"I don't find it's prison."

"You wouldn't. You're off to play ball with your friends, I see. By the way, my trunk still seems to be reposing upstairs. Would you send me a couple of fags?"

Carleton went along the corridor and through the Big School-room, where pandemonium still prevailed. A group of five was arguing loudly about something in the door to the outside. Boys only fagged for the first year, but Carleton knew all five to be eligible. Two of them were humorists, whom he had frequently beaten.

Metcalfe made a low bow and said, "Good morning, your Honor."

Trench Minor, who was noted for his ability to yawn and throw out a light shower of saliva, bowed even lower and said, "The carriage awaits."

Carleton managed not to smile and reflected that it was inconceivable that either remark could ever be made to his inferiors, Rogers and Pryde.

"You two. Johns wants you in the common room at once," he said. "You're to carry his trunk to the box room."

"Oh, *no!*" said Metcalfe.

"Oh, crikey," said Trench Minor, "why does it always have to be us?"

"Shut up, and do as you're told," said Carleton, and he stepped out onto the Chapel Square—so named because this gray simple building was at one side, with the wood behind it. Why *did* it have to be them? he wondered. Because they gave cheek? But to be honest, he found it preferable to the mute stupidity of their confreres. Indeed, they must have scented this fact before now: he found it difficult to keep order and depended on Dr. Rowles in the background. He had made the right choice: they had asked for it. Still, there was something wrong.

Gower was eating his nails close to the war memorial.

Carleton was startled enough to say, "What are you doing, Gower?"

"Nothing," said Gower, smiling faintly. "Why, what should I be doing?"

"Don't be cheeky."

"I'm *not*," said Gower, in his well-known whine. "What's cheeky about that?"

"Oh, shut up, Gower. You're a bore."

"I'm *not*."

Carleton had moved away across the square and was descend-

35

ing the stone steps that led to the front of the Head's House. Ashley was standing on the verge of a mown lawn that no one was supposed to stand on. He seemed to be frowning at the sky. Carleton wondered if he should say something about the Cambridge business, but it was an adult matter of whose meaning and importance he was uncertain. He was also shy, remembering the incident with Ashley's gown in the morning. It had been embarrassing.

"Barbarous custom," said Ashley, with disgust.

Carleton realized that he was watching the fire practice which the new boys were traditionally put through on the first day by McCaffrey, the gym instructor. From the considerable height of a window of the junior dormitory, which was above the dining hall, they were being lowered to the ground in a harness which came under their armpits.

He recognized at once the next candidate to come out of the little window. It was the black-haired boy called Allen, whom he had spoken to the previous night, because he had been put in Priestley House and in Carleton's dormitory. This boy was sixteen—two years older than the other eight—and he therefore avoided the Junior House. This also meant that he did not have to fag, and he could put his hands in his trouser pockets.

There was an immediate cheer from the crowd basking in the sunshine below. Carleton noticed with interest that a woman and a young girl—it was obvious to him who they must be—were watching up above from a side window of the Head's House.

The boy was wearing a brown sports coat, elegantly cut in a hacking style. He was well built and had some difficulty in getting through the window. His face was flushed. He was confused and hung onto the window. McCaffrey had obviously explained nothing. The man's hand came out and gave Allen a push. It must have been a hard one, because the boy not only lost his grip on the window and was dangling, correctly, in the air, but also swung out and was spun around, so that the back of his head hit the wall.

There were greatly amused shouts of "Hey! Steady on there!"

McCaffrey had begun to lower him. The pull of the harness twisted him around, so that he was now turned to the wall and his face was scraping against it. The trick was to keep oneself away from the wall with outstretched hands, but McCaffrey never had the wit to explain this.

The crowd gave its customary advice. "Kick out!" they shouted. "Kick the wall!"

The bewildered boy did so wildly, swung out, and came back hard against the wall. There was a cheer. His face was still against it. They advised him again. "Kick the wall!" It was hard to understand why one should trust to such advice again; but Carleton had been put through this four years ago, and he knew that one did. It was all too sudden and frightening, and there was the obvious thought that the last kick had been too hard. Allen kicked again, not so hard, but hard enough to send a slim triangular window of the dining hall flying onto the tables within, with a clatter of falling glass.

There was a tremendous cheer from the delighted crowd.

Carleton was paralyzed, but Ashley had rushed forward with an exclamation and broken into the middle of the group and was uttering a flow of abuse at three boys who had done most of the shouting. "Vicious little torturers . . . reporting you to your housemasters about this . . . yes, you three . . . going to have you beaten, and beaten hard. . . ."

Carleton heard it distantly, because he had gone forward to help Allen. Ashley had removed all attention from him, and he was struggling to get out of the harness.

"It's all right, Allen. Stand still," said Carleton, undoing the buckle. "It's all right. That wasn't your fault. There's nothing to worry about. Let's have a look at you."

He turned Allen round. The boy was red in the face. He kept his head down, and he was smaller than Carleton, and it was hard to see, especially since his black hair fell down on one side of his forehead. But there was a crimson bruise on the other side.

"You've got a bit of a bruise, but it'll be all right."

"What's going on down there?"

There was a shout from above. Carleton, looking up, first caught sight of Mrs. Crabtree, who had been seated in the window but was now standing and had evidently dispatched her daughter, because the girl disappeared. She then looked down with an expression of extreme indignation, and it struck Carleton as odd that her look was aimed at Ashley.

But the shout had come from McCaffrey, whose broken-nosed face was framed in the little window. He was pulling up the harness for the next victim.

"Come down here at once, McCaffrey," Ashley commanded.

"What for, sir?"

"Do as you're told, immediately. I want you down here at once. You're going to do this the decent way or not at all."

"Very well, sir," said McCaffrey, pulling up the harness and disappearing.

"Come on, let's get away from this," said Carleton, taking Allen by the shoulder for an instant to persuade him to move.

They walked toward the front of the Head's House. Allen kept his eyes to the ground.

"You know, it's funny, but exactly the same thing happened to me."

"Oh?"

"Even the window."

"Oh."

"The best thing is to forget it. Listen, are you keen on cricket?"

Allen looked up. He had recovered quickly. There was no sign of tears. "Yes, rather."

"Well, why don't you get changed and come down to the nets? I'll be there. They showed you the changing room, didn't they?"

"Yes. . . . I've no pads."

"That's all right. The school provides them. We have to get something for our money. You're a bit older than the others, aren't you?"

"Yes, I'm sixteen. I . . . was at Eton. My father and brother were killed in a car crash. My mother can't afford it now, so I came here."

"Oh, gosh. I'm sorry. . . . It's funny, I feel I've seen you before."

"At prep school. Glen Court."

"Oh?"

"You wouldn't remember me. I was a little weed."

Carleton had no answer to this; but he had to say something, and without thinking, he said, "Did you . . . know Mr. Brownlow?"

Allen blushed, but looked him straight in the eyes. "Yes."

There was understanding. First the broken window, and now this.

Mr. Brownlow.

As Carleton passed the Music Building and made his way down the slope toward the cricket field, Mr. Brownlow came horribly alive.

Extra Latin in Mr. Brownlow's room, on Mr. Brownlow's knee. Exercises corrected up at Mr. Brownlow's desk, in front of the whole class, and no one knows that Mr. Brownlow's left hand is on one's bottom. A sense of being special and privileged, and yet rather awful at the very same time. Such a damp and fleshy hand. He could bend his thumb right back and was proud of it. He would do it for you, not knowing that while it was jolly clever, it also looked nasty.

The never-to-be-forgotten smell of T.C.P. Little cuts and bruises. After rugger he said, "You'll need something on that." He didn't mean, "Go to Matron." He meant, "Come up to my room."

Seated on Mr. Brownlow's well-cut blue shorts and bare knees, in front of a one-barred electric stove, glowing red. Mr. Brownlow bending over in hairy white rugby club sweater and dabbing on T.C.P. Great gentleness and delicacy in those soft hands. He said he had wanted to be a doctor.

"Whose are you?"

"How do you mean?"

"Oh, come now, Terence. At home, you're your parents'. Whose are you here?"

"Yours."

Sense of comfort and being honored. But uneasy as well. A bit frightening. What the dickens was it all about? Was it wrong? One couldn't certainly mention it at home, but that meant nothing. Or to other masters. But after all, it was private.

"There's only one person I could ever marry."

"Oh."

"You know who that is, don't you?"

"My sister?"

A good guess.

"Right."

"She's coming for me on Sunday. I could introduce you."

"We'll see. Blast, there's that pest, Thatcher, coming across the yard. I'm afraid you'll have to slip out this way, or he'll knock the house down."

Raises my hand and kisses the back of it. Holds out this own. I take the soft hand and kiss the back of it. But not comfortably. Something funny. He is a grown-up man.

Smell of T.C.P. off Thatcher!

But Thatcher doesn't know he's been called a pest.

Thatcher in dorm: "Mr. Brownlow calls me Bruce when I'm up in his room."

"So what! He calls me Henry."

I stay quiet. Just shows how little they feel and how little he feels that they make public boasts. It's simply not the same thing at all.

Four ugly boys stay quiet, too. They've never been asked up to his room. Are they jealous? Ugly boys are never anything. They are just out of things, that's all.

"He gave me three with the bristly side of the brush. Whew! It hurt! He said it was for my own good, and he wouldn't bother to do it for anyone else."

"Sucks to you! He twice gave me four. He likes it."

He will never beat me.

No, and when he starts tremendous shouts at the class, he'll often shout at Thatcher and Woodgrove. It's terrifying, but not, in a way, because I know he'll never shout at me.

Best of all—the long summer evenings, on half-holidays, with bat and ball. The two of us away in some corner of the cricket field. He bowls to me—all kinds of spins. I bowl to him. For hour after hour. Nobody pays any attention. Nobody ever even makes a single remark. It is accepted. Boys come over with questions—"Can I do this, can I do that, sir?"—and are sent away. Alien beings. I would never call him sir. The warm evening goes on forever. It is perfect.

And now it is all horrible. Why? From the very moment of leaving Glen Court it was horrible. Why? Not just because one heard they'd sacked him for it, and he went into business and was caught stealing, and a criminal picture was completed.

Dr. Rowles came to watch a cricket match and meet the boys

who would eventually be going into his house at Weatherhill. Spread himself out on a rug beside me. Kindly, and made us all laugh, shyly. Smoked a pipe. Smell of heavy tweed jacket. Strong hand. The watch was buried in amazing hairs. He was older, of course, but he also seemed more . . . fatherly. He had more . . . He was bigger. As, of course, one would expect. Public schools were huge, unknown and important. A housemaster would be almost a great man. Certainly compared with here.

Somehow one knew that Mr. Brownlow was only for prep schools.

"Time for bed, Terence."

"Oh, no! . . . I wish we could be in the same bed."

Mr. Brownlow must have paused for a second.

"So do I, my dear. But I'm afraid we can't. I'll be around later. Your turn tonight, isn't it?"

In Mr. Brownlow's week of switching out the lights, he sat on a different bed each night and talked and told stories for a while. So did the other masters; but sometimes they would say "Not tonight," and everyone would groan. But Mr. Brownlow was never going out anywhere and never let them down. Also, he was the only one who put out the lights *before* they all talked —which was much better.

Thatcher and Woodgrove jumping up and down on their beds. "It's my turn, sir. It's my turn, sir!"

"Get into your beds. You know perfectly well it isn't."

He switches out the lights, and with nervous delight I hear him coming over.

Worrying sometimes that it could possibly be the same with Thatcher—horrible name, Bruce—because one can't see in the dark. But it couldn't; it couldn't. Thatcher would be bound to boast. And anyhow it's not the same with the others. Well, for one thing, he only *sits* on the other beds. One can see that, even in the dark.

He kind of half lies on mine, up on the pillow beside me, with his head against the wall (there's a hair-oil mark above my bed only) . . . and his left hand comes in and works its way inside the back of my pajamas, while he is talking, and none of them knows, and he takes my bottom between finger and

41

thumb and gives it a gentle pinch. Which is comforting, and flattering, and at the very same time somehow not entirely pleasant.

But this night, right in the middle of some reminiscence of Berry & Co. or Father Brown or whatever it was, Mr. Brownlow stops dead, for it seems several minutes, and there is a queer kind of tremor all over him beside me, and then he talks on, in a funny voice at first. Frightening, and horrible, and absolutely no explanation. But somehow one knows that one could never ask him. Perhaps he's really a very nervous person and has some awful worry occasionally and gets this horrible shudder, and for once one was present when it happened.

"I've had a wonderful letter, Terence."

DEAR MR. BROWNLOW,

I've been meaning to write to you for some time, because I owe you a real debt of gratitude. My son, Terence, has many times mentioned your name, and it is plain to me that you are proving an absolute boon to him as an adult companion at his school. He has always grown up among adults, and I was very much afraid that he would terribly miss their company, and in particular their conversation, at school. ("As I expected, he is a little scornful of his contemporaries!") It is frightfully valuable to a child of his intelligence. I see now that I need not have worried—and that is entirely due to you. Thank you so much for appreciating him and giving him the great benefit of your company.

In gratitude,
MARY CARLETON

I wonder if Allen's mother ever wrote to Mr. Brownlow.

The small cricket field was very much an artificial creation, in the sense that it had been built at much labor and expense right out of the slope, like a promontory. Once on the field, you could not see the lake below unless you walked over to the far side and looked down on it over the railings. The lake, too, was artificial and had provided an uninterrupted vista from the Big House until an eminent Victorian divine decided to turn it into a school for the sons of gentlemen, who would naturally need a cricket field.

The pavilion sat on the slope above, and from it stone steps descended to the green expanse. Carleton paused at the top and saw that four nets were in use.

"Come along now, Carleton boy!" called Jimmy Rich, and he ran up to bowl. It was funny to watch the little steps, the twinkling feet, the speed of this extremely heavy man, as he rushed forward with swoops of black hair bobbing on his head and bowled hard, crying out instantly on the "clock" of the bat, "Head down, boy! Keep that head down! Left elbow up!" Already he had collected the ball, licked his thumb, and was walking away fast, left right, left right, left right, preparatory to delivering it again.

There were about fifteen older boys at the four nets. "You're off to play ball with your friends," Johns had mocked. And the fact was that Carleton's position was unique. Not one of these fellows was in the sixth form. (There was a form called Remove, tactfully interspersed between fifth and sixth for boys too old to be seen in the fifth and insufficiently intelligent to attain the sixth.) Carleton felt alien. They were what Johns would call Hearties. They respected Carleton—it was the same at rugger and hockey in the other terms—but he was not one of them and always a little uncomfortable when they were together.

On the other hand, among the novice writers, painters, musicians, and the learned, Carleton was not entirely at home either. The inevitable scorn of games, indeed of the school itself, seemed to him obvious, boring, and mean-minded. They considered themselves Sensitives, as against Hearties, but very few of them were. They took pale glum boys for walks and communed about the place as a prison from which they awaited escape, and this was unattractive.

Carleton was the "typical" all-round public-school boy, except that he was in no way typical at Weatherhill. Perhaps at larger schools there really were all-rounders. Here he was almost alone.

At the same time, since he enjoyed work and enjoyed games, he was greatly enjoying school.

And this was marvelous—after a whole year! Laying his cap and blazer on the stone parapet, and rolling up his sleeves, and walking out onto the sweet-smelling springy grass, and picking

43

up one of the many old cricket balls that were lying around, and running up to bowl to a boy with crinkly blond hair and a rather crinkly old man's face, who was known, with good reason, as Sexy Sinnott. It was meant to be an offbreak; but it was a full toss, and Sinnott, a middling bat, hooked it hard into the netting.

The fact was that he had just thought, with an odd twinge of nervousness, that he had better give Jimmy Rich warning.

It was not easy to interrupt the flow, and Rich had bowled two more balls before he gained his attention.

"Jimmy"—he was the only staff member addressed by his Christian name—"I told one of the new boys he could come down. Allen."

"Ah, Carleton boy. I've no time for kids today. I'll have a look at them tomorrow."

"He's not. He's older. . . ." He was going to say, "He was at Eton," but strangely it seemed a betrayal. "I believe he's quite good." (An absolute fabrication. Why?)

"All right. All right."

Carleton bowled another offbreak at Sinnott, and it went wide. Jimmy Rich didn't see. Suppose the boy was no good at all. Why had he put himself in such a situation?

In silence, all fifteen of them went about the business of bowling and batting. Not a sound out of these noisy fellows. Not a sound except the dunk of the ball on the matting, the clock of the bat, and shouted advice from Jimmy Rich. This was about the only thing that they took seriously. So did Carleton. He felt in harmony, as long as they were quiet. He was concentrating now, and bowled Sinnott with a perfect leg-break, and was taken by surprise when he saw Allen, dressed in white (he wasn't entitled to a blazer), carrying a bat and coming down the steps.

He felt that alarming sense of responsibility again. Several of the bowlers had stopped, and somebody said, in an unpleasant tone, "What's this?"

Unfortunately, Jimmy Rich wasn't looking. So Carleton had to go over to the boy and say, "Come along."

"Jimmy, this is Allen I was telling you about."

"Hello, young man, do you bowl or bat?"

"A bit of both, sir."

"And which would be the better, now?"

"Um . . . batting, I think, sir."

"Right. Put on those pads, and we'll have a look at you. What are you slobs standing around for? Get on with it."

Carleton caught a glance, accompanied by an odd little whistle, from a lout called Merryman.

"What's the matter with *you*, Merryman?" he said.

"Nothing," said Merryman, and he grinned.

Allen was having trouble with one of the straps. But Carleton could not possibly help him. He was in suspense. He could not understand why.

"All right, come on out of that, Sinnott," called Rich from the neighboring net.

"Oh, Jimmy, for Christ's sake, I've only had about five minutes!"

"Come out when I tell you, boy! And mind that language, or I'll thrash it out of you. Go on up there, Allen, and we'll throw a few balls at you."

Looking sulky and dragging his bat, Sinnott came down the matting. They passed midway. He studied Allen up and down and then looked at Carleton. He glanced back at Allen, over his shoulder, and looked meaningfully at Carleton again. Carleton ignored it.

The strange fact was that until this moment he had not noticed that Allen was very attractive. Up at the school he had been impressed by the boy's calm and straight look, by the fact that he had lost both father and brother, and was able to say so, just like that, and especially by his admitting about the money. They never spoke of money. To confess to a shortage at home was downright extraordinary. But, being long accustomed to the sight of good-looking boys, he had not even noticed it. Carleton's ability at work and games had kept him far too occupied to be amorous in any serious sense. How people looked had never been a conscious interest, when they looked well.

But this boy was dazzling—black hair, brows, eyelashes, white teeth, a pinky-brown complexion. . . . Ridiculous. Were they all noticing it?

He had surely sat on Mr. Brownlow's knee. Horrible.

Jimmy Rich bowled a slow one. Allen seemed nervous, but he stopped it with a straight bat. And he did the same with balls

45

of good length from two first eleven fellows and another from Jimmy Rich.

"Watch out!" Carleton heard behind him, and he turned and saw the squat blond figure of Sexy Sinnott, enveloped in his big Sexy Sinnott sweater, coming up on a run of absurd length. He wore a furious expression and hurled the ball down the matting at Allen.

It was the first possible half-volley, and suddenly Allen had moved out, and the ball raced between them along the ground and away across the field to the far side, where it sprang back from the netting.

"Nice one, boy!" said Jimmy Rich.

"Shit," said Sinnott.

Carleton felt delight. It greatly surprised him. Sinnott was waddling away across the field. He had wide and very flexible hips under the thick folds of the sweater.

A perfect late cut. A leg glide. A hook to square leg. Another straight drive. "Get over it, boy. That's it, that's it."

"Carleton's not bowling."

Sinnott was back.

It was true.

"He is now," he said, and bowled the same leg-break that had defeated Sinnott. It was driven low and hard into the net.

He felt Rich's hand on his shoulder and heard a murmur in his ear. "You've found us a cricketer, me lad."

I have? thought Carleton.

CHAPTER SIX

Dr. Rowles and the Pedant came walking away from the reed-filled lake. A worn path in the grass went curving up the slope, around the cricket field, which stood out above them like the prow of an aircraft carrier, with its protective netting silhouetted against the blue sky. (If anyone hit a six over it, the fielder took ages to recover it. Many balls had disappeared into the lake.)

They were a well-matched pair of walkers. Roly's great round head came up to the Pedant's thin shoulders. The Pedant, or Mr. Milner, was aged fifty-three, and Rowles was seventy-two. They had addressed each other by their surnames for twenty-three years. (The third housemaster, the Cod, was younger and straightforward, and they avoided him.) In absolute contrast with Rowles, the Pedant had been wearing the same brown coat, with padded elbows, for at least ten years. He looked so like a schoolmaster that one might have suspected it of having been done by cunning design.

That he possessed a pointed nose and spectacles, unaltering short-cut hair, and an almost perpetual frown fitted the picture. That testiness—"You wretched child"—was his well-nigh invariable emotion, did, too. But a startling gift for obscene jokes and verses combined unexpectedly with sudden critical, though devotional, outbursts concerning the Church of England in the local press. And what on earth had the Pedant been doing in intimate conversation with the young barmaid in the Crown and Anchor Hotel in Marston?

Everything Dr. Rowles had to say to the Pedant was said, frequently with good reason, as if it were something to be passed on to no other quarter and might easily be overheard by someone lurking in the grass. He spoke with bent head, in a low murmur, out of the corner of his mouth, and Milner had difficulty in hearing.

"By the way, Milner, have you heard about our cynic Carleton's summing-up of the new administration?"

"Indeed, no. What does your prize exhibit have to say?"

" 'A tough nut' . . . tee-hee!"

Flushing a little and his face alight with humor, Rowles raised his pale blue eyes quickly to catch Milner's certain enjoyment.

"The boy is imbued with the gift of exaggeration, Rowles," said the Pedant, in his dry constrained voice.

Rowles darted a look to the left and to the right. But there was no one in sight. His question was almost inaudible. "Is that your considered opinion, Milner?"

"Are you referring to the subject or object?" said the Pedant, who was a painstaking, precise, and exceptional Latin teacher.

"Ah, come off it, Milner!" said Rowles, with thinly disguised irritation.

"Well, I'd say it was a little too early to tell, Rowles. The good man is due some surprises. That much is certain."

"Tee-hee!" (He loved Milner's dryness.)

"How about you?"

Rowles took the return poorly. He made his particular motion of uncertainty. He brought up his right hand and, with the frequently washed, perfectly cut and rounded pink thumbnail, scratched his right temple. He kept his other fingers folded well away from this strangely delicate motion, with whose implications the Pedant was well acquainted.

"One has scarcely had the opportunity as yet—"

"The scholastic record is unappealing," said the Pedant, who was now impatient in *his* turn. "Or rather, it seems to reside with the female line."

Appalled and delighted by Milner's daring, Rowles dropped his mouth open and looked in all directions. They were passing the nets, but no one could possibly have heard. Carleton was batting. Rowles liked very much to watch and would have paused, but Milner was only mildly interested.

"That's more your line than mine, Milner."

He had caught the infection: this was a daring one! At least, he was not absolutely certain whether Milner knew that the curious oaf Merryman had seen him last term through the saloon bar door of the Crown and Anchor and had spread the information at once. He himself had heard it with amazed horror but had dismissed it as a quickly passing aberration. Milner must have been ordering ginger beer, of which he was inexplicably fond.

"The meaning of that escapes me, Rowles," said the Pedant. "But there's an odd example ahead."

Rowles looked up. At the top of the hill, near the Music Building, the daughter, Lucretia, was leaning against a tree in dirty blue jeans, holding something white to her front.

She was starting at a nearby school next week, by the mercy of God. The Doctor thought this and then saw another figure, going across the drive in front of the Head's House and approaching the girl.

48

He half covered his mouth with his cupped hand, so that the Pedant, frowning testily, had to bend his head to catch a word.

"Oh, Lord," the Doctor whispered, "there's that unfortunate Ashley. I'll have to say something to him, Milner."

Lucretia, who was nursing a white rabbit, saw the peculiar man approaching and knew him for the master who had been in the study and had interfered with the fire practice and had angered her mother. (She had been sent to tell her father.) He walked with a slight bounce, his hands in his pockets, his face was sort of screwed up, as if he were going to sniff, and altogether he struck her as what she had come to know from a lifetime spent in prep schools as an absentminded professor. But the funny thing was that he wasn't so terribly old.

He stopped abruptly. He really *was* absentminded and had only just seen her. He inclined his head in a little bow and, with his jawbones all tight, said, "Good afternoon."

" 'Lo," she said, confused by all this, and held the rabbit closer, to protect herself rather than the rabbit.

"I like the rabbit," he said. "What's it called?"

"Persephone," she replied.

It was clear he knew nothing about rabbits, because if he did, he would have said, "What's she called?" or better still, "What's he called?"; better, because she could have corrected him. All the same, she didn't hate him. His blue eyes gave her the idea there was some kind of joke between them, and he made her feel almost the same age.

"You amaze me."

"It was my mother's idea. Some . . ."

"Go on."

"Someting to do with being let out of the underworld or a burrow or something."

She had never said so much to a strange adult in her life. And it was worth it. His whole face smiled, and he was different.

"Ingenious," he said, scratching his hair and nearly laughing. (She had no idea what that meant.) "Your mother is a clever woman."

If so, why was he laughing? He must be making fun. She began to hate him. "She's taught me everything."

"Everything?"

She knew exactly what that meant, and *did* hate him.

"Yes," she said and gave him the straight look that had terrified scores of small boys.

It didn't terrify Ashley. It filled him with a sudden revulsion. "I see. Will she teach you now?"

"She hasn't time and I'm too old. I'm going to day school next week."

(He could still tempt her to speech.)

"I think you'll like that."

He was trying to get around her, but he didn't do it very well. He merely gave away the fact that he thought it would be better than her mother.

"Why do the boys go in there?"

Ashley followed her glance, across the drive, toward the Music Building. It was prewar, and a memorial to an old boy, a gifted musician who had been killed, an expensive donation by his parents, which the bishop on the Board of Governors had ceremoniously named the Hugheson-Green Building. But nobody could remember that, so the memorial was called the Music Building.

"To practice the piano, I believe."

There were eight rooms off a corridor, just big enough for a piano and chair, and one big room with a piano at the end.

"Two boys went into number two," she said, and then counted along, nodding with her head. "And two boys went into number seven."

Their eyes met. She gave him the scare look and was thrilled to see him all tensed up and in trouble.

"They must be playing duets," he said.

She smiled, with contempt: she had disposed of this thought herself. It was something bad, and she wasn't sure what, and she couldn't think how to find out: the little windows were too high up.

"Why can't we hear any music?" she asked, playing her trump card.

"The rooms are soundproof," he replied, sharply and with truth.

She was taken aback, but no one could have guessed. They had become, in a matter of minutes, engaged in a duel of an intensity that astonished them both, and she had never suffered defeat, except by her mother.

She put her chin up, almost in imitation, and said, "My mother told me to keep a watch out. She said to report anything to her."

This absolutely knocked him out. His face was all tight, and she would have giggled if she hadn't been a bit frightened.

"She did, did she?"

His jawbones were working again.

She stroked Persephone's white head with one finger, saying, "They can't be playing duets. There's only one chair in each room."

There was no answer, and she scarcely dared look up.

"You're a master. Why don't *you* go and see?"

Ashley moved forward with the maniac intention of tearing the rabbit from her hands; but there was a loud and nervous cough, and he turned and saw Rowles and Milner coming up the slope.

"I'll see *you* another time," he said, and spun away.

"Tell *them*," she called after him, in one last daring fling that sent her heart scampering away under the rabbit.

It was necessary to get past these two. Milner he had never managed to approach. They were *not* made for each other. Rowles he rather admired, even with a feeling of affection. But while he suspected that both sentiments were returned, it was done in an intolerable manner: Rowles viewed him like an exhibit.

They halted before him.

"Ahh!" said Rowles, with his hands in his coat pockets jingling money and pushing up the thick tweed flaps. Going up and down on his soft heels, he studied Ashley—the latter thought—not merely as a case, but as one who provoked both apprehension and pity. "Well, at least the sun shines upon our enterprise."

"Yes. But we appear to have inherited a child from outer space."

"I beg your pardon, Ashley?"

Ashley nodded his head backward.

51

"What has she been saying?" asked the Pedant, leaning eagerly forward with a light sparkling in his eyes.

"It's not repeatable," said Ashley, and he felt suddenly uncomfortable. Why not?

The Music Building was an awkward ten yards away. The nauseating girl hadn't moved.

"Ahh . . . well, we won't inquire further. Listen here, Ashley"—Rowles lowered his head in obvious embarrassment, so that Ashley could only see the thin hairs on top, and moved his highly polished toe cap and studied it—"I was most distressed to hear your news. Damn bad luck!"

This was said strongly, and Ashley was touched.

"Yes. Very," said the Pedant, which was easier to answer.

"Thank you, gentlemen. I think I'll survive."

"I hope so, Ashley. I hope so."

Ashley listened and looked for a glint of the familiar Rowles humor but, to his mild shock, found none.

"See you later, gentlemen," he said, awkwardly raising a hand and moving on.

What had *that* meant?

Rowles couldn't have been serious.

But there was a lesser sense in which the problem of survival did have meaning. He was making a very unhappy debut with the Crabtree family.

CHAPTER SEVEN

The eminent Victorian divine had laid it down that the chapel was to be "the center of school life."

So it was. But not exactly in the religious sense.

On Sunday nights it was the place of assembly for this entire enclosed community; as with lunch in the dining hall (but then the chaplain stayed away), it was a time when all the protagonists, boys and staff, were on view—the boys in white surplices, all washed, brushed, and on display. Psalms and hymns and the controlling presence of the mesmeric and incomprehensible chaplain completed the feeling of theater. They sat poker-faced, one and all—especially the staff—but emotions were intensified, as the sentimental melodies swelled from the organ, and love, hope, sin, misery, glory and salvation were proclaimed in profusion within the space of an hour.

Chapel on Sunday nights was compulsory, except for poor Jacobs, a Jew, who wandered the Quad, kicking a tennis ball and listening to everybody else singing together within. Attendance was also required at a quarter to seven every evening before tea; but this was only a fifteen-minute affair, with no singing and no dressing up, and only the master on duty, apart from the chaplain, was obliged to be present.

Early on Sunday morning the chaplain sang holy communion on one trumpeting, relentlessly sustained note. Failure to attend was no offense, but many likely lie-abeds were tempted out because attendance, and no other excuse, freed one from the morning service at ten.

The latter was, therefore, a rather deserted and pale affair, and there was no sermon.

No, nothing was to be compared with Sunday night.

Even the devout would have agreed to this, in terms of its special pleasures, for there *was* a silent brotherhood of the devout—small but persistent, as the notable quantity of reverends and bishops in the *Old Weatherhillian* magazine testified. They could be identified by their presence at holy communion on Wednesdays and saints' days. Attendance was not obligatory, and it took some courage for a junior boy, however devout, to rise early in his dormitory and go to the chapel.

As for the baser Hearties, even they positively liked Sunday night: it was the end-of-the-week singsong, and in between the singing, the opportunities for whispered ribaldry about the staff, all present and asking for it, were manifold.

The only variant in the performance, the only likely flaw, was the sermon. Visiting clergy, in a rota so little changing as to afford almost word-for-word imitation in advance, came and bored the congregation close to hysterics. It was only the unusual vicar who believed that one could communicate with God by wireless waves who gave any satisfaction whatsoever.

But the perfection of this first Sunday—as of the last—was that on these two nights the Reverend Cyril Starr himself spoke. And while these polemics were also known in advance, they were a ceaseless delight.

Even new boys, who were still losing hope after the first week, suddenly found themselves cast into a region of storm and tempest in which they belonged just as much as everyone else. Many had gone to bed on the first Sunday night released, as by an explosion, from alienation and homesickness.

For them, it was a surprise. But the rest knew that the chaplain was going to give them, *must* give them, could not fail them by not giving them . . . the BURNING FIRE.

Mrs. Crabtree, like her husband, was new and not aware of this. Steele might have given warning, but it was not the sort of thing that occurred to his military mind. She did foresee the significance of the entire community in assembly, and she also foresaw the dominance which the Reverend Cyril Starr must inevitably exert over the proceedings. She had often wished that her husband was a clergyman, like her father, but never more so than now. She was deeply interested in the Church, as well as being an intense believer in its doctrines. She felt a pang of annoyance that it was not the headmaster but the chaplain who, as she was going up to change, came rustling past her on the stairs in a white cloud of ecclesiastical garments. His black eyes twinkled wickedly, and "played about his lips" was exactly right for his disturbing smile. She had the unpleasant impression that she was the object of amusement, but she consoled herself with the fact that he seemed to smile the whole time.

This man puzzled her, tantalized her—very nearly obsessed her. It was not solely the mystery of the sphinx. One had to admit that he was alarmingly handsome. She had several times caught her breath when there was a sudden squeak of buckled shoes and a Roman emperor came around the corner (or else the Grand Inquisitor), the face white as marble, the hair black as night. (He refrained entirely from speech—not even a "good morning.") And there was, too, the tendency to regard all men in orders as in some sort potential confessors. How unlikely and yet how dangerously possible with this one!

She was of the opinion that the chaplain had suffered and was suffering. She was even beginning to think that he *did* have to eat cold duck instead of shepherd's pie. But it was more than the stomach, more even than the pitiful ginger-haired boys leaping into blue water. He was a man of sorrows and acquainted with grief. And she was a woman of similar ilk.

She had accepted it now and was making the best—or worst —of it, but the one action Mrs. Crabtree could not understand on God's part was His giving her a brain, as well as her brown eyes. At Oxford and home at the vicarage in Dorset, her brown eyes had attracted, and the brain dispatched, all her contemporaries who were remotely human. It was not that the young men took unreasonable flight. The flight was fair. She had already, against her wishes, detected and been bored by their stupidity. In misery she had filled an entire exercise book with poems on the theme "I am not as other women are."

In her thirties, a classical scholar with an invalid father, she had met Philip Crabtree, who was headmaster of a Dorset prep school. He had fallen for both eyes and brain and persuaded her, correctly, that as educationalists, he and she would make an excellent pair. She had suffered frequent bouts of despair ever since. But she prayed much and fervently believed. Her husband did neither of these things. She would have wished him in vestments, handing her the bread and wine.

He had declared his intention of holding Scripture classes —he was teaching nothing else—but she knew perfectly well that it was merely to emphasize his patriarchal position and to deprive the chaplain of what would otherwise be a monopoly in their great founder's oft-quoted blueprint for Weatherhill.

As for Lucretia, the child had the eyes and her father's brain, but even so she appeared to take a sour view already of existence. Perhaps her mother had transferred it, unwittingly. Perhaps school would cure it.

"Why can't I go in these?"

"Because nobody goes to church in jeans. Where is your tartan skirt?"

"Why do I have to go at all?"

The headmaster, in his dressing room next door, was having difficulty in deciding among his six suits. He, too, could foresee the significance of the approaching ceremony and was not sure what kind of appearance to make. It was important, because he had always gone to church for this reason—of necessity, as a schoolmaster. His wife went for the other reason, and it was an increasingly disturbing division between them. As they grew apart, old accepted differences took on new life and developed alarmingly.

Not to be able to decide on a suit! In the last few days he had been afflicted by uncertainty for the first time in his life. He was noticing it now whenever it appeared, like spots on the body. Certainty was the essence of his whole reputation. Certainty, and the making of decisions.

There had been no rest this Sabbath: an alarming discussion with the bursar about the school's finances, a distressing visit from Lord Mountheath, who wanted quick results.

His narrow window looked out onto Buckinghamshire in the rain. All day, more than two hundred boys had occupied themselves indoors. At what? Where? In this, and in the larger sense, he felt that the place was existing without him and in ways unknown to him. He had made no decisions. He was set apart here, in this house. If he invaded their indoor world, silence fell, all motion ceased; eyes stared at him; questions received that dreadful, chilling reply, "Yes, sir."

His prep schools had been small, friendly places. He had never been set apart.

And what *was* going on? Outdoors, it was bewildering enough. He was haunted by a curiously disturbing little scene. On the first day he had taken a stick and gone for a walk in the wood and come suddenly on two boys in a clearing. They were wearing bathing togs and lying on a ridiculously wintry bearskin rug. The older boy—who looked much the older—was attending to the other's arm. A thorn or some such thing. He released it upon Mr. Crabtree's appearance.

"The weather is giving us a good start, eh?"

"Yes, sir."

"We must enjoy it while we can."

"Yes, sir. That's what *we* thought, sir."

It had developed that this boy was a prefect, and the other one had come only the previous term.

If there was anything of the sort that he suspected, he intended to destroy it instantly. It gave him a peculiar sense of horror.

There seemed to be no one to turn to. The staff was no less remote. Ashley had been excessively rude. The chaplain, whom one should have been able to consult about moral conduct, was unapproachable. He had accompanied the Head to the chapel and explained the seating arrangements in an aloof manner. A comment from Crabtree about the beauty of the stained glass had been greeted with a disagreeable smile and no response.

Nevertheless, the Head was noted for optimism as well as for certainty. In the approaching ceremony they would kneel as one. The captain and crew would be together—at the turning of the tide.

He realized that it mattered little which suit he selected; it would be almost entirely hidden by his gown.

He felt that in the old days he would have thought of that at the beginning.

Carleton and a boy from another house named Naylor had been made the two chapel prefects, because the chaplain had determined them to be the least religious of the available twelve. They were very nearly atheists. He had a theory that preoccupation with the objects of ritual, from altar cloth to bell rope, would effect a slow conversion. He was mildly amused to find himself wrong. They continued as stage directors with an interest in the performance, but little or none in the play itself.

The boy Carleton—brown wavy hair and those wide-apart eyes, but oh, dear, a player of games, a taker of showers—had been guilty of another deception two years previously. A declaration of the wish to be baptized at the age of sixteen, contrary to the viewpoint of parents who had deemed it unnecessary, had aroused the chaplain's sense of drama, not to mention his genuine pleasure at admitting one who was lost into the fold. He had enacted a remarkable scena by night, in secret in the chapel, to keep the child from embarrassment and mockery. Carleton had asked to leave the room, in the course of prep in the Big Schoolroom, and had come to the chapel where the Reverend Cyril Starr and his attendants were gathered together under a spotlight around a vast soup tureen, like so many witches about a caldron.

Resplendent in white lace, the chaplain had placed himself between the Matron and Dr. Rowles, who were standing in, so to speak, as godmother and godfather, and murmured incantations over the tureen and its glittering water. After much of this, he suddenly halted, fixed Carleton with piercing eyes, and inquired of the boy whether he renounced the Devil and all his works, the vain pomp and glory of the world, and the carnal desires of the flesh.

"I renounce them all," Carleton declared, not with the sweeping bravado that the words seemed to imply, but in a quavering voice, having no option.

There were more inquiries, more melodious sounds, and the chaplain prayed that the Old Adam in Carleton might be buried, and then he dipped a beringed finger in the water and elaborately crossed the boy's forehead. The degree of water was minimal; but in a second a white handkerchief of extreme elegance was in his hand, and he was lightly dabbing the boy's head.

The sense of awe that the chaplain had counted on had not been present. Afterward, all that Carleton remembered was wondering how Dr. Rowles on all occasions managed to keep a straight face. It had been plain that on this one he had been hard pressed, although he was a true believer.

There had been two reasons for that night's excursion, as the chaplain later realized. The boy disliked the nonconformity and feared the resulting exposure, as the only one of his year not available for confirmation. More practically, attendance at communion on Sunday, for which he would not otherwise have been eligible, excused one from the morning service. On the three Sunday "exeats" (four for prefects), this made all the difference to the day out.

Undismayed, the chaplain selected him as a chapel prefect. The boy accepted; he seemed mildly amused by the idea. The chaplain hoped that familiarity would breed devotion, but in vain.

Still, it was agreeable to see the two best-looking prefects taking the collection. It impressed the parents in the ante-chapel. Naylor had close-together eyes, but they were darkly alive, like the chaplain's. His black hair was not wavy, but it was crinkly in an exotic way. He had an olive complexion, brilliant white teeth, and a slim figure. He was not a games player, and it was difficult to tell whether he took showers or not, and he *had* come to tea for a while. But the others found him a little showy, he did not melt into the canvas, the irreligion was unattractive, and now he was too old. No prefects came to tea. Boys lost interest in chocolate cake at a certain age, and became semi-adult and unappealing. Pleasant enough, though, to observe some of them from afar.

Both in white surplices and feeling good in their dark blue suits, Carleton and Naylor had collected the altar cloth, moneybags, and a great gold plate like the sun from a cupboard on the landing outside the chaplain's rooms. They had disposed them about the chapel. Its pews faced each other across the aisle, on rising levels, with the exception of one row on each side, for the Head and housemasters, who looked across the whole school and onto the altar. The row on the Head's side ended at the organ, at which the precentor, Dr. Kingsly, was quietly playing. Both rows were backed by an ornate wooden screen, up to the roof, which cut off the antechapel—more simply referred to as the porch. The rain had moved away, and the late evening sun came into it, through the open doors, beside which the bell rope hung down to the pink-flagged floor.

Carleton had ushered a dozen or so parents and relatives into the four tiers of pews in the antechapel. It was not a good place to sit, but there was no room in the chapel proper. Only those at the center could see down the aisle; the rest saw only the wooden partitions and the backs of masters' heads on high. The parents did not appear to be able to grasp this, and it seemed irreverent to point it out, as if the service were a spectacle. So Carleton let them sit at either end. Visiting parents never seemed to be able to grasp anything. They were always cowed, and waited about to be told what to do, like babes. Thank goodness his own never came!

Naylor was standing in the high oaken doorway, by the bell rope, looking at his watch. Fortunately, he liked ringing the bell. A certain knack was required, as well as physical strength, and Carleton had never entirely mastered it. One could look a terrible fool if the thing went wrong. The whole school could hear it, and one could easily be pulled up in the air off one's feet.

His uncertainty probably dated from being told once, as a fag, to ring it. He couldn't manage it. He was nearly sick; it was terrible. Now he himself could command a fag, but luckily, as well as Naylor, that humorist, Metcalfe, positively liked doing it.

This was an odd thing: younger boys appropriated what Carleton considered most disagreeable tasks to themselves.

There was another who gave out the morning milk and biscuits, supposedly a prefect's duty. There were five or six who assisted Matron in the dispensary, though this was maybe different, because they all were more or less in love with her. It irked him on account of the vague possibility that they might be helping—that is, playing their parts as crew members. Something he had refused to do. But, no, no . . . it was because it made them feel important. Anyhow, Metcalfe understood the bell rope, and it was lucky.

Naylor had to do it now, since everyone except the chapel prefects had to assemble for roll call in the cloisters, in the fifteen-minute interval between bells. It was almost time for the first bell.

Naylor's dark foreignness was emphasized by the white surplice. There was a southern warmth about him. Carleton felt drawn. He had been conducting a humorous flirtation with Naylor for two terms. He was a quiet and tantalizing fellow, who showed amusement and neither encouraged nor dissuaded. They met seldom—only on chapel business. The chaplain had brought them together. (Naylor was six months older than Carleton, but he was in Remove and, surprisingly, did farming.)

Carleton was tempted to put an arm around him now. He thought if the silent group of parents seated in the wrong places could grasp *that,* they would really be beginning to grasp something.

"Right," said Naylor, and he raised his olive-skinned hands and pulled down the rope.

The bell boomed out. It was a splendid bell. (There were reports of salvage from the Spanish Armada.) It rang out over the organ. Old Kingsly went on extemporizing. He played wonderfully, and Carleton was looking forward to a series of late-Sunday-night Bach preludes and fugues, promised later in the term. It was also Old Kingsly who composed the end-of-term musicals.

Minutes later, the Chapel Square and the Quad and the cloisters below began to fill with boys in white. For timid souls, a surplice mislaid was a frightening experience. Extra ones were kept in the linen room, but this meant finding the fierce Miss Bull, confessing, and persuading her to open up. The alternative was complete exposure before all, including the Head, and a severe reprimand from the head prefect of one's house.

Lucretia Crabtree appeared in the doorway, in a gray pullover and tartan skirt, looking pretty except that her hair was unkempt and she was scowling.

"They told me to come ahead," she said.

She was old enough to make Carleton feel awkward.

"Oh. Do you know where to sit?"

Without answering, she went into the Head's pew and along it to the end, sitting behind Dr. Kingsly's back. Like the other masters, he wore his black gown and vividly colored hood. They all had degrees, even Jimmy Rich with his old B.A. The precentor was a doctor of music.

Carleton felt rather sorry for her, so much alone in this male academy.

Naylor let the bell ring itself out, and immediately they heard the senior prefect's sergeant-major bark, "Shut up! Silence!"

Since there was nothing more for him to do, Carleton wandered across and joined his fellow prefects in the two alcoves, overlooking the cloisters.

"Is it going to be a hit?" whispered Johns.

"Depends on Henry Irving," said Carleton.

Steele was standing alone, out in the middle, holding the roll-call list.

Down below, the boys were formed in two lines away to the oak door at the end, through which the staff would later emerge. Conventionally angelic they looked—even the worst rogues—all in white, with their hair combed.

At last the tumult petered out, in whispers, and Steele began:

"Allen."

"Present."

"Andrews."

"Present."

Carleton felt a little tug around about the heart and then a sense of guilt. It had been so prompt and unexpected, the first on the whole list. He was standing about halfway along. Black hair combed in a wave on his forehead. Whispering to the boy beside him. For heaven's sake, stop that; Steele will call you out. Whispering to Draper, an awful fool!

He couldn't look away from him and he thought that Johns must be noticing. Johns acted aloof—he really *was* the Cynic— but he didn't miss much.

"See you at the show," Carleton whispered, and he went back up to the chapel, where Naylor was getting ready to ring the second bell.

"Wainwright."

"Present.'

"Wallace."

"Present."

"Young."

"Present."

Naylor gripped the rope and pulled.

This whole little world moved silently into position, members of the choir occupying the first section of the chapel. Carleton, who was a bass, went up to an end seat at the back.

In the greater section of the chapel, older boys, though free from the demands of music, also gravitated to the back rows— where masters joined them. (There was similar positioning in classrooms.) These self-promotions occurred with strange ease and naturalness. No one ever moved back before his time. The knowledge of one's place in this society became instinctual.

An even odder fact was that the ability to sing—up to choir standard—went with a definite type. There wasn't a single Hearty in the choir; there wasn't even a player of games, except for Carleton. Once again, he was the only one.

At least, he *had* been. But he now saw that Allen was in the third choir row opposite, behind the altos and trebles. Old Kingsly had passed him as a tenor; he must have cracked.

All were standing. The masters were parading in now. Very colorful. Carleton watched Ashley go over to the far side and wondered what his hood represented. He had never wondered before, but he would soon be entering that other world. The trooping-in was now approaching its climax—namely, the chaplain. Roly, the Pedant, and the Cod, who was a robust and sporty type and a danger on the rugger field, came into the stall at Carleton's right hand and stood with their backs to the wooden screen. Roly, the first in, was within whispering distance and would often send Carleton about the place, distributing hymnbooks and so on. Opposite, the Crabtrees joined their daughter in the corresponding stall. Mrs. Crabtree was not sporting academic garments but wore her customary tweed suit. And then there was a hiatus.

The chaplain always left this gap for the purpose of his entrance. Its length was perfectly calculated between expectation and irritation. When the former had reached its peak, in he swept, in a tent of white lace, with his face set, and his buckled shoes squeaking with each step.

There was a theory that he had some method of putting those squeaks into his shoes. They were always there. And no more revealing comment on the man's presence in church could be made than this: while others would be deflated and put to ridicule by such an impediment, in the chaplain's case—and in a community in which ridicule was almost a way of life—the squeaks were a source of awe. Because the chaplain not only seemed impervious to them, but actually appeared to have embraced them as an addition to the ceremonial, they *increased* his importance. At several points in the service, more than two hundred silent people heard no other sound in the building. No one even smiled.

This was one such moment. But the squeaks stopped. The chaplain had halted in the aisle. He crossed himself elaborately, bowed low to the altar, spun away on his heels and up to a back row corner seat, opening the book he carried and announcing, in an unearthly voice, "Hide thy face from my sins and blot out all mine iniquities."

Adding to this ambiguous demand, or request: "Psalm Fifty-one. Verse Nine."

"I acknowledge my transgressions, and my sin is ever before

63

me," the chaplain announced. "Psalm Fifty-one. Verse Three."

Everybody knelt. Dr. Rowles was somehow the undeclared leader in all such moves. Anyone in doubt looked his way. In psalms and hymns his loud voice hit the first word, pronto.

"Dearly beloved brethren, the Scripture moveth us in sundry places to acknowledge and confess our manifold sins and wickedness. . . ."

An extraordinary baying sound: the words pronounced with impressive precision, but at an astonishing speed. The chaplain did not appear to wish them to hold any meaning, but to be rather a fast-running accompaniment to his one wailing note. So that it was only a moment before the company was confirming gross behavior of every possible kind.

Miserable offenders, with no health in them, they had been doing the wrong things and not doing the right things, and they had strayed from God's ways like lost sheep.

The number of boys disturbed about—never mind conscious of—manifold sins and wickedness must have been countable on one hand. But the mere vocal repetition of corruption, week after week, was calculated to create a conscience or sense of guilt which would last a lifetime, and this was perhaps the main idea.

The chaplain rose and absolved them all. They said the Lord's Prayer, and they sang a psalm, with Rowles coming in before anyone else—"Help Me, Lord, for There Is Not One Godly Man Left"—and then the hymn "Jerusalem, the Golden, with Milk and Honey Blest." Everyone let go on this. There had been no choir practice yet, and harmonies were uncertain. The Beard's quavering tenor rang out above everyone, and his beard quavered, too. (Mr. Dotterel could take this off to perfection.)

Then Rowles went up to read the first lesson, murmuring to Carleton behind his cupped hand, "We'd better have the lights."

It was true: it had been growing dark. Carleton slipped out into the antechapel and switched them on.

No squeaks from Rowles as he went up the aisle. No sound at all, even on pink flags, from his spongy shoes. His gown was huge, and it covered them. Boys in back rows just saw the great head moving past. He might have been running on wheels.

And now at last they could all sit down and examine one another!

As Rowles began reading, the Head—perhaps the only staff member not wearing a poker face—was not following in his Bible, but was looking about as if he wanted to see everybody and with a benevolent expression as if he wished to make friends with them all. His wife was staring at her Bible. Ashley was tweaking his nose. There was a note being passed along the row in front of him, to the accompaniment of suppressed giggles. Steele, sitting nearby, had noticed, and two of those involved were going to be in trouble.

The only people missing were the Matron and Miss Bull. There were two places for them in the Head's stall; but the late Greville Wilks having been unmarried, chapel had seemed to them an embarrassingly all-male affair, and they had attended seldom. The new dispensation left them in uncertainty; both awaited instructions.

Otherwise, everyone was here. They all were securely together. It was their world. It *was* the world. White and bright and warm and safe—with the sermon to come. New boys began to feel part of the company. The Head experienced an involvement and a new sense of pride.

Rowles was reading from the Book of Samuel, about the witch of Endor. Carleton was surprised, because he had always supposed her to be a witch from some rural English town or possibly one from the Macbeth country. He could not help thinking that Mrs. Crabtree would make a frightfully good witch. She was already known as Ma Crab, while her husband was the Crab and, sometimes, on account of his complexion, the Lobster.

"Here endeth the first lesson."

The chaplain rose. They knelt. The chaplain, having waited till Rowles was back in place, prayed. Rowles looked quickly across at Ashley. This prayer was possibly unfortunate, maybe a little curious—he would go no further—and Ashley always cleared his throat in an aggressive manner as soon as it began, and Rowles went in constant fear of some more specific demonstration. He had pointed out to Ashley that it was the founder's own composition, it summarized that good man's superior aspirations for Weatherhill, and there was no help for it. Ashley refused to listen. A very curious fellow.

That unfortunate hoicking noise had now, of course, become a school joke. Once they had made their point, these fellows could never resist performing. *He* never performed. He genuinely disliked noise . . . and so on. It was— The really curious thing was the way that quite extraordinary bird the chaplain carried on as if nothing had happened. He was a cool customer.

"O God, who hath caused our school to be set upon a hill—"

Ashley hoicked—louder than usual. There were snorts and giggles around the chapel. Mr. Crabtree's face came out of his hands, and he looked about, like a bewildered bird.

The chaplain's wailing monotone continued unabated. "—let us rise above the sins of avarice and envy which afflict the world below . . ."

The Head relaxed and tried to pray too. It was a prayer after his heart; it expressed his own aspirations. He had perhaps misjudged the chaplain.

So the service continued, and expectation grew. The Magnificat, Nunc Dimittis, the Creed (all turning toward the altar); Steele reading, with difficulty, from the New Testament (it would be Carleton's turn next week—he held the reader's prize); another hymn, "Strong Son of God, Immortal Love," by Lord Tennyson; and at last, as the final verse is sung, up he goes!

The chaplain always disdained the pulpit. He stood at the center of the altar step, and spoke directly down the aisle.

He read from the Bible, without informing them from whence: "Thou hast turned my heaviness into joy: thou hast put off my sackcloth, and girded me with gladness."

Mrs. Crabtree quietly raised her eyes from floor to roof.

The chaplain deposited the book on a stone ledge near the pulpit.

"This summer term is, as you should all know, the term in which certain among us will present themselves at the solemn and profound ritual of confirmation. They will be admitted to full communion, as Christians. They will come to share at last . . ."

This was mere preamble. Most of them let it pass. There

66

was no clue as yet to whether it *was* going to be the burning fire. He was clever; in order to keep them guessing, he never used the same text.

He had been speaking for quite a while, when two staccato utterances halted the flow and captured all ears.

Suddenly, recognition was spread in varying quantities among the audience. In fact, there were two or three brilliant imitators—one of them being Mr. Dotterel—who could carry on from here to the end.

"Christians . . . Christianity. . . ."

The chaplain let the words fall into the arena and slowly scanned the entire congregation; he appeared to be measuring the quality of reaction in each face. Many eyes were lowered before his dark stare.

"We cannot do better at such a time than to consider the true nature of this Christianity of ours. And as intelligent people"—a faint smile, meaning what?—"we shall approach the subject in a useful way if we first of all consider what it is *not*."

Yes, this was it—hurray! They had *known* he wouldn't disappoint. Almost the whole school braced for action. Hearts ticked faster under surplices.

"There are some . . . misguided persons—"

They watched keenly for his eyes to settle on some specific victim, but no, as always, he kept them slowly, alarmingly, roaming.

"—who labor under the impression that this Christianity of ours is a milk-and-water recipe—"

The chaplain spat it out and lingered so long on it that visions arose of mountainous rice puddings and other horrors.

"—for the good life. If you play the game—these regrettable persons maintain—if you keep your faces washed and your hands clean, if you conform to the accepted pattern of the society in which you find yourself, then you are leading the Christian life."

Mr. Rowles glanced over at the Head.

"It is my office to remind you . . . and to remind you forcibly . . . that such persons are . . . in their blindness, in their ignorance, and in their folly . . . CRUCIFYING CHRIST FOR THE SECOND TIME!"

Sudden as a thunderbolt, the words hit the back wall of the

antechapel, reverberated about the numbed figures of the parents and relatives, and came echoing along the sides up to the altar, and so filled the vault.

Embarrassment was the major reaction, holding them all motionless. Only one head moved: Mrs. Crabtree brought her eyes down and let them settle directly upon the ghastly white face of the speaker.

His right hand went up, with the long fingers outstretched and the blue ring flashing.

"No! No! No! This is not Christianity! This is the vapid *spawn* of misguided blasphemers. This comes not from Christ, but from small men too ignorant . . . nay, too cowardly . . . to embrace the true message. Cast your eyes upon the windows of this very *building!*"

Almost everyone had to turn his head around to do this comprehensively. Almost everyone knew what he was expected to see. But all acted under hypnosis. There was a stirring and rustling, and several hymnbooks fell.

Both the chaplain's hands were outstretched now and directed at the side walls, his garments issuing from his wrists like the wings of a great white bird.

He waited.

They had seen. They turned back to face him.

He cried out—a baying sound, wolflike and desperate—*"Look what they have done to Him!"*

The Head's mouth was down. He was scarlet.

Wrath took the place of grief in the chaplain's voice: "This pale . . . weak . . . *effeminate* . . . creature. This is *their Christ!*"

He reduced volume suddenly. His rubato.

"And fittingly so. For only such a one could tell us to accept the pattern . . . to become ciphers . . . to embrace . . . respectability."

The chaplain folded his white-winged arms across his front and uttered the word with searing disgust.

"But this is *not* Christ. This is *not* Christianity. This is not . . . *love.*"

Mrs. Crabtree dipped her chin several times, unconsciously. She had turned as white as the chaplain himself.

"What . . . you may well ask yourselves . . . what . . . is love to these people? I will tell you."

The chaplain paused and scowled, waiting to tell them what they knew, but in a manner which even Mr. Dotterel could never approach.

"It is some faint . . . wishy-washy . . . anemic little regard, for playing the game . . . for doing honor to these premises in which we reside."

The Head wondered if he could immediately halt the proceedings. But how? How?

"But this is not love. No, no, *no!* Christ is love. And Christ . . . is a BURNING FIRE."

Like spectators at *Hamlet* who know all the lines, they heard it explode with complete satisfaction, unmarred by familiarity. The chaplain's long thin mouth had opened into a dark cavern, and in his High English accent "fah" was like hot gas rushing out of it.

"Yes! Yes! Christ is a scorching flame of love! Such love that ravages the heart and soul of those who truly know Him. A love that burns its way to our very innards, reducing to dust and ashes our sackcloth, our pettiness, our pride, our ambition— all the vile balderdash of creed, class, and society—and leaving us naked and alone and free and *joyful* before Him. No, no, no, I tell you! Christ is not a milkmaid! Christ is not a bearded lady! Christ is not even a schoolmaster or a rural dean. Christ . . . is a BURNING FIRE."

His black eyes went along the pews, one by one, all through the building, and finally *appeared* to settle for a moment on the headmaster's pew.

They could hear the chaplain breathing.

Then he spun away from them and was facing the altar, making the sign of the cross. There was a rush of words too swift to be audible: "And-now-to-God-the-Father-God-the-Son-and-God-the-Holy-Ghost-Amen."

He spun back, took his skirt in his right hand and swept down from the altar step, moving rapidly along the aisle, which seemed to be entirely filled with his rustling white garments, his large buckled shoes squeaking as he went.

* * *

69

The rest was not entirely anticlimax. When Carleton and Naylor took up the collection, during the final hymn, the chaplain made great play with receiving it on the gold plate like the sun. Having allowed it to flash and glitter in the face of all, in various swooping movements, he then offered it up on high with dramatic ceremonial that put one in mind of the Aztecs. But otherwise, everyone was merely waiting to break forth and rejoice in the fulfillment of his expectations.

Night had fallen.

The boys paraded out first. This time they had the great satisfaction of standing aside, in the dimly lit cloisters, in two lines, and intently scrutinizing every face that passed down the middle and out the end door. The satisfaction would have been greater, were the masters not such born actors. Jimmy Rich could be relied on for a nod and a grin—even a quick wink—but the rest were expressionless.

The Crab was scarlet, with his chin up and mouth down. This was revealing, but no one suspected that he was dazed with shock and burning with rage, aggravated, if that were possible, by his having to give pride of place in the procession to the so-called man of God.

Ma Crab, beside him, walked with her eyes on the stone flags and her hands behind her back, revealing nothing. She walked with the new knowledge that the pain and all the hidden bitterness of her life were of infinite value and sanctified by the love of Christ. She could see nothing, save the face of the man who had made this plain.

The chaplain followed after them, faintly smiling, and went upstairs to eat a plate of smoked salmon.

The school broke ranks with a roar. (The Head heard it from the hall of his house, and his hand went straight to his heart; it sounded like revolution.) They stripped off their surplices and let themselves go.

The Chapel Square, the Quad, and the night resounded with running feet and repeated cries of "Christ . . . is a burning FAH!"

Blood was running faster. All things were intensified. Alone in the silent chapel, Carleton took one end of the white and gold altar cloth and Naylor the other, and as they moved together to fold it, Carleton let Naylor take his end of the cloth, and he put his hands instead around Naylor's waist. Naylor's face, close to his, blushed a little, and he said, mildly, "Tch, tch, Carleton, for heaven's sake!" Naylor was wonderfully slim and fresh in his dark blue suit. Turning away out of Carleton's hands, he folded the cloth again, with his back to him, and Carleton, feeling warm and happy, put his hands around Naylor's chest. They were the same height. Naylor did not move away. Carleton kissed the nape of his neck. "You're crazy," Naylor said suddenly. "Someone'll come in." He stepped away across the flags to a ledge on which was lying the tray containing the red velvet money-bags.

"I'll carry it," said Carleton.

"I saw you! I saw you!"

Seaton-Scott, with his spectacles glinting, had leaped out from under the altar table. Carleton nearly dropped the tray. They hadn't even noticed him crouching there.

"Caught in the act, caught in the act!" shouted Seaton-Scott, beaming and jumping up and down like an idiot.

"Oh, buzz off, Seaton-Scott!" said Naylor, as they started down the aisle with their burdens.

This was an old game with the altar cloth, and Seaton-Scott had been present at it in the past. They regarded his presence with indifference. He was round-faced, with specs. To have bothered to come back and secrete himself under the altar cloth was typically childish and typically Seaton-Scott.

"You're a bore, Seaton-Scott," said Carleton.

"I saw. I saw!" said Seaton-Scott, jumping about behind them. "Let *me* do it next time, Naylor, and I'll let you off."

"Not bloody likely," said Naylor.

"Cheeky little runt," said Carleton.

Naylor, who had only the altar cloth to carry, switched off the lights, and they went out onto the Chapel Square.

"FOR THE SECOND TAHM!" somebody shouted out of the dark.

"I'll think about it," Seaton-Scott called after them, but weakly.

They didn't bother to respond. They had forgotten him.

They went down the stone steps and along the cloisters.

Cloister cricket was permitted here, and the two light bulbs up above were in wire nets to protect them from hard-hit ten-

71

nis balls. There were flies buzzing around them in the warm night. The grass Quad was through the arches to their left, and someone called out, "Ooh, Carleton, can I have one of those?" —meaning the money-bags.

It was terribly boring and wasteful of one's youth, Carleton thought, to be surrounded by so many obvious minds. In a moment they were going past Lady Jane Grey's chest, and so upstairs.

There was an immense cupboard of dark wood grapes and flowers on the landing outside the chaplain's rooms, and Naylor carried the key. They put the altar cloth inside it, and following their usual practice, Naylor took out the bottle of communion wine, removed the cork, and had a long drink.

"Steady on," Carleton whispered, laying the gold tray on the carpet and taking the bottle from Naylor.

It was warm and sweet.

"It's jolly good stuff," said Carleton, wiping his mouth.

Carleton had to take the tray in and count the money with the chaplain. They took it in turns, and they had tossed for it, and he had lost. It was the only thing that Carleton did not like about Sunday nights: he was uneasy in this strange man's presence, and the deception over his delayed baptism had not helped.

As he raised his hand to knock on the door there was a weird cry, like a sob, from within.

"Come in!" the chaplain shouted.

Carleton went in.

The chaplain was seated in his usual chair, with the orange held to his nose.

It was not he who had sobbed. Huddled at his feet in front of the fire was Mrs. Crabtree. She was in tears, and she held the chaplain's poker in her right hand.

The chaplain lowered the orange. He was paler than ever, and he looked over toward Carleton with his expression of extreme disgust.

At the same moment Mrs. Crabtree's tearful eyes had come up and seemed to spell murderous revenge upon Carleton for this intrusion.

Carleton did not hesitate. He put the plate down on a table beside one of the Greek figurines and went out.

"Carleton!" the chaplain shouted.

Carleton closed the door behind him and made off.

There was a howl that not only filled the landing but must have been audible all through the Head's House: *"Will no one rid me of this turbulent woman?"*

CHAPTER EIGHT

 A letter arrived on Monday morning. Although Ashley had been in residence barely a week, it seemed to him that it came from a different, forgotten world.

MY DEAR ERIC,

Formal and more than apprehensive opening from erring friend. What a dreadful scene, and I only wanted to talk about your writing! Miss Godfrey gave me warning of eviction if it happens again. A certain irony in that, you must agree! I'm afraid I was overexpressive—it must have been the gin—but did you have to flee quite so far and for so long? You certainly live up to that strange thing on your notepaper—the birde flewe all right. The slam of the door rang in my ears all night, and I was blushing for weeks.

Your mother in Bryanston Square told me you were in the reading room, and I couldn't do much about *that!* After further pressing phone calls, and hearing no word from the master, she tells me suddenly you are in *Italy*, for Chrissake. I thought we'd finished with all that. Charming no doubt your Father Mancini may be, but I distrust his intentions. But I seem to have said that before. As you will have known, I'm having trouble in speaking of the hardest thing. Your mother told me of this too, and I'm terribly sorry—they don't know the best man when they see him. But whatever was going on in the reading room, certain that it will more than make up for temporary setback. Great faith in gifted author. Certain future. Don't care to think of you at all in that ghastly place. But that won't last—will it?

We suppose . . . uh . . . that our presence in the vicinity is not strictly to be considered? We find, once there, it has some mysterious hold, but could an exception not be made some London Sunday lunchtime? Someone feels awful and needs to make amends.

Love,
JOAN

P.S. I'm a dab hand at roast beef though I say it myself.

Ashley read it—and reread it—lying on the divan bed in his room, which was bright and sunny because it was another beautiful day. The room was on the upper floor in the new buildings, above a classroom. When he had swept out of the sixth form on the first day, he had merely needed to go upstairs and along a corridor. But Carleton's startling remark had sent him off absentmindedly into the outdoors. The room looked out not onto the herbaceous borders, but onto the other, northern side: a grass bank and lawns, and the wood, with a glimpse of the gorse-covered hills. On the lawn was a tall sycamore tree from whose branches he had occasionally taught the sixth form on fine spring days. (He was considering it today.) The other forms were impossible out of doors. The open sky for some reason made them uncontrollable.

The room was agreeable enough, with a desk by the window. On it was a photograph of his mother in a play by Terence Rattigan that had run for four years. There were books around the walls: much poetry, religion, philosophy; historical novels by his father, and a few others, mostly French.

It was the morning break, and the Matron and her admirers were dealing with a queue of invalids in the dispensary next door. It was true that there *was* a door, as well as the one to the corridor. He had hung a striped rug over it, when first coming here, to give more cheer to a room with a northern outlook. The thing had then vanished from sight and mind.

Was it solely because it came from the other world—the world below—that he found himself viewing this letter with such severe detachment?

She was an intelligent and generous and vital person, and though he had rarely proposed these long sessions of far from sweet or silent thought, once persuaded into them, he had

74

played the game with a will. My God, the talk! The revelations of self! The way she kept the gin and tonic moving!

And all after Cambridge, too. No excuse of youth. He had been scarcely involved with the opposite sex at Cambridge: only Mary, who wanted to be a soulmate, and Ruth, who wanted more and had sent him that bloody little book.

What *did* this one want? How much was it the gin?

Erring "friend."

Suddenly barring the door and throwing back the bedclothes right in the middle of his recent thoughts on the surface being all-important, and then a struggle—actual physical combat for a moment—and shouts, and the most amazing imprecations coming after him down the stairs.

As far as he was concerned, there was an impediment to the marriage of true minds: it did not admit to sexual intercourse.

Yes, his mother had told him that this "sweet girl" had called. Some drink had been taken. She was "rather intense, dear, but really very sweet. That sort of intelligence and honesty frightens men away, you know—that's why she's young for her age, like you. My God, she disagreed with *me* about two plays that I've *adored!* (We didn't talk about you *all* the time, you see.) She disagreed very sweetly. She blushed. The child blushed. But she was definite. Few men will stand for that, you know. One can see she finds you different. She's very fond of you, Eric."

"Sparring partner."

"No, no. On the contrary."

"Oh, nonsense."

"How blind you men are!"

"Mother, kindly—"

"Mind my own business. But if I can open your eyes. What was all that you told me about E. M. Forster and English people with undeveloped hearts? Now you wouldn't want to be found guilty yourself, would you? The "denial of love," wasn't it?

"It's my concern."

"This girl is full of heart . . . and body too, I wouldn't be surprised; she's most attractive in her own way, though it's not mine. All that intensity and intelligence didn't fool me. It genuinely fools her, though, that's what's so sweet. Still like a college girl—what is she, twenty-six? She genuinely believes herself impassioned about your career and your prose style."

"She works in a publishing house."

"Ha, ha!"

"How affectionately you women murder each other! You can't conceive of another member of your sex who isn't playing in a drawing room romance."

"I don't know where one plays it nowadays, dear, but it *is* in our nature, you know. Don't you think you should come to terms with that fairly soon?"

"I detest you sometimes."

"I don't believe you. I can't bear to think of having another confirmed bachelor in this house. One was enough. My dear, you're turning into your father thirty years before your time. I've felt for a long while now that I'm really living in an annex of the British Museum."

"Of Shaftesbury Avenue, more like it. The place seethes with your out-of-work contemporaries. How could he possibly have written or read history in this theatrical doss-house? My room is perpetually invaded by the stars of yesteryear."

"That's because I gave you all my best furniture. We seem to have got off the point."

"We always do, thank God."

What had Joan thought? A well-preserved enchantress. Full of heart. The dominant mother. Yes, classic situation. Dear God.

He had gone to Assisi, and the refreshment of Paolo's humor and immodest humility had worked a cure. They had laughed a good deal, savagely analyzing each other. It was Cambridge again. But if the Father had ever had any "intentions" (which was enigmatic—he jested about conversion), he had them no longer. He had sensed that mystery, ceremony, romance, comfort, whatever it was that had attracted Ashley, did so no more.

Ashley had himself only come to a complete realization of this when he found that he was actually encouraging the sixth form to mockery.

An essay which he had lately published on the Forsterian

knowledge of good-and-evil and on the panic and emptiness of the Malabar Cave—an experience he had lately tasted himself on several occasions, as in the Weatherhill Quad—had led him to a study of Eastern religions. Good-and-evil in an emptiness without panic was, crudely, the starting point.

That was what he had been doing in the reading room.

How disturbingly she touched on everything! The "mysterious hold." Was that possible?

A "ghastly place." Yes, women were surely bound to find it so. But there was a necessary lack of understanding.

In any case, his upbringing had equipped him for no other financial occupation.

No, there was no hold.

When he first came, he had feared there might just be.

But it was gone.

Carleton knocked and came in.

Immaculate, Ashley lay on the divan with his arm behind his head. One knee was up, and the other leg was crossed over it, so that Carleton had to look around the sole of Ashley's shoe in order to see him. Above his head, there was a primitive crucifix, which Carleton found embarrassing.

"Ah, dear boy. What can I do for you? Take my humble chair. What's this you bring? Further news from Caesar?"

"No, it's um—"

"Sit down. Sit down. This will evidently take awhile."

Carleton sat at the desk. "It's a story. I wrote it."

"Oh, God."

Ashley always disappointed on his own, Carleton thought. In class he could be crazy, funny, or sometimes exhilarating about a book which one would study later, trying in vain to recapture that same excitement. Alone, he was difficult.

"It's a long journey to that railway station in the snow," said Ashley. "Ought you not to reconsider while there is yet time?"

"I wasn't trying to be Tolstoy."

"In that case you may as well tear it up."

"Chekhov said the little dogs must bark as well."

Ashley almost smiled, and ran his fingers through his hair. "Where did you discover that, you wretched wench?"

77

"I think it was in a letter."

"Do you feel that there is an insufficiency of stories, in God's name?"

"No. And that's got nothing to do with it. Anyhow it doesn't matter."

"Sit down! Why bring it here?"

"I wondered if you'd correct it . . . I mean, look at it . . . for me, and tell me what you think."

"You assume that such a production cannot be corrected."

"Well, hardly."

"*Pourquoi pas?*" .

"Well, it's not an exercise or anything. I made it up."

"I see."

Ashley uncoiled and stretched out, gazing on the ceiling. Carleton wondered what he had said wrong.

"Freedom," Ashley murmured. "Sounds as if you were preparing for the rude world. You're leaving us, are you not?"

"Yes."

"*Sans bagages.* You seem to have slipped through here very neatly. I admire your agility. Perhaps you *are* a writer."

"I don't understand."

"It's a substitute. Or a natural defense, if you wish. Can be very valuable when in need. But *I'm* no artist, my dear fellow, so I'm afraid you've come to the wrong shop."

"That's silly—"

"How dare you, sir!"

"I mean, everyone knows you're a writer."

"Not creative, sir. A mere parasite, I regret. I regret it more than I can ever tell *you,* my boy."

"I don't know what you mean. I read that article on Yeats—"

"That's what I mean."

"I didn't understand it, to be honest."

"Ah. Let's hope I'm more fortunate, if I surrender. Why not show it to your mother?"

"Are you crazy?"

Ashley had rolled up the letter he was holding, and placed it to his right eye, and was scrutinizing the ceiling.

"You fear it might come short of perfection?"

78

Carleton considered this surprising idea, and was shocked to think it was probably true.

"We don't see her," Ashley remarked.

"No."

"Fortunately mine has no desire to visit. She considers my occupation beneath contempt. Ou-boom. Tell me, have you ever suffered from solitude?"

"No. . . . No, I quite like it."

"Really! Chekhov again? But perhaps you make friends. That Johns fellow."

"No. No, he's not."

"Dear me. Perhaps you're immune because untouched."

"I don't follow you."

"That's the luxury of being young. One should treasure it. But one can't, of course. We're determined to follow. We start to understand each other—and that's that!"

Carleton was anxious to leave. He disliked being called young, disliked gloomy thoughts he could not understand, and had another commission to execute in the break. Why did Ashley want to talk to him?

"I had two friends at Cambridge. I believe that's what they were. They found me entertaining, heaven help me. We used to laugh."

"You sound as if you were a hundred years old or something."

"I am now. We didn't understand each other at all. That was the good thing. That was our youth."

Ashley was silent.

"Well, will I—"

"Do you follow our incredible chaplain?"

"No."

"Nor do I. Is it conceivable he moves through depths we know not of?"

"I don't know."

"Nor do I, thank God."

"I have to see Matron about something."

"Oh? Are you among the stricken?"

"No! I'm not."

"It's a little unchivalrous to be so definite about it."

"Well, I mean . . . Jimmy Rich is her age. *I'm* not!"

"Ah. That's better."

Carleton was irritated by being repeatedly caught out. "Why do you have to make fun of everyone?"

Irritatingly personal, Ashley thought. He should have cut this conversation short at the beginning. The children were far more entertaining in the classroom. It was the surface or the particular in people that was precious. These children had developed none. But at least in class they had some outward forms—whether inherited or copied. In private, their lack of persona was painful. He himself had developed an outward form for class, to augment the pleasure there—or to make it bearable. How much it expressed his true self was now beyond discovery, as it was also beyond control.

"Go on. Leave your masterpiece there. I'll look at it when the mood strikes."

Carleton stood up. "Will that be long?"

"Don't use those eyes on me, dear child. Save it for next door. Farewell."

Carleton went out. He was hurt, and angry. What eyes? How use them? Ashley would talk to you straight, as man to man, and expect you to understand, and then he'd suddenly be sarcastic and treat you as a child. He wasn't going to come here alone again.

Some of these creatures were ridiculously beautiful, Ashley was thinking. Thank God it was a matter of no interest.

A short queue of boys, wearing hangdog expressions, stretched away from the dispensary, along the corridor. Some were unwell, and the rest feigned being unwell. Gower was not among them. But the break was nearly over, and he ought to have paid his customary call by now. He was usually first in the queue.

Rowles had sent Carleton along to check that all was well. He intended to put his as yet unrevealed plan into operation that afternoon. But it depended entirely upon Gower's having similar intentions. He did not operate every day. Had he come to ask leave off games or not?

Gower was useless at cricket. Games, for him, was more

likely to be the cross-country run—which almost everybody detested. A prefect went to the stipulated destination on a bicycle, to make sure that everyone completed the distance. Even if the prefect did *not* go, there was no means of knowing. Goody goodies, on their way back, would never tell you whether there was anyone there or not. If Gower *had* come with some complaint, Matron was to give him the afternoon off. Dr. Rowles had involved her in his plot.

The room was crowded, not merely with patients, but also Matron, three voluntary helpers/admirers, and, to Carleton's surprise, the Butcher.

Dr. Boucher's visits to the school, except in time of epidemic, were always a surprise. They were infrequent and followed no pattern. Matron hated them. They upset her routine and her authority.

The Butcher was standing with his back to the window—the sun making a halo round his short-cropped red hair—talking about his customary subject, starvation in India. Matron was bandaging a boy's ankle and saying "Really" and "How terrible" every now and then. Carleton thought her an awfully nice and gentle person in her white coat, and frightfully capable at the same time. He could not understand the grand passions that were aroused. She wore hardly any make-up! He gathered from the Hearties that she could be fun when not on duty. She laughed a lot and had lively blue eyes. But her hair was in old-fashioned permanent waves, and she must be over thirty!

Nevertheless, there were three seniors there, giving out tonics and things, and you could sense their adoration in the atmosphere. Strangely enough, one of them was his fellow prefect, Pryde, a hulking fellow with a poxy face. In the middle of last term, Pryde, who you'd think would never do anything unusual in his whole life and who had certainly never opened a book, had told Carleton he was going to read the entire Bible as a penance.

"Why?" Carleton asked.

"I'm hopelessly in love with her," Pryde replied.

"But why are you reading the Bible?" Carleton demanded.

"There's nothing else for it," Pryde replied. He had meant it too. He had very nearly finished the Old Testament.

". . . a mere bundle of flesh and bones . . . morning"—a nod to Carleton—"flies crawling all over the poor wretch . . . look here, I said, you're not going to leave that poor blighter sitting there, are you? By God, they were too! Bring him in at once, I said. . . ."

The Butcher was not entirely boasting. He had, in fact, led a medical mission to India that had met with remarkable successes, considering its size. A former university boxing champion, he was made for tough, adventurous, ginger-headed doctoring of this kind. He was certainly not made for attending to the manifold minor distresses of high-caste English boys at the most impressionable time of life.

Dr. Boucher cracked arms and legs back into place. A notable footballer himself, he believed that influenza and similar illnesses were best shaken off by getting the chap back into the scrum as soon as possible.

It was, therefore, not merely the convenience of his surname that had gained him the title of Butcher.

Dr. Boucher, who had just returned from his third Indian visit, was of the opinion that everything taking place in the dispensary at this very moment was preposterous.

Matron knew this.

She had finished with the bandage, and with a movement of the head she indicated that Carleton was to come over to the window. Doing so, he passed Pryde, and their eyes met, and Carleton felt keenly embarrassed on Pryde's behalf. He was in the act of spooning cough mixture into Finch Minor's mouth. If this was what love did to you, thought Carleton, heaven save him!

"Dr. Rowles sent me," he whispered. "Has he been?"

"Yes. I told him he could be off games," she said softly.

"What's all this?" boomed the Butcher.

"Ssh," said Matron, glancing round the room.

"Shush, shush? What the devil are we shushing about? Who's off games now?"

The Matron had colored a little. That great giant, Pryde, was looking across with moon-calf eyes.

"Um, Gower, Doctor—"

"Gower! Gower! What's that little blighter cooked up this time?"

"He has quite a bad rash, Doctor—"

"Nettles!" thundered Dr. Boucher. "We've had that one before. The little blighter goes out and rubs himself with nettles."

"That was not my opinion, Doctor."

Matron spoke very firmly indeed. The Butcher blinked, hesitated, and then relented, patting her on the shoulder.

"You're too kind to 'em, Nancy. You'd never do in India. It'd break your ruddy heart."

"Ah, Carleton! Come in. Close the door like a good fellow. Sit yourself down. What's the verdict?"

"It's all right. He has a rash."

"Good, good. Couldn't be better. A rash! Hee! Extra*ordinary* bird. Well, never mind," said Dr. Rowles, suddenly turning very solemn, "let's get down to business. now, listen here, Carleton, the whole essence of this thing is we're not going to catch the chap *flagrante delicto,* as it were. We've had you under the table rug."

"You mean when I lunged out and caught Johns around the ankle?" said Carleton, trying not to smile, because Rowles sounded so serious.

(After an hour in the dark under the rug, sweating with apprehension—a packet of biscuits being laid as bait on the table above—he had heard someone quietly enter. He lunged, shouting, "Got you, Gower!" Poor Johns had let out a shriek like a maniac. He had to lie down on the ottoman for a while to recover. The idiot had known all about it, but "forgot.")

"The extraordinary thing was that those damn biscuits had gone," ruminated the Doctor, more in his old style. "Now, listen, the only way we're going to catch him is to see him in possession. Ah, good, there's the bell. I was counting on that. Who have you got now?"

"Um, D . . . Mr. Dotterel."

"That's all right. You can tell him you were with me. The washroom, Carleton. Now! Ponder that for a moment."

"I don't quite see, sir."

"This extraordinary bird hovers about that room, leaves it, and returns to it again, like some damn jackdaw around its nest. For all I know, the poor chap may regard it as the womb, or the arsehole, or something. I'm no headshrinker. Now, Carleton, it's my strong hunch that the first thing our jackdaw does is to take the prize straight to its nest and gloat over it."

"He goes to the washroom?"

"Precisely. He wants to look at the damn thing. I mean, no one's suggesting that he's *eating* all those extraordinary foodstuffs of yours. If he is, he's more of a monster than I thought. At any rate, if he doesn't enter, he *must* pass the washroom door —which, as you know, has no door—and so out that way toward the jacks. He's only one other way out."

"Through the common-room window—or the two dormitory windows."

"Right. But you're going to be posted out there in the wood. You'll have to tackle him straight. He'll have it under his coat."

"Where are you going to be posted, sir?"

"If you think I'm going to be hanging around outside the jacks all afternoon, you're mistaken. I'll show you," said Rowles, glancing at his huge watch. "We'll just let those chaps get back into class."

They waited, and the Doctor puffed his pipe.

"What'll happen to him, sir, if we catch him?"

"He'll have to go. We'll have to tell the parents."

"I think I'd die if something like that happened to me."

"Really? Really, Carleton?"

"Yes."

"Ah, well, it's not quite what you have in mind. I mean, it's not the poor fellow's fault. He needs medical attention. I fear it's not exactly . . . within the scope of our own good Doctor, if you know what I mean."

"Yes. I do."

"Come along now."

Rowles eagerly led the way downstairs, into the corridor, and so into the washroom.

"Now then," he said.

They had paused by a wooden cubicle about six feet high, just inside, in a corner.

This was the Doctor's private shower.

Every morning at seven the boys left their towels on the washroom bench and scampered across the corridor into the shower room, which had a sliding door that clanged back and forth.

84

Anyone caught evading a cold shower immediately got three on the bare backside from a prefect or the Doctor himself.

At the same time, Rowles went into his own cold shower, and closed the door, and gasped and huffed and puffed, obtaining total cleanliness for what seemed an eternity to others who were rushing in and out of the icy waters.

"Have a look at this?"

Rowles had taken something from his sports coat pocket.

"What on earth is it?"

"It's one of these damn women's affairs. Matron lent it to me."

It was a lady's mirror, handbag size.

"See this."

To the back was affixed a little cardboard stand.

"I made it myself," said the Doctor, with evident pride.

"Now then, fetch me a chair from the common room."

"A chair?"

"Yes, yes, look smart."

Carleton hurried down the corridor and came back with one of their small wooden chairs.

Rowles had unlocked the shower door and was standing inside it.

"Put it there, in the corner."

"In the shower, sir?"

"Now then."

Rowles sat on the chair and bent forward, with an inadvertent grunt, and placed the mirror on the floor.

"Now, close the door."

"Shut you in, sir?"

"Yes, yes. Now then, can you see me in the mirror?"

He could. Presumably to save it from being rotted by the shower water, the door did not come down to the floor, but stopped some six inches above it. The mirror, at a slight angle, showed him the Doctor's great head.

"Yes, sir."

"And I can see *you*, which is more to the point!" said Rowles, and even through the door one could appreciate his triumph.

"Now go out, Carleton, walk past the door and out toward the jacks."

Carleton did so, and returned.

"I saw you all right." The Doctor's voice came rather muffled this time from his burrow.

"Well," he said, emerging, "what do you think of it?"

"It's brilliant, sir."

"I'll spring out on him, you see," said Rowles, looking almost bashful about Carleton's compliment. "Now there's only
one thing left—the bait."

"Um . . . I've got a can of mixed fruit salad, sir."

A flicker of disgust passed across the Doctor's face.

"Admirable," he said.

CHAPTER NINE

Even while involved in these unfamiliar happenings,
Carleton had been conscious that he would be sitting
beside Ma Crab at lunch. Work was no distraction:
there was neither Ashley nor Milner that morning—his favorite
lessons. Instead, Rowles did incomprehensible sums on the
blackboard, the Cod was equally bewildering with test tubes,
and Dotty waffled about the Wars of the Roses. None of it was
necessary in any case: schoolwork was over for Carleton.

The tinkling of the first lunchbell brought a renewal of apprehension.

The prefects stood behind their chairs along the high table,
up on the dais, while the school did likewise at the smaller
tables running crosswise out from the narrow windows of
the dining hall. Down the aisle, a master was due to sit at the
head of each table, and the boys moved around daily, so that
each had the opportunity of adult communion.

The prefects also moved around. The Head and his wife sat
together at the center, looking down the hall. Carleton had
been beside the Head the previous day, so he would now be
beside his wife.

Prefects across the table were free of embarrassment or

boredom, because the line of huge silver trophies running down the middle made conversation almost impossible. In any case, to hear Mrs. Crabtree you had to be up very close.

Over in a corner of the dais, the butler, Lloyd, waited beside the same soup tureen that had been employed at Carleton's baptism. Lloyd was a wonderfully grotesque creature, who had been there even longer than Dr. Rowles and had never been known to speak or smile. Tall and thin in his tailcoat, with a skeleton face and batlike ears, he was a butler from a horror film. From the point of view of Rowles, the man must know at least as much as himself—covering more than fifty years—but, damnation, the fellow would tell or share nothing!

Waiting for the school's usual pandemonium to cease, his mouth dry with dread, Carleton felt the need to confide. Unfortunately, Johns, who usually sat beside him, was today set apart by the Crabtrees' two regal chairs with high backs, while standing at Carleton's right elbow was the fourth prefect in Priestley House, Rogers, a square fellow with powerful spectacles and dandruff, with whom he had never been able to converse.

The strange fact was that he had decided not to confide in anybody about last night's astonishing tableau. The woman at the chaplain's feet, and in tears! And that look!

He had felt it unfair to pass this on. Cruel. They had been here only a week. He did not even know her. Roly and the Pedant—and, far worse, the school—could make murder out of it. Whatever it was—as he had frequently experienced with Ashley—he suspected that there was something more serious at stake than he could understand. But what? She couldn't *possibly* have fallen for Cyril Starr. Surely she must know, and anyway they were both about a hundred years old!

Pryde, who was prefect on duty for the day, struck the clapper a bang, down by the distant door, and the noise subsided.

They would be parading from the Head's hall, as they did for chapel. The masters' common room was across the hall from his study. He would put his head around the door and say, "Ready, gentlemen?"

She came in through the open door first—head down and hands behind her back. The Crab was following—head up, flushed, with his mouth down to show authority. Then the masters, standing at their places in the prevailing silence. (The chaplain was up in his room, eating duck.)

She rounded the end of the table, under the cavernous eyes of Lloyd. She's really terribly shy, Carleton thought; it's not just me. She approached. A murmured "good morning" might have helped, but no, she stood beside him, in silence, with eyes lowered.

On her left, her husband had his only moment which approached the role she would have wished for him.

"*Benedictus benedicat,*" he prayed, slowly drawing it out. "*Per Jesum Christum dominum nostrum.*"

Everyone sat down, with a noise like a barrage. The Crabtrees resembled royalty on their thrones. Since the Old Man's death, the matching chair for Mrs. Crabtree had been resurrected from a storeroom.

Conversation had broken out all about him. He could even hear the Crab talking with Johns. The ghostly Lloyd had inserted himself and expertly ladled soup onto Ma Crab's plate. Down the aisle, the skivvies rushed back and forth, some carrying seven soup plates at a time. Miss Bull, with her vast bosom above a steaming caldron near the entrance door, was rapidly dishing it out, with the experience of years.

The dipping action of Mrs. Crabtree's chin was ideally adaptable to the eating of soup. Down she went and up again. Not a word.

What could she say, for goodness sake? "About last night—"

He even turned to Rogers, but that ass was having a loud argument about Japanese motorbikes, of all things.

Her eyes came up for a second, but not toward him.

"Master Allen's dereliction is still with us."

She dipped so abruptly that the soup nearly spilled from her spoon.

He had only just caught her words, but he looked where she had looked and saw the triangular window, devoid of glass.

"We still await the parental check."

"Do you mean to say . . . you told his mother?"

"Naturally. . . . You know about his father, I see."

"But it wasn't his fault, Mrs. Crabtree."

"That is not our opinion."

Lloyd leaned over them again, exuding a supernatural odor

and removing the plates. It seemed to be a stalemate. In the silence, he could not resist searching down the room. Yes, there in the far corner. The black hair. Pinky brown face. The animation. Talking with enthusiasm . . . to Mr. Dotterel!

"I am perfectly well aware that Mr. Ashley holds other views. The headmaster was much distressed over his meddlesome behavior."

This took her so long to say that even before the end Lloyd had laid on the English landscape placemat, at which she had been staring, a plate of shepherd's pie. (It was Monday.)

"But—"

"We may be new here, but we are not as green as Mr. Ashley appears to assume. We are fully aware that fire practice for the new boys is an ancient tradition of the school. It was not our place to interfere, and it was certainly not his."

He thought it just as well that she only showed him her profile and did not see his face. She had a dark mole with hairs on it. He was looking and listening with such interest that he had forgotten everybody.

"I noted that *you* gave parental—" She turned a little away and must have glanced at the Head. Carleton could scarcely hear her now. "One trusts it was parental . . . attention to our little window breaker."

Carleton felt a blush rising and could not stop it. But at least she was not looking.

"He . . . Allen . . . got a fright. And he couldn't get out of the—"

"I hope that you and our Mr. Ashley are not founding some sort of adoption society for those temporarily out of favor."

Gleeful. It was almost meant to be a joke! He was very glad that there was a huge cup for cricket between them and the two prefects opposite.

"Mr. Ashley had nothing to do with it. He didn't even know it was . . . Allen. I thought he might like to go to the nets. He's very good, too. Mr. Rich said so."

Carleton found it strangely simple to speak so bluntly to her. In a crazy way, considering the conversation, she was easy to talk to. He would have liked to raise many other subjects. Among adults, women had always been far more approachable, when old enough, and this was the first one here in four years.

"I wonder that Mr. Rich has the time for such matters."

This from the headmaster's wife!

"How do you mean, Mrs. Crabtree?"

"I have already told you that one is better informed than you seem to imagine."

He noted that she said "one" this time, and not "we."

He wondered who had been doing the informing—Steele probably.

"Matron has been looking particularly pleased with herself."

"Oh?"

Mrs. Crabtree, who was evidently saying no more, did *not* sound pleased. The remark about the other lady was made with even more acidity than the remarks about Ashley. It was an entirely new experience to hear such alarmingly relevant comments coming from so high a quarter. Sitting beside the Old Man, one had never heard a word about other persons, least of all members of his own staff. Carleton was amazed, and equally so by her nerve. Was it bluff?

Was she challenging him to mention the unmentionable?

Lloyd had taken their plates and served them with bread and butter pudding.

"My daughter began at Gillingham this morning. I hope nothing fatal has occurred."

This was a surprise. Gillingham College was a girls' boarding school five miles away, but in fact mercifully remote. Occasionally, crocodiles in uniform gray, with helmetlike hats and male red ties, were seen on the roads, provoking embarrassed mockery and laughter.

"Oh. I thought she was going to a day school."

"She calls it that. She feels that in these circles going as a day pupil would be regarded as a disgrace. But it's only a bicycle ride away, and she likes the idea of dropping in and out. She's independent—to an almost sinister degree."

Carleton was very flattered by this domestic revelation and by her treating him to a sophisticated mode of address. It was a pity that having abandoned her pudding, she appeared to be concentrating on the portrait of their founder, which hung away in the distance, above the entrance door. One might almost have thought that she was bored by her neighbor.

With an excitement that made his knees tremble under the table, he was about to put the question "What did you think of the chaplain's sermon?" when unfortunately the Head rose to terminate the proceedings.

It would be twelve days before he sat beside her again. It was a surprise to discover that this was the source of positive regret.

After lunch the school lay down for half an hour. Carleton and Johns had to enforce silence up in that vast and chilly dormitory. He was glad that Allen was away in the Johns half, and he could not see him round the square pillars. He was not so glad that he was in a corner and the end of his bed met the side of Sexy Sinnott's.

Carleton lay next to a revolting specimen called Wolseley, who had a completely unique and vile body odor. But this was not all. He had lately taken to throwing back the sheets in the morning, standing on his pillow, scratching his greasy head in proud and mildly bashful wonderment, and announcing, "Gosh! Look! It's happened *again.*"

"Shut up, Wolseley, you're absolutely disgusting!"

"I'm not. I can't help it. Isn't it *amazing* though?"

"You're doing it yourself."

"I'm *not.* I swear."

"Stop whining, and clear off to the shower. At once!"

The usual spectators would approach. ("Oh, not again, Wolseley, you filthy beast.")

"And that goes for the rest of you, too!"

"It's *amazing.* I can't get over it. It never *stops.*"

"Clear off, Wolseley!"

The exterior of the wardrobe that separated Carleton from the bed on his other side was constantly hung with exposure meters and other mysteries of the photographic trade. Some of them were very expensive, and Carleton and Dr. Rowles had been trying to think of a way of warning their owner about Gower without naming names. The amateur expert was a comical boy named McIver who could make Eddie Cantor eyes behind his heavily framed eyeglasses. He had collected untold sums selling photographs of bijous at five shillings a picture and was forever pestering Carleton.

"What about it now, Carleton? I know there's somebody."
"There isn't. Go to hell, McIver."
"Ah, come on. I won't tell if you don't want. I never do. Ask anybody. Ask Sherriff."
(Sherriff was a prefect in Pryor!)
"Tell you what. I'll let you see the negative for nothing. Now. I can't say fairer than that. Come on, who is it?"
"Go to *hell*, McIver."

His head propped up on the two cold pillows, Carleton was trying to begin the *Life of Talleyrand* by Duff Cooper. He had taken it out from the library, remembering that Ashley had said something in admiration of it last term.

He found it hard to concentrate. Some people, like Johns, could bury themselves in books, right in the middle of everything. Schoolwork was easy enough, because it was enforced, and they all did it together and in competition. But he had always found it difficult to read outside the curriculum, there was so much going on. In the holidays there was nothing else to do, and he had read a lot.

How could one start considering this dead Frenchman when right across the dorm lay Gower, with his sallow face hidden behind some ghastly magazine—Gower, who was planning theft at that very moment, while he, Carleton, was planning arrest, and the terrible sentence of banishment?

The silence made him more jittery. You could hear nothing in that vast crowded room, save the sound of pages being turned. Someone's fountain pen was scratching out a letter. News home. What on earth was there to say? What was there to tell that would mean anything? McIver was reading a photography magazine. Wolseley was eating his thumbnail, and absorbed in some unspeakable comic cuts.

He was trying not to visualize someone who, night and morning, went back and forth from that far corner in a brown dressing gown.

The first night when he came from the shower (warm showers at night) and went past the beds, there had been some wolf whistles, and Sinnott had made a public overture that was supposed to be funny: "There's plenty of room in here." The somebody had merely smiled and got into bed. Such assurance! Was he actually flattered? Did he *enjoy* it?

Cautious Carleton felt suddenly terrified. What on earth would he do if this thing really developed inside him and forced him to declare himself?

But suppose it developed with another—under his very eyes. It seemed unlikely: the other had quickly established himself as a no-nonsense, "middle-aged," lively, popular fellow. (The Honorable Fitzmaurice was languishing about the place and looked to be just asking for it.)

Still, one could never be sure. . . .

He turned his head and whispered, "McIver."

"Uh? What?"

"Ssh. Have you been asked to take anybody in the past week?"

McIver did a mild roll of the eyes.

"Stop that, and answer me."

"One or two."

Carleton felt like murdering him.

"Who?"

The wretch started to laugh.

"Ssh!"

"You won't catch me out that easy. I told you I don't tell." McIver leaned forward, nearly falling off his bed, and said in an eager whisper, "Who do you want? I can do it this afternoon."

"Nobody, you fool. Stop talking!"

"Does that make any sense to *you,* Petty?"

The Pedant, leaning on leather elbows, frowned over his spectacles, with his eyes fixed on his own copy of the book in hand. His voice was thin, acid, and full of danger.

"Uh. Not really. No, sir."

"I do wish you people would do your blasted preparation when it's set."

They sat feeling frightened for Petty. He wasn't a prefect. The Pedant could keep him in and set hundreds of lines, but, more than that, Milner was in his person the most frightening of them all. The only one who never shouted. A master of sarcasm and cold ferocity. When he used the word "blasted," it was more alarming than all the thunder of his colleagues.

"I did do it, sir, but . . . I've forgotten."

"Let us not add falsehood to stupidity, damn you. Would you kindly explain it to him, Johns."

93

This first afternoon period in the summer always gave the most trouble. In the spring and winter terms, afternoon school came between games and tea, as darkness fell. But in the long summer days it came—it was got over with—before games and after a lunch and a lie-down that made everyone drowsy and irritable.

Milner had told them all to come from their desks and sit around a long table, so that he might spur them on at closer quarters. But it made little difference. It was Caesar, and Carleton, like the others, had never viewed these Romans as anything other than wraiths behaving in a meaningless manner. Horace and Virgil as well; it was all the same. The object was simply to get the words right. Carleton relished it when they came in single sentences as an exercise; there was a strange satisfaction in doing them. But these great paragraphs out of old and senseless books were death to pleasure and concentration.

"Oh, do stop that, you two!" The Pedant suddenly interrupted Johns testily. "If you can't wait till afterward, try to remember the old man of Peru."

The two kept their eyes down on Caesar and blushed—and smiled!

"Johns. Get on with it!"

Carleton was amazed. They had been doing something under the table. Two prefects from other houses. Both quite fat!

They didn't seem to care.

He would have died!

The Pedant didn't seem to care.

"No, boy! No, boy! No, boy! No, boy!"

It was Dotty next door.

Johns stopped.

"Oh, *get on with it,* Johns. That is none of our business," said the Pedant.

"I will not have it, boy! I will not have it! Do you hear? Do you hear?"

The Head was waiting apprehensively for the second period in his study. Ashley would be taking the sixth, in French. Crabtree had now heard all the others teach by entering their classrooms, saying, "Carry on," and discreetly seating himself at the back. He had been surprised. He had been impressed. Indeed, much that he had heard had been out of his ken. Unfortunately, the question was: was it also beyond the ken of the boys?

There remained Ashley. He had kept him to the last, in fear of some repetition of the man's excessive impertinence in the very classroom, in front of the boys.

The other one to be watched was plainly the chaplain. Having persuaded himself of the charitable conclusion that the man was out of his mind and might perhaps be shortly removed on medical grounds, the Head had been faced with entirely opposite sentiments by his wife, his former partner in all administrative matters. On the contrary, it seemed, he was a true vicar of Christ and a man who had, in her words, "achieved greatness." This baffling view of a lunatic insurrectionist might not have made him pause, merely on its own. Unfortunately, he had also discovered, on questioning Steele, that the same sermon had been delivered for many years, and that all the older governors on the board had heard it frequently.

He could scarcely invite Lord Mountheath and Sir Charles Pike and ask the chaplain to repeat his performance.

"Lucretia!" he called out, pushing up the lower half of the window.

She had ridden up the drive on her bicycle, looking almost unrecognizable in the gray dress, pot hat, and red tie.

"Come up here a moment, my dear," called her father.

The uniform was made of thick flannel, and the poor child looked hot and flustered on this glorious day. It had been a problem getting it on her, and she and her mother had tussled together in an upstairs room.

She was a mystery to him. He longed for some kind of communion or at least to see some indication of occasional happiness. Perhaps later these things would come. Devoting, as he did, his whole life to boys, he had very much wanted one of his own, but she could not possibly know that.

"Well, my dear, how did you get on?"

She was holding the hat.

"All right."

"Do you think you're going to like it?"

A hopeless question, he knew. She did not like things.

"They're all stupid in class."

95

"Oh, dear. Your mother's an excellent teacher. You must be patient with them."

"They're not allowed rabbits," she said, with satisfaction. "Miss Hutchins won't have it. I told them about mine."

"They must envy you."

"They do. They're silly, too."

"Oh?"

There was something indefinable that recalled her mother. Something shocking was on the way.

"They want me to deliver notes."

"How do you mean, Lucretia?"

"Here," she said. "They were all around me, silly asses. They want me to bring notes and photos backward and forward."

The Head was nonplussed. Life had become a series of perilous surprises.

"They said I could have cakes and sweets and things, and they'd pay for the photos. I said I'd think about it."

"Now, listen to me, Lucretia—"

"I know how to get the photos."

The Head paused. He looked like a lobster.

"How, my dear?"

"There's a boy goes round with a camera and stuff. He's called McIver."

"Are you suggesting that this boy be paid for this service to the young ladies of Gillingham?"

"I think he's paid already."

She made no ducks of the chin, but the downcast eyes, the relish, and the pleasure in evoking alarm were a direct inheritance.

"I beg your pardon?"

"He's always in the photographic room. I heard him saying something as I was passing the door. Mother knows. I told her."

Was it that he was an honorable man who would not seek information from his own child? Or was it that he could not bear to hear certain things? He was not sure.

But this must be halted at once.

"Now listen to me, Lucretia, you are not to have anything to do with this ridiculous, silly nonsense. I absolutely forbid it. Do you understand? You would put me into an impossible position with regard to Miss Hutchins. Do you understand that?"

"Yeh. I told them nobody here would write them notes anyhow."

He never really knew what she might say next or why.

"They were furious. One of them nearly had hysterics. I'm going to take off these prison clothes. Ugh, I hate them!"

"Very well. And don't you forget what I said!"

The bell was ringing for the end of the first period.

He put on his gown and, holding his mortarboard to his chest, went past Lady Jane's chest and out into the sunshine and the gardens with the borders. He walked slowly, so that the classes would be assembled for the second period by the time he arrived at the new buildings. He found himself looking ahead to October, when he would make his first appearance with two hundred colleagues, at the Headmasters' Conference. It would be the high mark of his career, and he intended to show a strongly conservative line. They were trying to call them independent schools now. Not Weatherhill, thank you very much! Nor was anyone ever going to come here on a grant.

They were all in class, behind closed doors. The sixth form room was at the end of the corridor. Feeling apprehensive about Ashley, he walked almost on tiptoe on the pink flags and put his ear to the door before entering.

A boy's voice said, "All I'm asking is whether you actually kiss your bijous or not."

Crabtree threw the door open.

A boy with his back to him, called Peters, was saying, "Sometimes. It all depends on the—"

"What is this?" demanded the Head.

"Extra art, sir," someone replied.

Five long-haired and—to the Head—offensively dressed youths were seated around a table, making senseless abstractions on large sheets of paper.

"I don't understand. Where is Mr. Ashley's French class?"

"Outside, sir."

"I beg your pardon."

"They're out at the back, sir. You have to go down the corridor and out the other door. Mr. Ashley likes to be out in fine weather. Mr. De Vere Clinton asked him could we come in here, as we don't have a table, and the others are behind us, and he likes us to improvise on our own."

"I find this very strange indeed."

"Yes, sir."

"Well, get on with it, and stop talking."

"Yes, sir."

For some reason, having left them, he was till almost on tip-toe. Things seemed to disintegrate daily, in this place. As far as he remembered, a "bijou" was either a jewel or a cabbage, and in either case there would appear to be only one interpretation of what had been said. At the corridor crossroads he turned right, instead of going out the way he had entered, and reached the open door and halted immediately.

The sixth form sat on the top of the grass bank, and perched high above them on the branch of a tree was Ashley.

The Head retreated a little, in order to observe without being observed. Ashley was comfortably placed on a lower bough. His gown hung down. His left hand was around the trunk to prevent his falling. His right held a book. Two elegant brown shoes dangled high above the grass.

"My task is the more difficult in that the play is about love—a subject of which you possess no knowledge or understanding whatsoever."

"How do you know?" Johns demanded.

"Silence, sir! It will also come as a surprise to devotees of the motion picture industry to learn that our heroine, Phèdre, is a lady by no means young—who is in love with her stepson. There are no bedroom scenes, Johns. No one even sits down. No one lays a finger upon anyone else. Yet this urgent, profound play is white hot with passion and sexuality."

The Head stood back closer to the wall. He could not yet accept that there was a man seated in a tree speaking this at the top of his voice.

"The French is extremely simple, strong as a horse, and of a beauty beyond description. That much at least I am going to *make* you appreciate, even if we have to spend the rest of the term on it. The love is forbidden. It is sin. The lady, though passionately desirous of the young man, knows it to be such. Her sense of shame and her dignity, in opposition to the intensity of her desire, give her greatness. '*Oui, Prince, je languis, je brûle pour Thésée,*' she lies. Come on now! All of you! Let's hear it!"

"What page is it, sir?"

"Oh, damn the page! Say it with me. You're on the stage in the Comédie Française. It's a play. It's for acting. You're beginning a confession of burning, hopeless passion."

The Head moved out into the doorway.

Ten loud voices in unison imitated Ashley from the slope above. " '*Oui, Prince, je languis, je brûle pour Thésée.*' "

"Again, again! Impassioned! Let yourselves go! You're burning for someone. Act!"

" '*Oui, Prince, je languis, je brûle pour Thésée.*' "

"That's it. '*Que dis-je?*' . . . page thirty-nine, eight lines from the bottom, damn you. Hurry up!"

The Head cleared his throat. No one heard. There was a rustling of pages.

" '*Que dis-je?*' . . . Come on, raise your voices, follow me, relish it, indulge yourselves, listen how they fall, listen to the word made beauty . . . '*Que dis-je? Il n'est point mort, puisqu'il respire en vous. Toujours devant mes yeux je crois voir mon époux. Je le vois, je lui parle; et mon coeur. . . . Je m'égare, Seigneur, ma folle ardeur malgré moi se déclare.*' We'll say that again . . ."

"Ashley!"

Heads turned. The Crab was at the bottom of the steps. Ashley frowned down at him from the tree.

"*What* do you think you're doing?" demanded the Head.

"What do you think I'm doing?" said Ashley.

"I'm sure I've no idea, but you will have to cease this noise at once."

"This what?" said Ashley quietly.

"It makes it quite impossible for anyone in these classrooms to do any work," said the Head, gesticulating at the windows.

"I've had no complaints."

"Apart from the fact that it is outrageous!" said the Head, pointing at the figure in the tree.

"*Vous brûlez, Seigneur.*"

The Head paused: one could not, in honor, speak before the boys—even if one could think of what to say.

"You will hear more about this."

He turned and went back through the building and out the other door.

"Come on, now. All together. Fling yourselves into it! *'Que dis-je? Il n'est point mort, puisqu'il respire en vous. Toujours devant mes yeux. . . .'* "

When the bell went, Johns proposed to Carleton that they go into an empty classroom and play their game on the blackboard. The game was Old Films, about which they both had an unusual knowledge, especially Johns, who hoped to be a film critic. Each wrote up for the other a title, with its four leading players underneath, omitting all the consonants. The opponent had to fill them in. Marks were scored.

Carleton had to remind Johns that Operation Gower was now proceeding. (He had been told already.) Carleton begged him not to forget and to stay away from the common room and its environs for the afternoon. Johns replied with a "Don't forget your deerstalker," made a scathing reference to "Dr. Watson in the shower," and went off to play the game against himself. He had memorized almost the whole history of film-making in this way.

Carleton had slipped his copy of *Phèdre* into his pocket. It was an odd thing to do. No one save the few out-and-out "swats" ever read a school book out of class. But Ashley had evoked his interest in several ways.

He went off quickly toward the wood.

Dr. Rowles had undertaken to put the bait out on their table and to be already in position at the bell. He must be in there now, wishing he could smoke his pipe.

Boys were disappearing rapidly. Except for a handful of languishers, they were very decisive and enthusiastic about leisure.

There was junior cricket that afternoon. McCaffrey was giving swimming lessons in the pool up on the hill. Farming and hobbies accounted for others, and the run for those with no alternative interest.

When Carleton lay down in the grass up among the trees, there was no one in sight. The grass in the wood was so tall that when he stretched out flat, he could not be seen. There was a direct view down to the common room window and the adjacent dormitory window. To the left of them, beyond Ashley's tree, was the new building with Ashley's room on the first floor. Far off, in the other direction, was the Chapel Square.

No sign of Gower.

He felt excited, as if he were a child again, playing a childish game: the ridiculous, yet keen excitement of hide-and-seek.

Imagine Gower emerging through one of those windows— or even going in through one of them!

Bringing *Phèdre* was a mistake. Raising himself on one elbow, he opened it, but it now meant nothing. The drama, the beauty of the words, too, which had seemed perfectly plain with Ashley, had vanished. What the dickens were these passions? The stepson, Hippolyte, was in the same state, too, about some princess. Boring and incomprehensible. Yet Ashley had seemed to make sense and life out of it. It had been very odd to hear him say "sexuality"—surely he didn't know anything about that. Or had he some other, adult's, life? During the holidays?

There was a ladybug on the page. Carleton lifted it off onto his fingernail and put it on a long blade of bright green grass. Huge white clouds were passing overhead, but they never seemed to cover the sun. It was very warm. He took off his coat and rolled up his shirt sleeves. An arty senior called Peters was walking slowly up the wood with the Honorable Fitzmaurice. They had their hands in their pockets and their eyes on the ground, and they weren't speaking. Why? What was the point? And for this nothing they risked all kinds of remarks.

As for Henderson and Finch Minor and the bearskin! Where did anyone get such profitless, insulting courage? A prefect! They—his fellow prefects—shunned him. He didn't seem to mind.

No sign of Gower.

Roly must be fed up in there. Carleton visualized him on his chair, cursing to himself.

Ashley had been very peculiar in the morning. Something about him, Carleton, slipping through with agility. Creative writing was a defense? Questions about solitude. Understanding each other was no good. There had seemed to be some connection with this play, though he could not make out what. Why had Ashley made so much fuss about this woman's wanting something forbidden and admitting it and being great? Why was that great anyhow?

It was beyond him.

Gower had come out of the door of the new building!

He had a folded penknife in his hand. He was throwing it up and down. He looked totally concerned with this and with his own thoughts, having no other plans whatever for the afternoon. He was as cunning as hell.

Was it his own penknife? No, that didn't matter. The fruit salad was the thing.

He was at the top of the steps now, still throwing the damn knife up and down.

Carleton lay flat, but Gower wasn't even looking about him.

This could go on forever.

Perhaps they had imagined the whole thing.

Perhaps it was someone else, not Gower at all.

Carleton's hands were wet. Get on with it, Gower!

Yes. He had put it in his pocket and was slopping along, kicking a pebble. He went out of sight, around the corner where the jacks—the bogs to everyone except Roly—were. He *must* have gone in that way.

He must either return that way, in Roly's mirror, or come out of a window. The farther dorm, on the bogs' side, had only an end window. Carleton would see him jumping out in profile.

But nothing happened.

Was the wretch sitting in the bogs?

Still nothing happened.

If Roly had made an arrest, he would surely have called out to his aide.

He wished he had looked at his watch. It must be nearly a quarter of an hour by now.

If only the common room wasn't so pitch dark from here, the window being so small, one could see him in the act.

He decided to wait another ten minutes.

The likeliest thing was that the Doctor had already captured Gower, and taken him up to his room. In his excitement he was perfectly capable of forgetting that Carleton was spending the afternoon in the long grass.

When the ten minutes were up, he put on his coat and, with his heart racing, approached the common room window and looked in.

The fruit salad can was gone!

He pulled himself up onto the sill and jumped into the room.

There was no one there. He dashed out into the empty corridor and threw open the doors of both the dormitories. There was no one in either of them. He ran down the corridor and turned and went into the washroom, and there was an immediate bark from behind the shower door, "Carleton, what in blazes do you think you're doing? Get back out there!"

"There's no point, sir." Carleton was trying to talk into the mirror.

"He came in from the jacks twenty minutes ago," came the Doctor's urgent whisper. "He must be in the common room. Get back outside, you damn fool!"

"It's no good, sir. It's gone. He's gone."

There was a long silence from the shower.

The door flew open. The Doctor looked explosive.

"How in arsehole *can* he be gone?"

"I don't know. I don't know. Come and see."

As they hurried down the corridor, Carleton felt a sharp rap on his back.

"Turn around!" said the Doctor.

He turned.

They were both looking along the corridor to the door at the end, opening into the Big Schoolroom.

"Why in hell didn't you think of that way out, Carleton?"

"Gosh, I don't know. . . . You didn't think of it either, sir."

"We must both be going stark arsehole crackers," said the Doctor.

Ashley was the master on duty that day, meaning that he had to preside over tea and also over prep afterward in the Big Schoolroom.

The late evening meal was called tea, because something resembling that beverage was poured out by the skivvies. They went along with huge teapots that were more like great kettles with long thin spouts, and as they bent between the boys, to pour, those superior beings would lean away or ostentatiously hold their noses, in defense against the proximity of black-garbed armpits. Miss Bull ladled baked beans onto toast from a steaming vat. It was altogether a more boisterous affair than lunch; voices were raised from table to table, and stale bread occasionally flew. Fresh air and exercise had raised everyone's temperature. There were no dampening presences: the high table was deserted. Instead, a prefect sat at the head of each of the commoners' tables, as the masters had sat at lunch. Ashley strolled benignly up and down the aisle, with a book tucked under one arm, running his fingers through his hair. His brown shoes were turned outward and moved in slow portentous steps from under his gown. His blond hair was straight and thick at the back. He would be evading the four demon barbers on their visit next week. Occasionally he paused, and looked down fixedly at someone with that tense half-sneer which they all found consistently entertaining, and said something sarcastic which even new boys could tell at once contained no sting. A sufficiently good riposte was likely to make him smile in a very satisfying way. At the same time he would always flush a little and seem embarrassed and make a mock-outraged retort, as if he felt he shouldn't be amused by a mere boy. In another way, they found that he was invariably, and with pleasure, *surprised* to find that they could amuse him. It was like no other master.

There was something a bit sad—no, a bit cut off—about old Ashley. Why was it that he was cut off from them and from almost everybody? Many had noticed that the only person he seemed not entirely cut off from was the most unlikely of all— Jimmy Rich.

Was he happy with it? Did he cultivate it? Those who thought about it thought not. The slow paced steps and the air of remoteness and the stiff and strained expressions did not convince. The boys were expert at separating true from assumed eccentricity. It may have been that Ashley was too young to have developed and surrendered to his own posture. Perhaps that would happen in time. At the moment there was a human being there who kept on emerging—with embarrassment and surprise.

No one had framed this verdict. But a perhaps surprising number among this rude assembly had sensed it.

"Is it absolutely necessary to remonstrate with your knife, Metcalfe?"

"'Fraid so, sir."

"Can you not command attention by voice alone?"

"No, sir, that's my awful problem, sir. It's been like that since I was very, very small. I remember my mother coming rustling into my room all dressed for the ball and wearing a bottle of scent, and she couldn't *find* me, sir . . . and I'd been shouting out . . . so I took out this . . . it's not a bit funny, sir, listen to me—"

"Silence, sir! We are not interested in the squalid details of your infancy. Keep your knife down, or I will have you savagely punished."

"Yes, sir."

At prep, Ashley paraded, too, but more out of necessity than as a performance. The Big Schoolroom was enormous, and it was very difficult to tell what was going on down at the far end or even in the middle distance, from the remoteness of the desk on the dais. So from time to time he descended and stalked slowly among their desks, glancing over shoulders to see that what they were doing was, in fact, prep.

As he did so, books, magazines, and bags of sweets went in under desk lids, and notes were thrown behind his back, with such address that it was almost impossible to spot any of it happening. There were too many of them; the whole school was there, except for the prefects, who did prep in the library.

A constant whispering also defied detection. Voices were raised only in requests—which had to be granted—to "leave the room." These were incessant and seldom genuine. Such was the sense of restraint and travail for some of them that a mere breath of the night air was irresistibly tempting.

Most of the time he sat at his desk and tried to write a letter:

My dear Joan,
    That astonishing interruption—for which you need not blush—came at a painfully inappropriate moment. I was about to state a thesis which I have since come upon in Wilde's *Decay of Lying*. What is interesting about people is "the mask that each one of them wears, not the reality that lies behind the mask." You can see, it was not exactly the moment for stripping.
    "Sooner or later one comes to that dreadful universal thing called human nature."
    I had thought that we were above—

"May I leave the room, please, sir?"

"Again, Pembroke?"

"I know. I can't help it, sir."

"Silence, all of you! Very well, but not again."

No, it was revolting. It bore a horrible resemblance to—"Let us rise above the sins. . . ."

She must be kept away, and he had no intention of going to London. The bird was determined to fly.

Where, finally, to?

Where to?

Later, when Carleton came wandering in from the library, Rowles caught him by the forearm, as they stood amid a bedlam of naked boys scampering in and out of the steaming shower room, and delivered an invitation in his customary words and in a lowered voice, "There'll be a kettle on later, Carleton, if you happen to be passing."

"Righto, sir. Thank you."

"Easy with that damn door, blast you! It goes right through my head!" shouted the Doctor, turning red and making a tentative gesture toward his ears with his cupped hands.

A boy with three straight bruise lines on his bottom had dashed in, sliding it after him with a bang. (Many of the Doctor's sudden barks went unheard, the boy having already flown. This made them all pretty certain that his idiosyncrasy was deliberately displayed.) This boy and three others had failed to turn up at the end of a run, where Pryde was waiting with his list. Carleton and the others had vacated the common room, and Pryde had dealt with them there in a morning break. He had hit them hard, because he was missing his session of love in the dispensary.

Carleton had beaten no one yet. This was bad. He would have to pick on someone soon, or Rowles would begin to notice.

Up in the dorm he had to tell Johns about the invitation. This was awkward, because there was a sense of competition about these night sessions. (What did Rowles and Johns talk about? Carleton had a suspicion that he himself might be the object of their irony.) However, Johns appreciated that this was altogether a Rowles-Carleton day.

"Naturally I assumed that you two would want to commune

about your afternoon effort. It's about the funniest thing I've ever heard. I'm writing a long poem about it for the mag."

"You'd better not."

Carleton shared the showers with the other three, when everyone else had finished: Pryde, the poxy-faced giant; Rogers, square and almost unrecognizable without his heavy eyeglasses and dandruff; Johns, tall and gangling. They had to raise their voices in all that noise and steam, and they didn't speak much anyhow, being paired off in disparity. Afterward, he waited till Johns had reached his bed down the far end and said, "Lights out! No more talking." He switched them off, and crossed the landing in pajamas, slippers and gray woolen dressing gown, and knocked on the Doctor's door.

"Come in! Sit yourself down there. I'll be with you in a moment."

Rowles was doing something at the desk, under the green lampshade.

Carleton sat in the one ancient brown leather armchair. There was a brick pile jutting out on the other side of the fireplace, with a flat hard cushion on which Rowles liked to squat. On the hearth, a kettle steamed on a gas ring, beside a brown teapot, sugar bowl, milk bottle, and two white mugs. Above the bookshelves were old school photographs, and above the mantelpiece was a photograph of the Old Man which he had not seen before.

He was pondering with surprise that Roly must, of course, have felt affection for his old headmaster of so many years when the Doctor swiveled round, saying, "Well, we made right idiots of ourselves this afternoon, Carleton."

"I'm afraid so, sir."

The Doctor's bottom obliterated the brick seat. He was crouched over, pouring the water into the teapot.

"I intend to persevere with my ambuscade, nevertheless."

"Do you mean you're going to sit in the shower again?"

"Whenever I have time. It's too damn good a dodge to let it go. I'll spare you your share in the performance—you have your own life to lead. I'll catch him myself, you'll see. There's milk and sugar there. You've seen him, I take it?"

"Well, naturally, I've seen him in the dorm. He looks very innocent."

"He would. He's an extraordinary creature. There are biscuits there in the can behind you, Carleton. I won't have any. Ah, that's a good cup of tea."

"Yes, very, sir."

The Doctor was leaning forward, looking into the empty fireplace, with his hairy hands around the hot white mug.

Carleton was thinking it was more fun in the winter, when there was a fire roaring there. It was easier to talk.

Rowles seldom made the openings in any case. Whether this was deliberate or not, it forced you to come out with things—to break the silence and be a worthwhile guest—which might not otherwise have been spoken.

"Another biscuit?"

"Um . . . no, thank you, sir."

"Ah."

This was too awkward. Carleton cleared his throat. "I was up in Mr. Ashley's room this morning. He was . . . a bit odd."

He had selected this subject as more interesting than the later incident concerning the tree. So far, the Crab had shown himself not to be a tough nut at all, but weak and ridiculous. It had been worth a laugh or two.

"Ah, hah." Rowles put down the mug, took a pipe from the mantelpiece and a tobacco pouch from his tweed pocket, and seemed to be going to enjoy this. "In what way, Carleton?"

"Well, I don't know exactly . . . He asked me did I mind solitude, and he said I'd slipped through here with agility, or something, and he keeps on saying ou-boom."

"Those damn Malabar caves." Rowles drew in, pensively, and blew out a cloud. "Panic and emptiness. He's quite a performer, our Ashley; his mother's an actress, you know; you don't want to pay too much— What did *he* have to say about solitude?"

"Nothing. I didn't like to ask."

The Doctor puffed. Time passed.

"Another cup of tea?"

"Thank you, sir."

"Good. Help yourself."

Carleton did so, trying to think of something else to say.

"You know, Carleton, in my opinion it's time Ashley left this Forster business to the undergraduates. It's time the man grew up. I understand he's now going in for yoga or some damn nonsense."

"Is that not grown-up?"

"Ah, no. There are biscuits in the can behind you, by the way."

"I'm all right, thanks."

"Of course, that other lunatic of his, Yeats, went Eastern, too. I don't believe in hero-worshiping myself, any more than I believe in seances or the rest of the codology. People should have more sense."

Carleton was wondering about a whole life of common sense, doing sums here in this room and smoking a pipe. How was it achieved, and was it valuable?

"You know we thought he was going to turn for a while?"

There was humor in Roly's eyes. ("We" always seemed to mean the Pedant.)

"He had some damn priest in tow. He had him up to the school once or twice. One of those Italian smilers. I didn't go for him. But I gather that's over now. He's on this other nonsense. Personally, Carleton, I don't mind if he wants to stand arse over tip and eat yogurt or whatever they do. It's no concern of mine. The only thing that troubles me is that it's a waste of a damn fine brain. It's a great pity he didn't get that job. It would have absorbed him and given him the best way of losing himself. By the way, you know the jacks is next door if you want it?"

"Yes, thanks, I'm all right."

They gazed into the empty fire, the Doctor leaning forward, with his hand around the bowl of his pipe. Carleton glanced at the great head in profile. The tea was black, and its effect stimulating. He said, "My mother once wrote a poem with a quotation at the top—I think it was from some book—'Serenity only comes after passion.'"

The Doctor slowly took his pipe out from between his teeth but continued to gaze at the fireplace.

"Have you . . . known passion, sir?"

The great head jerked up. The Doctor's mouth had dropped open. He examined Carleton as if he were mad.

"Well, I mean . . . otherwise where did you get all this serenity from?"

"You're a very curious bird, do you know that, Carleton?"

(This would go on to the Pedant. Or no, maybe not. Rowles was flushed. He seemed embarrassed.)

"Well, tell me, sir," said Carleton weakly, faintly smiling and unconsciously using the far-apart eyes to which Ashley had objected.

"My dear fellow, I'm not compelled to answer your extraordinary queries. I declare to goodness, Carleton, I think you must be a bit touched in the head."

"I'm sorry, sir."

This was painful.

"Ah, never mind. You're not the only lunatic in this place. More tea?"

"No, thanks. I've lots."

Carleton felt very uncomfortable. They sat looking away from each other.

Rowles scratched his temple delicately with his thumbnail. He said, "My passions have always been firstly mathematics and secondly Weatherhill, Carleton. I don't expect you to understand that."

There was, for once, a lack of serenity. There was feeling in his voice.

"I think I do, sir."

"I think you don't. Listen here, Carleton, if there is one thing it is necessary to learn—and as quickly as possible—in this life, it is this—"

Roly smoked and was tantalizingly slow.

"The one thing that is utterly useless . . . more than that, entirely destructive and to be avoided at all costs."

"What is that, sir?"

"The emotions."

Carleton was very surprised.

"I don't understand, sir."

"I don't expect you to. But you will later on. And the sooner, the better for you. I had hoped that Ashley had learned it unusually young. But I fear not. This is certainly not the place for him. Between you and me, I opposed his coming here at the time. But I couldn't in fairness explain to them why."

Carleton was baffled. He tried to imagine Ashley when he was unusually young, but he was one of those people with whom it was impossible.

"Where did *he* go to school, sir?"

Roly made his fish face.

"Ah, come off it, Carleton! Where do you think he went to school?"

"I've no idea."

"Here, man! Here."

"Here? Good Lord!"

"There's nothing unusual in that. Mr. Dotterel was here, too. The Old Man always preferred old boys to other candidates. They know the ropes."

"Which house was Ashley in?"

"This house."

"Good heavens."

The Doctor pointed with his pipe stem at one of the school photographs. Carleton rose and crossed the room. It took him awhile. But there was one fair-haired laughing boy who could just possibly be Ashley. Yet how he had changed! How he, too, would change! It was alarming.

"But why didn't you want—"

"Ah, he got himself involved here in one of these damn silly romances. I personally steer clear of that topic. Let them get it over with and learn better. Unfortunately this developed to ridiculous proportions. I damn nearly had to ask for their expulsion."

It was amazing to hear Roly admitting the existence of such a thing. But the way he did it made it curiously unembarrassing. Carleton felt man-to-man and adult.

"Gosh. And who was the other—"

"He was younger. Took orders. Now a respected rural vicar. Ashley has not only intelligence but a sense of humor. One would have imagined that. . . . Ah, never mind."

"But what makes you think—"

"The point is, Carleton, he only came temporarily on the understanding that he would be getting this appointment, for which we gathered from *him* that he was a red-hot favorite. Now that, too, has gone arse over tip, and I don't like the look of him. And your report of this morning's conversation doesn't improve matters. By God, it's late. You'd better be getting along. By the way, Carleton, I am not customarily given to in-discretion, but you will shortly be adventuring away from us, and into the bargain, you should perhaps do so with some un-derstanding. In short, put that under your hat and keep it there, would you?"

"Yes, sir. Of course, sir."

"Ssh!" someone whispered, as he opened the door and light fell across the dorm. There was a click as McIver's torch went out. He was always reading photography magazines under the bed-clothes. In the dark Carleton felt his way past the end of McIver's bed and then got in between his own cool sheets.

He usually went to sleep at once, but not tonight.

It was strange to think of thirty different individuals lying there in silence, in the dark.

There was an odd, regular rustling somewhere near. If Wolseley was really doing it—and doing it incessantly—he was going to tell Dr. Rowles. It was revolting. It stopped, thank goodness.

Was Gower, over there, still gloating? Or was he sleeping in forgetfulness?

Another day was over at Weatherhill.

It had been a good one, far from usual. Ashley, Ma Crab at lunch, Gower, Roly. In spite of its difficult beginning, their talk had been the best ever. He was sure that he had never talked with Johns about such matters, in so adult a way together. Im-agine it of Ashley! He could not. It was incredible. And any-how Ashley was grown-up, and it couldn't mean anything now. It was just one of Roly's hobby-horses, like Gower. Best of all, the Doctor had, for once, made no reference to his being a cynic. Perhaps he had at last realized that he was wrong.

And yet. . . .

When he thought of tomorrow, it presented itself as the same old round: the bell, cold shower, breakfast, school, break, more school, lunch, lie-down, afternoon school, games, chapel, tea, prep, hot shower, bed.

And it was his last term.

He didn't know what he wanted, but he wanted something more. He felt restless and empty.

There was someone infuriatingly beautiful in a corner bed, away in the dark, in that very room.

Would he go absolutely mad and ask McIver secretly to take a picture? Imagine having it in his wallet! Being able to take it out any time. This dark, happy, tantalizing face smiling back at him. Small, with square shoulders, in a brown jacket perfectly cut to show his narrow waist. The face speaking their secret back to him. Imagined conversations. Whispers. Yes, you're mine.

What rubbish! They had no such secret and would not have. He was astonished and alarmed to find that he was excited. He turned over and tried to think of something else. Eventually, he thought of Gower. He managed to visualize him slipping out of the Big Schoolroom and down the steps into the Quad. His face was an unwashed mask, with slanting eyes. Under that horrible dirty blue sports coat, there was a large can of mixed fruit salad. Where was he going?

It was his last vision before sleeping. But he had another in the form of a dream. He saw Ma Crab leaning over a steaming vat, stirring its contents and moaning the while. Her two hairpins were gone, and her graying hair hung over her face. She muttered curses now and then, and the chaplain, near at hand, was intoning something else. "Say it in French! Say it in French!" called Ashley. There was steam all about, and you couldn't see who was there. Suddenly, with a terrible look, Ma Crab lifted out a ladleful of baked beans and thrust it straight into the face of the chaplain, who threw up his hands and recoiled away, with an expression of horror and disgust. "This is all damn nonsense," shouted Dr. Rowles. "It will have to stop!"

CHAPTER TEN

The first match was away. The team, plus a twelfth man, was allowed off school, from morning break on. They had to take a train from Marston to Temborough, which was not only a

113

country town but also a public school of greater fame sixty miles away, where they would be given lunch, and immediately afterward play would commence.

There had been great jostling and excitement the previous evening when Jimmy Rich had pinned the list of the selected team on the notice board in the new buildings corridor, reducing noticeably as the unselected slipped quietly away, hiding their disappointment. Carleton had already been shown it. The sight of the name "Allen" at the bottom had made his heart leap with excitement and fear.

Now they were assembled in white, with blue blazers and caps, on the drive near the Music Building, while Lucretia Crabtree, who did not go to school on Saturdays, leaned against a distant tree, observing them. It was a blustery day, but there was no sign of rain. Jimmy Rich was talking away in the middle of the group. Carleton stood on the outskirts. He was glad to see that Allen had the company of a boy of the same age, Hamilton Minor, a comical little flirt, who was twelfth man. These two, as the most junior, had been deputized to carry the huge bag, containing all their bats and pads, and they were just starting down the drive when Jimmy Rich said, "Hey, steady on there! Wait a minute, lads. Nancy's coming."

"Good-oh!" someone said with enthusiasm, and Rich looked delighted.

"She's probably bringing Eric Ashley," he said.

"*What?*"

"We thought it would cheer him up," said Rich. "You can grow moldy in this old place, eh, lads?"

"You sure can!"

They appreciated this. They all were silly with excitement about getting out of confinement. At the same time they couldn't see any earthly connection between Jimmy and Nancy and Eric Ashley, a man so remote that nobody had ever been able to think of a nickname for him. "Jimmy Boy" was about all they had for Rich; but he was more like one of them.

"But don't take that as an excuse for breaking the rules, boys, or I'll have the hide off you. We'll be coming away straight on the seven fifty. There'll be no messing around the town. Merryman . . . Bewick . . . I have my eye on you, boy!"

"Why us, sir?"

114

"Ah, here's herself."

Rich went forward, grinning. He was wearing his flaming sports coat. He kissed her and said, "So she persuaded you, Eric?"

"She did, indeed. To my great surprise."

"She'd persuade the divil out of hell, this one."

"Ah, go on with you," said Nancy.

"Lead on there, lads! We haven't all day. Come on, come on, come on!"

Chanting "Come on, come on, come on," they set off down the hill, following Allen and Hamilton Minor and the bag.

Nancy walked between the men and took their arms. Ashley was touched. He would have expected it to be irritating. He could not think why he was liked, and he was confused.

Only a few moments ago she had appeared in his room, saying that they knew he had no more classes that morning, she had noticed he had been looking "a bit seedy," the change would help, she knew nothing about cricket, and he would keep her company. "So come on, Eric, do!"

"Very well. But it's madness."

"Nonsense."

Now she walked brightly between them, saying, "God, I can't tell you chaps what it's like to get away from that old dispensary."

They were departing down the superior of the two drives. The other one went away in the opposite direction, near the lake. This one prided itself on an erratic concrete surface laid down by the boys under the vigorous supervision of the Cod. A muddy lane, off to the left, led to three pink bungalows, set rather peculiarly in a field, for the benefit of married members of the staff. Dr. Kingsly, the precentor, and his wife occupied one of them, their children having long since departed. There were only two other candidates, and they both had, by preference, small houses in Marston. So two of the bungalows were let to outsiders. Jimmy Rich and Nancy had their eye on one of them. Away beyond, among trees, was a gray gloomy building, which Matron could not look at without foreboding: the sanatorium, or san. At any moment, epidemics could alter her existence and create extreme responsibility. The last one had been measles. On the other side of the drive there was a grunting of pigs from the gray stucco farm buildings. Cows lay in the field beyond.

Finally, they passed the dark and silent Gate Lodge, where old Gregory lived with his wife and a semimoronic son of fifty. Then they were out. In Buckinghamshire. Where a different life had been going on all this time. Persons of parental age sped by in fast cars on the main road, headed for who knew what or where. The junior company, on the grass border, had to walk most of the way in Indian file until they reached the wide red brick main street of Marston. Very elegant, but also empty and oddly depressing, the street was enlivened halfway along by the still older whitewash and black beams of the Crown and Anchor Hotel. Merryman called it the Pedant's Pumphouse, and there were obscenities and shouts of laughter, drawing from Jimmy Rich a quiet "Now then, lads, now then." Bewick made a humorous attempt to slip into a tobacconist's and was rewarded with a "Watch it boy, watch it."

Their protector's responsibility was more seriously tested at the deserted station. They had to get across to the other side, and there was a covered bridge, affording a laborious climb upstairs and down again. But there was an easier way: at one point wooden planks had been set between the lines for the convenience of railway workers. It was tempting, and dangerous because the trains from one direction came unexpectedly around a treelined bend in the fields.

"The bag's awfully heavy, sir," said Hamilton Minor. "Can we just nip across here?"

"Certainly not, boy! Up the stairs with you."

Carleton was glad it wasn't Allen who had made such a stupid request. He had been walking in silence beside Pryde, who had been looking moody and lovelorn since the arrival of Matron. He was cricket captain, though otherwise Carleton's inferior. This was not unusual: Steele, the senior prefect, was also on the team. Carleton was a more likely candidate than Steele, a rather wild hitter, but ever since his rejection of the highest office, it had been accepted that he wanted, in no sense, to be a leader of men. He was, in fact, captain of tennis; but that only involved six people, and matches took place only occasionally, when cricket permitted.

They stood on the windy platform.

116

"Now then, lads, we can bring this off today. We've beaten them before. I hear they've a good team, but so have we. Carleton and Southwell, you'll be opening as usual, take it easy, don't rush it, play yourselves in, there's plenty of time. Hawke, bowl like you did on Wednesday, pitch 'em up, don't mind the full tosses, you'll find your length. Berry, vary it, boy, don't overdo that leg break. Sinnott, for God's sake keep that left elbow up. Merryman, when we field, *try* to stay awake, boy. Let's start the season off with a win, lads!"

"We'll do our best, Jimmy," said Pryde, solemnly.

The train was half empty. Carleton waited to see which compartment Allen would be in. With mild dismay he saw Sinnott going in there, too. But even so he chose another, where he pretended to be part of the boisterous company. It was a poor pretense, but they were scarcely aware of him. He had been tempted to join the grown-ups; but they seemed an oddly complete trio, and he didn't want to be faced with Ashley's badinage in front of the other two.

The three adults felt like children out on a spree. Jimmy Rich produced cigarettes. To such a degree were they part of the community that both men were aware that they were doing something forbidden to the other two compartments, and to make this sensation complete, two boys exploring along the corridor seemed to glance at them with envy as they went past. Or were they on the way to do the same in the lavatory?

"This is fun. I love trains," said Nancy.

"So do I," said Ashley.

"I'm only used to them with the old teams of men and boys," said Jimmy Rich. "This is much better."

She sat opposite by the window, with Rich beside her. He had his arm around her. Fresh and homely and freckled she was, in a simple light brown tweed dress. How did one begin to feel desire for such a person? Ashley looked on them as if they were the victims of an inexplicable aberration and with no envy at all. He felt far older and more secure.

The high wind was driving clouds across the flat fields of England. He wondered what he was doing here. But Temborough boasted an interesting folly by Kent which he had never seen. . . .

"Listen, did you notice that girl standing there as we were coming out?" said Nancy.

"Lucretia?" he said. "It's an extraordinary and alarming phenomenon."

"It's more than that. I'm quite certain that child is following us around, Jimmy. I saw her go behind a gorse bush when we were up the hill the other evening."

"Silly kid. Why didn't you say? I'd have had her out."

"Silly?"

"Yes," Ashley said, "I must agree there. I'm afraid Lucretia is a lot of things, but not silly."

"You'll say I'm mad, Jimmy, but I don't think she's doing it on her own account."

"Go on. Tell me. Is it the F.B.I.?"

"No, don't be stupid. Her mother!"

Rich laughed so wholeheartedly that Ashley couldn't help smiling, even though he remembered what Lucretia had said to him.

"Do you know that the child demon actually told me that she was under her mother's orders in these matters?"

"There!" said Nancy. "You're such a blooming innocent, Jimmy."

"Oh, go on! Why, in the name of God?"

"It's hard to tell you."

"Oh, for the Lord's sake. What's come over you, woman?"

"Tell us," said Ashley.

"She's jealous. Mrs. Crabtree has thrown four or five remarks at me. Nothing definite. But she makes her point all right, the old so-and-so. The other evening I was doing the blessed laundry—I know you people think I don't do anything but hand out medicines, but I'm responsible for all the linen and laundry in this place—"

"Yes, yes, we know that, love."

"Well, she was hanging around, pretending to help. And this maid, Philomena, you know the one, she's about ten feet high, was bringing in piles of sheets and dropping them here and there like an idiot. Anyhow, when she'd gone, Mrs. Crabtree says—you know, with the old head going like this—'I'm afraid, Matron, that the much vaunted heart's affections are responsible for that grotesque spectacle.' 'How do you mean?' I asked. 'Miss Philomena Maguire,' she said, 'is enamored of our chaplain.' "

Jimmy Rich roared, with his head back.

Ashley suddenly laughed, too.

"Shut up! Shut up, the two of you. This isn't funny."

Rich had a fresh attack.

"That's not the point! It's what she said next. She said, 'It may be perfectly understandable—' "

"Oh, Christ, no!"

"Shut up, Jimmy. 'But it can't be forgiven . . . or something like that . . . in women who have reached a certain age that they should permit themselves such sentiments. It is of no significance with this creature. But with others it matters a great deal. An example must be set. You understand me?' 'No,' I said, 'I don't think I do. I can see it's ridiculous, but, as for age, Philomena must be in her thirties.' 'That is what I mean,' she said."

"I don't get it," said Jimmy Rich.

"Oh, come on, she meant *me!*"

"The old bitch!"

"Yes, and how old was *she* when she married, I'd like to know! I tell you she's wildly jealous for some reason, and she's dangerous."

They were evidently in Oxfordshire: the train had stopped at Banbury Station. Youths with long curls and dressed in black leather were noisily climbing on board. Ashley reflected how innocent and vulnerable even the toughest of their white-clad protégés must appear by comparison. Delicate souls, straight from the shower room. Darlings away from home.

"It might help if she knew your intentions," said Ashley as the train moved out. "Which I must admit I'm rather curious about myself. Are you intending to be spliced?"

They grinned at each other.

"We're going to announce it at the end of term," she said.

"Congratulations. Delighted to hear it. Don't you think you should do it now? She might call off her bloodhound, for one thing."

"Nancy doesn't want cracks from the lads all term. And there's the matter of getting them out of one of the bungalows

—which has to be approached with tact and caution, if you know what I mean. Besides, we thought we'd have a bit of gas over it at the end of term. A bit of a do."

"You'll invite me, I hope."

"Oh, of course, a partygoer like you, Eric!"

"Don't you make fun of Eric, now!"

"I wouldn't dream of it. What about yourself? You old mystery man. I bet you've got some little piece hidden away from us?"

"No. No."

"He has plenty of time," said Nancy quickly. "Not like us old fogeys. That's right, Eric?"

"Yes."

"Well, thank you very much for that!" said Rich. "Christ, from all this talk you'd think we were a hundred."

Really, their lives were as remote as those of the Banbury youths.

"Are we nearly there, Jimmy?"

"Another half hour."

"Mind you, I may like trains, but I'm not going to be doing this every away match. I hate your old cricket. If you weren't the blooming games master we'd have the half-holidays off together."

"You've made that point before, love. It can't be helped. Cheer up."

There was some memory—also from miles away.

His eyes were on the open fields, but he was not seeing them. The world passed quickly by, demanding no attention. It came to him suddenly, for the first time, that his four years at Cambridge had been like this. Leaving nothing. A scholarly vacuum. Somehow he had immediately adopted the role traditionally associated with his elders: as an undergraduate he had looked like a don; indeed, he had felt like one. And on top of his achievements this had perhaps been a part cause of his optimism —now so harshly disappointed. But in all that time absolutely nothing could be said to have occurred. Except work. The absorption, the excitement, of learning. His passion! What had happened to it? Did one have to be challenged? Encouraged? Now then, lads. . . .

He had returned here with some apprehension, which had

resolved itself almost at once into a faint and sad recollection of childhood.

But was it childhood?

The extraordinary fact was that—now that he made a calculation—it was only six years ago.

Yes, that was it! Six years ago he himself had said to another child . . . to someone else, "If you didn't play games, we'd have the half-holidays off together."

"Eric!"

"What?"

"We've been talking to you for the past ten minutes."

There were two tall Temborough chaps—one of them the captain—to meet them at the station. They had posh white blazers with red edges, and they seemed a bit snooty. Perhaps they were shy. There was no reason why they should feel superior to fellows from Weatherhill. Maybe it was because Jimmy Rich went on talking to them in his Irish way, without realizing how he must sound. "Well, I hope you lads are going to give us a game . . ." and all that. Carleton could see that they didn't think it amusing, and they obviously didn't like being called lads. He seemed pretty crude all of a sudden. And that coat of his! Carleton imagined that they had some horribly distinguished Oxford blue or something as their games master.

The school was some distance away, and they had come with three big hired cars with drivers, which was jolly decent. (Could they have conjured them up at Weatherhill?) Carleton watched Allen get into one, and this time he did join the grown-ups in another car. He sat facing them on the pull-down seat, and he was greatly taken aback when Nancy, in the middle, said, "Hello, handsome." He didn't know where to look and unfortunately caught a mocking expression on Ashley's face. Gazing out of the window at the old Temborough houses, he thought, Am I?

It was a pretty good thing to be told and well worth the embarrassment.

He went into lunch feeling handsome and wondering if Somebody thought he was handsome.

But then it became confusing. They were shown to a table with their opponents—all in white, too—but there were hundreds of other boys standing there, waiting, and the little Weatherhill group went through a sharp scrutiny, and he thought he heard some rude comments. A lot of them, of course, probably never played cricket and considered their arrival silly. It seemed that they had kept them waiting; some master said grace immediately.

There was the same uproar. The hall was similar but much bigger. There were prefects up at the high table. (No Head's wife. No butler.) Yet it was disturbingly different. A huge alien community. They probably had all kinds of different traditions and rules and slang and everything.

Somehow one always assumed that Weatherhill life was the only life. He felt an affection for their own place. Probably he had felt this before on away matches, but he couldn't remember. He felt it very keenly now, partly because he was wondering if this was how he would feel when he left. Was it this that made one write an old boy's letter? Had the good fortune to bump into the Reverend S. J. Sinnott, 196—. We had quite a chinwag about old times at. . . . Weatherhill was his own smaller, friendly place. He looked along the table—they had been seated alternately—and liked them all—yes, even Sexy Sinnott. His own crowd. How dreadful of him to have felt ashamed of Jimmy Rich!

"We call this hog's swill," said the strange boy beside him, and he began spooning it up.

He couldn't remember exactly, but he was sure that none of *them* had ever called soup anything so obvious, and certainly no one of the age of this fellow, who was obviously a senior. Anyhow, though he wasn't a bit hungry, the soup was quite nice.

As he looked down the table, he saw that everyone else seemed to be getting on awfully well with conversation. How on earth did the others manage to get chattering with complete strangers like this? With adults it would have been different— and how easy with Ma Crab! But he couldn't think of anything. Pryde, across the way, was going on and on with both his neighbors about a forthcoming test match. But he wasn't alone: Allen was staring at the table, like himself. This was a change, and one that made him feel close and protective. Allen usually appeared animated, though it had always been at a distance.

It occurred to him now that he had never yet heard what Allen was saying. He might be stupid. No, he couldn't be.

Were all the others untouched by the thought of the match? Never mind the difficulty of talking . . . when the roast lamb was presented, he couldn't eat either. He felt slightly sick. But his neighbors were eating with amazing zest. He tried to force it down; it might look as though he thought their own roast lamb superior. The terrible possibility of being bowled out in the first over of the game! It must be even worse for Allen—his first match.

Lunch seemed to go on forever. But at last the two teams were on their way out, passing along dark oak-paneled corridors, which Carleton had to admit were impressive, with the studs of their white boots making the devil of a clatter. Strange boys in gowns stood aside and examined the Weatherhill group as if they were convicts on parole. They were being led by the games master, a little red-faced man with a ginger moustache, who looked as if he had been through hard times. Jimmy Rich, walking beside him, seemed positively distinguished. "We call him Foxy Fred," a boy murmured to Carleton. How frightfully feeble, he thought. The line of huge portraits of men in gowns was pretty imposing, but all in all, Weatherhill was far more homely. He wouldn't have liked it here.

The field, so green in the bright sunshine, was overlooked by the rear of these ancient red brick buildings, which were curious when one was used to the old Weatherhill gray. Boys were sitting under the great trees on the far side, and the low grass bank on the near side was becoming quickly occupied by more of them lying on rugs. Carleton was surprised and a little alarmed to find that contrary to what he had assumed, the match was evidently the event of the day. However, the wind had not abated, and boys dashing in pursuit of flying comics and other reading matter, gave evidence that the game would not be claiming their entire attention.

Not far from the pavilion, to which they were proceeding, there was a peculiar circular building, set on high, up stone steps, with a pink dome. He saw Ashley wandering in and out of its white columns, in a state of abstraction. It was crazy of him to have come.

A table and two chairs were brought out for Hamilton Minor and the boy who was scoring for Temborough. Pryde tossed up with the rival captain, and won, and elected to field—thank goodness. It was too sudden and upsetting when one had to go in and bat in completely strange surroundings immediately after lunch.

They went out onto the field, and there was some polite clapping from the distant observers. Jimmy Rich and Foxy Fred came out with them, in long white umpire's coats. Jimmy stood near Carleton at square leg, as they chucked the new shiny red ball about, and he spoke in a lowered voice, as if aware of his position as an impartial umpire, "Now then, Carleton boy, keep off those heels, on your toes, leaning forward, ready to run in. I'm watching you, boy."

"And I'm watching her, too," he added, grinning.

He was looking toward the pavilion, where two Temborough boys were setting up a deck chair for Nancy—who was laughing —with elaborate comic display.

There was loud clapping all around the field as the two batsmen walked out.

Ashley came wandering among the deck chairs, which were being taken by masters and the Temborough team and several unexplained ladies.

"Eric!"

Nancy patted the chair beside her.

"Now for a good snooze, eh?"

"Is that quite the right attitude?"

"Oh, why not. How was your folly?"

"Charming."

"Hey, what's the matter with you? You look funny. I couldn't get a word out of you at lunch."

"Nothing. Have your snooze."

"I think I'll have to prescribe a tonic for you," she said, lying back and closing her eyes against the sun.

It was hours later, after the tea interval, with Temborough all out for 178, that this day began to be an unforgettable one for Carleton. He had taken the last two wickets, Pryde having put him on to bowl near the end. (One of them was an amazing

124

catch by Allen in the slips.) But batting with the real joy, when it went well.

The score was not enormous, but it was pretty high by Weatherhill standards. Jimmy Rich didn't seem worried, but then he never did. Carleton and Southwell went in first together, trying to look confident, and parted toward either end, with a "good luck" from Southwell that sounded like doom. They had tossed up, and Carleton was facing the first ball. Jimmy Rich gave him his guard. Behind Jimmy, a tall fellow with high frizzy hair who had not distinguished himself in the batting—always a dangerous sign—was preparing an alarmingly long run. Oh, Lord, the responsibility. One had to start well, for the sake of the side. If the others saw you demolished easily, they all could lose their nerve. The fielders were in close; it was going to be fast. Yes, the enemy—probably a decent chap really—was coming up in a most ungainly manner, but quickly and determined, and he hurled the ball from a height, and it looked to be a good length, and Carleton had, instantly, to move forward or back. He made a rapid decision and chose the safer course, stepping out to it, and the ball seemed to disappear. But no, he had come down on it just right—in the center of the bat by the feel and sound of it—gently returning it along the pitch.

There was the first faint hope of confidence.

And perhaps the reverse for the bowler, because the second one went wide and was snapped up by the wicketkeeper. Carleton had begun to lunge out, but luckily stopped in time. Even so, he sensed that Jimmy Rich must have been on the point of exclaiming out loud.

The third was very fast and high, and both Carleton and the wicketkeeper missed it. "Yes," shouted Southwell, and they took two runs as the fielder just caught up with the ball before the boundary.

The fourth was a half volley on the off—his favorite—and he went for it. Oh, yes! Exactly right. The thrilling full-blooded contact, the marvelously right sound, the ball racing away from him not an inch above the ground, straight between two fielders and off to the boundary where the boys sat under the trees.

There was loud clapping from his colleagues over by the pavilion. The Temborough captain moved two of his fielders farther out, possibly a hasty move, giving Carleton the definite sense that confidence was possible.

He played a leg glide to the next one, with the delightful feeling that he had lots of time—which he hadn't—and they took two runs.

The sixth ball was as good as the first, and he stopped it in the same way.

One of the best beginnings he could remember. Keep your head. Don't count on it. Slowly improve. Jimmy said there was plenty of time. Till seven. What time is it now? Don't look at your watch; it will only put you off. What's this other devil like?

He looked small, dark, and devious and was obviously going to be slow and spinning. Southwell made ready to face him with apparent nonchalance. He was a silent fellow and almost too careful a batsman.

Southwell was darn nearly out first ball! A fierce leg-break just over the top of the wicket. The wicketkeeper whipped off the bails, and there were roars of "How's that?" But Foxy Fred shook his head impassively. Southwell looked about him in disdain.

Surprisingly, for Southwell, he took a run off the next—a neat little cut. And it was Carleton's turn. It was not his intention to steal the bowling; but it seemed to be working out that way, and he knew it didn't worry Southwell.

And it was somewhere in the next four balls that the marvel happened. Impossible to say when or which. He had very rarely experienced it. The ball became huge. It floated up, giving one all the time in the world to belt it where one pleased. There was no need for thought: the bat itself dealt with the large round object. Two first-class leg-breaks went hard to the boundary—one of them darn nearly a six over square leg's head.

Would it be different with the fast bowler? No. He didn't seem to be fast at all. Mysteriously—and none of Carleton's doing—the game was, suddenly, supremely easy. The fellow was lobbying up this great object for him to belt about the place. It was absolutely impossible to miss it.

It was happiness. And pride. He was trying not to look cocky about treating them so ruthlessly (including two new bowlers), but one couldn't help feeling a little superior.

Especially— Well, what on earth was wrong with everyone else? Southwell was caught, Pryde was stumped, and Bewick and Steele were bowled. It was so easy. He watched them go with shocked surprise. And all the while they were cheering. A current—a communion—was created between himself and his schoolmates away at the pavilion: a true expression of the team spirit. He was usually a small scorer, and they knew that this thing had happened and shared the excitement. And to cap it all, Steele—Steele, of all people!—who was hitting wildly, when they were 130, of which Carleton had made 90, said, as they passed on one of their runs, "Great stuff, Terry!"

In his whole time at Weatherhill no one had ever called him that!

How did Steele even know it?

There was an unknown warmth in people.

And now it came up. Yes, his 100. They were shouting and clapping at the pavilion—and even all the way round the field!

He tried to raise a hand. He was now shy about the whole thing.

But all the same they were more than 30 runs behind, and yes, now Steele was gone—a skyer, an easy catch. And soon afterward, Merryman, the idiot—a crazy stroke.

Stupidly, he had forgotten to look at the batting order, and he never knew who was coming next.

But it was Allen.

How terrible—he had forgotten him. So small and dark and alone. Come on. You can do it. Do it as you did it at the nets.

And it's the first bowler, back on again. Be calm. You can do it. He's easy!

Oh, gosh, here it comes.

Oh, my beautiful! You impetuous, raving madman, how could you do it? The very first ball, struck full belt. And we're running past each other, and I want to shout, "Marvelous, but for heaven's sake be careful." Yes, it's a 4, but don't do it again. Wait, wait. He stops it calmly. Yes, yes. We can do it together. Twenty-three to go.

Whew! Just missed the off stump.

He's blushing. I can see it from here. Calm down, calm down. It's Sinnott and the dear knows who next—we wouldn't have a hope.

Glorious! A late cut. Right through them.
This will be 3. Yes. Now it's me. It's still a huge balloon. I'm
going to wallop this one!
I have.
There's a fielder after it. But it's another 3. Your turn. This
is the last ball of the over. Do you *know* that? Don't try any-
thing. Leave it to me. We can do this together. No, I can't ex-
pect you to have worked that out. It's pitched right up; he'll be
tempted. He just stops it. Oh, you marvel!
We need 17. We must do it. We're going to.
There's another 3, at least!
Up to you. Ouch! Be careful.
Glorious! "Come on!"
He smiled at me as he passed. He smiled! We have it. He
knows it. We have it.
They're shouting their heads off by the pavilion.
We're down to 6.
"Yes, come on! Yes. Yes, again!"
We're down to 3.
And it's you.
Watch these slow ones. Watch these slow ones.
Yes, that was wise.
What about this? Gosh, he's going to try it.
Yes! It's a 4. It must be. A certain 4. We've won!
He's grinning and blushing, and I'm running down the pitch
to him. What am I doing? What on earth am I doing? I've
grasped him by his bare brown arm—these awful clumsy bat-
ting gloves!
"Well done, marvelous, marvelous!"
"I didn't. You did."
He thinks I'm mad.
The whole field is watching me, but they're all clapping.
Perhaps it's all right.
"Well played, Allen."
That was better.
Carleton started off, thinking they would walk out together.
But Allen wasn't with him. He stopped and looked around,
confused. The two umpires were communing. Yes, of course, it
wasn't necessarily over: there was Sinnott and someone else,

and it wasn't nearly time up. "We'll carry on for a wee while, Carleton," called out Jimmy Rich.

"Oh. Well, then. . . ."

He didn't like to shout this across the field. It seemed immodest. So he went over to Jimmy, and said, "In that case, I think I should retire, and give the others their turn."

"Righto. Great going, Carleton boy. Whatever came over you at all?"

"I don't know."

As he began to walk off, the clapping began again all around. He thought there had been too much now and wanted it to be over. All the same, one couldn't deny the glow of delight. What have I made? I don't even know what I've made. Lost track there at the end. But it must be 120 something. Not out. I've never made more than 50 in my life. Wait till my father hears! There were happy faces ahead of him and shouts of "Hurray!" and "Well done, Carleton!" The nearest was Sinnott, who was going in to bat, and though he must have hated being put in after Allen, even he looked admiring. "You must feel pretty good," he said, with a smile on his wrinkled, sexy face. It was perhaps a little too perceptive.

Carleton had instinctively made his way toward the Matron and Ashley—as the persons least likely to keep up the performance. But as he sat, taking off his pads, she kept on bubbling away, "Honestly, I never thought I'd be interested in a cricket match. You were marvelous. I've never been so excited in my life."

"You're embarrassing the hero of the day," said Ashley.

And normality returned, like a cold shower.

But not for long. They all foregathered outside the great main door at seven. Merryman and Bewick and Sinnott turned up at the last minute with two of the Temborough players, trying to look innocent. They had actually asked Carleton to come away with them for a smoke—an amazing compliment. But it wasn't worth risking with Steele around. Jimmy Rich said nothing. There was too much confusion going on. Foxy Fred was all flustered and apologetic. Only two cars had turned up, and he was in such a state that he had put everyone in a fever, on top of the general excitement of leaving, with Rich shouting, "Don't worry, old boy. Sure, what does it matter? We can all squeeze in. Come on, Nancy, on me knee. Pile in, lads, pile in!"

Ashley had cunningly got himself the seat by the driver. There was a scramble for places. Carleton was in the back corner, with someone between him and Rich. On a pull-down seat, Sinnott had quickly and calmly gathered little Hamilton Minor onto his lap—the nerve of them! There were people still outside, and the other car must be just as full. There was a face at the door. "Come on," he said. Allen sat on his knees. Oh, gosh . . . as they drove away, waving and cheering. On the very points of his knees. Everyone was shouting and laughing, but he couldn't hear what anyone was saying. Not even Allen, who was joining in. Did he know? Did he know that if he moved down, it would be unbearable? Impossible to tell, he was a cool cricketer. And this was ecstasy enough. Such absolute unimagined joy. He was afraid to raise his hands to hold him. No, he had laid his right hand gently on Allen's soft blue blazer. On his waist. Oh, heavens, has he felt my hand; does he know? The black hair came out in a wave from under the back of his blue cap. His neck was brown. His beautiful shoulder blades moved inside his blazer, as he turned at an angle to join in the talk. He had a faint sweet smell. He is on *my* knees! He is on my knees, and you can all see, and nobody, nobody cares . . . and nobody really knows. Good luck to you, Sinnott and your little friend; you don't feel what I feel; you don't know what I feel. May these moments of bliss go on and on forever!

CHAPTER ELEVEN

It was even windier as they struggled in the dark up past the front of the Head's House. God had set the school on a hill and given it no protection against the elements. Hence its name. The front door opened, and Lloyd stood there, with his batlike ears silhouetted against the hall light, looking like a character in some Gothic mystery.

"Mr. Rich."

The hollow sound came clearly to them, out of the gale, even though the butler had scarcely raised his voice. It sounded like an invitation to disaster.

They followed Jimmy Rich uncertainly up the steps. Lloyd was murmuring something to him. He turned and said, "Come along in, lads, the Head wants to see us."

They crowded awkwardly into the hall. A faded carpet ran down the center; but it was narrow, and their boots mostly resounded on gray stone flags. There was a small dusty chandelier on high. Lloyd had gone into the Head's study to announce their capture, and the Crab came out at once.

"Well, what's the news?" he said, looking benevolently at Rich and at all of them, but sounding almost apprehensive.

"We licked them, sir," said Rich.

"Really!" The Head was surprised. He looked around them, and he appeared startled again when his eyes fell on the Matron and Ashley.

"Well done. Well done," he said.

"This is the hero of the day," said Rich. "Tell him what you made, Carleton boy."

"Um . . . a hundred and twenty-eight, not out, sir."

"Really! Well done, indeed, Carleton, well done!"

Carleton felt he was being examined in an entirely new light. Of course, the Crab was an old ass. But even so—

There was a faint cough from the staircase.

"They've had a great victory, Cecilia," called out the Head.

She had paused halfway down, looking strange. Carleton wondered if she had been visiting the Reverend Cyril Starr.

"I see that supporters were in attendance," she said, and everyone glanced at the Matron and Ashley.

"You people cricket fans?" asked the Head, and somebody giggled.

"Yes. We were very excited," said Nancy, blushing. Ashley was running fingers through his hair and looking as if he were going to commit murder.

"I trust no medical attention was required?" said Ma Crab.

"No. There were no injuries, Mrs. Crabtree," said Matron.

"Well, we're very pleased," said the Head. "Carleton, Dr. Kingsly asked me to tell you that he wants you and Allen right away at choir practice. Allen, you'll be excused the rest of prep." "Yes, sir."

They thought he was pretty silly, but it had been decent of him to see them. Maybe he wasn't such a bad sort.

They clattered out past Lady Jane Grey's chest and then past the door of the dining hall and into the Quad. Allen had to relinquish his side of the bag, which Jimmy Rich had agreed could be taken up to his room for the night, to save their bringing it all the way down to the cricket pavilion in the dark. There was no one obviously junior as a substitute, and Sinnott promptly took hold of it, with the air of being a great help. When he and Hamilton Minor had delivered it, they would be alone together in the night. Carleton envied and wondered at Sinnott's daring and promptness. But he and Allen had parted from the others now and were walking along the cloisters together, under the two lights.

He had escaped again when they boarded the train and told himself that it was all dangerous nonsense, to be forgotten at once. But his heart was fluttering, and the ache to stretch out a hand and touch was a marvelous pain. To be singled out by the Head! He had thought for a second that the whole world must know. But in fact they *were* the only two choir members on the first eleven, Old Kingsly *did* hold his choir practices on Saturday nights, in preparation for Sunday and because Saturday night prep was shorter and not very serious, and it was perfectly natural. They went up the steps without a word, and the Chapel Square was dark, and he thought, oh, gosh, I'm going to put my arm around him, what will he say, what will he do, will he be horrified or will he accept, does he know, did he know in the car, can this possibly exist in one of two people only, mustn't it surely be something created between two, is it possible it would come to him as a complete surprise?

Carleton thought of so many questions that they reached the open doors without incident and passed through the antechapel.

The lights seemed terribly bright. Carleton was dazzled. Kingsly—known as the Beatle—was perched on the narrow front rail of one side, conducting the trebles across the aisle.

The voices ceased as he turned his round spectacles on the new-comers.

"Your cap, Carleton," he said. "Your cap, man."

"Oh. Sorry."

Allen, who was no prefect, least of all a chapel prefect, had remembered to take his off. Damn everyone for being so calm and sensible.

"To whom was the victory?"

"To us, sir."

"Good for you. I'm afraid we've nearly finished, but of course, in this place music bows to cricket," said Dr. Kingsly, who was usually the best tempered of men. "You and . . . uh, Allen, had better stay behind after chapel in the morning, and I'll run through the anthem with you."

"Thank you, sir."

"Now then, let's have all of you together." The precentor sprang from his perch into the middle of the aisle. "Beginning of the second verse. O.O.O.O."

He sang out the note for the basses, the tenors, the altos, and trebles. The Beatle could sing any note. He could sing a whole soprano solo if anybody wanted it. He raised a hand to conduct, and they all began:

O loving wisdom of our God!
When all . . .

A funny thing happened as Carleton went to find a place. A boy named Ferguson moved out to let him in beside Naylor, murmuring, "I expect you two want to sit together."

Really, something acknowledged like this was so much easier, so much more real, than the other, and Naylor was looking very good in a dark green coat. Carleton was still in an excited state. But everything was now translated into Naylor's elbow, which was pressing on his. Was it deliberate? Yes, it was. He glanced across the aisle and saw Allen studying his hymnbook. Of course, the boy had shared and noticed nothing! In any case, it was out of the question. There was no hymnbook in front of Carleton, and he was singing out of Naylor's:

A second Adam to the fight
And to the rescue came.

"Quiet, you tenors, quiet! Ssh!"

O wisest love! that . . .

The Beatle was comic to watch, for those who were not used to him. He was extremely imitable—a tiny man, tense and springy in all his movements, and always exhibiting the utmost enthusiasm for the work in hand. He was seldom caught in repose, and had formerly been known as the Sprite. His black hair took years off his age, which was fifty-five. It fell down on his forehead in a thick wild fringe. But his round specs, his enthusiasm, and his innocence were all boyish, too.

He was suddenly singing with the trebles, in a voice purer and more piping and more like a young boy's than any of theirs: "Should strive and should prevail."

Naylor had moved the hymnbook, lying on his open right hand, onto Carleton's white trousers. The back of his hand pressed firmly down on Carleton's leg.

And that a higher gift than grace . . .

This was very unlike Naylor, who was always the impassive recipient of Carleton's little advances.

Carleton was surprised by his own calm. He sang exactly as before.

Kingsly clapped his hands together, and they were silent.

"You must go down *cleanly* there, trebles. This isn't some dreadful pop song or whatever they're called. Again, please. Trebles only. *And.*"

And Eh-eh-ssence aw-aw-all . . .

"Once more!"

And Eh-eh-ssence . . .

"Better. Everybody!"

And Eh-eh-ssence aw-aw-all dee-vine.

"Better. Now we'll finish with the last verse, and let's hear your very best this time. Tenors, up! 'Praise to the *Ho*-liest.' Some of you were flat. Now then."

Praise to the *Ho*-liest . . .

Naylor moved the hymnbook again, so that the back of his hand rested firmly between Carleton's legs.

. . . in the height.

Carleton found himself responding. As he did so, there was a slight extra pressure from the back of Naylor's hand. It was extraordinary; no one had ever done such a thing to him, and yet he sang on, coolly and calmly. So did Naylor. There was a cool, but thrilling complicity between them. He thought for a second that there might be some terrible blasphemy in this; but the hymn meant nothing; the words meant nothing, not, at any rate, to this rather unusual pair of chapel prefects.

In all His words most . . .

Why, suddenly, this initiative from Naylor? Could it be something to do with his being in his cricket clothes? There was nothing else different. Never mind, it was so simple and so exciting.

"Most sure in all His ways."

"Good, good. Sing it like that tomorrow. Good night to you."
Naylor put the book away. Carleton glanced at his profile. He was impassive.
One might almost think he had done nothing. Noticed nothing.

Later, there was a curious silence between them as they made the chapel ready for the morning's sung communion. There was something a little uncomfortable, and the few things they said were cold—almost curt, almost hostile.
The chaplain was in his room, reading a book. He made some

comment about Carleton's cricket clothes. They set off with
the altar cloth, the gold communion cup, the bread and wine.
In the chapel they laid a damp cloth over the wafers. There
was none of the usual nonsense. Carleton felt constrained.

Naylor locked the big oaken doors with a large key, which
he put in his pocket. They had switched out the light above the
door. It was inky dark. The wind was making a wild noise
among the trees of the wood.

Carleton was walking away toward his own house, over the
square, but for some reason he had not said "good night," and
for some reason Naylor was walking that way, too, beside him.
And he realized he was excited again. Somehow Naylor knew
it. Or did he? At any rate, Naylor suddenly grabbed at him.
Fiercely. No, no, impatiently—perhaps that was it. Carleton
was in no condition to analyze. He heard himself say, pushing
Naylor's hand away, "Wait a minute." And it seemed to con-
firm that Naylor was merely impatient. It was extraordinary:
he had made a decision, instantly, and with this amazing calm,
as if from experience. "Over here," he said. He was leading the
way toward the storm-tossed wood. Naylor was somewhere behind him, obedient.

Cool as he thought he was, he knew that he must really be
eager too, because their feet were scarcely in the long grass when
he lay down, and it was right under the upper window of Roly's
room. The light was on, but far up and of no importance. All
the other lights were out. Naylor was down beside him and
scrabbling at his buttons. There was something not so good
about this. He had to help. Naylor *was* being fierce now. It was
as if . . . as if this were some kind of revenge for all Carleton's
attentions. Naylor had touched no other part of him. There
was no affection at all. No love? Yes, it was like some kind of
vengeful attack.

Something had gone. The pleasure had gone. He was not
there. Naylor was just attacking him. And failing. His own
voice, cold and clear, and with a detached and mild animosity,
was heard in the wind, directly under his housemaster's cham-
bers: "You don't seem to be having much success."

"We'll soon see about that," was Naylor's harsh reply, right
in his ear. And he went at it with renewed ferocity.

It had to be seen through now, if it was possible. The funny thing was, he felt a bit sorry for Naylor and his failure, and maybe disappointment, though his detachment was complete.

He waited for news.

Naylor stopped.

Was it possible? Yes, it was. He was wet.

He buttoned his trousers. Naylor was still there beside him, but miles away. Yet for some reason, in spite of everything, he felt a tenderness. He wanted to turn and embrace Naylor. But only for a moment. It made no sense, after this unpleasantness. Naylor would probably push him away. Or would he? Was he expecting something? No, it was a washout. They were apart.

"I think we'd better go."

"I think we had," Naylor said, not doubtingly, but with—almost—bitterness.

They were getting to their feet.

Carleton's home was the nearer.

"Good night," he said, and this was quite fond. After all, there was now an understanding between them and them alone. There had been an unmasking, even though it had been a fiasco. They shared a secret, even if it was only a failure.

"Good night," said Naylor, and it was sharper, but almost sarcastic and almost amused—which Carleton thought was a good thing. All was over. This would never be mentioned between them. But they would still be quite good companions. Perhaps better.

Naylor had disappeared.

Yes, Carleton thought, going into his house, we are both older and wiser. We have both disposed of something. We have learned something. It was what they called experience.

He felt good. He felt more grown-up. He wiped himself with a handkerchief, and went into the Big Schoolroom, which was in darkness. Feeling his way, he struck his hip painfully on a corner of the Ping-Pong table. There was a light falling into the corridor. It must come from the washroom. It shouldn't be on. He turned the corner and glanced in, with his hand on the light switch.

Dr. Rowles was there.

He was polishing his shoes. At this hour of the night!

It must be nearly eleven.

He was bent over, with his large behind under the sports coat directed toward Carleton and with one foot up on the bench. He always kept his shoes on for this performance, to leave both hands free to whip a cloth back and forth across the shoe, occasionally grunting as he did so.

"Sorry, sir, I didn't know—"

"Look here!" roared the Doctor, standing bolt upright, but with one foot still on the bench. He turned. He was flushed with exertion and fright.

"Look here, Carleton," he said faintly, "don't do that again, damn you. Do you want to give me a blasted heart attack?"

"I'm very sorry, sir. I thought you heard me."

"I see you're still in your regalia," said Rowles, turning away and polishing again, but with less vigor.

"Yes, sir."

Carleton went across and stood looking down in fascination at the astonishing shine that was appearing on the round-capped, slightly creased brown shoe.

"I've heard all about your apotheosis," murmured Rowles, rather breathlessly. "I'd very much like to have seen it."

This was kind and flattering—about something which Carleton felt had happened years ago. Yet the Doctor seemed unusually tense.

"They tell me Ashley was there. What in God's name induced *him* to travel?"

"Well, I don't know, sir. He was with Mr. Rich and Matron."

"He'll get small change out of that bright pair," said the Doctor, putting his foot down on the pink flags and substituting the other foot with a clonk that shook the whole bench. "The man should learn to live with himself."

Why couldn't people one admired speak kindly of each other?

"They say that no man is an island, sir."

(He was putting in the "sirs" tonight, because the Doctor's mood was a little frightening.)

"Balls. Come off it, Carleton! All men are. Thank God," said Rowles, attacking the second shoe with his former vigor.

"I don't see that, sir. And I don't see why it'd be something to be thankful for."

(He couldn't help thinking Roly's remark had a very odd relevance to what had just happened with Naylor.)

138

"You don't? You really are a curious bird, Carleton. If you're going in for platitudes, why don't you try 'the bliss of solitude,' which at least is real, unlike yours?"

"I don't know such bliss, sir."

"No. And I'm afraid Ashley doesn't either," said the Doctor, standing now on his two shining feet and throwing the cloths, brushes, and polish into a large wooden box, on which were the initials W. R. "Or he's forgetting. The whole world is afflicted now with the notion that bliss and even mere contentment are only obtained by running after each other's arseholes. Whereas, in fact, that's the last place they're to be found."

Rowles had moved across the floor on his silent spongy soles, and was running the taps in one of the basins.

Carleton had felt a moment of fright. Was it possible that Rowles had seen something from his window? What else could he be talking about? What on earth had it to do with Ashley going out with the other two?

"Where are they to be found, sir?"

"In solitude. In yourself. It's so bloody easy—that's what gets my dander up." He had stopped the taps and washed his hands with the bar of soap at least three times. "We are islands anyhow, and as islands, by God's good grace, we can find joy. It couldn't be made more easy. But people prefer to put their trust in fornication. Well, that's all right by me, but let it not be suggested that they are living life at its richest, and I am not. Because the exact reverse is the truth."

The doctor lowered his great head, cupped his hands, and splashed the water on his face. And did so again, snorting through his nose.

"No one would suggest that, sir."

"*You* have, Carleton! Or you've come damn close to it."

Rowles was going blindly across the room, with his hands held on high, towards the roller towel.

"I never—"

He pulled the towel down with a sharp jerk.

"You tackled me there with some balls about passion and serenity. I knew your game all right."

"Oh, sir, I never meant—"

Rowles jerked the towel down again.

"Ah, skip it, Carleton, you won't fool *me*. Listen here." He took a nail-file from his pocket and worked deftly on nails. "That creature's got my goat. I was in the shower for a while this afternoon, and I saw him go in and out; but he appeared unencumbered. Find out discreetly if anyone's lost anything. In future, you'll have to put out large articles—like cake—so it's *quite clear* to me in the mirror if he's encumbered."

"Yes, sir."

"It's damn late. Where have you been, by the way?"

"At choir practice, sir. And then we had to put out the things for communion tomorrow."

"Mm. . . . Well, I should do up your flies properly, if I were you. Why you chaps have to go round pissing in the dark —and on your pants, too, I see—when there's a perfectly good jacks, I'll never know. I put in two new bulbs myself there yes- terday. You'd better get up to bed."

"Yes, sir. Good night, sir."

"Good night."

He went upstairs, blushing and with the shaming suspicion that somehow Rowles knew or had guessed. He was in such a state—could it be merely because of Gower? And maybe miss- ing the cricket? He always seemed to know everything. No, he couldn't. He would have said much more. It must be just Gower.

He opened the door. A light clicked off somewhere. His hand found the end of McIver's bed. Wolseley was, mercifully, asleep —but snoring.

He lay on his back and remembered Someone at the end of the dorm. Sitting on his knees. How could it all have turned into this? Was this what they meant by the treachery of the hu- man heart? No, there had been no treachery. It had been some- thing entirely different. One of his mother's many incompre- hensible poems had been called "Love: Sacred and Profane." That was what it was, and from now on it would be sacred or nothing.

Having made his solemn decision and being tired out after a long eventful day, young Carleton fell into a deep and dream- less sleep.

CHAPTER TWELVE

After chapel next morning, the Beatle was unable to take them through the anthem for that night's service, to Carleton's great disappointment, because it had begun to seem like a marvelous stroke of fortune.

Mr. Crabtree had decided that this was the Sunday for delivering his conclusions to the entire and fully available staff, though the chaplain—perverse as ever—chose to remain above in his eyrie. Dr. Kingsly's plea for absence was rejected. Steele had arranged for the placing of high-backed chairs along two walls of the study, and the gentlemen of the teaching body sat uncomfortably in line. Occasional glints of sunshine through the tall windows illuminated this ill-assorted company. There were peculiar pairings, most of them cases of *faute de mieux*. De Vere Clinton was muttering through his beard at Dotterel, who was keeping a straight face. Ashley sat next to Jimmy Rich. The Beatle was beside white-haired old Mr. Wall, with whom he shared an ever-youthful innocence, though without the aura of Mr. Chips. Rowles smoked his pipe next to the Pedant and ignored the Cod on his other side. The Doctor looked stern; he was very aggrieved indeed that contrary to the precedent of forty-seven years, the headmaster had omitted to consult with him in advance.

The Head was behind his desk, which again displayed *Old Weatherhillian* magazines. The four demon barbers had recently visited (How was it that the hair of De Vere Clinton's artists appeared to be unaltered? He would have to look into it) , and the high sweep above the ears always gave him an extra confidence. All the same, he was apprehensive. Some of these men held him in disdain, for his lack of scholarship. None of them had been particularly friendly. Ashley, with his nose wrinkled, and his hand going continuously through his hair, was examining him like some unwelcome and incomprehensible freak.

"Gentlemen," the Head began, "the term is now well advanced, and I don't think you can accuse me of being hasty in coming to conclusions. I wanted—as did my wife—to get the feeling of this ancient and celebrated school before making any judgments. I believe that we have achieved that. It was not difficult. As you will all agree, Weatherhill has a very definite character, a combination of history and tradition, of loyalty and Christian fellowship, in this truly wonderful setting.

"At the same time, I will not disguise from you that I came here forearmed with reports that all was not entirely well. Lord Mountheath and Sir Charles Pike, whom I hope you will all shortly have the good fortune to meet, had expressed their concern to me on several occasions. A number of parents have been confiding doubts and fears over the past few years. The yearly admissions have been perceptibly diminishing. I consider that nine new boys this summer term is definitely not enough. It is true that it is gratifying that Lord Fitzmaurice has seen fit to trust us with his son's education, but we can do much better than this. Lord Mountheath and Sir Charles have in confidence mentioned to me the names of friends and colleagues of still greater renown who are merely awaiting a sign that Weatherhill is what she was always reputed to be.

"There have been too many failures in examinations, gentlemen. There have been too many defeats on the field (though I may say we were delighted with yesterday's victory). And there have been rumors—notably in Marston—of a more serious and disturbing nature, some of which have been echoed in the correspondence of parents themselves.

"All these things point to a laxity, a lack of earnestness and of the ambitions proper to the young men whose lives it is our duty to shape. Failure is popular nowadays. Inferiority becomes a source of pride. Not here, please, gentlemen. We are here to produce superior young men—not commercial travelers.

"In this context I want to read you out some alarming and, I fear, representative contributions to recent issues of our old boys' magazine.

"Consider this, for instance. . . ."

You were seeking an escape from these tiresome platitudes, thought Ashley. Now you have it. Satisfied?

For is it not true that for the past six years you have opened every copy of that damned magazine, when it came in the post, with excitement and dread, and looked for a name beginning with M?

Yes, you. A grown man and scholar.

And only once has it been there. And "J. L. Manson (the Reverend)" came right out of the page. And when the sense of guilt —yes, guilt—had passed, you were filled with memories and longing. "The Reverend"—and there was no other information save his parish and address—after the first shock was meaningless. Farcical. As you envisioned his small square figure, with a hard white collar, up in a pulpit, pontificating down at rows of elderly ladies in hats. Impossible.

Is he married? Yes, confess, you have wondered every time. You have even thought that at the end he had a strangely high voice.

Hoping him a child forever?

Only six years ago. And are not these hills, the wood, yes, come on, the corner nook made by the buttress at the rear of the chapel, and oh, God, the small room in the san where the innocents put you alone together for a whole week, all still part of your love?

And in the interim? Much study. But evasions—rejection of "human nature" underneath, as against the persona above. And consolations—great religions of the world!

That sense of futility. How "philosophical" has it been?

Are you afraid—have you always been—of what this may mean? Of the future?

How dreadful an expression—a "dab hand"! Should you perhaps accept?

Another evasion?

"Laxity," said the Head. "This brings me, first and foremost, I'm afraid, to a subject upon which I find it extremely difficult to speak. I shall call it 'moral laxity.' "

The Head reddened, pulled down the corners of his mouth, and looked slowly along the ranks.

It was difficult to tell whether he was examining the accused or asking them to share his embarrassment and face this awesome problem together.

"As you all know, I have hitherto been responsible for younger boys, and some of you may regard me as inexperienced in these matters. Nevertheless, you may rest assured that I have the very strongest view on the subject. From what I and my family have heard and seen in these weeks, it is plain that the rumors have not been entirely fictitious. There is an element—I hope and believe a small one—among the boys, which evidently indulges in the kind of behavior to which I refer and does so without a sense of wrong, but rather with a kind of brazen conceit, actually speaking of this disgusting subject as if it was a matter of ordinary everyday acceptance. My reaction is one of horror and also of astonishment, because it is impossible for me to close my eyes to the fact that it is you, gentlemen, who have permitted this state of affairs to persist, or at least you have done nothing to stop it."

They gazed back at him. Silent, they were embarrassed *for* him, except for the Beatle, who glanced at Mr. Wall, hoping for some elucidation of the incomprehensible.

To the Head they merely appeared embarrassed. It gave him a sense of satisfaction and confidence.

"*I*, however, intend to do something to stop it."

"What do you propose, Headmaster," said Ashley, in a dry voice. "Castration?"

A muffled noise from Jimmy Rich in the corner was the only sound. The Head looked quickly his way and saw a hand over a mouth and directed himself toward Ashley. He was crimson.

"Mr. Ashley, I'm going to have to ask you to leave—"

"Hrrmph."

Dr. Rowles had cleared his throat and was leaning forward, with his arms on his knees and his pipe in his hand.

"I think, Headmaster, that Mr. Ashley was implying—in a quite inexcusable manner, to my mind—something which I believe most of us nevertheless feel in this matter."

"And what is that, Dr. Rowles?"

"That there is no remedy, Headmaster," said the Doctor, being careful not to look in Ashley's direction, "for something

144

which, whether we like it or not, is evidently natural to some
—not to all. You may punish, expel, what you will, sir. But I
fear you won't eradicate. I have been here quite awhile, Headmaster—"

"I know that, Dr. Rowles. But I still don't agree with you. At
the moment I don't contemplate these extremes you mention. I
intend to make a start of a more imaginative kind and one
which I fear will not be any more to your liking. I've come to a
decision, gentlemen."

"May we know it, sir?" inquired Rowles, controlling, with
difficulty, his anger that he did not know it already.

"Certainly. That is one of the main reasons why I have asked
you here. It is an idea that has been given to me—quite indi-
rectly—by my daughter."

"By your daughter?" said the Pedant, with his eyes bright-
ening.

"Yes. I am inviting the senior girls of Gillingham College
here for the day, gentlemen."

At length, Dr. Rowles, who had turned very pale, said, "I beg
your pardon, Headmaster."

"There will be a tennis match and tea outdoors under the
supervision of Miss Bull," said the Head rather stridently.

Dr. Rowles said, "Headmaster, I would like to say at once—"

"I'm sorry, Dr. Rowles. As you know, there are only three
weeks now to Weatherhill Day. I want to be able to announce
this, I hope, permanent innovation in my speech *and* to report
that it has taken place. So that we have no time to lose in argument. I hope also to be able to announce a reciprocal visit to
Gillingham and many more in the future. I have already sent
on to the board a letter from Miss Hutchins expressing full co-
operation. And we're all quite certain that our parents will applaud my decision without reservation."

"I can only say—" began Rowles.

"Our life here may be of a monastic nature, but we are not a
monastery, Dr. Rowles. It can do our boys nothing but good to
know that the tender sex not only exists, but is worthy of respect. I want everyone behaving like little hosts and gentlemen
on the day. And I have no doubt that those who are at present a
disgrace among us will begin to see the error of their unnatu-
ral ways, and at the same time it will certainly be made more

145

plain to them by the majority. And, I must insist, by you too, gentlemen."

"Tell me," the chaplain was saying, in his room above, "since communication seems inescapable, have you always preferred the floor?"

Mrs. Crabtree continued to poke the fire and gaze into its flames. The truth was, she had not sat on a hearth rug since university days. But for that very reason it evoked happy memories.

"I mean, is it not a trifle indecorous at one's age?"

She turned her brown eyes toward him, enthroned in black in his chair, and jerking them up to the ceiling, said, "You are less perceptive than you imagine. Your excessive ill manners merely put one at ease."

"Heaven preserve me," said the chaplain, who was holding the orange at the ready. "Do you suggest that if I were more amenable you might take a chair—or, better still, cease these infernal visitations altogether?"

"I might take a chair."

"It is not much to hope for, God knows," said the chaplain miserably.

He had tried everything. The woman was unbearable and beyond comprehension. Only one consolation had been salvaged: the Starlings were more than mildly amused by his scathing accounts of the latest persecutions. ("The good lady appears to be enamored of me. I cannot begin to express to you my extreme revulsion.") There were shouts of laughter, and on the last occasion young Robert had choked over a piece of cake, while the others slapped him rather too vigorously on the back. The hope that some of this might reach her husband had been vain. To have been beyond rumor in *this* academy was going to be that wretched man's final epitaph.

"Within a few moments I shall be holding a private confirmation class. Ought you not to be upstanding and preferably absent when the boy arrives?"

"I'm going in a moment."

The chaplain sighed.

"What if your husband enters?" he demanded, with daring born of extreme impatience.

"He's with the staff. Why aren't you?"

"Had I known the alternative—"

"Why will you not cooperate? He is doing his best. He's a good man. I know that I've said things—"

He brought the orange to his nose.

"My good woman, if I have to endure another tasteless word about your husband's inadequacies—"

"You won't. I promise that."

She was pushing the cedarwood and coals about. Philomena laid an excellent fire. It was beyond endurance.

"Shall I tell you what he is saying?"

"No. I have already extracted a confession. We are to become a school for girls. The man is to be pitied, if one had the capacity. His stay here will be brief."

"In my opinion yours will," she said, dipping up and down, "unless you make alterations."

"Alterations?"

"To this room for a start," she said.

It is possible to have murder in one's heart. She had lately given a new and terrifying meaning to many sections of the Old Testament.

"I understand your vision," she said. "He does not. He was in here on Friday."

"With two inane propositions relating to my services."

"He said nothing, but I could tell."

"Tell what, may I ask?"

"Your décor is not consonant with his beliefs or intentions," she replied. "It is too naked."

"Now will you leave?"

"I wish to help. There are a number of Impressionist reproductions in the attic."

"Kindly rise and—" he began. But the knife entered his stomach, and it was impossible not to grimace, and the woman had seen it.

"You *are* in pain," she said. "I've always known it. I have known it since you spoke of the fire. Why will you not see Dr. Boucher?"

This was beyond answering.

"Or someone. You must. You must!"

"We are all in pain," he said, and it happened again, but less

147

severely. "The thing is not to turn it into *La Traviata*. Now would you mind leaving me in peace?"

"I'm going," she said, disposing of the poker and rising awkwardly to her feet. "How *you* can turn suffering into a tea party! You!"

"It's an achievement you might emulate."

"I'm not interested in tea parties."

"No. You're interested in upsetting other people's. But it seems to give little satisfaction. You would be wise to adopt some other occupation."

"It is for people's good. Do you intend to sit here and die then? When you could be cured. When you have so much to give us, so much to say?"

"I can't be cured. And I have nothing to give—except confirmation classes. Please leave."

"I heard your sermon," she said.

"One hears what one wants. It has nothing to do with me."

She paused at the door. "And moral standards," she said, "in our school. Is it all to be put on the headmaster? Are you not the chaplain?"

"You must be jesting."

"How blind are you? How blind are you, for instance," she said, with a sudden onrush of bitterness, "with regard to the shameless example being set by the Matron and Mr. Rich?"

The chaplain was smiling: wretchedness had turned to farce.

"I have seen no signs of what you speak of. Quite the contrary."

"You should talk to my daughter."

"Heaven forfend."

There was a knock. Allen came in. Mrs. Crabtree went out without a word. Allen closed the door. The chaplain made his more familiar grimace.

"Another visit from Medusa," he remarked, and shuddered, only partly for the boy's benefit.

Allen smiled and said, "Poor you."

"Yes, indeed. Pull up a chair, Nicholas."

Rowles and Milner were walking between the borders toward the new buildings. The sun had gone in. It was a sad

148

gray Sunday morning. The Pedant at length said, "It seems as if your Cynic may have been right after all, Rowles. In his own way he may well be a tough nut."

Rowles, who was breathing deeply, merely gave Milner a quick cold glance.

"I said he was due some surprises," the Pedant went on. "It seems it is *we* who are due the surprises."

Rowles continued to be self-absorbed. The Pedant was secretly enjoying himself. They passed under the arch, made by the ancient vine, and on between the borders.

"Listen here, Milner, if I wasn't fast approaching retirement in any case, I'd resign now. On the spot."

"Oh, come now, Rowles!" The Pedant couldn't help smiling. "You take it too hard."

"I don't, I assure you. I assure you I don't. Do you realize I wasn't even consulted on this outrageous, damnable, and farcical decision?"

"He's not a fool, Rowles. He knew it was profitless."

"But my position, Milner! My position!"

The Pedant looked solemn. "Yes, I agree with you there. Naturally."

"In forty-seven years—"

"I feel we should approach him more closely, if only to teach him better manners. We've perhaps been a little aloof. We haven't helped."

"Pah!"

Gower was slouching ahead.

"What the devil are you doing, Gower?" the Doctor barked.

"Ooh, sir. You gave me a fright."

Gower smiled: fear and taunting.

"Well?"

"Nothing, sir. What should I be doing, sir?"

"Something, damn you, something. Go and exercise that fat body of yours. Go and do something with your brain before it atrophies."

"It what, sir?"

"Listen, Gower, you give me cheek and I'll boot you right up your fat arse, do you understand. Now clear off!"

"Yes, sir."

"A very curious child," said Milner.

It was the Doctor's phrase, and it should not have come from the Pedant.

"As for the event itself, it is the end of Weatherhill and all it stands for," said Rowles. "It is the end of my entire life's work."

"Oh, Rowles! Come now!"

"I mean it, Milner."

"I think it should be rather amusing."

"It what?"

"You have always taken an excessively severe attitude toward the fairer sex, if I may say so, Rowles."

"It has been exactly the same as yours, Milner," said Rowles, "until recently. Might one know why?"

The Pedant was not answering.

Lucretia Crabtree was balancing in gym shoes and jeans on top of one of the round stones at the edge of the border.

"Go away," the Doctor said.

"Pardon?"

"Go away."

She gave him the look, but it was no use. She slouched away, vowing vengeance.

Everyone else engaged in activities, except these two bored and nefarious souls. Idleness the Doctor detested above all else. The refusal to progress. Here in his beloved school, where progression was the one requirement.

Everything seemed to be going wrong of late; and it was all on account of the new regime.

He had a sense of approaching doom.

```
      — — E  — A — —   — A — I — — E —
 W:   — A — — A — E —   — O — — — OO —
 W:   — A — — A — E —   — U — — E — — O — —
 M:   — I — — AE —   — E — — — — A — E
 M:   — A — I —   — A — — O — —
 M:   — AU — — O —   — A — — E
```

"There's a dead easy one, since you seem to be losing heavily," said Johns, moving away from the blackboard and throwing the chalk back on the master's desk.

Sunday afternoons when you hadn't taken an "exeat"—Carleton was saving his up till later—were dreary and difficult to pass. He and Johns used to go for bicycle rides and walks, but in the end they found they had nothing to say to each other. This game was better, though Johns always won.

It was raining now. They had picked classroom Number 2 in the new buildings, and unfortunately Sexy Sinnott and another senior, called Blondie Beauchamp, had come in out of the rain and were passing the time outrageously on a chair in the back row. It was hard to concentrate, though Johns had been treating them with complete disinterest.

"Well, the *M* for man gives the *A E* away," said Carleton. "It must be Michael. Michael who? Can't think. It's the something something. Do the two women have the same Christian name?"

"Looks like it," Johns replied.

"Ossie is coming for me next Sunday in the new Austin-Healey. It's milk white, I believe, and very, very fast," said Beauchamp, who was seated on Sinnott's lap, even though he was considerably the taller of the two. "Freddie Ainslie may come too. He's sweet, but quite mad, and he drinks like a fish. I hope the dear little Crab is peering out of his window as we zoom away."

It seemed unbelievable; but Beauchamp did go off on his "exeats" with these grown men, in vivid check caps, and he was always talking about the one called Ossie. What on earth did his parents think—who never saw him? But everything about this quite clever fellow with sleek blond hair spoke of an unpleasant, adult, sophisticated existence beyond Carleton's ken. He was even more careless of public opinion than Sinnott, who was a much cruder specimen. This was all they had in common: it must have brought them together; it was a brand-new lineup. how did these things suddenly happen?

"The double *O* and the *AU*," said Carleton. "What *is* that Christian name? It must end in an *R*. No, not an *R*. Um."

"Hey, easy on, dear," said Beauchamp, giggling.

Sinnott, who had scarcely spoken a word, had his hands in Beauchamp's pockets. This was the final futility, Carleton thought, when there was no love, when nothing was sacred. Shocking and pointless.

"Ossie has this glorious motor-cruiser at Henley. The bar's the size of this room. Last time I fell in with some very dubious people. My God, was I wet!"

"A *T*. It could be a *T*. *E T*. Margaret. It must be Margaret. Margaret who? Double *O*."

"I'd ask you, dear, but I'm afraid Ossie gets so terribly jealous. Besides, there won't be any room in the white elephant if Freddie turns up. Hey, for Christ's sake go easy, or I'll come off."

"Look, could you two not take your disgusting performance somewhere else?" said Johns. But he spoke with his usual weariness.

"How crude you are, my dear Johns! Certainly not. We like company. Don't we, dearest?"

"It's Margaret Lockwood," said Carleton, writing it on the blackboard. "Um . . . *The Wicked Lady*. . . No. But 'The Lady' would fit. *The Lady Vanishes*, of course!"

"I wish you two would play your infantile game next door," said Beauchamp. "It upsets our concentration."

"So it's Michael Redgrave. And who is that marvelous woman? . . . Margaret Rutherford!"

"Carleton's pretending not to be shocked," said Beauchamp.

"I know," mumbled Sinnott.

"Ossie once asked me who the pretty boy was with the wide eyes. Not your type, my dear, I said. That's nice."

Carleton turned around. "You're a revolting fool, Beauchamp."

"Tch, tch. Language, dear."

"Pay no attention," said Johns. "Who are the men?"

"The two funny men. I know them well, but I can't remember. . . . A *U* should be easy. . . . Yes, I have it, Naunton Wayne. Now what the devil was the name of the big man with the moustache?"

"He's our public school type," I said. "He has played the game, and leaves us without a stain on his character. Respectable to the last. Oh, but let's talk about something less boring."

"I've got it. Basil Radford!"

"Let's talk about this weird thing someone told me at lunch. My dear, would you believe it, the little Crabs are worried about our genes going wrong. The invitation has gone forth to a horde of muscular young women who are coming here to beat us with tennis rackets. Well, really! One knows that

Mother is repressed, but this is going too far. I can't wait to tell Ossie and the crowd."

"Let's chuck it," said Johns. "I can't listen to any more of this rubbish."

"Good-bye for now," said Beauchamp. "Don't do anything we wouldn't do."

"You're a disgusting little twit, Beauchamp," said Johns.

"Oh, charming. Have a look at yourself in the mirror sometime."

In the corridor, Carleton suggested they continue in another classroom. But Johns, who seemed upset, was going to the library. They parted at the corridor crossroads. The library was down by the Pedant's Palace; Johns put up his coat collar and went off with loping strides between the dripping borders. Carleton got as far as the other door out, intending to return to the common room. He stood looking up at Ashley's tree and the wood beyond. The rain was coming straight down, with a sizzling sound, out of a dull gray sky.

It was quite cool. He shivered. No noise, except for the rain. It was extraordinary how more than two hundred people could disappear. He was sorry now he had not picked this Sunday for one of his exeats: they would be having tea, his mother talking with friends, his father reading the Sunday papers. It was very odd; but even now, at the end, it was still possible to feel moments of homesickness, and when one was being left back, in the car, from Sundays out, there was still the faint recurrence of his first year's feelings, when these seemed to be prison walls.

Who had a home here? Not poor Ashley, who was probably now up in his room, directly above where he was standing. Not Rowles at his desk, with his little bedroom and "jacks" next door. The Crabtrees had a house, but it scarcely seemed to be a home. Curiously enough, the chaplain's warm apartments, with their entirely personal furnishings, seemed to come nearest.

But it was an institution, and cold. It was funny that this was most obvious on Sundays. The place was work and games, and without them it was nothing. He felt depressed and lonely. He had perhaps not spoken the truth to Ashley about solitude. He wondered if he'd go upstairs and ask him if he had looked at his story yet.

But he didn't like to intrude.

Where were Jimmy Rich and the Matron? Some Sundays they went to London. There was an early morning train. Distant, magical, enormous, mysterious place. He had stayed there a few times with a wealthy uncle.

Dotty, the Beard and the chaplain all were probably giving tea. Dotterel had tried to tempt him into his group once, but he hated their crude talk and the way the man caught one's arm in bony fingers or let a hand fall tightly around one's neck.

How did he come to be standing alone and friendless here, on a hill, in the rain?

With his collar up, he bounded up the stone steps and dashed along past the bogs, and so into his own house. Gower was in the washroom alone, combing his lank black hair. He appeared unencumbered. With the utmost caution, Carleton glanced down at the mirror which remained in place in Roly's shower, but he could not tell quickly enough whether Rowles was in there. Gower was saying, "Is anything wrong?"

"I hope not, for your sake."

That was a bit cruel. Why did one badger Gower so? And, on second thoughts, risky. He hoped Rowles had not heard.

In the dark corridor, a blast of sound came out from the Big Schoolroom—and it was most welcome—and through the open door he saw Rowles playing table tennis with that comedian, Metcalfe. The Doctor, with his pen-handle grip, scarcely ever missed a shot; he moved fast on his spongy soles, concentrating intently even in the midst of the bedlam he so much detested, and was almost unbeatable.

Carleton was just turning to go down to the common room, when a boy dashed out of the Big Schoolroom with another in pursuit. The first turned the corner and had gone out, into the rain. The second halted, a yard away from Carleton. He was flushed and out of breath. It was Allen. He whispered, "In your mackintosh pocket." And was gone.

Carleton was dazed. Allen had spoken with a peculiar intimacy, as if there were something between them.

His mackintosh was hanging in the fifth wooden locker down on the left.

He moved along to it and undid the latch. He felt afraid. He thought, Gower must feel just like this when he does it. What if he comes out and sees me? Well, after all, it's my *own* locker.

There was a small piece of paper in one pocket, folded up very neatly.

He held it tight in his hand, and went on tiptoe to the common room. Reynolds or Pryde might easily be in there.

But there was no one; it was dark, and smelly, and empty, with that awful rug on the table.

He took out the note and unfolded it. His stomach felt sick. The message consisted of two little pages from some lined notebook, with three little holes down each side. The writing was big, and wild, and all over the lines:

"I know you think it's great to have so much blasted sex appeal you can make other people miserable! You go your own sweet way and they can go to hell. I know you're laughing at me already. I can see you reading this out to Johns for your amusement. Well, I don't care. I can't keep quiet any longer. I've *got* to see you. *Please* meet me, if only once. I will be in No. 4 classroom after chapel tonight. If you don't come and meet me there, I don't know what I'll do. Allen."

CHAPTER THIRTEEN

 Fear was cautious Carleton's overwhelming reaction. Out-and-out fright at being caught in something forbidden and—if he had anything to do with it—easily discoverable.

Could it be some mad joke? The boy had given no signs of anything at all—and now suddenly this! As if it had been going on for weeks. From someone who had been laughing, and chattering, and chasing other people about the place—apparently perfectly happy.

It was so peculiar too. It was kind of tough. Positive abuse—

of the second prefect! From a new boy, who was almost a junior.

And what was this extraordinary accusation, using a phrase that had always puzzled him, that adults used, that he had never seen used by anyone younger before? People had accused and admired him on astonishing grounds lately, and this one was the most surprising of all. He stood and examined himself in the dirty cracked mirror that hung beside the half-naked cutie. Perhaps he was good-looking. There had been remarks about his eyes. Was that sex appeal? How the deuce was one supposed to know? What was the value of something that only others could see? Nothing. Had the cutie sex appeal? Surely not.

He was feeling better. Well, one couldn't help feeling a bit puffed up. And this crazy note seemed to say that other people were being affected as well.

But that he could be "amused." . . . Allen must be nuts. Imagine being so puffed up as to go around being amused at other people's being affected. It came from distress, of course. The boy really *was* worried. It was frightening.

Yes, he was afraid again. He was not going near Number 4; that was certain. It was all very well he and Naylor making asses of themselves. But this didn't sound the same thing at all. He would stop it at once.

But how was he going to face Allen for the next couple of months?

And what would Allen do?

He wished to goodness he'd never received the blasted note. Everything had been so pleasant and easy till now.

He thought about this.

It was his last term.

Well, why shouldn't it be pleasant?

The huge figure of Pryde came through the open door in a brutal check sports' coat.

"It's pissing cats and dogs," he said.

"I know."

Quickly, and with a poor pretense at being casual, Carleton had pocketed the note. Pryde had seen. Had he the wit to guess anything? No.

Pryde's back was turned to him as he leaned over the gas cooker. The kettle was on, and he had thrown a piece of stale sliced bread onto the hot plate. A demon barber had shaved his brown head, and there was a large red something or other on his thick neck. It was surprising that Matron had not put a dressing over it.

"What's the matter with you?" he said, crossing the room. "You look as if you'd swallowed a ghost."

"Nothing. A wet Sunday."

"It's a bugger."

He had taken down a plate of butter and a jar of strawberry jam and thrown them onto the rug on the table. They were kept on a dusty wall shelf. So was Pryde's Bible, just above them. He had not been doing penance for a week or more. Perhaps the romance was over. The toast was burning already: Dr. Rowles would be down at any moment. No, Pryde had noticed and turned it over.

"I've an appointment at five with a couple of brats."

"Oh. Well, I'll leave you so."

"Stay. It impresses them. The more the merrier. It scares the shit out of them."

Pryde poured the water straight into a teacup, threw the toast on a plate, and sat at the table, facing the door, in a round-backed wooden chair. He ate as if he were starving. The butter was covered with week-old jam and crumbs. A knife protruded from the lidless jampot. He had provided himself with a half-empty bottle of almost stale milk. He had red lumps and spots on his face, too, and thick brows that went right across the top of his nose.

Carleton was trying to think of a reason to leave. The terrifying thought had struck him that it might be Allen and the boy he was chasing. It was too late; there was a very soft rap on the door.

"Enter!" shouted Pryde through a mouthful of toast.

They had trouble with the handle for a moment, and then two boys sidled in and stood against the wall by the cooker. The first—fair and wan—was the Honorable Fitzmaurice. The second—smaller and reddish-haired—was Hamilton Minor, the twelfth man on the first eleven.

Pryde concentrated on his food—for hours, it seemed. They watched him. They never once glanced at Carleton.

"If the door isn't closed in two seconds, Hamilton Minor,"

said Pryde, in a surprisingly quiet voice, "I'm going to make you bleed."

"Oh. Sorry."

Hamilton Minor closed the door.

"We are charmed by your apology. Are we not, Carleton?"

"Yes," said Carleton, who wanted no share in this. So much came back—the many real terrors of one's first year, so easily forgotten. What was a note from a junior compared with this? Now one had pride and privilege. It was the good time. There were inferiors now who had once been a nightmare: Merryman, for instance, who had given him three terms of it in the shower—"Pigeon chest!" and the inevitable smack of Merryman's fist on his two front bones.

Entirely in the past. Merryman wasn't even a prefect. He would certainly have forgotten. Carleton had a chest now that he could show with no shame at all. So much that was frightfully important happened so quickly here.

"Unfortunately it will not help your situation."

Pryde threw his plate across the rug and leaned back so that his feet were up against the table. Casually, he stretched out an arm and picked up one of their canes, which stood against the wall in the corner.

"Let us hear your offense, Fitzmaurice."

"Um . . . we . . . we had—"

"Well, well," Pryde interrupted, "I do declare the Honorable Fitzmaurice is frightened, Carleton. In fact, our noble aristocrat is so scared he's about to shit in his pants. What is our country coming to? Tut, tut. You disgust me, Fitzmaurice, do you know that? Do you?"

"Yes."

"Good. Good. . . . Am I right to be disgusted?"

"Um."

"Answer the question!"

"Yes."

"That's better. . . . Hamilton Minor, are you also too shit-scared to speak?"

"No."

"Well, speak then!"

So saying, Pryde whipped down the cane and struck the table a fierce crack, just missing the teacup.

"We had our hands in our pockets," Hamilton whispered.
Hamilton Minor is beautiful, Carleton thought, to his great
surprise. Am I going mad these days? Am I going like Sexy Sinnott? With one move of my right foot I could tip Pryde's chair
over backward.

"Which is forbidden to first-year warts. Correct? Correct,
your Honorable?"

"Yes."

Fitzmaurice kept biting his quivering lower lip.

Carleton hated this. He was also powerless. Did Pryde know
his hate? Had he deliberately involved him?

"So the question is, what are we going to do about it?"

Pryde held the cane above his head at either end. He slowly
worked it up into a bow and released it again.

This was one of the few offenses for which one could not be
beaten, at least not without a previous warning. But they probably didn't know this.

"That is the question, is it not?"

They nodded.

"Well, let's see . . . let's see. . . . Very well." Pryde
seemed suddenly to be bored with it, or else he had merely run
out of tortures. "You will write out one hundred times: "I must
not put my hands in my trouser pockets," and you will give it
in to me here before chapel tonight, and no later. And if I ever
catch you at it again, we will think of something else. . . . Do
you understand?"

"Yes," said Hamilton Minor.

They shuffled out and had difficulty in closing the door.

At least the performance had been quick.

They would have to write quickly, too.

"That should settle them," said Pryde. He put his hands behind his head and yawned. "Nancy and Jimmy went to London," he said.

"Oh?"

"Lucky sods."

They both glanced at their watches.

"Are you going to do some reading?"

"Are you trying to take the mickey out of me, Carleton?"

"No."

"You'd better not."

"Oh, dry up, Pryde."

Pryde looked at him, in slight surprise, and then knifed some jam into his mouth.

That whole evening was dreadful: sitting at the head of a nearby table at tea, and trying to look as if nothing had happened, and noticing that Allen was silent, with his eyes downcast; putting on a blue suit in the same dorm afterward and pretending not to see him; and all the time wondering what to do.

For something had happened. That was inescapable. By placing your hand in a coat pocket, you could become involved with another life. The two of them were now separated, in this, from the whole school. He and the dark boy down at the far end of the dorm.

This beautiful boy was going to be waiting for *him,* in the night, in the silent classroom. And waiting. And waiting.

Was this not what you wanted?

No. No. That was just daydreaming.

He will turn to someone else. Will you be able to bear that?

Naylor was no problem at all. It was just as he had known it would be. Naylor smiled wryly when they met. He was certainly a good-looking chap, but Carleton couldn't think how he had ever been attracted. They let themselves be separated in the choir. It was perfectly simple.

But the agony of having to look across the way, without apparently seeing Allen, who kept his head down as before!

And when they stood for the anthem, they were the only two who had to pretend they knew it.

The sermon he did not hear at all. But very few did. It was old Pettifer who came twice a year from some church in Oxford. They could imitate his shaky head, but not his sermons, because no one could remember them. The chaplain looked scornful, and the squeaks of his shoes seemed somehow to express contempt.

Carleton hated to see them file out. This was final. It was now. What would he do?

Naylor must have found him even more detached than he had expected. Indeed, he hardly noticed Naylor. There was even no embarrassment at all in folding the altar cloth.

160

They drank wine, as usual, on the chaplain's landing, and it seemed almost a toast to mutual understanding.

It was Naylor's turn to help count the collection

So he was free.

He walked straight into the senior prefect, turning a corner by the dining hall, and Steele said, "Hey, look out!" and examined him in a puzzled way.

He was in the dark Quad. The rain had stopped. It was a warm night.

He found he had not gone into his house through the Big Schoolroom door. He had passed it and passed the window of his common room. The light was on. The other three were inside, making toast.

There was no one about. He was at the top of the steps, looking down at the new buildings. There was a very dim light above the entrance door. Number 4 was quite a long way down. Allen probably couldn't see him. There was still time to turn back.

But it wasn't fair. He would meet and tell the boy it was all impossible and put an end to it. There was no alternative.

He went quietly down the stairs, through the hall, and turned left down the corridor.

The door of Number 4 was open. It was very dark. There was a movement, of someone coming forward and standing close.

"Now listen," he whispered, "I don't know what this is all about, but it's impossible."

There was no reply.

"Allen. Do you hear me? Do you understand?"

A hand touched his and then came softly inside his.

He pressed it, intending a sympathetic dismissal. But he found that he was still holding it, because it seemed to be the most marvelous thing that had ever happened to him. He was terrified and amazingly happy.

He could not help it: he had raised his other hand and put his arm around Allen and brought him gently closer. His hand was on that wonderful shoulder-blade. Allen's dark sweet-smelling hair was against his cheek. It was ecstasy. His legs were trembling. Allen was his. This marvelous boy was his.

A door slammed, and there were feet clacking along somewhere in the corridor.

Carleton was startled. They stood listening. He had lowered his arm.

The feet stopped.

There was silence.

"I'll have to go," he whispered.

"Don't."

"I must."

Allen's whispered appeal touched his heart. He had never imagined anything like this in his life.

"Listen, we can't. I'm sorry, but we can't. I'm the second prefect. You must forget it. I'm going."

He released Allen's hand and went quickly out. He hurried softly along the corridor.

It seemed safer to go out the different door. There was a light bulb here, too. Four tennis balls in a lidless box lay on a ledge. The warm damp night had brought out midges, which were circling under the light bulb. He went down between the borders. There were distant lights in the Pedant's Palace as his house went to bed, and Carleton could just see the path leading toward the archway made by the vine.

There was a giggle or a teasing laugh, and something hit him lightly in the back, and someone rushed past. He looked down and saw a tennis ball bouncing at his feet, and without hesitation—and somehow freed, and released, and feeling light of heart and joyous—he caught it up and flung it at Allen's broad back. Yes, it was Allen running ahead. It was a hit. Allen stopped for a second, and the ball struck Carleton in the chest.

He was dashing on under the vine, with the ball in his hand. He had caught up a little. This time it hit Allen again in the back, but he did not stop.

He picked up the ball—and Allen had gone. But he must be just ahead. Flushed with excitement and happiness, Carleton came suddenly to a halt.

There was a railing and a light high above it. Ashley was leaning against the railing, talking with two boys. Beside them, steep concrete steps descended down to the yard where the photographic and other rooms were. Allen must have gone down them.

Ashley stopped talking. They were looking at him. Ashley had a funny, surprised, quizzical kind of half-sneering expression. Carleton went boldly forward, to go down the stairs, intending to say, "Good night, gentlemen," but he could not bring it out. As he passed, Ashley said, in a very peculiar voice, "Carleton's in love."

So they *had* just seen Allen, he thought. So he must be down here ahead of me.

It was only as he arrived at the bottom that he considered the full meaning of Ashley's remark.

He had taken it for granted as correct!

Could it be?

His first love, the one they say affects a whole life. Was this what it was like?

No time to think. He was in the dark, in the yard, walking softly on the wet slippery cobbles. His heart was racing. He said, quietly, "Allen?"

No answer. A starless night. But he could just make out the high hay-barns on one side, and on the other the ghostly white doors of the photographic room, the senior Ping-Pong room and the printing room, where he and Johns produced their magazine.

"Where are you?"

Oh, come to me now; this may never happen again, thought Carleton, losing all caution.

"Allen, where are you? *Please.*"

But he had gone.

It was baffling—not so much that he had gone, but that this strange younger boy seemed to have taken charge.

CHAPTER FOURTEEN

The lesser of the two gates was nearer Gillingham. It was, therefore, a likely bet that the two coaches would come up the back drive. They did. Entering between the tall stone pillars, with an eager face under a gray helmet at each window, they passed below a white banner six feet in width, on which were written the words, in red, BEWARE OF RAPE.

There was a gasp—and then shrieks.

"Girls! Girls!"

Miss Hutchins was sitting in the first coach, wearing a tweed suit and a brown helmet. She turned quickly, and looked out the back window, and read it in reverse. It was true. Miss Moffit, the little games mistress beside her, was ashen white. And rightly.

But the girls were scarlet and beyond restraint. The green coaches sounded like parrot houses as they went up the bumpy uncemented back drive, and very slowly, too, because the ancient driver in the front was weeping with laughter and could scarcely see.

Yet they were suddenly hushed as they turned up in front of the Head's House. More than a hundred boys of the senior school were standing about on the grass, examining them as if they were indeed a traveling zoo.

Blushing greatly, and some of them taken with renewed seizures, they descended to the ground. Mr. Crabtree stepped forward. Miss Hutchins spoke at once, "I don't know that we can stay, Headmaster. There is a quite disgusting notice over your gateway."

The Head stared at her, quickly coloring, and at last brought out, "What? What is this, Steele?"

Steele looked military, and almost came to attention, but had to confess, "I don't know, sir."

"I hardly expected you to know." Miss Hutchins paused. She had been interrupted by wolf whistles. The Head spun around, scarlet, and attempted to wither his charges with a glance. His wife, beside him, was gazing at the sunny blue sky, which was not helpful.

"But I insist it come down at once, and I'll have a letter of apology from the culprits, who, I trust, will be severely punished."

"By all means, Miss Hutchins," said the Head.

Now they put the week's planning to the test. Ten girls had come in white, for mixed doubles. There was the Head's court (for prefects only), just across the drive near the Music Building, and there were four more courts down the hill near the lake, with benches around them. Adjacent to these was a large marquee, within which Miss Bull was already supervising the distribution of strawberries.

Dr. Rowles had announced that he would be staying in his room for the afternoon.

The chaplain was doing the same—indeed he was at home for tea—without feeling any need to announce it.

But the Pedant and the Cod and a number of junior masters were active. Everyone noticed that the Pedant was in uncommonly lively form. They told prefects to take parties off on tours of the school. They saw that some watched tennis on the Head's court and that the other courts were not neglected. Jimmy Rich was keeping the juniors out of the way on the cricket field, and more of them were up at the swimming pool under McCaffrey. Mixed bathing had been vetoed: Miss Hutchins was doubtful about the problem of changing, and the Head himself considered it a little too ambitious for their first meeting.

Still, they were to mix; that was the thing. Tennis, and tea, and so on were means to that sole end.

The only guide who was not silent with embarrassment was Lucretia Crabtree. She took—she commanded—a party of eight up into the wood, to see her rabbits which were kept in numerous cages. With them went a Starling named Lawson. He was—even for a Starling—very ugly and unwashed. He had lately been helping with the rabbits and had otherwise been seen in attendance. It was a liaison that was generally regarded as revolting, and also damn cheek, since one did not associate with girls.

In this respect, Sexy Sinnott, whose tastes seemed indiscriminate, was probably the boldest among the few sinners. He sprawled amid a group of four or five, lying on a grass bank above the Head's court. But it was noticeable that the more he talked, the more he faltered and the more he blushed.

They watched with mocking eyes. They whispered comments behind hands to each other—*even while one was speaking.*

Yes, it became uncomfortably plain very soon that though

the visitors might have lost the first round, the day was going to be theirs. Together in groups, they talked, they whispered, they discussed; they made selections on Darwinian principles. Their hosts suffered. "Rape" looked a sorry threat.

"I'm Peggy Wyckham. I'm Captain. You're Terence Carleton?"

"Yes."

Carleton was in agony. She was some inches taller than he was, gingery, freckled, with a full bosom. She had happy blue eyes that he knew should have seemed nice and friendly. But no, they were too frighteningly alive, and—did he imagine it? —they were laughing at him for being a shy child.

"This is Antonia Naylor."

"Hello."

Antonia was worse. She was bored and superior, maybe contemptuous. She was slim, dark, and supple. The news had somehow gone right through the school beforehand that she would be the beauty of the day. She was Naylor's sister.

"This is . . . Bewick."

(He had no idea of Bewick's Christian name.)

"Gerald," said Bewick, in a quavering voice.

"Hi," said Peggy Wyckham.

The four of them went on court. Carleton was playing with Antonia.

There were staring faces all around. Male and female eyes, in entirely separate groups. He saw Ashley in the distance, on some lone walk or prowl, pause and narrow his eyes, studying what was presumably a preposterous scene. The Crabs, Miss Hutchins, and Miss Moffit sat in a row of deck chairs by the net. Red-haired Hamilton Minor was up on the umpire's ladder. He loved being scorer. His ambition was to be an accountant.

"You serve," said Antonia, for some reason in a dry, apparently hostile voice. It was the one thing he did not want to do, but the instruction was imperative. She patted two balls back without looking. She crouched at the net, slim and limber in a neat white dress, with a young girl's legs and shiny black hair. Somehow incredible to think of her as being Naylor's sister. She was another being, supposed to be beautiful, but that was what Naylor was. How did one tackle, how was one ever likely to be tempted to tackle, this different creature, so thin in the middle, with those breasts . . . and such a fierce face?

The ball went sideward, away to the right, and he only just reached it and struck it into the net. Which was pretty silly, since he himself had thrown it up. The second time it went up so high he thought it would never come down. He waited too long but just managed to push it over. Peggy came in heavily, all white and pink, and hit it calmly and hard to his backhand. He scooped it up. Peggy banged it down, just missing Antonia, who was in retreat.

"Love—fifteen," said Hamilton Minor.

Antonia tossed her hair.

He had just spotted his darling, his still undeclared and apparently much recovered darling, chatting with friends behind the end netting.

Purgatory must be like this.

"We must see that they mix."

The Head had leaned toward Miss Hutchins with this sudden original thought.

"Quite," she said.

Mrs. Crabtree spoke for the first time, dipping like a bird, "I fear it's less important for you than for us."

Miss Hutchins had no response. The Head's mouth went down. Miss Moffit delicately cleared her throat.

"Do you ride?" asked Antonia, in a bored voice.

Everyone was standing on the grass outside the marquee, in distinct groups. He was one of the few boys trapped by a visitor. He wished they were still playing tennis: it had not been so bad; they had been defeated by Peggy Wyckham's steadiness, but only just.

"No. No, I don't."

He was watching Allen out of the corner of his eye. As a younger senior, he had been deputed to hand around the strawberries. Carleton could bear the heartache and the apartness no longer. He decided he was going to act.

"You should take it up," said Antonia.

Allen passed just behind her.

"What?"

"Riding. It's the only sport."

She was examining him in a peculiarly cold way. It was very embarrassing to be observed by nearly the whole staff, not to mention everyone else, talking with the beauty of the day. It was true; there was a kind of radiance about her, a different and definitely unapproachable kind. He supposed he should have been getting a kick out of this. He only wanted to escape.

"There's a school two miles from here. I go on Wednesday afternoons."

"Oh."

"They have some pretty bloody horses. But Daisy and Nigger are O.K."

"Oh."

"What do *you* do on Wednesday afternoons?"

"Me? Well, we've a half-holiday. There's usually cricket."

She spooned in a strawberry.

"Always?"

"No. Not always."

"Would they let you have a riding lesson?"

This was unbelievable. She looked so bored. He was afraid.

"But I don't want one," he said quickly.

She inserted another strawberry.

How surprised she would be, he thought, if I gave her an account of her brother.

She raised her head, looked him straight, coldly, in the eye, and said, "Where *will* you meet me then?"

His legs seemed to disappear beneath him.

"What for?" he murmured.

"Don't be a bloody fool," was her reply.

It was unkind, since his question had been largely genuine. It was almost impossible to comprehend that one was supposed to enter into some sort of relationship with this strangely constructed creature.

"I'm sorry. I can't," he muttered, and was thinking, I've said that before, when luckily there was a "Hi," and Peggy came up with Bewick.

The Head had been watching, while half-listening to Miss Hutchins. He more than suspected that Carleton lacked the school spirit, but even so, it was one of the few rewarding sights of the afternoon. Pretty girl, too. No, they were *not* mixing, and Miss Hutchins kept telling him so.

"Steele . . . the uh . . . is it removed?"

"Yes, sir."

"I shall need to know what it said."

"Beware of rape, sir," said Steele.

Miss Hutchins bristled. The Head's mouth had clamped down. He had meant at another time. Steele was a rock, but he could be monumentally unsubtle.

And at that moment, from that same gateway, which was near at hand, there came a roar, as of a jet engine, and a white sports car halted on the driveway.

A mad-looking individual in a cap was standing up in the passenger seat and shouting, "Hurray for the Sabines!"

Everyone watched in silent astonishment.

The driver was grinning like an idiot.

"Steady the Buffs!" roared his companion. "Come over here, Blondie, you bastard child!"

Beauchamp was hurrying over to the car. He looked flustered, for once.

The Head glanced at Miss Hutchins and saw that this was probably the beginning of the end.

"It's an orgy, I tell you! A veritable orgy!"

Beauchamp could be heard expostulating, "Shut up, Freddie, for God's sake!"

But suddenly he was perched up in the back of the car, and it was roaring away up the drive. The Head's House, the whole school, seemed to be reverberating. There was a flash of white, out from among trees, and the car was speeding away, past the farm, down the other drive, and so out the main gates.

Instinctively, they awaited its reappearance. A grounding in British comic films told them that it would repeat the circuit almost indefinitely. But no. Even odder, considering that Beauchamp was a passenger, it did not return.

"Girls! Time to go!"

These were very nearly the last words that Miss Hutchins was prepared to speak.

The Head himself could find little to say. This outrageous incident had destroyed his already diminishing confidence.

They straggled up the slope—girls in one group ahead, boys in another group behind.

The Head was not sure now what he had expected. Even

without those two gross eventualities, the day would not have been a success. He suspected—correctly—that Miss Hutchins was planning to cancel their reciprocal visit. Something else, something more, was required to wipe the slate clean at Weatherhill.

The planned farewell was almost a mockery. Steele gave three cheers for Gillingham, and Peggy Wyckham for Weatherhill, and their cheers were feeble indeed. Miss Hutchins shook his hand and said, "You'll be hearing from me, Headmaster," and followed her girls into the coach. There was an uncomfortable silence as the two vehicles departed—and then uproar.

Yes, even in his presence, while he and his wife were still climbing the steps to enter their own abode, there were shouts of "Steady the Buffs!" and "It's an *orgy!*"

They were scattering.

Carleton had deliberately stood close by. He said quietly, "Allen."

He stopped. His companions went ahead.

"I've got to see you. After tea."

"Where?"

How calm! How expressionless! But there was intimacy somehow. Yes, he was blushing. There was love.

How stupid! He couldn't think of anywhere.

Allen solved it.

"The Music Building. I'll be practicing in Number five."

He ran away.

Fired by their cries, the Head was making angry resolutions as he went through his front door: six for Beauchamp, and a threat of future expulsion; an address to the whole school in the morning, demanding the culprits' names, or else all exeats would be canceled. But above and beyond all that—sterner measures, yes, much more severe measures.

CHAPTER FIFTEEN

Two hours later it was tea proper. Miss Bull was la- dling baked beans again, behind the vast hot plate by the door, but only the junior school, who had missed the strawberries, had much appetite.

Carleton, seated at the head of his table for the day, was sur- prised to hear that, in spite of everything, certain connections had been made. Several notes had been received and were passed about the dining hall. He was not interested; he had committed himself now and was waiting excitedly—and with apprehension—for their meeting afterward. Sexy Sinnott had received one, signed Phoebe French, which said simply, "I'm crazy about you. Send me your photo and I'll send you mine."

This was shown to Jimmy Rich, who was parading as the mas- ter on duty. He read it and handed it back, without a smile, without a word.

This was extraordinary. They had never seen Jimmy Rich in a bad mood before. He looked peculiar. He looked flushed and angry.

There was a crash. Rich had banged a silver cup down on the unattended high table. He was standing on the dais with his back to it.

At last the voices ceased.

They assumed he was about to give them leave to go.

But no.

"Silence now, silence now. I want no more talking now, lads, till you hear what I have to say."

They began to be excited already. Something was brewing. Something good.

"Carleton boy."

"Yes, sir."

"There's the key."

A large rusty object came flying down to Carleton. He caught it.

"Lock the door, boy!"

He hesitated. He glanced at Steele for possible guidance. Something subversive was in the air. But Steele just looked stunned.

"Do as you're told, boy. I haven't all night!"

The entire school watched as Carleton walked down the aisle. As he locked the door, he heard Rich say, from the distance, "That's it, boy. We don't want the old Crab poking his nose into our business, do we, lads?"

There was an astonished silence, and then a brave voice said faintly, "That's right, Jimmy."

Carleton went back to his place—a conspirator. Steele gave him a nasty glance.

"Now then, lads, I've a wee statement to make. It's not a pleasant matter, and I'll try to get it over with as quickly as I can. There's a state of affairs going on, and I want you lads to know all about it. And when you've heard what I have to say, you're going to tell me that *you're* not standing for it any longer either."

Super. It was thrilling. It was going to be some drama which left them safe. This was great!

Steele rose.

"Mr. Rich, I'm afraid—"

"Sit down, boy, or I'll larrup you!"

Steele sat.

"Now then, to start with—and I'm sorry you lads have got to hear this, but I've no alternative—Ma Crab has been going round spreading filthy lies about me and Nancy."

You could have heard a baked bean drop. This was incredible. It was terrific.

"I want you to listen to this, lads. I want you to listen to this. She has been paying her own daughter to follow us around the grounds!" Suddenly his voice was raised to a shout—his fist struck the air—"*Two and sixpence an hour!*"

They gasped. This was big money. They went for long walks.

"Now I've nothing against Lucretia, lads. The girl has owned up. She's decided to chuck it in. She's owned up to Lawson, over here. She took him up an oak tree when Nancy and me were sitting by the lake below. Lawson, boy, stand up; tell us what happened."

Baffled, deeply envious, they watched as this wretched Starling rose embarrassedly to his feet.

"She said. . . ."

"Go on, lad, let's have it."

"She said we'd watch you from there, and I said why, and then she came out with it and said it was worth a lot of cash. But she said she was tired of it, so I persuaded her to give it up, and she said she was owed seven and six, but she wouldn't claim it."

"Thank you, lad, and Nancy wants to thank you, too. Sit down, lad. Boys, this is only the half of it!"

Hurray.

"I want you all to know now, lads, what that old witch has been saying in extra Latin. Bolton, Forrester, stand up lads!"

Two members of Remove were on their feet.

"Come on, now, tell them!"

"She said—" began Bolton.

"Come on."

"She said—" began Forrester.

"She said we'd been fornicating by the lake. Right?"

They nodded.

"Sit down, men."

They sat down.

He waited for them to take it in, for their shock to be complete.

A large minority longed to know what it meant. You couldn't ask; you'd be savagely mocked, probably by boys who didn't know either. Parents said nothing. There were rumors you did something face to face, but it seemed incredible. Did women have nothing or what? How rotten for them! Impossible to find out.

"Now I want to tell you, lads—and Nancy wanted to come and tell you too, but she's too shy, God bless her—that this is nothing but a dirty rotten lie."

All at once there was a gentle, inquisitive knocking on the door.

Steele rose again.

173

"Sit down, or I'll have the hide off you, Steele!"

Steele sat.

"That's the old Crab. He'll stay out till I'm done. Now then, this is what I want to tell you, lads. I fell for this lovely girl last Guy Fawkes Night. I daresay I'm not the only one, but I'm the lucky one. Nancy's wild about Jimmy."

Suddenly, a total change. He was beaming. It was Jimmy Rich!

Someone shouted, from the far end, "Good for you, Jimmy!"

"Ssh, lad, ssh. And do you know what I'm going to tell you, lads?"

The knocking began again. It was slightly louder.

"Do you know what I'm going to tell you? . . . We're in love, lads, and we're going to be married!"

There were several voices this time: "Hurray!"

"Ssh, lads, ssh."

There was louder, insistent knocking.

"And this is what I want to say. That girl is something wonderful to me, lads, and *I wouldn't harm a hair on her head!*"

"Good for you, Jimmy!"

"And I only hope that you'll be as happy in later life," shouted Rich above the growing tumult of voices.

There was fierce banging on the door.

"Pay no heed to that. And this is what I'm going to ask of you now. Next time that old cow comes to you with her wicked lying tales, you'll tell her where she gets off; you'll send her away with a flea in her ear. I want this promise from you, and I want it now. I want to hear one great big "Yes" from you, and I want to hear it now. Will you do it, lads, will you do it for me and Nancy?"

"YES!"

Their instant roar even drowned the maniacal hammering at the wooden panels.

"Let's hear you say that again, lads!"

"YE—SS!!"

"Right, lads."

He was grinning with delight. And suddenly they were singing, while a number were rushing up to shake him by the hand,

"For he's a jolly good fellow, for he's a jolly good fellow, for he's. . . .

Steele strode down the aisle, forging a way against the growing stream of admirers, and unlocked and opened the door.

Philomena Maguire stood there, with a troupe of maids about her. She spoke from behind her hair. "What's the big idea?" she said.

"None of your business. Stand back!" said Steele, pushing through them in disgust.

"It *is* our business," a small figure in black shouted after him. "We've got to clear!"

He had gone to the Head to report.

CHAPTER SIXTEEN

 "Oh, gosh, I can't believe it, somehow," said Carleton, squeezing Allen's waist as he spoke, relishing his own intense happiness.

His darling was seated across his lap, with an arm around his shoulders, so that his dark eyes looked down and looked bashfully away.

There was this one rickety chair in front of the upright. The room was so small that the door struck the piano if you opened it too far.

"Are you happy?" he whispered, delighting in knowing the answer.

"Yes."

Carleton felt both their happinesses, enjoyed both at once.

"What have we been doing all term?"

"I don't know."

They were very safe here, because they were the only two boys not willingly embroiled in the evening's drama. (Except for Beauchamp. He had skipped tea: his friends had returned him soon enough, but the Crab had struck him very hard six times. He was sulking and smarting in his dormitory.)

"What's this ring?"

"It's a family crest. It was my brother's."

"Oh. Sorry."

"It's all right."

Carleton was thinking, I wonder how you'd look older, if you were the dead brother. Did his black hair go up that way, in thick waves? Had he this complexion like sunburn? These eyes: shy, but wise, laughing . . . maybe mocking. No, he'd have been older and duller.

"What are you looking at?"

"You," Carleton said.

They examined each other, and they both smiled.

"Stinker."

"Why?"

"I don't know. . . . Yes, I do know. Where the dickens did you go to that night?"

"There's a way up past the linen room."

"Goodness, you seem to know everything."

"How do you mean?"

"You're supposed to be a new boy. You seem to . . . know things. You make *me* feel— Have you been in love before?"

"No."

"Promise?"

"Yes. . . . Have you?"

"Never. Never."

He looked down and stroked Allen's slim brownish hand. He felt sad suddenly, in a wonderful way.

"I wonder what'll happen?"

There's nothing to wonder, Carleton thought, a little surprised by such a remark. We're together forever, that's all.

"How do you mean?"

"Jimmy Rich."

"Oh. . . . Oh, I'm afraid he'll be thrown out. He's crazy. . . . Anyhow, how can you think about that?"

"I can't, really," Allen said, in the most marvelous, delicate, funny, silently happy way.

"Oh, I do love you. I love you, my darling. Don't be shy, look at me. Do you love me?"

"Yes."

"Do you swear?"

"Yes."

He leaned up and kissed Allen softly on his blushing cheek. He felt a new sweetness enter him. He felt he had become, instantly, a more tender person. He felt older, with a purpose, someone to look after, to cherish and love, for always.

Ashley knocked and entered, and the great head at the desk turned. Two cupped hands went up over the ears, and there was a quiet, melancholy exclamation, "Oh, Lord. Oh, spare me, Ashley, my dear fellow, I beg of you. Not one of your crusades, if you please! Not now."

Ashley moved forward and stood over Rowles.

"You've heard?"

The Doctor kept his head protected, with his eyes fixed on a sheaf of foolscap, covered with figures.

"I've received a report of a kind. The head of my house has unaccountably disappeared. . . . But I've heard enough."

"And what are you going to do about it?"

"Nothing."

"What!"

Rowles twisted his protected head, raising pale blue eyes to study Ashley.

"Look here, Ashley, what in arsehole do you expect me to do? That idiot has cooked his own goose."

"On the contrary, it's been cooked for him."

"Balls."

Ashley walked to the hearth. There was a picture of the Old Man that he had never seen before. It was an affection they had shared. He glanced at Rowles, who was aware of his discovery without seeming to look.

"This has been my worst day in this place. I've been incarcerated for the past six hours. Don't press me, Ashley. I've no time for fools."

"Fools? These are the only two sane, normal people in the whole school."

"That's their bad luck."

"There's no room for the sane and ordinary here?"

"There has never been much, I'm afraid."

"You amaze me, Rowles."

"You flatter me, Ashley."

Rowles picked up a pencil and wrote off a series of numbers. He was not exactly terminating the meeting. Ashley felt faintly encouraged.

"And what about the school? Your school?"

"Ah, what do you mean, man?"

"Writs for slander and wrongful dismissal and publicity in the national press."

Rowles made a noise of amusement, very nearly a "tee-hee!"

"And why would he bother and what hope would he have? A public oration to children, destructive of a lady's character. Come off it, Ashley!"

"That's no lady. That's the headmaster's wife."

"I see you recognize the element of farce in all this as well as I do."

"Farce is only tragedy seen in a particular way."

"Tragedy? Oh, come, come, man."

"Some people must have work, you know. And some people may be just as fond of working here as *you* are."

The Doctor was silent. Ashley felt he had scored.

"You're a very curious bird, you know, Ashley. . . . Has someone put you up to this?"

"Matron has just been to see me in tears. But she didn't need to put me up to it. Unfortunately, my popularity is such that I can do nothing on my own."

"And what the devil did they expect?"

"Rich expected nothing. He thought it would clear the air. She tried to persuade him against it. He's with the headmaster now, to his surprise."

"Jumping Jehovah! And you say he's not a fool?"

"He's an innocent. And he lost his head. He also *is* innocent. Assuming it matters a damn how people lead their own lives, do you believe the lady's allegations; do you countenance her attitude and her daughter's employment?"

"No. Nor do I countenance folly. People should grow up. . . . Look here, man, what do you imagine that I can possibly do?"

"I'm going to the Head now. Come. I don't say, support me. But come, and judge. You can't go on hiding here, because the Old Man is dead. You've been hiding here all day—all term!"

It was a sudden thought, and it was out before Ashley could stop it.

"Damn your blasted impertinence, Ashley!"

The Doctor's fervor took him by surprise.

"I apologize. I really mean that without your participation this school is likely to become a monster."

He listened to Rowles breathing.

"You needn't try to butter me up. . . . Listen here, what do these people mean to you?"

"It's not important. I'm merely concerned with injustice."

"Oh, come on, damn you," said the Doctor, rising. "But remember, I promise you no support of any kind."

They went downstairs, through the Big Schoolroom, and across the Quad in the evening sunshine.

"You're a very odd bird. I'll never make you out. Here, clear off the lot of you!"

An excited group of whisperers scattered before the Doctor's approach.

"We're doing no harm, sir."

"You're an old woman, Metcalfe. Take your ladies somewhere else."

"Yes, sir."

They passed the famous chest, and came into the rear of the Head's hall.

A dense crowd, and uproar.

Pryde was there.

"What the blazes is going on here?"

"It's a deputation, sir. We're going in to protest."

Faces pressed forward out of the throng. There were piping cries.

"It's not fair, sir!"

"We're for Mr. Rich, sir!"

"He's done nothing wrong, sir!"

"Silence!"

He protected his ears again.

"You must have gone clean round the bend, Pryde. Where is Carleton?"

"I don't know, sir."

179

"Where's Steele?"

"He's in the study. So is Mr. Rich. I'm not the only prefect, sir—"

"So I see. Well, you can all—"

There was a shocked silence. Jimmy Rich had broken out into the mob, distraught, disheveled. His carefully waved hair had fallen down the sides of his face. It was horrible to them. He was elbowing everyone away. He was going straight to Ashley. He seized his arm.

"He's throwing me out! Me and Nancy! Now! The bastard's throwing us out. He's throwing us *out!*"

Some felt they ought to shout something. No one did. Dr. Rowles said, "I want every one of you out of here within ten seconds. If it's any gratification, you're giving no help. You're doing the reverse. Now hop it! Rich, you go to your room. We'll see what we can do."

They slouched away. A few hung around Jimmy Rich, but he did not seem to hear what they were saying.

Nicely timed, the tinny bell for prep began to ring, calling them back to the curriculum.

Mrs. Crabtree was standing before the mantelpiece, her hands joined, as ever, behind her back. She looked pale, but surprisingly calm in comparison with the scarlet figure behind the desk. Steele was seated in a chair, nodding in response to the Head's directives. He was dazed: a military commander who has just suffered an unexpected defeat. Mr. Crabtree paused and looked at the two arrivals, with consternation still on his face. The Doctor said, glancing at his wife, "I'm extremely sorry to hear of this occurrence."

"It seems I've been defamed in public, Dr. Rowles," said Mrs. Crabtree. "Mr. Rich has delivered an unexpected dissertation on the facts of life. My request for an apology has just been dismissed. So has Mr. Rich."

"Ah . . . yes, well, uh . . . it appears Mr. Ashley here has views on this matter, and I undertook to accompany him. They're not mine, I may say."

"I suggest you reconsider this decision, sir—" Ashley began.

"Silence!" The Head struck his desk. "Ashley, I've warned you before. I will not have you meddling in my affairs. The decision is final. Nor is it the only one. We have at last made a start in bringing a sense of decency back to Weatherhill. I will be taking other decisions. After Weatherhill Day is over, I intend to do a great deal more. In a way we are grateful for this outrage by Rich. The boys will appreciate the lesson."

"A crucifixion," said Ashley.

"Ah, here, steady on, man," said Rowles.

"I'd be obliged if you'd leave my study at once, Ashley," said the Head.

"I'll have to run," Allen whispered, looking up at Carleton, with his hand on the doorknob.

Carleton placed his cheek softly against Allen's cheek and closed his eyes. He had already said, "Don't go," twice, which was selfish, because being a prefect, he himself didn't have to attend prep. Their cheeks were burning.

"O.K. When will we meet?"

"I've an exeat tomorrow," said Allen.

"So have I, dammit."

"After chapel then."

"Right. Where? I feel a bit trapped here."

Allen was thinking. They had been whispering into each other's ears. Carleton felt *he* should be dominating these places, but he could not think of anywhere.

"There's a corner around the buttress at the back of the chapel. No one goes there."

How the devil did Allen know that?

"Isn't it a bit close?"

He was stroking Allen's hair over his ear.

"That's why," Allen said. "No one need see us walking anywhere. Just go around the back when the coast's clear."

How the deuce? Was it conceivable that Allen could have been through this already with someone else? No. He was just terrifically bright.

"If anything's wrong, put a note in my mack. My locker's Number nine. We must have a sign."

Carleton moved away a little and looked at him. "How do you mean?" he whispered. "How do you mean, darling?"

"So we know one of us has left a note. When I see you, I'll put my right hand in my coat pocket, like this. And you do the same."

"Righto. I don't know how you think of these things."

Allen smiled. "It's just common sense."

It sounded a bit like Rowles; but the context could hardly be less apt, and this made Carleton smile, too.

"Oh, I do love you."

"I love you terribly," Allen said, and he had gone quickly out of the door and closed it carefully behind him

He waited a few minutes and then stepped into the corridor. The bell had stopped. There was no one to see him. But up in front of the Head's House he came on Pryde and several other prefects. They looked morose and angry. They stopped talking and watched him. Pryde said, "Where the blazes have *you* been? Roly has searched the school for you."

"Where is he?"

"With the Crab."

He left them wondering and went up the steps through the open front door.

Rowles and Ashley were standing in the hall. They appeared to have been having a row. Ashley was scowling. He looked awful.

"I was told you wanted me, sir."

"Where the devil have you been, Carleton?"

"Uh . . . how do you mean, sir?"

"You've been noticeably absent from our latest variety show."

"He's in love," Ashley said.

"I beg your pardon!"

Ashley was looking at him with the most horrible expression. He wanted to run.

"You're going crackers, Ashley. I've work to do."

The Doctor turned and walked away.

"True, is it not?" Ashley said.

"I don't know what you're talking about," Carleton murmured.

"So we haven't escaped after all. You don't know what danger you're in, child."

"I'm not a child."

"No. No, perhaps not. But that is the danger."

Suddenly—and luckily—Rowles was back. He said, "By the way, Ashley, there's been a letter lying in the common room

for you most of the week. If you used it like the rest of us, I'm
sure your correspondents would be grateful."

He was gone again.

Carleton escaped out the front door.

The common room faced the study, across the hall. Oblivious
of everything, old Mr. Wall was asleep in a brown leather armchair. There was one letter on the central table. He recognized
the writing with distaste and alarm. He opened it and read:

DEAR ERIC,

I thought not answering was pretty damn mean. A blast in
the teeth would have been preferable.

Your mother says she hasn't heard from you either. She is
not a celebrated actress for nothing, but I still don't think she's
as worried as I am.

I'm nerving myself on vodka for the next bit. But I'm determined to brave it.

It seems you passed your boyhood years at this same damn
place! When she told me, I laughed hoarsely. There appears
to have been a greenhouse period of vegetation at Cambridge,
involving overheated rooms, joss-sticks, sherry, the lot—and
two characters called—ye gods—Walter and Clive. She seemed
to place particular emphasis on the Clive one, but I may well
have reached the state of hearing things. It is not for a mere
girl to pass judgment on how the better-heeled males, if that is
what they are, choose to educate themselves in this country,
but I do feel you should have called a halt. I mean, I believe
you may have done something worse than foolish in going
back to school.

I would give a great deal to know why the birde flewe.

There is worse. Read on.

I have booked a room in a hotel called the Crown and Anchor in Marston for next Saturday night. I am inviting you to
dinner at seven.

And having topped up my glass again and taken a long gulp,
I'm telling you that in my opinion—and I believe you know
what I mean—if you do not meet me there, you will be *lost*.

Love,
JOAN

Ashley tried to laugh hoarsely but failed.

He tore up the letter instead.

183

CHAPTER SEVENTEEN

This is going to be something better to do in rest than reading *Talleyrand*, if I can keep to it.

I'm on the blanket and cold pillow, with my knees up and this empty hard-cover exercise book propped against them. I'm going to write a memory of the most important event in my life. (I have a key to the drawer in the bottom of my wardrobe.) McIver has given me a suspicious look and rolled his eyes, but he can't see from there. I don't need a photo now. No, that's not true; I'd like one as well. I'd like to be able to look at him all the time or any time I wanted. But I'm not going to ask.

I love writing. I don't suppose that necessarily makes you a writer.

Home was an absolute blank. I wonder did I seem odd. I thought my mother was looking at me. I longed to be back. I could only think of him.

And not really being able to imagine him, see him . . . isn't that funny? Only someone small, dark, laughing, warm, and excitingly, bewilderingly, mine. Perhaps that's why I mean I'd like a photo too.

The Crab was surprising really. He was frightening at breakfast, telling us this would be the last exeat unless the culprits owned up. Beware of Rape. (Everything seems to happen in the dining hall these days.) Three oafs confessed and were given six. Jimmy Rich and Nancy have gone. The Cod is taking games for the rest of this term, and some old crone is coming as Matron.

There was a moon. But no one could see us around the buttress. We stayed until the bell went for A. to go to bed. We could have stayed forever. Bach was going on inside. The Beatle was playing the Prelude and Fugue in A minor. It was all just magical and marvelous. I told him he had beautiful ears. It didn't sound soppy then, but maybe it does a bit now. He says hardly anything. We both stood there for ages without speaking at all. Which is something I could never have imagined. It's funny—there's something special about being together in love *out-of-doors,* particularly at night. Maybe because it's so real and natural—and nature is too.

I nearly forgot. I'd taken two cigarettes out of my mother's packet when I was home, and we lit up. It sounds silly, but there was something extra special about being a prefect and smoking with my darling. A kind of trust. It removed the only possible division between us.

After he'd gone, I slipped round the chapel—straight into the Beatle. He didn't wonder where I'd been. He said he'd decided to resurrect one of his early musicals—*Peter Piper,* before my time—for the end of term, and as usual he wanted me for the male lead. I said that was marvelous as it was my last term. I certainly meant it.

He's amazing. How did he know we'd *have* to write notes? Meeting isn't so easy, and we couldn't endure a day without getting at least one. He's amazing. He runs by, with his friends, and he doesn't even seem to notice me; but he puts his hand in his coat pocket. It's tricky; his locker is nowhere near mine. Gower has turned the corner twice, and the second time I think he saw me closing the wrong locker. To be suspected by Gower! Roly never mentions him now. I don't know what's happening. Anyhow, his little notes seem alive in my hand. My heart races. "Don't worry, I love you, I love you, I love you. N.A." "Yes, I'm longing for tomorrow too. Be patient. I'll be in your arms. N.A."

Nicholas, his name is. The funny thing is, I can't say it. He doesn't call me anything either. We say "you." A couple of times I heard his friends, or whatever they are, say "Nicky." (He's frightfully popular.) I was furiously jealous. I think of him now as Nicky. I long to call him Nicky. But I can't say it.

It's somehow crazy to think he's away down in a corner of this very same room each time I am writing this.

* * *

185

Thank goodness Nicky has a bike! There's a heat wave going on. It's glorious. He looks absolutely brown in his white shirt. He's going to be terrifically handsome when we're older, which is exciting. Not that I'm going to be able to love him any more than I do now. It was the half-holiday, and we met on bikes up near Little Hammerton. It has a funny old pub, and I nearly went crazy and suggested we go in. We left and returned separately, of course. It looked odd, so I pedaled like mad. Blast it, but on the way back up the drive I had to pass Roly and the Pedant. I rang my bell. They turned and stared, but I was going like the wind. I have a three-speed gear.

It's hard to write this, but as I sat looking down at him as he lay on the grass, I heard myself say something very strange, without thinking. No, not really—in fact I'd always thought it and always thought I should say it. I remembered Naylor. But I want to be absolutely honest—I think there was a little bit of a question in it as well.

I said, "We must never do anything."

My goodness, it seemed ages before he answered!

"It's up to you," he said.

It didn't seem to be exactly a complete agreement. I couldn't think what to say.

"Anyhow," he said, "I don't want ever again to have to turn away whenever I see somebody. Never again."

I nearly collapsed. I didn't dare question him.

But it did seem this time to mean that he agreed.

I got over it quickly. But for a moment I thought—and it wasn't the first occasion I'd thought it—and I was furious, What the dickens goes on at Eton?

I've asked him about Mr. Brownlow. He thinks he was horrible. But he *did* sit on his knee.

Ma Crab was on several times about "Allen" and that wretched window at lunch, even though it's been put in ages ago. She also remarked—twice—on how I wasn't eating anything. (I can't these days; my stomach's all fluttery, my heart, too. I feel kind of nervous all the time. *And* I'm glad.) Can she know? How? Lucretia still wanders around, but I thought she'd given it up.

I think there's no doubt a few others know. I can't imagine how.

186

This morning Beauchamp and Sinnott went past, and Beauchamp said, "I never thought our Carleton had it in him, did you?"

A nice compliment!

But to be honest, I'd be a bit fed up if nobody knew. If only it were possible, I'd like every single one of them to know. When you score a hundred, they cheer. To have fallen in love seems a far greater achievement. And to have won him—this, surely, Desired of All, as they say—is another.

But wait, it's more than that. I want my New Self known. I want to reintroduce myself, because now I'm a completely different person. I like them all suddenly. I even like Sinnott. I even like Beauchamp. It's the way I felt at the match, only more so. I like everyone. I'm not Carleton anymore.

As a matter of fact, I've always hated my surname. I wonder does anyone else have the same feeling. We're all stuck with surnames here.

I'm still worried about Eton. We were lying in a place we've found behind the san yesterday, and I had put my hand inside his open shirt collar, and there were little black hairs running right down his back. I liked them. But he said, bashfully and at once, "I've horrible hairs going down my back."

How did he know?

Who told him?

Speaking of the san, Henderson and Finch Minor are both in there, without their bearskin, but with gastric flu. And there's no one else there! Everyone is talking about it. But the old crone is not likely to understand. It's a bit sad—no one helps her in dispensary.

Nicky is quite a gossip himself. He can be very funny. He seems to be far more in the thick of things than I am. Perhaps it's being a prefect. Perhaps it's just me. He's in a much bigger form, of course. All kinds of things seem to get said and done in the middle part of the school that we've lost. All kinds of people seem to confide in him. Too many. It makes me nervous. I've no one but him. In the world.

I suppose the best piece of news I'm ever likely to hear in my whole life!

187

Nicky is coming to Oxford, too.

He's aiming for some kind of grant or other.

This settles everything. I'm going to have the luckiest life anyone ever had.

CHAPTER EIGHTEEN

Outside the Music Building a visiting cricket team in red blazers was climbing up into a coach and preparing to depart. The home side stood about, in blue, vaguely and embarrassedly saying good-bye. The Cod and a visiting master were doing it with more address and more talk. Curious that hellos, good-byes, thank yous, and handshakes were "adult." Did the young dislike them for their falsity, or was it that egoism as yet unassailed ruled out such tributes to strangers? Or just shyness? (Always a dull solution.)

Carleton, in the blue group, looked over his shoulder and at once looked away.

Why had he been so cruel?

My God, surely not envy?

No, it was a recognition of folly and a knowledge that for Carleton's sake it should be stopped. Extremely ill expressed. True. He must try to make amends.

The other creature was there, too, fooling about on the outskirts. A dark little self-satisfied piece of apparently angelic nogood. Dangerous.

He was conscious of subjecting the handmade shoes to the ill-laid concrete, which had ripples in it all the way. It was another perfect and interminable summer evening. Still and hazy—the aftermath of heat. His forehead and nose felt sore. The oaks at either side of the drive threw no shadows. It was dry and dusty; the farmers had dumped hay in the almost brown field for the cattle. A church bell was ringing far away. Soon their tinnier bell would be ringing for tea. They would drink it in absurd quantity and gobble mountains of bread in the dark noisy refuge of the dining hall, while outside this long summer ache went on.

I am becoming a self-pitying bore. And why the devil am I walking into this challenge after all? Because at least it is a challenge, and rage and rejection seem tempting negatives as things are now.

"Taking the air, sir?"

Old Gregory, in a filthy shirt, was doing something to his three rose bushes in front of the Gate Lodge.

"Good evening. Yes, indeed."

A fatuous question. There wasn't any air.

A black Rover swooshed past (though in fact Ashley didn't know the makes of cars), bearing homeward a tired, sunburnt family. The road was warm and sticky, and the tires made a peculiar sound.

The monastery infected even him, to the extent that always on stepping forth, he felt for a time a deep antipathy to this other existence. Freed from thought. Running on petrol. Nowhere. No more Latin, no more French. . . . The enemy. Escaped. Smug about it. Crass, vulgar, and inane.

Especially in Buckinghamshire.

Ashley walked along the very dusty path, detesting Bucks.

A particular hell in summer.

The Thames Valley. The river—polluted by humanity.

And *they* were set, absurdly, on a hill in the middle of it. In a county of assistant film producers. At Sunday lunchtime in the Crown and Anchor, toward which he was now heading, there was the babel of prosperous cretins, amid horse brasses and mock parchment lamps. And in the public bar, building laborers—experts in mock Tudor—looking by comparison like dockers from Port Said.

While on a hill—down the road—in a stale stench of ink and exercise books, one stood behind a filthy desk, at the same wage as the clapper-boy in their studios. And spoke of Racine.

Which was the more real?

It was a short walk, and he found he could still plump for Caesar, algebra, and Magna Carta.

Perhaps they did rise, just a little, above the avarice and envy down here, after all.

There was no one in the wide street that was Marston—only the passers-through in cars. Old red brick pretty houses faced one another across this main road. They had not built a bypass yet. When they did, there would be no sense of loss. The place seemed to have cut itself off already; the houses seemed uninhabited. True, there was a new little shop selling pottery and brassware, but Ashley had never seen anyone in it. Marston was a long way from the river. There was no water to pollute.

But there were large and shiny cars outside the Crown and Anchor, and there were more parked in the lovely old courtyard at the back. It was approached under an archway, which had signs to left and right—SALOON BAR and PUBLIC BAR. Ashley went into the saloon. It was confusingly dark, having mullioned windows on the street and with walls of almost black paneling. The portentous publican, with the R.A.F. tie, or else his wife, in the black frock and pearls, had found it necessary to switch on the small parchment lamp on the counter. Quite a group of friends, neighbors, fellow customers, or whatever they considered themselves had assembled. Their talk was loud but not all-absorbing; not one of them, male or female, missed Ashley's entrance.

She was sitting at a small table in the corner, in a light brown tweed dress, simple and presumably expensive. A glass of Campari, like blood, was on the table, and the butts of several tipped cigarettes were in an ashtray. His first reaction contradicted all he had formulated on the walk down. Here was company. Here was company at last, after the solitude of the monastery. The prepared hostility had gone. He looked down at her rather as he did at the boys, teasing, with a kind of affection. He understood how much nerve this had taken. He also knew why it was company; every word spoken on the hill had its connotation in respect to school. But their words would be free. The word "alone" is certain good. (She thought Yeats "a phony" —and another bad influence.) No, on second thoughts it was also company for the reason that they had found they could talk together.

"You know this is mad. And pointless," he said.

190

"Well!" she said, with some humor, and patting her brown hair, which was cut rather short and newly done. "Let's not come to any hasty decisions. What are you drinking? I'm sure you don't these days, but let's say it's Christmas or something."

That tone won't serve your cause, he thought. Yet at the same time straight talk had always brought them closest.

"A gin and tonic," he said, to a youth in a dirty white coat. "Large."

She lit a cigarette with a lighter. Her hand was shaking slightly. He wanted to help, a little.

"What's all the drama about?"

"I just thought"—she was tapping the cigarette on the ashtray—"things should be made a little clearer."

There is nothing to clear, he thought. How do I say that?

She looks like a young businesswoman. She partly is. But mostly it is courage. She can be hurt, but there is a spirit of recovery that says a day later, "Christ, that hurt," and so off to work. She would not be destroyed. But, of course . . . she was here to save him.

He should not have come.

"Is there anything to clear?"

"What do *you* say?"

She looked at him directly. She had greenish eyes, rather close together, and a slightly tilted nose. He was antagonized. What did the bar think of this girl? Pretty? Not exactly. Good figure. Very good legs. Interesting? Yes. Nice to look at, dressed like this. Would they guess she had until recently let go in the latest dances with a boyfriend called John who was now being evaded as a bore? No. The woman-of-the-world exterior was well done, even antagonizing.

"I've been clear enough, heaven knows," he said.

"Will you tell me something?"

He was almost afraid. Why? Because they were not of the same world. She was alien, pushing in. For God's sake, let her go back to John. He had been flattered, yes—for a day or so.

"Probably not. What is it?"

"Why have we spent hours together, and I thought we were at one, and I thought you said things to me you'd say to no one else, and I don't believe I'm a complete bloody fool?"

"Slightly similar minds, and neuroses, and humor. Both seekers maybe. Also, too much drink."

"Thank you."

"Oh, come on, Joan. It's not worth being intense. We're not important. Are we having dinner? What's it like here?"

"Ghastly."

Ashley looked at the half-dozen large men in check coats at the bar and their painted ladies on stools. It was the world outside, and yet even they must at one time have been to schools. Life was incredibly long, if one was prepared to pursue it.

"I think we are *all* important. And I'm afraid I don't believe you."

"What?"

"It's possible I'm extremely stupid, and I'm making a mistake which will be with me forever, but I feel there's more between us."

"If there was, I would know."

He thought this might be the end of the evening, but she said, "Not necessarily," and, "I'll have another of these," drinking down the Campari.

"How's school? You look tired, if you don't mind my saying so."

"Well, it's supposed to be ruining me, isn't it?"

"I think so."

Another drink was ordered, and for himself also. He considered it unwise, but he could see no other way of enduring the evening. She lit another cigarette, with a calm hand. He had once smoked a pipe at Cambridge, but nothing now. It gave him no sense of advantage. It gave her a sophisticated air of meaning business.

Yet she is vulnerable, and she is in a very awkward spot, and she believes me vital to her existence—yes, that has become plain enough—and she doesn't know that she will survive without a scar. Or rather, with a scar that she treasures.

"Why don't you go into publishing?"

He very nearly laughed.

"You smile?"

"It was unexpected."

The drinks seemed astonishingly expensive. But his life was sheltered.

"Listen, *Eric*—"

They had always been very bad indeed at Christian names. She could only use his with an emphasis—a pleading note, a sentimentality. It was unpleasant.

"—you must get another job."

"Why?"

"Because this will destroy you."

Across her shoulder a figure had appeared in profile at the end of the bar, wearing a leather-patched coat. Ashley was astounded. It was Milner. He was talking with the blond assistant behind the counter.

"What's wrong?"

"Nothing. I don't really like it here."

"Oh, for God's sake, who does? . . . Your mother agrees."

"Oh, no."

"Eric, if you don't listen to people who . . . care, who are you going to—"

"I don't require anyone's advice."

She is addicted to mistakes. She is a mistake maker. There was some undergraduate called Tom who seemed so nice and turned out a cad and left her with an abortion. It made her no older or wiser. She is twenty-seven and a bit afraid of it and the future, and still an emotional child, an innocent. She waits to be surprised. She refuses to know or grow, because then there would be no surprise or mistake, no sudden blow in the face to carry back to the flat and grieve over.

But she thinks she is waiting for me, oh, God. And may well spend a life on it.

"Let's talk about Spinoza or something," she said.

Loss of temper will end this. She knows that. She is now controlling herself, and except when the shouting starts, she is admirably good at it. The curious part is that she does talk about Spinoza, like a college girl. She was at some strange college where there was a handsome man with silver hair who was a father to her. She uses his Christian name with ease and freedom. She did a thesis on Spinoza. And another one on Eliot.

She also makes fun of herself on both counts: "As I remarked about Eliot. . . ."

Intellectually uncertain, she admires and is a little afraid of me. In that sphere.

I am being absolutely detached and therefore a swine. And will always be with this other person. Can she not see that?

"I'd prefer it," he said. "I hate . . . pairs of people who talk intensely and desperately in corners of bars."

Had Milner seen? He was cunning. His hand was now out, and the barmaid was telling him his fortune. Well, he too had seen, and it was almost incredible.

"Come upstairs a minute," she said abruptly. "I have a letter I want to give you."

"What?"

"It's all right; it's all right. I won't assault you. My God, never again, thank you very much! This is important. Then we can have dinner. I share your views on bars."

"What is it? What letter?"

"I'll show you."

She stood up and, taking her glass, led the way across the bar, passing perilously close to Milner. A brute with a gingery moustache scrutinized her—and particularly her legs. Milner did not turn his head, but he must obviously have seen them. She passed through the miniature foyer—a chintz sofa and sporting magazines and a huge fireplace bedecked with horse-brasses—and so up the stairs.

Talking about letters, he was thinking, do you remember that you wrote me this insulting, superficial drivel about joss-sticks? This college girl's Freud? Am I not being overkind in pretending that it did not happen?

They went up on a hideous crimson floral carpet. There were pink gladioli on the landing in a highly polished brass pot. Nothing seemed real, Ashley thought, including this encounter.

When they were in her room, she closed the door. She also dexterously locked it and kept the key, without his seeing. This move was assisted by a pink dressing gown hanging on the back of the door, very feminine, very unlike her, or rather, like a part of her that he did not care to know about. A smell of perfume. A pair of stockings hanging on the back of the chair. A woman's bedroom. It was all rather shocking. There were other feminine adornments on the dressing table, and a letter which she handed him. It was from her employer, the managing director of a publishing house.

194

DEAR MR. ASHLEY,

I learn from Miss Taylor that she will be seeing you at the weekend and also that you are contemplating other employment more suited to your talents. I happen to know about these: not merely your reputation at Cambridge, but also your critical writing in *New Arts Review*. It so happens that we are looking out for someone at this moment who would join our editorial side, with the prospect of becoming editorial director when the present holder of that position retires, as he shortly intends to do. If you are ever in London, it would be very agreeable to meet you and talk further about this.

Yours sincerely,

J. DENHAM WALKER

Ashley crumpled it up and flung it to the ground.

"How dare you!" he said. "How bloody well dare you!"

It was like hatred. She flinched and backed against the dressing table in surprise.

"How dare you interfere with my life in this vile, lying manner!"

"Don't," she said. "Don't."

She was blushing, and to his amazement he saw tears in her eyes.

"It sounded such a marvelous chance. I thought I was helping."

"Oh, God. Never mind."

"I'm sorry."

Her hands were on his shoulders, and her cheek was against his. She had moved very swiftly, but all the same he cursed himself for not being more agile.

"Stay with me, Eric," she said into his ear. "Stay with me."

"How do you mean?" he inquired. His arms were around her; there was nowhere else to put them. For answer, she kissed him desperately, silencing any possible protest, particularly as she was busy with her tongue. He tried, as there was no alternative. But it was of no interest at all. They were standing close to the bed, and she caught him off balance, so that they were sitting on the side of the bed, and she was running her hands through his hair and kissing him. He tried again. If she was going to work as hard as this, maybe she was right. It was again

195

useless, but it was evidently enough to convince her: she even uttered a few seemingly spontaneous moans.

"Wait a minute," she whispered and broke free and stood up. She whisked the chintz curtain across the tiny window, making the room almost dark, and went into her bathroom. His blood ran cold.

He shouted, "That's enough. Good-bye!" and hurried over and put his hand under the dressing gown and found the doorknob. The door refused to move. "What the blazes!" he said.

He struck the bathroom door and said, "Where's that key?"

"Never mind!" came from behind the door.

"Tell me where that key is," he threatened.

"I can't remember," was the reply.

"Give me that key!" he shouted.

"Not yet," she replied.

"This is a preposterous farce."

"No, it isn't," she said, emerging. She was wearing nothing whatever. He averted his eyes from the two vast white alien presences on her chest. They had no connection with any Joan Taylor that he had ever known. For a moment they had a life of their own, with huge nipples, but they were part of her, all right, for she had turned into Mother Earth. She had taken off his tie before he even noticed. "It's all so simple," she murmured, in a special voice, and his coat was on the floor. Another useless kiss, and she had taken him by the hand and led him to the bed. He was in two minds. He actually assisted the final removals. An appalled glance had taken in what seemed like a huge white stomach, and hairs, on a lady, but otherwise he kept his eyes away. So did she. He lay on top of her, because that was what they said. She made all possible motions under him and finally an assault on his backside which struck him as a damnable insult. He was cold as any stone.

He sat up and ran his fingers through his hair and said, "Where's that bloody key?"

He was not looking at her. There was no reply.

Then she jumped up, crossed the room, and put on the dressing gown, pulling the belt round her.

He was reassembling his clothing.

"At your feet. Under the bed."

He picked it up. She sat on the only chair and crossed her legs and lit a cigarette. She was staring at him with a maddening, worried frown—"brows knit." He was putting on his tie.

"Eric, have you never—"

"No!"

"*Never?*"

"No."

He felt curiously at ease. It was almost a relief to have been stripped, even to no purpose. It was almost a relief to have been able to say it. Not that it had even seemed an admission . . . an inadequacy, a need. Not at all. It was merely him. After all, he had loved. But it lasted for several minutes only, because she said, "My dear, I think you ought to see a doctor. I can give you the name—"

"Blast you," he said quietly.

"But, Eric, you *must*—"

"The comedy is over," he said. "Good-bye."

"Eric, wait! Don't go."

He inserted the key and opened the door.

"All right," she said, approaching. "But at least . . . listen, there's a little book I'd like to send you."

"WHAT?"

She blinked and stepped back and tripped on the end of her gown, throwing out a hand against the dressing table.

He departed and slammed the door.

There was a crash of something being thrown within. He was hurrying down the stairs and nearly at the bottom when he heard the door above opening, and her voice, almost unrecognizable, rending the Crown and Anchor, "God blast you to *hell!*"

Alarmed eyes gazed on him through the open door of the saloon bar. One pair belonged to Milner.

Then he was out in the street.

It had been a considerable sound, but he could not contemplate her pain at all. What had happened down here had not been real. A relaxing, or at least releasing, companion of the mind, she had for the second time made a conscious and therefore preposterous attempt at therapy of another kind. One of her mistakes. Not his failure.

Yet the emptiness was back—and the accompanying panic. An absolute hollowness, joined with alarm. He scarcely realized where he was going.

He was returning up the hill.

CHAPTER NINETEEN

Such happiness.

The weather continues without a cloud. It seems to be helping to make a kind of magic out of my last term. Never will I forget it!

There's an awful crowd always in the pool—which is too small and has slimy green stuff around the sides. I'm glad I'm not mad on swimming, as Nicky goes there a lot and I wouldn't dare go in at the same time. He has dark red togs. I hate Sinnott and Co. watching him dive, but I can't say anything.

There's an organized group now who seem to get a great kick out of jumping out and stoning the hooligans who come over the wall for a free swim. The lower orders don't seem to be very bright! They can't work out when we're in class and when we're not. I wouldn't have anything to do with it myself. But they're a filthy lot, and they've certainly no right to come over our wall.

Sometimes Nicky puzzles me, and frightens me. From the start he has at times—after we've been quiet for a while—come out with what I call his gloomy talk. At first I thought he was just flirting—and he does that too, and I love it. But he's not. He means it.

"It's funny. With us it's different from everyone else."

"How do you mean?"

"It's nearly always the older one who loves more. But with us it isn't so. It's *me* who loves *you* more."

"That's not true, darling, and you know it."

"Yes, it is."

"Why do you say that? I love you more."

"No. I have. From the start."

"Well, maybe at the start. But that changed very quickly."

"No, not really. You don't understand how it is with me. You're everything. Everything."

"But that's exactly the same with me."

"No. Not really."

He was so absolutely certain. That's what I couldn't understand. Why? Why? He nearly made me doubt myself. I tried to imagine something totally more—overwhelmingly—that he claimed. But it was merely what I felt already.

Then he'd go on—"You'll get tired of me."

"Never, never, never."

"Oh yes. You will. Even before the term is over."

"That's just ridiculous. I wish you wouldn't say it. It's just potty."

"It can't be helped. You will. It's the way it happens. It can't last. I know."

(Another souvenir of Eton?!)

"Yes, it can, and it will, always. Unless *you* change."

"You'll get bored with me. You're bound to. It's bound to end."

"It's not, it's not!"

But he had shaken me again. I couldn't understand such certainty . . . such kind of grown-up knowledge, and such grown-up, smiling acceptance of something which, if it was true, *I* couldn't bear.

And then he'd say, "Anyhow, you're leaving."

"Oh, that makes no difference. We'll always be together. We'll be together all the holiday. I want to go sailing. Wouldn't that be marvelous? And then I'll write. And then you'll be coming to Oxford. . . ."

"No. You'll forget. You won't want to once you've gone. I know. It'll be over. It's all right. I'll be O.K. You'll be in another world. You'll write and tell me."

"It's not! It's all nonsense! We can *never* be apart, you and I. How could we be?"

"You'll see how."

"Oh don't. Please don't."

And my mind was churning over. *Can* we, in fact, sail? Will people see he's younger? Will my mother and father see?

Oh for heaven's sake, only two years! And he's such company, and fun, and everyone likes him, and so good to look at. And they'll jolly well have to accept it, because I'm going to be much braver and more definite about such things, as an ex-public schoolboy. Gosh, I'll be a young man. Introducing fellow grown-ups to a marvelous friend.

Johns, now, is leaving too. Imagine sailing with Johns!

We've had two home matches now, and lost them both. I made 16 and a duck. Unless I smarten up my father is not going to be as proud of me as he was when I was home. Nicky made 32 and 48. There are so many of us leaving, he may easily be captain next year. I don't know why, but I'm a bit afraid to think of him being older, and in authority. Just imagine—if he agrees in the end to be senior prefect!

We passed in the Quad yesterday, and to my horror Nicky stopped and talked to me!

I thought he'd gone nuts!

"You may have to beat me," he said, and my heart seemed to drop out of my chest. "Sherriff caught me smoking with Metcalfe and McIver. He's told Roly."

"Oh Lord."

He ran away.

I was trembling. I couldn't. It was unthinkable. What was I going to do?

Sherriff (for whom McIver had taken a photo) was within his rights. They were all in this house—Priestley. The only prefect who could punish boys in other houses was Steele.

Roly would ask me to do it.

What could I say? What could I say?

He sent for me after tea. I was in a state.

He said: "Those idiots Allen, Metcalfe and McIver have been smoking. Give our two M's four on the backside, would you?"

"Yes, sir. Uh. . . ."

"I'll deal with Allen."

"Oh."

Did he sense my relief? Was he looking at me in a funny way? Did he remember what Ashley said? Yes, I think so.

"He's new. I'm not having him start like this. I'll have something to say to him."

"Yes, sir."

Gosh I nearly said, "Thanks awfully, sir." I'm sure he knew. It was jolly kind, if so.

Metcalfe and McIver were both smirking. I tried to make it hard, but I know it wasn't. One of Metcalfe's strokes was nearly a clean miss. I don't mind him so much, because he doesn't give a damn. But McIver's quite bright, with his cameras and all that, and I felt silly and embarrassed. It was like beating almost an equal. Also, when I told him to bend over the table he stopped smirking, and looked scared.

The funny thing is I hit him harder and more accurately than Metcalfe. It seems a peculiar thing to say, but I think it's because I wanted him to respect me.

Even so, I find it hard to imagine Nicky going off with either of them. What does he say? What is this life he has that I can never know?

Never mind. One thing I *do* know. It was nothing like smoking with me!

I've had two more "exeats." It's funny, once upon a time—and not so long ago—home used to be the real place and this was just somewhere I had to be. Now it's exactly the other way around.

Weatherhill Day is coming close. It begins with the confirmation service. Several times I've met Nicky after he's been with Cyril Starr for private instruction. He never says anything about it, and always seems a bit more subdued and thoughtful. I've never dared question him. But yesterday afternoon my curiosity became so great I couldn't resist it.

We were in a perfect little nook we've found in a clump of blazing yellow gorse away at the top of the hill. You can see anybody coming from miles away.

I said, "What exactly does Cyril Starr talk to you about in these sessions?"

Nicky was so quiet and pensive I thought he wasn't going to

201

answer. But at last he said—and he seemed to be perfectly serious, "Well, just now he talked mostly about temptation."

"Indeed!"

I was already feeling frightfully sarcastic. I couldn't understand why Nicky was sounding so solemn. "And what, pray, did our chaplain have to say about that?"

"He said if I was tempted to sin I was to get up at once and move around."

"This was your confirmation class?"

"Yes. He said it was only boredom. Sitting in the one place. He said if you get up and move around, temptation goes away."

"Crikey! I take it he was seated in his usual chair?"

"What? Yes. Of course."

"Did he get up and move around?"

"Don't joke. It's . . . serious."

"What?!"

All this time he had been talking with his brown back to me. We had taken off our shirts. He was propped up on an elbow, and playing with some gorse blossom. Weatherhill lay below us, beyond the swimming pool, directly in our line of vision: all there, in one neat clump, from the chapel to the Pedant's Palace; and looking extraordinarily small, this place where no less than two hundred of us were leading our young lives.

Anyhow, the point is, I couldn't see his face; I could only hear his tone of voice—sounding so strangely solemn.

"I think I'm going to confess," he said.

"I beg your pardon?"

"He says it's best. One should be in a state of grace."

"Confess to Cyril Starr? You're codding me."

"No. I'm not. I'm very serious."

"Confess what, might I ask?"

Nicky pulled the petals off the gorse blossom.

"About us."

I felt as if I'd been hit over the head with a mallet.

"But there isn't anything to confess!" I shouted—and for an awful moment I thought, I admit it, No, there isn't, and maybe we've made a big mistake, maybe we've been wasting our time, maybe we should have given that old fool something to make him sit up and walk around the room.

"I know," Nicky said. "But I think I should mention it all the same. I don't know what the Church would say."

"The Church? Have you gone cuckoo?"

"You don't understand," he said. "I believe in it. Very much. I'm going to be a clergyman."

Well, I was really flabbergasted! "How *can* you have decided such a thing at your age?" I said.

"I decided it when my father and brother were killed. I decided it at the burial service."

I couldn't think what to say. It was beyond me. The whole glorious afternoon seemed to have gone sad and gray.

"Well, I'm sorry. I don't understand. I was only baptized at your age—and for all the wrong reasons."

He sounded very surprised, turning his head to look at me— "But you're a chapel prefect."

"I know. . . ."

"I always thought that was . . . fine."

"Gosh, you don't mean . . . that has anything to do with us?"

"No, but . . . it was partly why I . . . first noticed you."

"Before that match? Even before that match?"

"Long before."

All at once, we were both smiling. It was nice news—never mind the reason.

"*You* don't have to believe," he said, putting his hand on my bare arm. "It won't come between us. The opposite, in fact. It's why I'm going to Oxford. I want to go to Keble College."

This, as I've said already, was the best news of all.

I decided never to mention the subject again.

"I have a confession," I said. "I more or less flirted with Hamilton Minor in the pavilion today, when we were putting on our pads for Nets."

"So what?" Nicky said, smiling at me.

"Well. . . ." I said, a bit taken aback, "I thought you should know. It's just that since loving you I feel a bit in love with everyone. But it meant nothing."

"I don't mind. You can do whatever you like."

"Aren't you jealous?" (I suppose this is what I hoped for—though I *did* feel guilty).

"Don't be silly."

What the devil?!

I don't think I'll ever understand him.

But I know, somehow, he's *better* than me.

I wonder did that awful accident give Nicky some kind of wisdom, make him philosophical, even religious, so that he can't be jealous or anything. Can it have made him good, and ready to endure anything bravely? He seems somehow different from all the rest of us.

I thought this writing would . . . not improve on things, for that's impossible, but sort them out, make them clear, and make them alive for me forever. Most of all, I wanted to make a picture of him . . . and us.

But now, when I read my own words they don't describe him or us at all.

Words are no use. Words don't describe anything. *They only make something new.*

And less. Yes, I know writing is supposed to make something more. But this is much less than the actual thing . . . much.

Perhaps it's because I'm not going to be a writer.

Perhaps I'll give it up.

But not till I *make* Eric Ashley tell me what he thinks about that story of mine!

CHAPTER TWENTY

"I know we polished off Phèdre," said Johns. "But I've been thinking. I still don't know why you say she accepted. It seems to me she never stopped complaining for a minute."

"I beg your pardon?"

Ashley was looking very peculiar, Carleton thought. The afternoon was gray and heavy. Johns was pretty insensitive. Or was he deliberately provoking trouble?

"Phèdre. I think she was half enjoying not being able to do anything about it."

"It is a possibility that has escaped Sainte-Beuve."

"Maybe so."

Ashley was gazing down at Johns with his expression of fierce contempt. How real? How much assumed? He was snarling, "Montesquieu . . . Voltaire. . . ."

"Maybe so." Johns was meeting his gaze. But he was blushing a little.

"Boileau . . . Fenelon . . . not to mention Euripides and the greatest intelligences of the most supreme civilization the world has ever KNOWN!"

"Ssh," said Petty.

"Maybe they missed something," said Johns.

Ashley's face was dreadfully white. His cheekbones were grinding away.

"Maybe we know more about these things nowadays."

"Yes," Ashley jeered. "Beautiful lofty things."

"If that's your Yeats, there aren't any beautiful lofty things anymore."

"How cheerful you sound about this good news."

Extraordinary, but Carleton had been feeling almost jealous . . . of Johns!

"Didn't Yeats say so himself?" he chipped in.

"And what rough beast its hour come around at last, slouches to Bethlehem to be born?" said Ashley, with venom, and transfering his gaze to Carleton.

"Exactly," Carleton said. But he wasn't sure whether Ashley had meant agreement. Much in Ashley's classes was incomprehensible. They were never sure whether he was many steps ahead of them on the same path, or whether he was merely being cussed and confusing. Just lately, it haad become more confusing than ever.

"As a matter of fact," said Johns, not to be outdone, "Phèdre reminds me a bit of Yeats, the way he went on about Maud Gonne."

"Be careful," Ashley said quietly.

"They half enjoy their frustrations. It makes them very chatty."

"Look at Dante and Beatrice," said Petty in a voice more piping than he had intended, so that all ten of them burst out into giggles.

"What precisely do you mean by 'Look at . . .'" began Ashley, who was very nearly smiling.

"Except that this is all so French," said Carelton.

"So 'French'?"

"Yes. Grim and tough and hopeless."

"That's 'French,' is it?" said Ashley. "That's 'French'?"

"Yes," said Carleton. "They all seem to accept being kind of trapped, and don't really try and get out of it."

"Had you been present you could have offered them some simple solution?"

"No, I suppose there isn't any. It's like that thing I saw in Oxford. Sartre. Three people stuck in a room."

"That was Hell," said Ashley.

"Maybe this is, too," said Carleton. He didn't really know what it meant—if anything—but Ashley looked almost interested, instead of angry. "Anyhow, they're both French," he added, to keep things simple.

"Write me an essay on that," said Ashley.

"What!! Oh, listen here—"

"Write me an essay. It might just be interesting."

"That's not fair! Merely because I said something, I'm made to . . . I'm penalized. What about everyone else?"

"The essay is not generally regarded as punitive, you idle fool. Write it! Do as I say!"

"There's not much point in his doing so," Johns interposed. "You never correct them anyhow. You have a pile of them up there!"

"You insolent wench."

"That's true," Carleton shouted out excitedly, "That's true. And what about my story?"

"Of what do you speak?"

"I gave it to you ages ago. Do you even know where it is?"

"No."

"This is costing our parents money," said Johns.

There was a long silence—with a few suppressed giggles. They would normally have expected a smile here, at their common predicament. But he was not cooperating. At length he said: "The virtues of youth are much exaggerated. You are vain, ruthless, shallow, ignorant of the precipice upon which you stand, and unacquainted with grief."

Carleton thought, Except for Nicky, and the bell went.

"Aren't you flying today?" Johns inquired.

"You will all retire, except Carleton," said Ashley.

"Me?"

"Retire! Leave my sight! Go and play ball or whatever it is you do."

There were cheers and a few desk lids were banged; and they were gone.

They stood in silence. Ashley made his face. Contemptuous? Mocking? Merely a way of covering shyness? Carleton could not tell.

"You are persevering in this romance?"

Carleton was astonished.

"How do you mean?"

"Have no fear. I am sealing my lips. I suggest, very seriously, for your own future, that you stop it."

"Why should I?" Carelton said. "Anyhow, I couldn't."

"You are 'kind of trapped,' " said Ashley, with a nasty smile, "and you're not really trying to get out of it."

"If you like. Though I don't see it that way."

"Our friend Johns would have it that you're half enjoying not being able to do anything about it."

"I'm entirely enjoying it."

"In that case, God help you. We'd better have a look at your story."

"What? Why? I don't see any connection."

"Maybe you will later," said Ashley. "If it has no merit, five minutes will do. If it has—can you give me two hours?"

"What!! Two hours? For heaven's sake, it's only ten pages."

"Really? Two and a half hours then. Tomorrow afternoon?"

"Um . . . there's no cricket . . ."

"You had other plans?"

Carleton was blushing deeply.

207

"Cancel them. Unless, of course, it has no merit. In which case I don't envy you. Art as solitude must be your expectation, my boy. The best way back to isolation. Art before life."

"Serenity after . . . ?" Carleton began, but it sounded silly, and he was not sure if it was the same thing.

"Begone," Ashley said, though he had wondered what was coming.

Ashley stood there alone, playing with the detestable chalk. I suppose it's possible to look like a Michelangelo and still be able to write, he thought.

She had not even asked him about his own creative venture in the reading room. She had not even remembered.

Yes, it was harsh to have left her for the night in that ghastly place. But she had asked for it. A pathetic clown she had made of him. A naked child.

It was over, such as it was.

And now?

Strange, he found that he missed Jimmy Rich. An element of sanity. It seemed years since they left. The only two normal people had been briskly dispensed with.

Dotterel and De Vere Clinton. How did they maintain their ineffable good cheer? Strange paradox: it seemed that there was no emptiness if one was superficial enough.

Ashley went out into the corridor and upstairs. He was feeling genuinely curious about that story. Well, after all, work was the popular prescription; and though this was not art it was at least work.

CHAPTER TWENTY-ONE

 It was called "Carter and McCracken."

On the following afternoon, Ashley held it in his hand as he stood against the window, and flicked over the pages.

Carleton sat on a chair, feeling apprehensive, and tried to decipher Ashley's expression, but he was only a silhouette against the sunny window. Not a word had been spoken. He had pressed for this, but now it was terribly embarrassing to be there while somebody else looked at something so personal.

For it was about himself as a small boy. And a true experience. It was about loss of innocence, and the destruction of illusion by reality. A small and evidently solitary child was indoors on a summer day, playing his own invented game of throwing dice and racing motor cars across the carpet. The villain, who was always named Carter, competed ruthlessly against the hero—on this occasion named Bill McCracken. Creatures of the innocent imagination, they were doomed to be crushed underfoot.

"I must confess," Ashley said, his face dark against the light, "I went to the trouble of looking up your Chekhov about the little dogs barking as well. Perhaps I had some notion of applying it to myself—a delusion, if so. Never mind. It continues very relevantly. They must bark as well, 'and bark with the voice God gave them.' The surprising fact is that you do this."

"How do you mean?" Carleton asked. "What other voice could one bark with?"

"Many, I assure you. You seem to have underestimated your hero. But the unexpected feature is that underneath this rubbish you have a voice. That is the thing I couldn't have given you. The rest is easy."

"How do you mean? . . . Do you mean . . . I'm a writer?"

"Yes."

Goose pimples ran up his legs and arms. For some reason tears came into his eyes. Ashley saw in embarrassment and surprise, and was impressed. They both felt he had said something almost holy. Ashley had not foreseen this. He said quickly, "As it stands, the story is indescribably bad."

"But . . . how can it be?" said Carleton. But he knew, or thought he knew, and he was smiling with happiness.

"We shall need all of our time."

"I thought you said the rest was easy."

"Comparatively. Merely hard work and nothing to smile about. All right. Bring that chair over."

They sat elbow to elbow at the desk in the window. Ashley

ran a finger through his hair and scrutinized the careful handwriting.

"Now, the cardinal point is that any final alterations made in this must be yours. It belongs to you and it's your voice. I can only suggest. I like the title. Now, let's see. . . ."

Carleton felt marvelous. He felt they were seated there together, doing something really important: an entire new opera, a joint production, for the Metropolitan, New York; a major play, in collaboration, for the West End. Artists. Dedicated together to the one true faith. Nothing to do with school. A new and adult life. Ashley was reading to himself very quickly:

" 'Owen was lying on the carpet in the warm sunlight, playing a game he had invented for himself. He used to cut out car advertisements from *The Motor* magazine, paste them onto cardboard, and stick a little stand at the back. Then he threw the dice and raced them by moving them so many lengths on. Of course, the cars were never exactly the same length, so he had to make allowances for the shorter ones, to make it fair. . . .' "

"Mm," said Ashley, "This is curiously fresh—against the odds. It's helped, of course, by being a rather original image. But it could be fresher. It could be much more immediate. The odds you've set against yourself are that it's all statement. You've opened a short story with an explanation. You've asked the reader to endure with you awhile at the very outset. You've added insult to injury by assuming that he will not be able to grasp this game—I wonder is 'game' quite right—on his own. Do you see?"

"I think so."

"Let's try it, shall we, with Owen in action, doing it. No explanation. No apology. Put the reader on the floor beside him. Would you like to . . . here, use this pen."

"Um. I'm not sure what . . ."

"All right, I'll jot something down and we'll see what we think of it."

" 'Owen' . . . first word, yes, good . . . 'was lying' . . . 'lay,' I think, more immediate. . . . How? Let's make it precise. Let's show our certainty of vision, our authority, and put the reader in our pocket at once. 'A small boy. Lay on his stomach,' perhaps. On the carpet, you say. Yes. But if we're going to specify the carpet, let's give it a reason to be there—let's make it do some work for us. More certainty of vision. Let's give it a color. What would you like?" Ashley smiled. "What was it?"

(Gosh, he knows it's true. How?)

"Green."

" 'On the green carpet. In the warm sunlight.' It's clumsy. Never mind, we'll come back to it. 'Warm.' Did you need that?"

"Uh . . . well, there could be cold sunlight."

"Good. All right. Now, I'd like him in action at once. And I think one could convey that this has been going on for some time. Repetition, or boredom, is part of your plot. Let's insinuate it at once, without the reader even knowing he's been hooked. How about this? 'He cast the dice again.' All right for the present?"

"Uh . . . yes. . . ."

"Now what happened then? Let's not explain. Merely the sight, the action. You have them down here. . . . I don't know what they call these things . . . a Bentley. Yes, you have it here. 'The Bentley, a closed coupé, came again past the sports Alvis.' Excellent. Couldn't be better. We've lost a whole paragraph. Splendid!"

"What?"

" 'Owen lay on his stomach on the green carpet, in the warm sunlight. He cast the dice again. The Bentley, a closed coupé, came again past the sports Alvis.' I still don't like it enough, do you? But at least we've lost a whole paragraph and nevertheless told . . . no, suggested . . . in three short sentences, the age and nature of our hero, his mood of the moment, the state of the weather, the occupation in progress, and possibly even the social status of his home and parents. That's not bad, is it? I still don't like the first sentence, do you? Do you see why?"

"Yes, I think so. The two 'on's,' and the 'in.' "

"What do you suggest?"

"Um . . . 'Owen lay on his stomach in the warm sunlight that spread across the green carpet'?"

"Yes. Wait . . . 'Across' is a little heavy. Distracting. 'Over' is enough. Let's write that out. . . . We're a pair of amateurs without a typewriter. . . ."

My next birthday, Carleton thought. "But I'd no idea you were supposed to go through all this," he said. "Nobody ever told me."

"But it's exciting, isn't it?"

"Yes. Yes."

"Now then. . . . Look what's happened. We've two 'agains.' The sense that this has gone on for some time is good. The second one helps. How can we keep them both? Only by splitting them apart a bit. I know. We haven't said what the dice did. Visual and immediate. Must be a big number but not too big to distract. 'Six and four.' How about that? And he's a small boy and, even though bored, he will still retain some childish enthusiasm, so let's give it an exclamation mark. All right, what have we got—for the moment? Here . . . you write it this time."

Such delicate brown fingers, Ashley thought. " 'Owen lay on his stomach in the warm sunlight that spread over the green carpet. He cast the dice again. Six and four! The Bentley, a closed coupé, came again past the sports Alvis.' "

"Right. We may have to scrub all that, because we don't know what will follow. It may not combine. As a complete paragraph it may not flow. It may even refuse to adapt itself to the *next* paragraph. There may be no personal rhythm. Your voice may be lost."

"But *you* seem to be doing everything."

"No, I'm not. You're there, in the middle of it. This is only method. You'll see. Now then, what have you got next? . . ."

They were rather like lovers.

Lucretia Crabtree, on a half-holiday from Gillingham, had been standing under the sycamore, looking up at the window, and she thought so. She wandered away with a mind to report the fact. She had long ago dismissed her Starling. She was bored, and she was contemplating going back into business; though the two and sixpence had been a lie.

The other wanderer looked down from the war memorial and saw her crossing the Quad toward the Head's House.

Gower liked no one, and no one liked Gower. But he felt a distant affinity with this other creature. They were rivals in boredom. Frequently they passed each other, as they mooned away their days, and shared a look that was apparently icily detached, but was in fact an unwanted but inescapable admission of understanding.

They never spoke. But she was the one person he might very nearly have told. Even Gower occasionally felt this need. To carry on an occupation of infinite skill and subtlety without the plaudits of a single other human being was hard indeed.

He was waiting to see if his housemaster was in his shower. He had given Rowles nearly an hour since afternoon school to get settled in there.

He had even selected the most visible of his ailments—a twisted ankle—to rouse them to activity; and had been limping heavily past his housemaster all day.

Oh yes, Rowles knew, and that cleverboots, Carleton, knew, and the other three beastly prefects, but you could hardly call them appreciators.

With a slight quickening of his very steady heart, Gower dawdled up the five stone steps into the Big Schoolroom. They were worn down at the center by thousands of young feet. He skirted the Ping-Pong table, entered the corridor, and turned right for the washroom.

The slanting eyes were now very useful. He could see into the little mirror on the floor without apparently looking anywhere near it.

Today, it did *not* reflect Dr. Rowles.

Gower felt damply disappointed.

The spice had gone out of the afternoon. The way of business was all too open. There had been three juniors reading books at desks in the dusty darkness of the Big Schoolroom. But they looked settled. Not a soul in his territory. A cold corridor of lockers. He had the notion, for the first time, of going for the highest available prize. Carleton's was Number 5. There might be something transportable. Slouching along, all innocence, he swiftly raised the latch and darted a hand into the pocket of a mackintosh. Nothing. The other pocket. Nothing. Well, a piece of paper. He took it out and closed the locker door, and without expectation unfolded the paper and read: "Every time I see you—you're more wonderful than ever. Love, love, love. . . . N.A."

Baffled for a moment by these alien words, and then excited by various possibilities, and then back in control again as a mastermind, Gower finally smiled. This time it was all taunting. No fear at all. Swiftly, for a creature of sluggish habit, he went up the stone stairs, paused on the landing, glanced into the upper dormitory—empty—and knelt with one slanting eye to the keyhole of Rowles' door. There was no key. (There never was.) Nor was there anyone at home.

"What the devil is eating you today, Milner?" said Rowles as they emerged from the wood. The yellow of the gorse made him blink. Boys in bathing togs lay about on the vivid grass. There was the twang of the diving board and an instant splash, as one curious creature after another leaped into the noisome pool. The sky was deep blue. No breeze. In belated deference to the summer, Rowles sported a fat walking stick and Milner a white hat which he had owned for twenty years.

A paradisical afternoon, but the Pedant was speechless and odd.

"I'd other plans when you came and persuaded me out," Rowles said. "I understood you'd something to impart, but I was evidently mistaken. Furthermore, it may surprise you to hear I have an appointment with the headmaster in half an hour."

He glanced up quickly. The Pedant was frowning

"I haven't told you about our friend Ashley," he said.

After so much solemn silence, there was a skittishness that disturbed the Doctor. There had always been this element in Milner, and it was never quite tolerable. He walked with his leather elbows in, and his hands in the pockets of that sports coat, despite the heat, with the two thumbs showing. A neatness. Little elegant steps with the toes turned in. Something elegantly under control. The faint danger that it might break forth into the dance. Jack Buchanan moving suddenly, carefree, over the grass. That white hat. It didn't accord entirely with what the Doctor would have preferred. The gift for limericks. The gift for gossip—yes. But gossip had a seriousness for the Doctor. It was a study of mankind at its most curious. Next to the chapel, it was the center of Weatherhill life. It was not a dancing matter. The Pedant had, centuries ago, taught in India, and he possessed a permanently crumpled fawn linen summer suit. At any moment it, too, might appear. When it did, the Doctor always found himself immediately removed, a yard or so, from his customary companion. Thick tweed was sanity.

"What? What, Milner?" said the Doctor, already perturbed, and prodding at the grass with his stick.

"A misadventure of a public nature in the Crown and Anchor on Saturday night."

"Where? I don't believe it."

"One presumes . . . how can I phrase it for you . . . a flight . . . an inadequacy in an upper room."

"Look here," said Rowles, seeming pale, though they were both reluctantly pink, "what in arsehole are you talking about?"

"A lady," said the Pedant.

"Oh no," said Rowles.

"I speak euphemistically. She delivered herself of some downstairs . . . or rather upstairs . . . castigations. After our fleeing hero. They were public property."

They walked on. The Doctor was breathing loudly.

"Please, sir. Sorry, sir. Can I come and see you about permission to get a new cricket bat in Marston, or can I ask you now, sir?"

"Get what you want. Keep out of my way. Clear off."

"Oh thanks awfully, sir."

"He's a fool," said Rowles. "As if it were necessary!"

The Pedant glanced uneasily at him.

There was a long silence.

"Is that what you had to say?" Rowles inquired. (They were near the pool.) "Listen here, let's turn back out of this. It goes right through my head. If they want to jump into cold dirty water why can't they do it without screaming like hyenas?"

They began to descend toward the wood.

"You know that De Vere Clinton has rented a Volkswagen autobus today, and taken five artists out sketching in the woods above Little Hammerton?" said Milner.

"I heard he was granted permission. I was surprised, I may say."

"They are thought to have left with a large supply of ginger beer. Clinton, with some ingenuity, made me agent and witness in the matter, as I happen to have a permanent order, being particularly fond of the liquid, as you may know."

"I am aware of that."

"What you are not aware of is that Clinton subsequently and secretly altered the order to an equally large supply of light ale."

Rowles halted, dropped his mouth open a little, without intending it, and said: "Is this true, Milner?"

"Absolutely."

"And why did you not put a stop to it?"

"I only discovered it an hour ago."

They walked on.

The question was long delayed.

"How did you discover it?"

The Pedant cleared his throat.

"You may have detected that both my pieces of news originate in a particular locality."

"The Crown and Anchor."

"This is difficult, Rowles. I wanted you to be the first to know. Now don't fly off the handle, old man. I have proposed marriage . . . and I have been accepted."

"Your mind is going, Milner. It must be."

"Alice is an employee of the hotel in question—a position to which she is infinitely superior. I'm fully aware of the thirty years diff—"

"Come off it, Milner! You can't be serious. You're throwing away a housemastership for this!"

"What the deuce are you talking about, Rowles?"

"You . . . you don't mean that you plan to bring the woman *here?*"

"Oh, don't be impossible!" said Milner, very testily indeed. "Of course I do. I intend to ask the Head for one of the bungalows."

"Then good day to you," said Rowles, and he walked away.

"Rowles!" Milner called after him, in vain.

His great head was swirling. He stumbled once in the long grass, in spite of the stick, and then marched stoutly away, down toward the Chapel Square.

"Do you want to rest for a minute?" said Ashley.

"No, no. It's just . . . it's terribly hot. Can I take off my coat and tie?"

"Certainly. I don't really notice it. My old bones."

Ashley felt a small pang. A regret for his own lost youth, that was all. Yes, that was it. The boy had rolled up each of his white shirt sleeves. Brown forearms with golden hairs. Strong, but young somehow. The creature was fresh as a baby, and at the same time he was almost a young man.

"I presume the mother is . . . entirely fictional?" he said.

"How do you mean?"

"This remote and silly lady who talks about chintzes. It's not possible that . . . ?"

"Oh no, I made her as different as I could."

"I see. It's just that you've otherwise written from knowledge. Which was the right instinct. And the other thing you've done, uninstructed, is to stay with one character—almost. It's as well you've made her like this. Her role is small. We don't need her. No, we don't need her at all."

"What's up?"

"Nothing. Now then . . . where were we? . . . 'He tiptoed to the door and saw that Ellen was sitting on the window-sill, polishing the outside of the window. As often before, he pretended to himself that she was that villain, Carter. She was heavily armed, probably with a six-shooter. She. . . .' Is there anything *you* don't like there?"

"The second sentence."

"I agree," said Ashley. "Why?"

" 'As often before'. . . . It seems to slow things down. And, 'he pretended to himself'. . . . The reader knows already that he does that. And the reader also knows that Carter is a villain."

"Excellent. What do you propose?"

" 'She was Carter.' No, that's *too* blunt. 'Immediately, she was Carter.' "

"Fine."

" 'She was heavily armed. . . .' "

"I wonder . . . sorry . . . dare we risk a repeat of that? Let's see. . . . 'Immediately, she was Carter. She was Carter, and she was heavily armed, probably with a six-shooter.' It adds emphasis, and confirms this sudden decision, don't you think?"

"Yes. I see."

"Let's go on. Notice how you improve as you get into it.

Starts are often self-conscious. I believe your friend Chekhov used to throw them away. 'He ran into the room and screamed "stick 'em up!" at this old woman on a windowsill sixty feet above the ground. She was a marvel. Ellen never let you down . . .' (Good. Exactly what she's going to do). . . . 'She feigned a look of wild terror and exclaimed, "Glory be to God, you're not goin' to kill me, are you?" '

" 'Dismissing the suspicion that Carter would not talk with an Irish accent, he seized a pipe from his father's pipe rack, leveled it at her through the glass and said, "I probably am. You've certainly asked for it." '

" 'She cowered before him.'

" ' "Oh please, sir, please don't kill me." '

" ' "We'll see," he said, walking up and down. She should not have said "sir," but this was an error which he had long ago accepted, eventually coming to believe that Carter was as servile even as this.'

" 'She dipped her rag again into the bucket of water. Ellen always went on with what she was doing. She had to, in the end. They both knew it made no difference. They were still who they were.'

" 'Strands of gray hair had come out of her bun, and she pushed them away from her eyes with the back of her fat hand, which was red and swollen. He wondered why, though she looked horrible and he would have hated her to touch him'
—"Good. She's going to"—'he liked to be near her. He even liked her smell.'

" ' "I'll tell you one thing," he said. "You've asked for it. The sheriff's after you too. I just happened to get here a bit faster. I guess I know the way better." '

" ' "Haven't you a better horse too?" she asked, cajoling.'

" ' "Of course I have," he said, only half deceived. "I've a chestnut colt." '

" ' "Gracious!" she said.'

" ' "I may have to hand you over to Jim Butler." '

" ' "And who might he be?" she asked.'

" ' "He's my buddy," he replied. "He knows all about torturing." '

" 'He knew well that there was no torturing in the Wild

West, but at times one had to make things up for Ellen: otherwise she would be lost—even she.'

"'"Oh please don't do that," she begged. "I'll do anything, anything."'

"'But he was dreadfully bored, and prayed for something new and exciting to happen. . . .'"

"Yes . . ." said Ashley, interrupting his own reading. "One of those prayers which unfortunately get answered. Now then . . . what do you feel about all that?"

"I . . . can't honestly think what to . . ."

"I agree. I like it. A lot. What's wrong?"

"Nothing."

They smiled, and for a moment looked each other directly in the eyes. The boy felt older, and the man younger. It made them close.

"Famous last words," said Ashley. "Here comes your big mistake. 'Ellen watched him through the rainbow circles that her rag. . . .' My dear boy, we can't switch over to Ellen now. We really can't. Agreed?"

"Yes. O.K."

"Now let's see. . . ."

Lucretia, who had returned to the tree, moved away. This time she was confident that a striptease was being enacted.

She crossed the Quad again, but with certainty now. She had been looking for something like this. She had been out in the cold for too long; ever since that silly ass, Lawson, had not only believed about the half crowns, but passed it on. Her father was remote. Her mother was worse. She would recapture them. She would show her willingness to cooperate. She would sink this Mr. Ashley without trace.

Lucretia put her ear to the door of the study, and heard two male voices. She opened the adjacent door and went into the sitting room. Her mother was seated with her stockinged feet up on the large chintz sofa. She was knitting herself a somber jumper in dark gray wool.

Lucretia sulked across the room and leaned her blue-jeaned bottom against the piano. Her mother said, "Well?"

"I wanted to tell you something."

It was a tremendous statement.

The knitting needles were still.

At last her mother accepted. She banished the past. She said, "What is it?"

"Carleton's been up in Mr. Ashley's room since class."

"Mr. Ashley?"

"Yes."

"For two hours?"

"Yes."

"How do you know?"

"I can see them through the window. They're sitting together. Carleton's taken his clothes off."

This went down very well! Her mother flinched. She paled.

"What did you say?"

"Well . . . he's in his shirt."

"I see. . . . Why do you . . . report this?"

"It looks funny. They look peculiar. I can't explain exactly. It's a long time."

"Yes . . . our Mr. Ashley . . . I think your father would be grateful if you went back and observed this curious scene to the end."

"Righto."

Lucretia slouched out. With great difficulty she subdued the desire to bound and leap.

Her mother fought with temptations too: a conflict of emotions.

She had just passed a wearying tea with a Mrs. Benthall, who had gained the impression from her son Harry, on his last exeat, that his extreme sensitivity was making him the victim of others. Harry was a dirty-minded, lying little bully.

But it was in this same room, over tea with her husband, some days ago, that something remarkable had happened. Without preparation, with awareness only after it had occurred, she leaned across the table and placed her hand in his.

They were astounded.

She took her hand away. They said nothing. But the apartness of years had gone in that one moment.

She knew why. She was not one to endure love denied for very long. The chaplain had undoubtedly achieved greatness. But he was dark and forbidding, and his manners were bad. He had set her heart in motion. She had looked about, to give it occupation, and begun to think that her husband was really rather handsome. It was a little late for a second honeymoon, but she could put her mind to his service. She had nothing else to put it to, except extra Latin. She was offering outright support against all opposition.

Mr. Ashley had shown himself to be among the opposition.

In the neighboring room, the Head and Dr. Rowles had been discussing arrangements for Weatherhill Day. The Doctor, pleasantly aware of his superior knowledge, had written out an agenda in his scrupulous hand:

> Confirmation.
> Old Boys' Cricket Match.
> Lunch. The Loyal Toast.
> Headmaster's Speech and Prize-giving
>   (in Big Schoolroom).
> Cricket Match.
> Tea Outdoors.

Rowles had already prevailed upon the bishop, who was confirming, to stay and preside at the prize-giving. His role had been active, as assistant headmaster. The two men were finding each other much improved.

"There is another matter, Dr. Rowles, which I hope we shall settle as agreeably."

The Doctor was seated on his large posterior, leaning well forward in his customary way, with his pipe held between his knees, so that he had to raise his eyes to see his rubicund companion at the desk. The Crab was sporting a linen summer suit rather like Milner's. (Horrific, well-nigh incredible news!)

"What is that, Headmaster?"

"As you know, I had an unnecessarily abrupt letter from Miss Hutchins. She believes our experiment to have been premature. She withdraws. Very well, she may be right. Meanwhile, our problem persists. I intend to solve it. I've come to a decision."

"May one know it?"

"Commencing the morning after W. Day"—Rowles closed his eyes in pain. This had already happened before—"an investigation will be conducted daily. Younger boys will be questioned about older boys, and vice versa. Boys may even be questioned about masters—we shall see. In strict privacy, you understand. There will be no half measures. Finally, we shall conduct a purging of the few baser elements. Few, I believe them to be. They will be expelled. Immediately."

"I fear I may go crackers," said the Doctor softly. "Who conducts this . . . ?"

"Against the advice of my wife, who otherwise fully supports me in this matter, I consulted with the obvious candidate. Our chaplain."

"You did? With the chaplain?"

"Certainly."

The Head pulled down his lips.

"He was not only reluctant. He was insulting. Well . . . he may have his reasons. There is another and more fitting candidate. *Mens sana in corpore sano*. I have asked him, and he has consented. With an enthusiasm even beyond my expectations."

"Who is that?"

"Well, naturally, Dr. Boucher."

Never before had the Doctor seen the hand holding the bowl of his pipe quivering as if from some tropical disease. He tried to bring it to his mouth, but could not do so.

"He tells me that he has known of this evil, and wished for such a remedy, for many years. He will call daily. I am putting my study at his disposal. I take it you approve?"

"I most certainly do not. But let me say one thing. The term is far advanced. There are not many weeks to run. Might I ask for a postponement?"

"I'm afraid not. It is urgent."

"By expulsion I take it, at this late date, you mean that you would merely ask boy or . . . great Scott, Master . . . not to join us next term?"

"You take me wrong, Dr. Rowles. I said 'immediately.' The example is the whole point."

"The case is different from that of Mr. Rich," said Rowles. "One might do great harm."

"It would be deserved," said the Head. "The harm being done to the school is the one that counts."

* * *

"Sit, Nicholas," said the chaplain.

The day was now advanced. The sun had moved away from his green satin curtains; which was as well for "Nicholas," since Philomena had lit a particularly good fire.

"This will be our last time before your great experience."

"Yes," said Allen, who was looking nervous, bashful, and quite charming, though over-clean.

"You have something you wish to tell me?"

"Yes."

"You seek absolution, Nicholas?"

"Well, I'm not sure if it's anything or not."

The boy's beautiful eyes were fixed on the chaplain's buckled shoes, emerging from the black habit. The orange lay on his black skirted lap. Rather regrettably, he was not likely to need it. No odor of pig; and that black head was wavy and alive without a hint of Brylcreem.

"Look at me, child. Don't be afraid. What is it?"

"It's just . . . we're in love. Someone older. Carleton. I don't know if it's wrong or not."

The chaplain fingered his great blue ring. The only surprise was always the other name. One never knew who would drop out of the sky. Carleton! One would never have suspected him of sentiment, or of daring to transgress.

"Does it feel wrong?"

"No."

"Then it almost certainly isn't. Does it feel right?"

"Yes. . . . But other people mightn't think so."

"That's called morality, my dear Nicholas. We needn't trouble about that. I take it you meet?"

"Yes, all the time. And we write notes. There's one waiting for him now."

"Has there been temptation?"

"Yes, but we agreed we'd never . . . I mean . . ."

"And kept to it?"

"Yes."

A strange child. Somehow wise and direct beyond his years. He was going to make an admirable clergyman.

"How much does it mean to you?"

"It means everything."

Oh dear, the chaplain thought. Oh dear, oh dear. "I don't

think there's anything to worry about, Nicholas, though you were right to tell me. Love is no sin. The contrary. Is he not leaving this term?" I, too, the chaplain thought. Let them wait. Let them be surprised.

"Yes. . . . He thinks it'll go on. Just the same."

"He does?"

"Yes."

"And you don't?"

Allen looked at the carpet. "No."

The chaplain turned his head and gazed into the burning fire. Love in the terrestrial sphere was more than mildly alarming. Thank God he had been spared it, man and boy. The headmaster's unspeakable proposition came to mind. How many were to fall? How many would perhaps be hurt for life?

"Tell me, frankly, Nicholas, have others put this temptation your way? For your own sake, tell me. My cloth is the guarantee of secrecy."

"Well, when I first came, Mr. Dotterel and Mr. De Vere Clinton both asked me to tea, with other boys. They said it was for new boys, but Fitzmaurice and I were the only ones there."

"At both receptions?"

"Yes. I didn't like them. I didn't like the jokes."

"You have good taste, Nicholas."

"Ever since, seniors who were there have asked me would I go for walks. I've always said I wouldn't. One of them has taken a down on me. A prefect."

"Who, Nicholas?"

"Well . . . Sherriff. He's had me beaten, and so on. He's got my photo in his wallet. He paid McIver to take it. I didn't even know it was being done."

"McIver?"

"He . . . takes them."

"I see. . . . Dear me. Do you tell Carleton these things?"

"No. They'd only upset him."

It was like resting by some riverbank, the chaplain thought, and some damned naturalist comes along and chatters about reality, mercilessly elucidating the turbulence underground, underwater, in the trees, in the sky, all about.

But then he smiled, and his eyes twinkled wickedly. He had

just thought what an excellent inquisitor he would have made, had the idea not been abhorrent.

"Anything else, Nicholas?"

"Yes. Yes, there is. I was going to say it first, but. . . ."

The chaplain ceased smiling. Pride before a fall, he thought, and he found that the fingers on his right hand were closing gently, in anticipation, around the orange.

"Oh?"

He was back in the confessional. It was truly necessary: the child must achieve grace. What others would be unlikely to understand was that he did not enjoy it. Not at all. He enjoyed peace and mild amusements. He disliked what was known as reality. (Fortunately what others thought had never been of the slightest interest.) There was a dull pain in his stomach, and a sense of nausea. How long, oh Lord, how long? The absolute peace.

"Tell me, Nicholas."

"The other night. We were waiting for the bell for dorm. I was playing Ping-Pong with Caldicott."

"Oh?"

A new name. No. The chaplain remembered. Rather appealing. There were so many in this place—outside of one's circle.

"I don't mean in the schoolroom. In the senior Ping-Pong room, down in the yard."

"I've heard of it."

The senior Ping-Pong room. To what had one devoted twenty-three years? Never mind—it would soon be over. Without regret. Sure? Yes, yes.

"Sinnott and Beauchamp came in. They sat on the bench. They . . . compared us. We went on playing. We couldn't do anything else. We were a bit scared. But they weren't really nasty. They flattered us, really. Everyone was . . . more or less smiling."

"Everyone?" the chaplain's fingers closed around the orange.

"Yes, we played quite well."

The chaplain looked like the Grand Inquisitor, and felt terrible.

"The bell went, and we finished the game—I don't remember who won—and Caldicott just suddenly ran off, and Beauchamp said 'I'm leaving you children' or something, and he went, and I was left standing with Sinnott. There was the light up at the top of the steps. And I said—"

"Yes?"

"I said 'all right.' I don't know why. . . . And he said kind of roughly, 'I'll see you in the dorm,' and just walked off. He has a funny walk. He waddles. And I was scared."

The chaplain sniffed the delicately colored globe.

"I wished to goodness I hadn't . . . I thought he was going to . . . jump into my bed or something awful and crazy."

Told with such address! Or was it just absolute confidence? In a father. A father confessor. The chaplain had never bargained for so much, or been so alarmingly rewarded.

"Before lights out he gave me a funny look, but he didn't say anything. He was in his red dressing gown. I was scared . . ."

Yes, an abominable little blond animal in red.

"Carleton. . . . He put the lights out. Nothing happened. I must have been nearly asleep when. . . ."

The peace that passeth all understanding.

"The foot of my bed is up against his. His hand came in and he took my foot and tugged it down. It was kind of fierce. And he began stroking my leg. And it wasn't fierce at all. It wasn't . . . like Sinnott at all. It was kind of . . . delicate. He stopped and I . . . I stroked his hand with my toes."

If not orders, then certainly the stage. The chaplain inhaled the fruit.

"That was all. In the morning I was in the shower . . . and he must have told some of them. He must have told lies. They were making cracks. They were saying . . . how I'd got bigger, and so on. It was horrible."

"Yes. Yes, indeed."

"I couldn't believe he'd do that. What I think is, somebody must have heard, and he *had* to make up something. So he boasted instead. He told lies."

The child was almost in tears. Belated though it might be.

"Charity may be your saving grace, Nicholas. It suffereth long indeed when it is extended to Master Sinnott."

"Maybe. Because he did it again next night."

The chaplain filled his nostrils.

"I drove my toenails into his hand. Well . . . as best I

could. It wasn't easy. Anyhow, he took it away. He must have been completely surprised. Because he didn't even seem to understand. He and Beauchamp walked past me the next day. They were laughing. Sinnott stopped for a minute and said seriously—and he seemed really puzzled—'What on earth's the matter with *you?*' "

"Is that all?"

"Yes."

" 'Twill suffice," said the chaplain. "Have you told Carleton this?"

"No. I couldn't."

"I think perhaps you should; though that's outside my territory. It's very serious that you said"—the chaplain suffered a spasm—" 'All right.' "

"Yes. He was like the devil tempting me. And as well . . . I just wondered what . . . just for once . . . what it was. It's harder to resist something you don't even know."

The chaplain had always found the opposite to be true. Nevertheless, they were extremes that touched. The child was remarkable.

"I've sinned, haven't I?"

"I think so. Mildly, Nicholas. Have you repented?"

"Yes. . . . It was terrible to Carleton."

"Oh? Is that repentance?"

"Well, I did him a wrong."

"But, my dear, that's not the sin."

"Isn't it?"

The boy looked him in the eyes. He felt himself challenged by an infant. It was astonishing.

"Come now," he said. "You hope to enter the Church, don't you?"

"Yes. But I'm muddled. He seemed . . . I mean even Sinnott . . . he seemed . . . almost loving. I know that afterward . . . I don't know what I mean."

"There, there. Listen to me, Nicholas, it was lust. Before confirmation, you abjure the carnal desires of the flesh. You must assure me that you do this."

"Yes. I do."

"Very well," said the chaplain abruptly. "You'd better run along now. I'll see you in chapel."

Allen stood up. He looked humbled. The chaplain felt uneasy. He almost felt uncertain of his advice; and even more so of his role. Confessor or inquisitor?

"And by the way, I should be very careful. Our headmaster is not happy. Though love is no sin, it banished Mr. Rich and our Matron. You are at the mercy of others—unlike myself."

"Yes, sir. Thank you, sir."

Allen went out.

Sir! How unexpected, how merciless.

The chaplain sat staring into the fire. His mood was very dark. He thought, These are not children. This is not a rough draft for adulthood. Later life is a copy. These are not childish things, and they are not put away.

They had come to the "realities"—two young men, framed by the window for Lucretia's inspection.

" 'Her straying hairs and the smell of her—she was sweating—made a disgust rise up in him, but he could not move away.'

" ' "For twenty years," she whispered, "I've fooled the lot of them. If you could see my little room . . . but they'll all see it when I'm gone. I've two dozen glasses there. And I've two sets of crockery, and more of your precious mother's jewelery than she ever remembers she had, and silver spoons, and . . ." ' "

Ashley was reading out their agreed final version; which was not easy to do, since it had to be extracted from a maze of alterations in two different handwritings.

" 'Owen realized that without thinking he had lifted her case off the table in order to give it to her. She saw this, looked slyly at him, and said in her cajoling way, "Thank you, Master Owen." '

" 'He gave it into her hands. It was not from fear. It was as if there was something between them that could not be denied.'

" 'Julia came with the brandy, and his mother, in the voice she always used for servants, said: "Drink this down, Ellen, and you'll feel better." ' "

There was something strangely close to perfection, Ashley thought, in sitting beside this silent and beautiful young man, and relishing their joint creation. "Now then," he said, "does our last paragraph stand up?"

" 'Owen did not reply. He left the kitchen and went above. A terrible sense of guilt had overtaken him. He had helped. He had held the case in his hands. He felt dirty and guilty. He went upstairs to where the wretched sun was still making everything bright and hot, and he ran the cold water into the basin. He put out his hands and splashed the water all over his face and hair, and he seemed to be washing away at least some of his sin. He went along the corridor and into the sitting room. He was not crying. His face was wet and cold. On the carpet he saw the Bentley and the Alvis—Carter and McCracken. They were two bits of paper—nothing more. He walked over to them, over the green carpet, and crushed them flat with his foot, one after the other.' "

They were quiet for a moment. Ashley murmured—"Yes, indeed. Well, at least he's not bored any more. One can say that much for reality, if nothing else. Do you know E. M. Forster's *The Longest Journey?*"

"Yes, it's very difficult."

"It's the most interesting of them all."

Ashley turned his head. Carleton was still looking down at the writing. With shock and then alarm, Ashley was aware of a sharp desire to put his hand on the square back of that brown head and run it down to the brown neck inside the white collar. "Well," he was saying, in an odd voice, "I think that's quite a nice little story."

Those eyes had come around, smiling at him. Was it deliberate? Yes, it was. It was deliberate. That look was flirtation. A detestable thing. Neither hot nor cold. The boy had known his temptation. Had provoked it. He stood up abruptly, and said, almost with ferocity: "Make a final copy. Make two, if you can find a typewriter in this ancient academy. I'll send it to the *New Arts Review* with a covering note to my friend, the editor."

"Gosh! Do you mean we'd try to have it *published?*"

"Only a fool would write for any other reason," said Ashley, sitting on the divan bed. "You'd better put your home address. They're not too quick. You may be out in the rude world by then. Have you written anything else?"

Carleton had twisted around on the chair. Those eyes were less definable against the light. But it was undeniable, and appalling: Ashley wanted to go over and embrace the figure seated in the window.

"No . . . except in the Mag. I've been keeping . . . a sort of diary, but I'm going to give that up. This is much more exciting. Making something that wasn't there before."

"Even diaries do that."

"Gosh, that's what *I* thought! But this is more. This is something really new."

"The word is 'creative,' " said Ashley, gazing at the carpet and running fingers through his hair. "Or art. What Owen was doing with the cars. In solitude. Until life refused to be rejected any longer."

"Oh? I suppose so."

"This little story contains quite a lot."

Carleton felt the first shadow fall in the most wonderful hours of his life. He didn't care to think that his story contained more than he knew. Mental effort had excited and tired them both. He thought he should leave, but didn't know how. Half an hour still before the bell for tea. Sometimes one really wanted the bells by which they lived to ring out. There was a long, uncomfortable silence. A change of subject perhaps—

"Did you ever find the door to the dispensary?"

Carleton found he had said it like one young man to another. A little mocking. It was very odd.

"Yes. I had forgotten my wall decoration."

Given an inch, they always turn to impertinence, thought Ashley. "You'd better get along and get started on that," he said. "The sooner the better."

"Right."

Carleton rose, and took his coat and tie, and at the door said, "I don't know how to thank . . ."

"None of that. Leave. Just leave."

Carleton heard it in bewilderment. What had gone wrong? Ashley had his head in his hands. It was too difficult to understand.

"Right," he said, and went out.

Ashley surrendered to self-pity.

Yes, it had been more than affection, more than tenderness. My God, it had been waiting for him. She had been right.

The illusion that it was a Michelangelo was destroyed. It

was not. It was a person. Flesh and blood, and of the same sex. The love was forbidden, and he had wanted to touch.

Carleton bounced out of the new building; and Lucretia dodged behind the tree. He had recaptured the whole sense of marvel: the wonder of the afternoon. He walked on air, heading for his house, via the bogs. There was time to start the first page in the common room, on that awful rug. How much one could learn from older people! Seemingly from nowhere the thought came—maybe his mother had been right, after all, about the value of Mr. Brownlow's company; in spite of everything. As for Eric Ashley—this one chance afternoon with this one person had given him a life's wonderful occupation.

Boys were standing about in groups, waiting for the bell; hungry, as ever. In one group a boy looked at him meaningfully and put his hand in his coat pocket. Who was this junior, this kid, making signs to *him*?

Yes, the connection returned. Nicky, of course. But something had been very nearly lost.

He felt more fatherly than before.

But his heart had quickened all the same.

He felt especially bad now, because they had been going to meet that afternoon and he had canceled it.

He passed the washroom door. There was no one in the corridor; not even Gower. He opened the locker door and put his hand in each pocket of the mackintosh.

There was no note.

He knew now that nothing was lost, because he was bereft. And alarmed. Was Nicky fooling him? It had never gone wrong before.

Again, he was conscience-stricken about the moment's alienation. It was as if Fate and Nicky were paying him back.

"Carleton!"

He was startled. Rowles was standing at the foot of the stairs. "Come here a minute."

He followed the Doctor up the stone steps and into his room. "Close the door."

Rowles stood with his back to the fireplace, looking at him in a curiously intent way and breathing deeply. If the Doctor could ever have been said to be in a state, he was in one now.

"Nothing rational seems to be happening here any longer, Carleton," he said.

"Oh? . . . Maybe that's no harm, sir."

Rowles was too worked up even to drop his lower lip in his customary expression of surprise.

"I beg your pardon?"

"Well . . . maybe we need both. The irrational as well, I mean."

"Are *you* feeling all right, Carleton?"

"Yes, indeed. I've had an amazing afternoon."

"You're not the only one. I've just seen Clinton's long-haired ladies falling about in the Quad. They stink of beer. Unfortunately, none of them is in my house, or I'd have had the arse off him. They went to the woods and took young Fitzmaurice with them. The worst of it is, I begin to wonder if the headmaster isn't right."

"In what way, sir?"

The Doctor breathed, and stared, and evidently decided not to say something.

"I've seen a lot here, Carleton. I've seen poor old Mr. Pritchard, who taught geometry better than *I* do, dead in the bath. But I've never seen anything like this."

"Yes, sir. What else, sir?"

It seemed ages before Rowles was able to speak.

"Mr. Milner has proposed marriage to a barmaid, and the lady has indicated acceptance. They intend to live here."

"Gosh!"

The Doctor watched and waited for the total horror to be appreciated. Carleton, aware of this, and feeling inadequate, added, "Goodness!"

"He didn't need to do it, Carleton. That's the pity and the folly of it."

Carleton had no idea what this meant.

"Oh."

The Doctor had watched him keenly enough to think, He's not really concerned. These curious birds are concerned solely with themselves. They take what you give, and eagerly accept dismissal, and are gone. "And what is this 'amazing' afternoon you've been giving yourself?"

"Not me. Eric Ashley. He's taught me how to be a writer.

232

For hours. I never knew. It's the most wonderful thing. He's the most wonderful teacher."

"Ashley? Ah come off it, Carleton! Ashley couldn't teach a duck to swim."

"Oh, *sir!*"

Carleton had cried out with such feeling that they were both taken aback.

Rowles was quite impressed, and puzzled. Self-centered, yes, but this curious creature had, for some reason, lately ceased to be a cynic.

They were saved by the bell.

"There's your tea. You'd better be off."

"Yes, sir."

He was going out the door.

"Carleton!"

He turned.

Rowles was suddenly looking desperate—even a little mad.

"He didn't need to do it, you know. He didn't need to do it."

"No, sir."

Carleton went out, completely bewildered.

The Doctor stood there, and felt that there was no hope for Weatherhill. After forty-seven years. Why now? Why suddenly? Why this term? These new people, certainly. But their share was small. That the place was everywhere yielding to that lethal adversary, the emotions, could scarcely be put at their door. It must be the weather: this damn, endless sunshine, which even at this hour was blazing across his desk.

There was something lying there on the blotting paper. Someone had written him a note.

He walked over, and looked down at it.

"Every time I see you—you're more wonderful than ever," he read, and his whole great head flushed with embrrassment. "Love, love, love. . . . N.A."

CHAPTER TWENTY-TWO

"Almighty and ever-living God, who has vouchsafed to regenerate these thy servants by water and the Holy Ghost, and hast given unto them forgiveness of all their sins; strengthen them, we beseech thee, O Lord, with the Holy Ghost the Comforter, and daily increase in them thy manifold gifts of grace. . . ."

The small white figures stood in line before the altar.

The bishop had white tufts above either ear and a ring that rivaled the chaplain's. He was enormous.

Ashley wondered about water and the Holy Ghost.

Carleton was jealous of both: Nicky was removed from him, submitting himself to something else, something incomprehensible. Still, Weatherhill Day was exciting: they could forego each other more easily; the Day dominated. His last—yes, his last. Everyone was, at the least, a little nervous. He even felt a bit out of it that *he* did not have the awful expectation of his parents appearing on the scene. Perhaps this last time he should have submitted himself to more than a fluttering stomach. Perhaps he should have shared with others this true and ultimate nausea.

Dr. Rowles believed in the regeneration, but it was up to the curious birds, and one never knew what was going on in their heads. The most seemingly devout of the group must have written that note: there was only one N.A. at Weatherhill at the moment. After the first flush it had been clear that it was unlikely to be for him. But for whom, then? And who the devil had put it on his desk?

It was a minor matter. Behind him, the other sex packed the antechapel. One could sense the cherries and feathers. On the chapel step, Milner had introduced him to a young woman, covered in bows, and called her his fiancée. He had nodded, incapable of speaking.

"We make our humble supplications unto thee, for these thy servants upon whom (after the example of the holy Apostles) we have now laid our hands, to certify them (by this sign), of thy favor and gracious goodness toward them. . . ."

His hand on Nicky's head. Carleton saw the fat old man as almost a rival. Ashley had looked across at him and held his eyes for an awkward moment. Why?

The Reverend Cyril Starr, removed at some distance along the altar step, scrutinized the faces of his charges. His expression seemed black, but this was merely repose. There was a remote contempt for the bishop, and a mild amusement at these passionate young children wishing for grace; and some hair-raising recollections which would not depart.

Mrs. Crabtree, with her chin right up, watched the ceiling and wished for grace too.

At her side, the Head let his eye rove until it fell upon Dr. Boucher with satisfaction. He looked sturdy enough for the task.

But first there was W. Day to be gone through: the highest peak of his life; and his nervous excitement about it was identical to that of the boys. Both Lord Mountheath and Sir Charles Pike were now modestly seated in the antechapel. He had asked them to breakfast, and would reveal his plans. They would need to know of Milner's astonishing digression, but the young lady's origin had best be kept secret.

Ashley debated it, and decided that there could be no doubt about the look he had just received. He wondered about his confreres. Dotterel, Clinton, the chaplain. . . . How did they resist—or did they? How did they survive? Tough? Superficial? Shameless? People lucky enough to possess no heart? He felt faint, and afraid. He thought about resigning. But where to? Was this something that would travel with him or not? After all, the place was an emotional hothouse. Was this thing not equally unreal? What was his history? Not promising. Even if Joan was to be regarded as merely wrong for him. My God, was it not possible that Clive at Cambridge had borne a definite resemblance to J. L. Manson (the Reverend)? (Charming, shallow, vain Clive, of whom he had been so—as it was finally revealed—absurdly fond). And Carleton to both of them? Great heaven, was it possible that his emotional life was already fixed, way back, as merely looking for copies of J.L.M.?

"O Almighty Lord, and everlasting God, vouchsafe, we beseech thee, to direct, sanctify, and govern, both our hearts and bodies, in the ways of thy laws. . . ."

Carleton wondered if the Pedant's love was sacred or profane. And Jimmy Rich?

What *were* the ways of the laws?

"The Blessing of God Almighty. . . ."

Gower! Of course!

Carleton almost spoke the words out loud.

Yes. It must be. No one else would search his mack. It must be that fiend. But what had he done with it?

How the dickens could one find out? Challenging Gower was always useless, and in this case would be downright embarrassing.

They would have to think of another hiding place.

The fiend, in an innocent white surplice for disguise, was filing out now with the rest of them; dirty skin and slanting eyes, and enigmatic as ever. But probably filled with glee. Carleton would like to have seen him hanged from a height.

Following at the end, with Naylor, he glanced nervously at the parents in the antechapel, with the mad thought that his own might have slipped in. But no. Breakfast at the Crown and Anchor was the tradition. The other visitors came mostly in the afternoon. New faces, ignorant of everything, invaded the grounds. Their sons put away their secrets for the Day. They allowed the invaders the assumption that there was some connection between here and home; whereas, of course, there was none whatever. Tomorrow, normality again.

Standing in the alcove with his fellow prefects, looking down the steps along the cloisters, Carleton fixed Nicky with a penetrating gaze. Had he lost him? Had the rival gained? Had the Church swallowed him up?

My goodness, Nicky looked away! He stared at the stony ground. For heaven's sake, you'd think he'd been canonized.

Johns had murmured something, something horribly unexpected.

"I suppose it could happen to a bishop."

Johns had been watching him. Johns was looking him in the eyes. That beaky face. Johns was pitying him, patronizing him. Gosh, he was almost succeeding in making him feel guilty—caught out. By what right? Johns had never felt a wound; never would. It certainly couldn't happen to *him,* not with that ugly mug. For an instant they looked at each other with animosity. It came mostly from Carleton.

"What do you mean?" he said, not as boldly as he had hoped.

"Will you never grow up?" said Johns.

Right. That was the end of Johns. Good riddance.

How had they ever been companions?

Carleton had the curious intuition that there would always be a Johns in his life. Copies of this one. The passive companion. The scrutinizer. The one who let him do the living, and make the mistakes. "Will you never be young?" he should have said, but it was too late. There was a common need—which was infuriating. Another Johns would turn up like a shadow, and he would not be able to say "Go away."

But I'm the one who has sent a story to an adult magazine, he thought, not you.

The bishop came last. The chaplain, just ahead, was smiling a smile for all to see—and every one of them watched with fascination—a smile of demonic contempt.

But the chaplain's expressions were always overestimated. The smile expressed mild amusement.

They had changed from surplices to gowns—torn, and covered with food and shoe polish—and Carleton was breakfasting at the head of a senior table.

Ashley was slowly stomping up and down the aisle, seemingly in a dream. It appeared fitting, to those who thought about it, that he turned out to be the master on duty. The most removed from the place and its ethos, he was there as he might be on any other old day.

But it was not any other old day, and there were three sausages each to establish that point. Also, the din was far greater than usual. Cold showers and work ahead always dampened them. But this was different. The prospect of no classes had such a releasing effect that one might have imagined hard labor under the lash to be their customary fate.

This table came low on Carleton's preference list, because it was dominated by Beauchamp and Sinnott. They had been separated once, but since whatever it was that had happened they had switched places and were now elbow to elbow.

"Just *wait* till I tell all you dear children the latest!"

Beauchamp was down at the far end, but there was something about his voice that cut through everyone else's.

"Our dear pastor has let it out of his bag. Our heavenly Starr has spilled the nasty beans."

"Oh, get on with it, for Christ's sake," said Sinnott.

"Now, dear, just because I've let you in on the great joke. . . ."

"It may be no joke."

"Oh, come off it, you fool, it's the funniest thing that has happened in the entire history of this godforsaken jail. I can't wait to tell Ossie. It's far better than Miss Hutchins. My dears, there is to be what our heavenly Starr terms—with the utmost distaste, I may say, God bless the dear sweet man—a purge."

"A what?"

There was mild interest, and savage attention to the food.

"We are to be investigated, my little chicks. We are to be questioned as to what we do with our spare parts."

"What do you mean?"

"You're codding."

"You're making it up."

"Questioned by whom?"

Carleton felt strangely uneasy, and then saw that Beauchamp was leaning forward and looking down the table at him. An unnaturally healthy and provocative creature. He kept a sunlamp in the dorm. He had been a Starling for a while, and found it a little too tepid, but had later graduated into an almost adult friendship with the chaplain.

"But Carleton can tell you all about it."

"I can't. I don't know what you're talking about."

"Ah. Excellent. Dear me, are our prefects losing favor?"

"Shut up, Beauchamp."

"My dears, according to the Starr in the East, we are to be questioned, young and old, the halt and the lame, staff and school, and those found with a stain on their whatever are to be decontaminated, disinfected, hung, drawn, quartered and, in short, expelled forthwith."

Carleton was suddenly afraid. It was obviously the truth. He tried to eat, but the sausages and fried bread were sickening. Just suppose. His mother's amazement. Her hostility for the first time in his life. His father's horror, and shame; both profound, and forever. No home any more.

My Lord—the note! What had Gower done with the note?

"Look at Carleton! My dears, I declare he's turned quite pale. Just look at him."

"I haven't turned anything. Shut your blasted mouth, Beauchamp."

"Oh yes, you have. We're beastly scared about Barbara Allen."

The table was shocked. Even at the best of times, most of them found Beauchamp crazy and frighteningly sophisticated. Their silence would have been unbearable if the rest of the hall hadn't been thunderous. Carleton was appalled, but the funny thing was at the very same moment he felt a little proud. He still wanted everyone to know. He even suspected that Beauchamp was a little admiring. This pleased him. Why, for goodness sake?

But it was nasty all the same.

"Oh, chuck it, for Christ's sake," Sinnott murmured.

To be defended by Sinnott!

"I don't know what you're talking about," Carleton said. "And I don't know why *you're* feeling so cheerful."

"Oh, I don't tamper with the young. Only with contemporaries and elders. That doesn't concern the little Crab. He doesn't understand it. He couldn't imagine it, poor sweet. And even if he could—I'm just dying to be expelled. It would solve everything. Perhaps we should explain it to him, dear."

"Oh, shut up," said Sinnott.

"You're very dreary today. Confirmation must have upset you. You're all as disappointing as ever. No one's asked me the question."

"I'll ask it then," said Sinnott. "Who's doing the purge?"

"Thank you. The Butcher, my dears! Can you believe it?"

"The Butcher?"

"How do you mean?"

"Who?"

"Dr. Kinsey in person," said Beauchamp. "Isn't it marvelous?"

"Cripes."

"They must be nuts."

"Of course they are," said Beauchamp. "Oh, you're all such bores. Nobody's mentioned the future Mrs. Milner. Did you see? Did you all see? Isn't it glorious? Buttons and bows, my dear. The Pedant's wife. What a tale she'll have to tell! What a pilgrimage! Canterbury, here I come. . . ."

How could he get it from Gower? There seemed to be no way.

It was a funny feeling, changing in the dorm at ten in the morning. Unreal. It seemed, disturbingly, in this vast chilly place that he might be the only one in the whole school putting on cricket togs. But, of course, the Old Boys were probably going on to the field by now. Hurry up. Being late. Being late was the one and only terror that remained. They're all waiting and I'm late. The bell's ringing and I'm late. Yes, even now as a prefect. Even now his fingers would scarcely button up his white shirt. It wasn't very white: he kept it inside his blazer. And he had forgotten to tell a fag to blanco his boots. Never mind, it was only the Old Boys; and they were only concerned with themselves.

He clattered down the stone stairs, holding carefully onto the banisters, because his studs were slippy. Gosh, am I late? Metcalfe and his pals were cluttering up the Big Schoolroom doorway. Metcalfe bowed low. "Good morning, your Worship." He brushed past them, ignoring the tribute. It *was* a kind of tribute. He had always been popular. He liked that. It wasn't really lack of courage, or conceit: it was the wish for human connection, however small. Yes, even with juniors. Something which the senior prefectship would have destroyed. Was that an excuse? No, no it wasn't. That some were called "fags," and had to behave as such, was nonsense and inhuman.

Thank heaven, there was someone on the Chapel Square in whites. But it was only Hamilton Minor and he was only

240

twelfth man. No, he was also scorer, and nothing could happen without him.

He hurried on. "I am *not* walking down with Hamilton Minor." Why? Because he is small, and junior, and beautiful even though his head is red.

Gosh, what had Beauchamp said!

Some cars were drawing up in front of the Head's House already. It was sunny and windy, with white clouds. It must have brought them out early. But it wasn't a heat wave any more. Lucretia was sprawled on the steps, making no attempt to receive them. Never mind, he had other duties.

More cars, belonging to Old Boys, were parked on the drive outside the Music Building, and these gentlemen were unloading pads and bats. He went down the slope, with most of the school ambling down beside him. Spectators always seemed like lazy lumps: you even had Clinton's artists, who you knew perfectly well weren't even watching. There were men and boys in white, bowling at each other all over the field. One of them was Nicky.

He felt an immediate sense of defiance. He quite forgot Gower. He felt a greater closeness than ever, and a new pride that his love was stronger than fear. He experienced a keen desire that made his heart race, as he ran down the stone steps that cut into the spectators' grass bank, threw off his cap and blazer, and strode out onto the springy grass.

"Sling us down a few, like a good chap."

A tall, bald man even older than his own father threw a ball over to Carleton.

He remembered all this: it was a question of the Old Boys limbering up.

The man struck the ball with a kind of flourish when Carleton bowled it to him, a fanciful weaving of the bat; as if to demonstrate, and be sure, that the old style was still there.

There was much laughter and shouting. You'd think they had taken everything over and the school Eleven didn't even exist.

They seemed to be bandying Christian names about to show that *they* had gone out into the world and learned them, and learned how to use them freely.

241

"Another century today, Harry, what?"

"Ah, ha, I don't know about that, Geoffrey."

"Got you, my boy!"

"Morning, Frank. Cutting it a bit fine, what? At the tables last night, eh?"

"Not exactly, George."

"Hah, hah, hah!"

They were bouncing about in their club sweaters and, Carleton thought, trying to seem young and vigorous. But these ones were all old. He remembered them vaguely from past years, and remembered well the invariable Captain, Sir Gregory ("Greg") Waltham, who had played for the Gentlemen of England and was said to be nearly seventy. His voice was the loudest of all.

The Eleven was always alarmed at first by these unabashed adult men, who came from gambling and late nights to take on mere children. But they weren't so brilliant in the end.

The other, smaller group were all very recent Old Boys, and shy about it. The quick change of status unnerved them. They were not at ease with their former colleagues, who were now recognizably schoolboys, and they were silenced by their new companions. They had found the outer world unattractive and had come smartly back. But it was not somehow what they had expected. Having become an Old Boy, the last thing one anticipates is being humbled.

The pattern with regard to letters to the *Old Weatherhillian* magazine was exactly the same. Reaching the mid-twenties, volunteers for this match suddenly were missing. Then around about fifty a number bounced back again, and stayed on until they dropped. They were in the world, but they were back at Weatherhill, and always had been. They took to the field as if it was theirs again, as if they were residents and slept in the dorm. The only thing to do was to bowl them out.

"Hm. Miss Lucretia!"

She idly turned her head and looked up at the open doorway. Lloyd, the medieval manservant, was standing there.

"I must get on with luncheon. I am preparing the cup for the loyal toast. If there are any further inquiries for Headmas-

242

ter and Mrs. Crabtree, would you kindly explain that they have gone down to the cricket?"

"I suppose so."

"That is gracious of you."

She wondered if he was getting at her, and if so whether at his age he was worth destroying. This was a dreadful day for her: she had no role to perform. She had stayed home and exchanged her jeans for the tartan skirt with fierce reluctance; but what was she dressed up *for?* To do Lloyd's job for him? Yet another car was approaching. They kept on striding up into her house as if they expected a party or something. Her parents had fled into the open. It was a small black car, driven by a lone lady in a large hat, and it had come to rest quite close to the steps on which she sprawled.

The lady got smartly out and slammed the door. Lucretia liked the way she did that. There was something about her. Lucretia was almost never impressed, but this lady was somehow different. She had a light blue dress with a full, pleated skirt which swished as she walked. Her walk was elegant and commanding, as if she was used to people watching her. The front brim of the big hat was turned up, as if she liked her face to be seen clearly. It was frightfully made up, and she was pretty old, and probably not really a blonde at all, but even so Lucretia thought she looked a bit like a film star.

The nose was too long and thin. It reminded her of someone.

"Good morning," the lady said, with a false but nevertheless dazzling smile. "You look comfortable."

"I'm the headmaster's daughter," Lucretia replied.

"Ah, that would explain it," the lady said, seeming a bit too motherly and patronizing. All the same her voice was very special, kind of rich.

"If you want them they're not in," Lucretia said. "They're down at the cricket."

"It was really my son that I wanted. Can you direct me to his room?"

"They don't have rooms," Lucretia said. "Only dormitories."

"You flatter me, my dear," the lady said, and she certainly looked as if she meant it. "My son is a master. Eric Ashley."

Astonishment, bewilderment and animosity left Lucretia without words. She had very nearly inadvertently produced the scare look.

"My name is Helena Ashley. What's yours?"

"Lucretia Crabtree."

"Really!"

"Yes. Really. He's not in his room, in any case. He's at the cricket too. He walked past a few minutes ago."

"I see. I didn't know he watched cricket."

"Depends who's playing," said Lucretia.

Their eyes met for ages. It was well worth it. The lady was a picture. Her face went through all kinds of expressions. First surprise, and then doubt, and then suspicion, and then worry, and then—yes, almost—fear.

"I don't understand you. But I can find my own way. Don't trouble to get up."

"Righto."

Lucretia hugged her victory to herself. A tremendous adversary. Her own daring had left her quite shaken. She felt she couldn't have stood up even if she had wanted to.

Mrs. Ashley—who was still celebrated as Helena Parrish—swung down the drive toward the Music Building, saying to herself, "Bloody child." She clenched her right fist for a moment, and found she was slightly breathless with anger. What had that last remark meant?

There was an open iron gate in the railings, leading to the long grass slope down to the cricket field. One boy nudged another, and they stood politely aside, watching her with awe. "Thank you," she said, and smiled on them, thinking, Eric looked like this once. It was hard to remember. But there was enough memory to cause a pang. She felt sad. Her emotions always changed rapidly. It was partly theatrical training, though to what degree she herself no longer knew. Impossible, her son had once said, in mild accusation, to tell the dancer from the dance. Yes, there was the back of his fair head appearing over a deck chair, something known and intimate, and also for some reason sad.

He looked rather solitary and odd, sitting there halfway down the slope. Everyone else was sprawling on the mown bank above the field, or else on deck chairs close to it. Passers-by collected these chairs from two great piles, sons bearing the burden for fathers, mothers and sisters. Very few brothers—they tended to stay away. The school had opened the batting, and Carleton and Southwell were still in. The rest sat on the bank in front of the pavilion; which was also occupied by people of distinction: the two new governors, one of them dark-suited and military, the other tweedy and county—only the Head seemed to be quite sure which was which; and also the bishop and Lord Fitzmaurice and others.

It was windy: she had to hold on to her hat, and her skirt was a mistake. She knew he was going to be startled, but could see no alternative.

"Hello, darling."

"Good God."

He was more startled than she had expected. He was running his fingers quickly through his hair. She was shocked by his appearance.

"Can I sit on something?"

"Uh . . . yes," said Ashley, standing up and looking around dazedly for an unaccompanied boy. Watson-Wyatt was passing, with his Gleneagles golfing parents. One couldn't command them when in company: they were somehow protected. Disturbing for Mother to hear her boy compelled to obedience and service at the drop of his surname. Another hyphen, Seaton-Scott, was unencumbered.

"Seaton-Scott, you idle knave, come here!"

The round face and specs seemed to light up, as if complimented. He approached quickly, as one delighted to be put to use.

"Yes, sir."

"Fetch us one of those chairs, would you, like a good fellow."

"Righto, sir."

She had never heard him speak to a child before and was pleasantly impressed: a kind of reluctant detachment, almost an intimacy. They must like him.

"What are you doing, child?"

"I don't quite see which way it goes, sir."

"The other way around, you idiot."

He said it in a funny way, and Seaton-Scott began laughing.

"How, sir?"

"Give it to me, you ass. Go away, you abominable creature."

"Righto, sir."

She saw his angry expression as they sat down.

"You might at least. . . ."

"Now don't, Eric. I'm only staying five minutes. I'm expected at Henley. As I was passing, and I suddenly remembered the Day from of old, it seemed logical."

"What do you mean 'expected'?"

"A chance of a film part, darling. About ten lines, but one isn't a chooser any more. Now tell me—what's happening?"

"I don't know what that means."

"I had a very odd note from Joan. Good-bye and all that. She said I should have a look at you. I can see what she means."

He actually seemed to have half an eye to the cricket. Could it be that he was really accepting this place?

"Which is the new man?"

"Down there—fawning. The mortarboard and red face."

"I expect you miss old—"

"Yes."

"But he can't have been very active in his position. Is that glorious clergyman still here?"

"Yes."

"What a loss to the theater! I don't really understand any of it. I never did. We mothers are kept out. The sons say nothing. The fathers are silent. Should we really send him to a public school? What's it *like* there? What was yours like? They evade it always. There's some conspiracy."

Ashley wanted to speak. He wanted to be close, as they had for a long time been. There's a conspiracy down there, running up and down the pitch, while they applaud. It seemed rather preposterous in her presence. Infantile. She made him feel like a schoolmaster, in a school: a fact he always tried to ignore.

"There's something I never dared ask *you*. Are some of these children as romantic, to put it politely, as one reads in books?"

"More."

"More what?"

246

"More so than in any of the books I've read."

She turned and looked at his profile, holding on to her hat. She felt a little ridiculous. The wind was blowing right across the slope and she had to hold on to her skirt as well. It seemed to emphasize the point that ladies were not required, and could not decently exist, on these premises.

"Darling, there are only a few weeks more, aren't there? Are you coming back to the flat?"

"I don't know."

"I hate to try to influence . . . but it's fairly lonely. Especially without work."

"We are both educated to one job only. That's the misfortune."

"Not you. Not you."

"Yes."

"Nonsense. Eric, why don't you leave this blasted place?"

"Don't start that, Mother. I've had enough of that."

"You don't look well. You must know that."

"Maybe not."

She glanced at her watch and felt the urgency to achieve something out of this. He had grown terribly difficult.

"I wonder does it ever occur to you that I'm a widow and you're my only child, and if something happens to you, it happens to me too. It's a role I've never acted, so perhaps you'll accept it."

"I do. I do, Mrs. Alving." He placed his hand on hers, and smiled.

"Perhaps rather heavy, but I'm glad I said it. What's wrong?"

"Nothing."

"Oh, Eric, for God's sake what's it all about?"

"Mother, have you ever waked up at eight o'clock on a clear summer morning and experienced terror?"

"Yes."

"What?"

"Yes. But Dr. Henry gives me pills for it."

"Pills."

"Yes. Why not? But you're young. What do you do—put your head under the bedclothes?"

"Yes."

"I get up. You should try it."

"What for?"

"Eric, being morbid is an Ashley specialty, and one gets sick of it. Your father was bad enough."

"What are you?"

"I'm a Parrish. We enjoy. None of you seems to have ever known how."

She was sorry. She realized that she had crudely rejected something.

"Mother . . . I'm beginning to find there are moments when I can't be alone."

"My God, that's not new to me either," she said, unable to stop herself.

"But I don't mean loneliness. I mean . . . a panic necessity for the company of another."

"Any other?"

"No. I think there must be love."

"Well, that's the first healthy piece of news I've heard yet."

"Is it?"

"Of course. But what do you mean 'panic'? That's just the Ashley line."

"No. A gathering fear. A racing heart. Something is going to happen—I don't know what."

"Stop it, Eric. Now you're frightening me."

"The only hope is a faint one—that I'll be rescued by unconsciousness."

"That's no rescue."

"It's peace, of a kind."

"Who is the doctor here now?"

He nearly smiled the way she remembered.

"I bought a bottle of whisky in the Crown and Anchor. It's better."

"You? No, not that. Not for you. You know, I think you have too much peace. You need to fight—like I have had to."

"I fought for Cambridge and lost."

"Fight again, for heaven's sake."

"I fought for two good people here. I lost."

"I think you always expect to win, Eric. It's perhaps my fault. You always had everything. You always had me."

"I seem to remember you were invariably on stage."

"Your memory is poor, Eric. We were together all day. Every

day. You even came to rehearsals. Until you left for this place. And even then in the holidays. I never went anywhere without you. You wouldn't allow it. Your father wasn't much help."

"Perhaps you wouldn't let him be."

She was quiet for a moment.

"You're making me angry now," she said.

"Father loved children."

"If they were small enough. When they started to develop he got out of the way. Your father lost all interest in you from the age of eight."

"What did you say?"

"I'm sorry, but it's true. He went back to his books."

"Do you swear to that?"

"Yes."

"Why did you have to say it?"

"I'm sorry, but I'm tired of being always the villain. It's true."

"Classic situation," Ashley murmured. "Oh God."

"How do you mean?"

"They all are, I suppose. There's nothing new under the sun."

"If you're starting on your father's dreadful friend, Ecclesiastes, it's time to go. No, I'm joking. I'll be late. Keep in touch, darling. Let me know what you decide."

They were standing.

"Good-bye," Ashley said. "It was nice to see you."

"Do you mean that?"

"Yes. Yes, I do."

She turned, rather shyly, and went away up the slope.

She heard shouts behind her in the distance, and clapping, but without interest. She was touched by their parting. Perhaps she shouldn't have said that about his father. But he seemed to have taken it. She turned to wave when she reached the gate.

He was not looking. He was standing with his back to her, and his hands in his coat pockets. Everyone else was clapping the boy with a bat who was coming quickly up the steps from the field: a handsome, brown-headed boy.

There was something disturbing. She felt uneasy.

That dreadful child was still lying on the steps.

"Depends who's playing."

She averted her eyes and walked straight to the car. But she sat in it for a moment before putting in the key, and found that she was being drawn to the steps.

It was unnerving, even sinister. The child stared back at her, unblinkingly, in a strangely cold and meaningful way.

She shivered. She had always disliked this place. She turned the key and started the engine.

"A panic necessity for another," she remembered, driving away. What did it mean? She had never lost interest, never ceased loving deeply, but she had lost real connection and understanding. Whatever it meant, it was frightening. He must *not* come back next term.

Forty-two. It wasn't bad. Everyone seemed to approve. Carleton felt pleased with himself. "Well done," murmured Dr. Rowles, who was sprawled on the bank in his best tweed coat, with Nicky close beside him. It was bewildering: all kinds of people here clapping; the Crab, Ma Crab, the bishop, strange men and women. . . . Bewick, who was passing, looked at him questioningly. "The slow man's easy," Carleton said. "Nearly all off-breaks. Watch out for the fast. He swings them in from the leg." He went into the deserted pavilion, to take off his pads, feeling important, and almost relieved that it was over and with dignity.

A long musty room, with a nice wood smell. He sat on the bag. He had flirted here with Hamilton Minor. "Are you going to do up my pads for me?" "Not likely," Hamilton Minor had replied—which was cheeky. As well as the photographs, there were teams of the past, for years, written in gold on the wooden panels. His name would soon be there. An Old Boy.

He wasn't going to sit near Nicky, but Rowles barked out— "Carleton!" and nodded at him to come over.

He sat on the bank, so that Rowles lay sprawled between them. He said nothing, but chewed a blade of grass. As with conversations at night, it was his pose to keep you waiting. His watch, among hairs, lay on the grass, and Carleton remembered: yes, when he came to Glen Court, and I was to be in his house. A hundred years ago. Nicky's school too. How small their world was!

"Did that swing in?"

"Yes."

He wasn't going to call him "sir" in front of Nicky, who was looking at him with blushing admiration. God seemed to be losing at the moment. It was wonderful.

"It was a good ball. Ah, watch it, Bewick, you ass!"

The Doctor was extremely uncomfortable and trying to appear calm. Normally he endured this Day of ladies, hats and social hell, by adhering to the Pedant; and it was not easy to accept that his place had been taken by a barmaid. They were seated among the school, over on the other bank, and the Pedant had added injury to insult by putting on his crumpled summer suit. Rowles had passed some social moments with this crowd here: for the Head and his two sycophants, who knew absolutely none of the Old Boys. But he had wearied of it: he was awkwardly shy at this sort of nonsense, and above all he was deeply disgusted by their plans for the morrow. Forty-seven years gave him the confidence to lie down and ignore them and watch the cricket.

He had watched the Ashleys too. He had a reputation for eyes in the back of his great head. He had met her several times, as a mother, and formed the impression that she was an improvement on that unfortunate breed; though she had shared, even to excess, the notion that her own was an angel beyond reproach. She had intelligence and a presence. She followed a lunatic trade, but that was not her fault. All the worthwhile plays were to be read in one's study. He knew Shakespeare almost in its entirety, and it was pitiful to think that egocentric cretins with painted faces imagined themselves to be of any use to that superlative fellow. Ashley's mother was a cut above them too, but she had the emotional nature common to these puppets, and it had caused him concern in the past. She might have been greatly hurt.

She might still be.

What had they said?

He had for a moment experienced the curious temptation to intervene.

To say what?

To say what he had nearly said before?

Take him away?

251

And now beside him sat this dark, religious, decidedly curious creature, Allen, who was professing love in unnecessary repetition for God knows who.

There was no end to it.

Almost perfect, the morning was, Carleton was thinking, as he glanced repeatedly across at Nicky; perfect except for one frightening fact—Gower. How was he to convey it to Nicky? Its urgency, and something delightfully warm and pleasant about the three of them sitting together, made him reckless.

"I was just thinking this is an ideal day for Gower."

The Doctor's mouth fell open and he slowly turned his head, flushing a little.

Carleton suddenly realized that, of course, Nicky wasn't supposed to know about Gower, though they had discussed him many times.

"Oh dear," Carleton said.

"I really don't know what you're talking about, Carleton."

"I mean, he likes doing nothing, and wandering about and taking notes . . . of what goes on."

It was very flustered, but he had caught Nicky's eye, and Nicky was thinking. He was worried. He had understood.

Rowles did not respond to this extraordinary statement. He appeared to have returned to the cricket. But in fact he had received the message too; Carleton having overemphasized the "taking notes." Yes, of course, Gower must be the culprit; from a locker, presumably. Rowles had eyes in the sides of his head as well: he was aware that they had exchanged a glance. And what was it Ashley had said in an unbelievable, shocking moment? "Carleton's in love." Rowles had walked away. But there was no escape now. He held the blade of grass between his teeth, and gazed dismally at Bewick and Southwell running up and down the pitch. Carleton! The one-time cynic. Imagine *him* being vulnerable to that stinking mishmash of destruction—the emotions.

The Doctor picked out the blade of grass and flicked it away.

"I'm the beneficiary, I regret to say."

"Of what, sir?" said Carleton in a nervous voice.

"Of what you guess to be . . . I presume it's a guess, and I grant you I never thought of it myself . . . Gower's latest activity. It was on my desk. I tore it up. Bewick won't last long if he plays another stroke like that."

Carleton saw that Nicky was scarlet. He himself was dumb with embarrassment. There was something particularly awful about its being Rowles: a person from another world. Ashley had been perfectly understanding, though horribly outspoken and scornful, about it. Even Ma Crab had hinted. But Rowles simply couldn't know what it meant. No common language whatever.

"I'm going to insist on it being the last of such excrescences." Rowles was pale. He was getting angry. "In fact, I'm asking you to cut the whole thing out, now, and once and for all. Do you understand?"

Carleton understood, though it was out of the question. "The whole thing." How easily the sense of wrongdoing and indulgence was created by these words! Were guilt, and shame, really part of it? Was it really something one confessed to Cyril Starr? Why was Rowles necessarily right, and why were they wrong?

"Well, Carleton?"

"Uh . . . yes, sir."

"*You* amaze me, I must say. The head of my house, damn you. I could have you out, you know that?"

"Yes, sir."

My Gosh. His mother. His father. Sin and shame. Take him away. Expelled.

"You'll go, in any case, if you keep this up. You may as well know, Dr. Boucher is starting an investigation into this sort of muck and carry-on tomorrow. God knows what he'll unearth about you. Personally, I don't intend to assist. You may rely on that, though you don't deserve it. It's nearly time for lunch. I'm going up for a wash."

Rowles got to his feet, with a grunt.

"Thank you, sir."

"Don't thank me. Chuck it in. That's my advice. No, those are my orders."

The Doctor walked up the slope, taking care to steer a course a long way from Ashley.

It was a disappointment, and depressing, that some of them simply couldn't help going in for arse-licking. It was not really disturbing. It was not even interesting. What *was* interesting, by Jove, was that extraordinary creature, Gower. What a masterly little conception! What infernal and extraordinary cheek. "Tee-hee!" Ashley heard him quietly exclaim, as he passed at a distance. My God, he regards me now as a figure of fun, Ashley thought. We'll see about that!

Carleton was looking across at Nicky, feeling hopeless, absolutely hopeless.

"Well?" he said.

"There's a crack in the buttress behind the chapel," Nicky said. "It's about my height. We'll leave the notes there. Don't put your initials."

The lunch of the year.

Lloyd's waxen face conveyed nothing, but this event was the apex of his entire existence. It mattered little to him that the Head was now of inferior stock. Lloyd served the school, and this was his libation. Scarcely had he given the high table soup, than he was back at his altar, bending over the cricket cup, with his ears sticking out of his head like Ping-Pong bats. He sniffed. And sniffed again at the other silver cup containing a refill in case of need. He stirred with a ladle. It was good. His own creation for half a century: cider and nameless white wine.

All was reversed. The staff occupied the high table: fourteen bachelors, three husbands, and Ma Crab. It was the prefects, instead of the masters, who sat at the head of the tables below. There was quite a crush: one table had been abandoned to the Old Boys' team. Most remarkable change of all, the chaplain graced the high table. He sat, by careful choice, at one end; at the farthest possible distance from the Crabtrees, and between the Beatle and old Mr. Wall, who was getting vaguer every day. He was regaling them, to his own mild amusement, with memories of an unspeakable lady organist in a church over which he had once presided in the Outer Hebrides.

Ashley as master on duty had the curious privilege of sitting beside Mrs. Crabtree. She had been dipping in and out of her soup, without a word. On his other side, the Cod was elaborating some new theory he had formulated with McCaffrey about fire practices.

Down at the end of the hall, Miss Bull was already tackling

a vast roast of beef with a knife like a scimitar. The skivvies in black were queuing up like a funeral party. Lloyd had his own smaller roast for the high table. One had to get everyone started on the second course, because waiting for the cup to go around would have taken too long. Possibly the most placid man alive, Lloyd was showing signs of excitement: his hands trembled slightly as he collected and delivered the plates. Until at last his moment had arrived.

The Head was waiting: he had cleared a place. Lloyd carried his treasure across, bent between the Crabtrees, and set it on the table; and as he did so the din subsided, because everyone had really been waiting for this. He backed away, and became a tall black statue in his own private corner.

The Head, Mrs. Crabtree and Dr. Rowles stood up together in the profound silence, with all heads turned their way. Whoever gave the toast always had a supporter at either side. It was the Head. Coloring a little, he raised the extremely heavy cup and pronounced the words—"*Floreat* Weatherhill. *Et floreant* the Weatherhillians."

He brought the rim to his lips and drank.

There was a marvelous hush. Most of the boys were impressed. They seemed to be all together, all at one, in their own private place, which they wanted to flourish, in defiance of everybody.

The Pedant was always testy about this: he had tried to Latinize the school name but had been outvoted.

Ma Crab had taken the cup, and nearly missed it, because her chin had jerked up and her eyes were on the ceiling. Her voice was quavering and almost inaudible.

"*Floreat* Weatherhill. *Et floreant* the Weatherhillians."

She dipped into it. She handed it to Ashley, who was standing at her side, and dropped her eyes to the table. The Cod had risen. Ashley looked into the pale brown liquid with silver flashing through it, and with embarrassment forced himself to speak what were to him fatuous words: "*Floreat* Weatherhill. *Et floreant* the Weatherhillians."

He tasted the noxious liquid and handed the cup to the Cod with sharp relief.

The Cod boomed. Excessive and preposterous, Ashley thought. He sat down and tried to stomach the roast beef.

There was a gentle rattle of knives and forks. *"Floreat* Weatherhill,"* said the Pedant very testily indeed, *"et floreant* the Weatherhillians."

"Matron disapproves," Mrs. Crabtree murmured, with several nervous dips. "She fears an epidemic. She does not appreciate our traditions."

"Floreat Weatherhill"—the chaplain worked it out of the corner of a wickedly enigmatic smile, and appeared to add further mockery—*"et floreant* the Weatherhillians." Mrs. Crabtree cleared her throat and threw her head right back.

Rowles made it sound loyal but surprisingly abrupt, and he had scarcely taken a sip of the extraordinary concoction when he was nodding to Lloyd to remove it.

Lloyd bore it to the Old Boys' table. And muted conversation began all down the hall. Very few people knew who these invaders were, and the ceremony had lost its solemnity. There were even some giggles when old Sir Gregory ("Greg") Waltham absolutely shouted it out.

"Our chaplain seems amused," said Mrs. Crabtree drily.

It was curious: Ashley had also been studying him and wondering about him.

"What, in your opinion," he said, "if it is not too naïve a question, *is* this burning fire?"

She was playing with some peas on her plate.

"I believe, in our dear chaplain's terms, it is a deliverance through pain."

"Really?"

They were talking in muted voices. No one was attending. Dotterel and Clinton, opposite, had turned their backs to them and were looking down the hall.

"We each bear a cross," said Mrs. Crabtree. "It must be acknowledged, not evaded. Once it is truly faced and admitted, it is then scourged in the fire, which is Christ. And the fire is His love. But I speak like a child's guide. You know all this perfectly well, Mr. Ashley."

"Floreat Weatherhill." It was Carleton's voice.

"I'm afraid I can't believe in this fire."

"I'm sorry."

"Floreat Weatherhill," cried a very piping voice, and there were high-pitched imitations. More of the juniors were in-

volved now, and it was becoming quite rowdy. The Head's paternal and jovial watch down the hall was mixed with an expression of faint alarm. Was this all right with the Old Boys? Was it usual?

"Does the acknowledgment of the cross not bring its own salvation?"

"Not to a Christian." She smiled wanly. "Not even, I suspect, to a Freudian. Certainly not to the chaplain. His cross is purely abdominal."

Ashley was amazed, and nearly laughed out loud for the first time in weeks. But there was something coldly merciless about it.

"Can one be sure of that?"

"Oh yes."

"*Floreat* Weatherhill. . . ." Carleton watched Nicky with wonder and pride: something sincere about him, some strange dignity, had silenced his noisy neighbors as soon as he spoke. The next speaker was promptly mocked.

"I looked out some of your writings, Mr. Ashley, when I heard you'd be teaching here."

"Really?"

"That's why I was interested in meeting you. That essay on Forster. 'The unforeseeing multitudes who remain aloof from sympathy, neither rejoicing in human joy nor mourning with human grief, and are the world's bane.' I'm not sure that I quote correctly. . . ."

"Word for word," said Ashley, in surprised admiration.

"Well . . . the chaplain holds a membership card."

Ashley marveled at such venom.

"Hey, Finch Minor, don't swig the lot!"

As if at a signal, Lloyd was going solemnly down the aisle with his second cup.

"You remember," said Mrs. Crabtree, "you point out that these unattached have, logically, one vice: curiosity. The chaplain sits up there, asking incessant questions of his admirers."

"You make the cap fit," Ashley said. "Myself, I begin to envy the truly unattached. I'm not sure any longer that they are either baneful or multitudinous. They may well be few, and possessed of rare virtues."

"What virtues would you suggest?"

"Freedoms mostly," Ashley said. "Curiosity is a very small vice. The chaplain is free of argument, competition, envy, blame, conflict, and he makes no assertions—save one. And even though you ascribe it, in his case, to the abdomen, you seem to acknowledge it to be the greatest of all."

"Certainly his assertion achieves greatness, if you speak of the fire . . ." said Mrs. Crabtree; and Ashley wondered at such a reaction to the school jest.

The toast was over and Lloyd was contentedly serving semolina.

"But as for your freedoms . . . from Mr. Connolly in the guise of Palinurus, are they not? . . ."

"You are well read."

"I have nothing else to do. That is my cross. Your freedoms . . . they strike me merely as negatives."

"They allow one to live at peace, in a room."

"Pascal's ideal always struck me as outstandingly undesirable. I gather you are losing the gift, Mr. Ashley. The point about attachments is that one has to be so careful with whom they are formed, don't you think?"

Ashley had no chance to answer. The Head rose and pronounced, *"Benedictus benedicatur, per Jesum Christum dominum nostrum."* And his wife, with bent head, eyes on the floor, and hands behind her back, followed him down the hall without another word.

Instead of being up front, with the staff, Ashley lounged on a kitchen chair close to the narrow, open, arched door of the Big Schoolroom. Now and then he glanced out onto the Chapel Square, where the innocent invaders were beginning to swarm in even greater number than in the morning. Clouds of dust blew about them, and among the hats only the white-petaled helmets of the debutantes seemed secure.

Within, boys sat on high behind Ashley, with their legs dangling from tables that had been piled up to make more room. They had the best view of the dais and the prize-giving. Ashley only saw the backs of heads.

Everyone had been getting prizes, he felt. The team spirit. Under advice from the Pedant, the bishop had handed out numerous silver cups, a football, a cricket ball and bat, a hockey stick, and countless leather-bound books.

It was over, and now the bishop was speaking. A slow rumbling from this ancient mountain of a man:

"Each of you spends only a few years here. That may seem like nothing compared with a lifetime. But a great many will feel that they have been the most important of all. Even the few months of a term, when one is young, are equal to years when one is grown up. All the time your characters, your views and ideas, are being formed, and your feelings developed. You are being developed to go out and take your place as citizens of the world. . . ."

Ashley thought he might faint. His heart was racing.

He was standing near the war memorial, talking with two young women in print frocks covered with large flowers; talking very easily, smiling, showing his white teeth. He wore a gray herringbone sports coat with gray flannels and a dog collar.

He looked exactly the same.

"Most of all, from my own time at Weatherhill," the bishop said, "I remember our classics master, Blewitt, an absolutely legendary figure in his day. Some of us may have thought him severe, even irascible, by nature. But that was our ignorance, as youngsters. Those fiery, even flaming outbursts of his which would undoubtedly have taken him to the top in politics—or any of the more public professions—were far from being what they seemed to the victim. They were merely expressions of a mercurial and generous nature. Quite simply, Blewitt loved Weatherhill. He had no ambitions outside. He loved the place and all that it stood for. Blewitt was a simple, honest Christian. That was his secret, and most of us came to know it. That was the essence of the towering legend that was Blewitt. . . ."

Yes, short and square, with wide-apart eyes, and even now that blushing child's complexion. How dare you smile! How dare you appear so stupidly well! How dare you deny my existence and all that has been! Who are these women?

"And so the years roll by," the bishop said. "There have been changes. New buildings which we would have envied. But essentially Weatherhill remains the same. The same principles apply. The same sort of fellow, Christian, upstanding, clean-

living, ready to pull his weight and more, ready to take responsibility, ready to command those less fortunately favored, goes
forth into the world. That world may be changing. But Old
Weatherhillians remain the same, thank God. You find 'em in
the Church, you find 'em in the army—nine major generals to
date, I believe—you even find 'em in the art game. A bit long in
the hair, what? Yes, yes, you laugh. We have our little laugh.
But never mind. They're Weatherhillians—like the rest of us.
We've had our characters developed on the same old lines . . .
the best lines. . . ."

Yes, apparently no older, no taller, and that rather high
voice, just audible against the bishop's. Only the preposterous
collar. And a certain poise in adult company. My God, was it
possible that one of them was a wife?

"I once had a dog called Hubert," the bishop said. "A scruffy
little fellow he was, when he came to us as a puppy. But my wife
and I took him in hand. We didn't bully him. We guided him.
We let him find his own feet, and then we began to show him
the right way of going about it. We said, in a manner of speaking, 'Look here Hubert. . . .' "

It was incredible, and overwhelming. It was just as before.
The same ache. I persuaded you to read Jane Austen, remember? I started you off on *Pride and Prejudice*. I may be ridiculous, but what are *you* now? Do you feel you've developed or
something, damn you? Have you any memory? My God, you
must have!

Applause. And more applause. The Head had stood up, apprehensive and flushed with his mouth pulled down. The visiting audience was suddenly on the alert—eager to help.

"Your Grace, I envy you your memories. As you all know, I
am what you might call a new boy. . . ." (Laughter rippled in
the front rows.) "Like other new boys, it is my proud boast that
I am now at an English public school. . . ." (More laughter
and some clapping. There were a number of parents up there.)
"I was at one more years ago than I care to remember, by the
way, in case you have any doubts on that score." (An explosion
of laughter and applause. Mrs. Crabtree glowed and smiled
wanly, with her head thrown back.) "I cannot resist returning
to the bishop's splendid simile concerning his dog, Hubert. . . ."

260

What are you now? Are you a dull, commonplace, self-satisfied, sporting parson? How can you be, you who wrote those poems to me? Yes, you did. You want to deny it. But you *can't* deny it.

". . . the character is formed," the Head said, "the feelings developed, but they must also be guided. They must not be allowed, so to speak, to run about the streets—and become a danger to others. There must be Christian discipline. . . ."

Will I approach and try to speak? No, never. You will look at me blankly and say "Hello, Ashley." Lying. Denying. And realizing at once, to your embarrassment and maybe even guilt, that *I* do not deny.

"Young people develop feelings before they develop the moral sense," said the Head. "It is our duty to curb them. Or rather, it is the duty of myself and my colleagues, and of course of our chaplain, to see that the sense of morality is also developed and runs parallel. I want to give the parents now an undertaking that this will be done—or should I say, will continue to be done. . . ."

There was a bemused and embarrassed stillness in the front rows.

The trio was walking away. They were laughing. He walked between them. The same back to his head, the same shoulders. . . .

In the san you lay naked and adoring in my arms.

"As for our numbers, our achievements in the classroom, and in the field, they are well up to standard. But I believe we can, and will, improve. . . ."

CHAPTER TWENTY-THREE

"Ah, Carleton. Come in. Take a pew," said the Butcher.

He sat behind the Head's desk with a pipe in his hand and notes in front of him. With his closeshaven ginger

261

head, broken nose and curious ears, you might think he
was still a boxer. But he had retired from the amateur ring
twenty years ago.

The study was cold. It was a dark grim morning. The rain
hit the two tall windows in sudden gusts.

"Sorry about taking you from class, but I don't imagine
that'll worry you, eh?"

"Uh. . . . No, sir."

"I'm starting by seeing the head of each house. Now then
. . . as head of Priestley, not to mention second prefect, have
you anything you'd like to tell me?"

"Um . . . no, sir. I can't think of anything."

The Butcher swiveled until he faced one of the dark windows and relit his pipe. He suddenly swiveled back again.

"Now then. Let's not be mealy-mouthed about this, Carleton. We want healthy minds and healthy bodies at Weatherhill.
The fellows that haven't got them may go and bugger somewhere else. The Head wants a clean start. I'm with him all the
way."

"Oh."

"I hear you sleep next to McIver?"

"Me? Yes . . . I do."

"What have you got to say about him?"

"Uh . . . I can't think of anything."

"In that case, all my thanks go to Steele."

The Butcher had turned to a small white cardboard box on
the desk, and was taking something out of it.

"The senior prefect took me to the photographic room last
night. We collected these."

The Butcher placed the pile of negatives in front of Carleton.

"He tells me they're taken by McIver for cash. I find it hard
to think of anything more filthy. Have a look at the top five.
They're all in your house."

Carleton took the top negative from the pile and held it up.
It was black against the rainwashed windows.

"I can't . . ."

The Butcher leaned forward and clicked on the table lamp.
Carleton held the negative against the green shade.

It was Hamilton Minor, grinning, with trees behind him.

Evidently he had knowingly posed for it. For whom? Carleton felt a slight and inexplicable shock, as if he were implicated.

"Carry on," the Butcher said.

He also felt shame, but he could hardly refuse.

Henderson and Finch Minor together! Also somewhere in the wood. And very definitely posing. In their bathing togs, with Finch Minor carrying the bearskin rug.

"Henderson's a prefect," said the Butcher. "They've shared a room in the san. Carry on."

Sexy Sinnott. In his favor, he had not known of it. He was running up to bowl in his big sweater. Beauchamp? Surely Beauchamp wouldn't bother with a photo. Wait a minute. . . .

"What are you thinking?"

"These may all be for Gillingham, sir. I heard a rumor that Lucretia . . ."

"All?" said the Butcher. "Are you looking for excuses, Carleton?"

"No. . . . No. But . . ."

"Carry on."

It was Nicky.

Carleton could scarcely hold it steady against the lampshade. He seemed to be coming out of the front door of the Music Building. His head was down. Thoughtful maybe—it was hard to see. Anyhow he didn't know, thank goodness. McIver was cunning as hell. He must have taken it from across the drive, from behind a tree or something. For whom? It was trembling in his hand. He had forgotten what he was doing.

"You seem interested."

"No. No," Carleton said. "I was just surprised."

"Surprised! I've stopped being surprised, Carleton. There are twenty-four snaps there. The Honorable Fitzmaurice appears three times—once in company with Peters."

Steele was a cad, Carleton thought. An absolute stinking, dangerous fool. What was it for? The school? The army?

"But. . . ."

"But what?"

"I mean, they're only photos, sir. Maybe they don't do any harm. It's just . . . silly."

"Silly! I. . . . Have a look at the next one."

Carleton held it up. He was looking at himself. It was a

nightmare. He felt sick and terrified. He was standing crouched at the net. There was a crowd in the background. It was at the tennis match with Gillingham College.

His hand was so wet the negative was sticking to his fingers when he tried to put it down.

"Any ideas about that?" asked the Butcher.

Carleton's voice was quavering.

"No. . . . No, I don't. But . . ."

"But what?"

"But why shouldn't McIver just take photos anyhow, sir? I mean, for memories of school or something. I mean, he *is* crazy about taking photos."

It sounded terrible: like a plea from someone guilty.

The Butcher was putting them back in the box.

"That's possible. But not likely. We'll soon know. I'm having a chat with McIver. And the others. Thanks for coming, Carleton. If you think of anything helpful, I'll be grateful. This isn't a pleasant job. I'm getting it over quickly."

"Yes, sir."

Carleton rose and walked to the door. His knees were wobbly.

"Oh, Carleton!"

"Yes, sir."

"Mrs. Crabtree tells me you're having extra tuition with Ashley."

"What, sir?"

"For hours at a time."

"Oh. . . . That was just once, sir."

"Ah. . . . She said there were no extras down on your fees, and you've passed your leaving exam. She was curious, of course. And worried, too, because she feels that Ashley has been looking overworked."

"Oh, that had nothing to do with school, sir."

The Butcher put his pipe stem into his ear.

"Can you explain that?"

"Um . . . he was helping me to write a story."

"Really?!"

"Yes, sir."

"It must be a long one."

"No. . . . Well, yes, quite."

"I see. Right. Off you go. Oh, send McIver along to me, would you."

"Uh . . . now?"

"Yes. Straight away."

"He's in class, sir."

"No matter. Our Head has laid down that any boy shall be released to me. Good for the others too. Put them on their toes. I want everyone to know I mean business. Any chap who decides to help can see me at once."

"Yes."

He went out into the hall, feeling weak and bewildered, and there was a cry of "Here, watch out!"

Philomena Maguire was looking down on him from a height through her hair, over a silver tray of morning delicacies that she was bringing up to the chaplain.

"Watch where you're going," she said.

"Sorry," he murmured, vaguely wondering how she was able to do so. It was dark as night at the back of the hall past Lady Jane Grey's chest. The rain was streaming down the gray stone of the old buildings, and turning them black. He was going along between the borders, with his gown pulled over his head. Though he was being drenched, he wasn't running. McIver. What would McIver say? Nicky. He was going to see Nicky. Eric Ashley. A long story. Ma Crab had said something. What on earth had Ashley got to do with anything? He passed under the arch of the vine. He felt cold and shivery. Could he be expelled? And Nicky? What for? He went up to the new buildings, through the open door. Four tennis balls had lain here, on a ledge, in an open brown box. He trod softly on the pink flags of the corridor, taking his gown down, off his head, and smoothing his hair. There were murmurs behind each green door. There were cricket and other notices pinned to green baize. A shout behind one door—"No, boy, no!"—Dotty. The fifth form was McIver's. He paused at the door and for a moment thought that he just couldn't enter. Who was taking class? He stood closer, but he couldn't hear. He knocked gently.

"Come in!"

A very testy voice. The Pedant.

Milner had his back to the class, and was writing on the blackboard in his small, very clear hand, "Having conquered the city, he inquired who their leader might be."

Carleton watched him write to the end, hypnotically, while conscious that the whole class had turned in his direction. Conquering, and cities, how completely meaningless it all was.

The Pedant faced him, frowning.

"Well, come on, come on, what is it?"

"Um . . . Dr. Boucher wants to see . . . someone, sir."

"Someone? Someone? Look here, man, do you think I've all the time in the blasted world . . ."

"Um, McIver, sir."

Carleton sensed a kind of gasp from the company, though there was really no sound.

"Very well. Cut along. and hurry back. Your present progress, McIver, is such that you cannot afford to mess about."

McIver went out in front of him, and he closed the door carefully. McIver was looking up at him. He was not making Eddie Cantor eyes. His face had turned white.

"What . . . ?"

"Ssh," Carleton said. "Come away. . . ."

They moved along the corridor.

"He's got your negatives," Carleton whispered.

"Oh, gosh. . . ."

"There's one of me. Who did you take it for?"

"I can't . . ."

"Listen, McIver, you've got us all in a blasted mess. We've got to get ourselves out of it."

"It was . . . Allen."

Carleton was amazed. Bewildered, and then relief, and then fear.

"What are you going to say? What are you going to say?"

McIver was maddeningly pathetic and dumb and sickly behind his glasses.

"I don't know."

He's so small and young, Carleton thought, with sudden compassion, up against that great brute.

"Listen, there's only one thing you *can* say. You must say you took all these photos, because it's your hobby, and you just

266

like taking photos of everyone. Can you do that? Can you do that, McIver?"

"I don't know."

"There's one of him. Of . . . um . . . Allen. Who was that for?"

"Uh . . . Sherriff."

Carleton, in the midst of astonishment, felt a stab of hatred for Sherriff.

"McIver, you've got to say that you just like taking photos of anyone. It's your own skin too. You'll be thrown out. Do you understand?"

"Yes . . . I'll try."

"Try damn hard," Carleton said. "Good luck."

McIver went out into the rain.

There was ten minutes between class and lunch—a warning and then a final tinny bell. It hung from the wall outside the dining hall. Metcalfe liked doing it and was curiously reliable.

Among the mob, emptying into the corridor, Carleton spotted Nicky, who at once put his hand in his pocket.

Everyone was sprinting away, with gowns over their heads. Carleton ran out, under Ashley's window, and along past the bogs and into his house. Gower was in the washroom combing his hair. He hurried through the door into the Big Schoolroom, which was crammed yet curiously quiet. He hesitated and then dashed down the steps and across the Chapel Square, pretending to head for the chapel. The great oaken doors were open, and there was one light on, over the organ, in the midday darkness. The Beatle, who was practicing something, sensed him standing in the antechapel, stopped and called out his name.

Carleton approached this little dark-haired sprite, perched on high on the organ bench.

"We must get cracking, Carleton."

His fringe was almost over his eyeglasses.

"I beg your pardon, sir?"

"I've picked my twelve," the Beatle said. "They've all permission off from rest. First rehearsal in the Music Building after lunch. Silly of me not to have told you, but I was so concerned with getting the others off rest, and you're a prefect so I'd no trouble there."

"That's all right, sir."

"See you then, after lunch."

"Yes, sir."

Carleton moved back to the door. There was a river running down the cement strip to the cloisters and spilling over the top step. He peered out: there was no one in sight, and no one in the Big Schoolroom doorway. He suddenly dashed out and around the end of the chapel, into the long, soaking wet grass. A tall clump of nettles made the buttress difficult to approach, and he thought it safer not to trample them down. His hand was stung as he reached forward and took the paper out of the crack. The ink was running already as he read:

"*Can't* meet at any of the old places. Too dangerous. But I can't *bear* it if we don't. We've *got* to think of somewhere???

"One piece of good news. Has the Beatle told you? He tried me alone in the Music Building after tea last night and I'm to be Alice. We're meant to be in love. Isn't that a laugh!! I could hardly keep my face straight. Anyhow, we'll be together. And I *do* love you. Terribly."

He had to tell. He searched in his wallet and found a letter from his mother which had a blank space at the end. He tore it off. It was almost impossible to write in the rain, but under his gown he managed to say: "The Butcher is seeing you. Photo of you by McIver. Not me. That sod, Sherriff. Of me too—taken for you! Why on earth did you need that? Just say you're a friend of McIver's and you remember him taking it. He's saying the same. *Don't worry. It's easy.* I love you terribly too."

He inserted it in the crack in the buttress. He crumpled up Nicky's note in his pocket, reminding himself that he must get rid of it safely. Yes, Nicky would find it easy. Silly, maybe, to have said it. He'd manage it much better than McIver— or me. Metcalfe was ringing the bell. Edging up to the corner of the chapel, he thought, A laugh? A laugh? Nicky must be crazy. Or crazy brave. There was no one to be seen. Peter and Alice, up on the stage! His mind was all confused. He could not even visualize it. He didn't want to, and he dashed across the square, and then walked slowly down the cloister steps, which were turning into a mild waterfall. He could hear them all pouring into the dining hall, behind the stained-glass windows.

The skivvies were waiting in a black body just outside the

door. And just inside Clinton, the master on duty, was talking quietly with Miss Bull, who stood behind her hotplate with her vast bosom sailing out over it.

The funny thing was, theirs were almost the only voices to be heard. There was something in the air. Everyone knew now. There was an awe, a hush, even a fear; something sinister. They were all waiting to see the Head come in.

Carleton, going up the aisle with his fellow prefects, was looking for Nicky. He caught his eye, and at once put his hand in his right coat pocket. Then next he looked for McIver, who was at the usually rowdy comedians' table, with Metcalfe and company. He was as pale as before, and stood with his eyes fixed on the table. The others standing beside him appeared uneasy. It was agony not to know what had happened.

Thank goodness he was at the end of the high table today, and nowhere near the Head and Ma Crab. Everyone was watching the open door at the end. Carleton found himself studying Steele. He had a German military head, which was going to help him in the army. What was going to happen to Steele when he ceased to be senior prefect? Surely someone was going to order him about . . . tell him to look smart and so on. Though it was difficult not to think of Steele being made an officer in command straight away. Would it hurt when he found himself under orders? Could one hurt Steele? Had Steele got a mother? A home? Did she march about the place, paying no attention to Steele, while Steele marched about contentedly too in the opposite direction? It was the only possible vision.

But what was this? Steele was next to the Head, and there were three empty places beside him, not two. A smaller chair beside the two thrones. And three rolled napkins in silver rings.

There was absolute silence down the hall. Ma Crab had come up the two steps and through the door—head down and hands behind her back—and—yes—she was accompanied. The Butcher walked proudly beside her, with the Head following behind.

Gosh, they were having the cheek, the nerve, to bring him in! Guest of honor. Was he aware of the effect . . . of the horrible atmosphere? He was smiling. He looked delighted with himself. But the Head, behind, was putting on a show; his face decidedly redder, his chin up, and the corners of his mouth pulled right down to show defiance, determination, authority. . . . He held his mortarboard higher against his chest than usual, almost at his neck.

The trio stood together. The Head was saying grace when Carleton spotted something wrong down the hall. There was a master missing from the head of one of the tables. He inspected them all and realized it was Ashley. Why? Had something happened? What had the Butcher meant? What had it to do with him?

Lloyd was serving oxtail soup.

"Oh, no. Oh God no."

Rowles put his tweed elbows down on the problem on his desk, and cupped his hands over his ears. It was a time of mercy . . . almost of bliss . . . when the creatures were silenced by rest.

Now it was ruined.

"I beg of you, my dear fellow. Not this time. No more crusades. No, please."

"You've heard?" Ashley said, closing the door behind him.

The Doctor sighed deeply. "Your absence at lunch was noted."

"I imagine you ate a hearty meal."

Raindrops peppered the small window, making the Doctor feel more thoroughly trapped than usual.

"I asked if you've heard."

"Of course."

"This little jack-in-office who employs a pugilist with a stethoscope to determine sin and dispatch the sinners—who will never forget it, never! It's done with your support, is it?"

Rowles lowered his hands and looked up for the first time. There was something odder than usual about Ashley. He had run his fingers through his hair so vigorously that it stood on end in several places. But there was something even odder than that.

"No," he replied. "Sit down, man, you'll drive me crackers marching around."

Ashley fell into the chair by the fire, and worked at his hair so that it looked even worse.

"No?" Ashley said. "What do you mean 'no'? You've opposed it?"

"Not since you heard me before. It's not in my power to do more. It's extreme, I grant you. He needs quick results. He wants to impress. I don't care for the method, but I think we may have been getting slack. I'm beginning to think so."

"I pity you, Rowles."

"That's kind of you, but I don't require it. No thank you." Rowles put his pipe between his teeth, preparatory to lighting it, and took it out again.

"Have you been drinking, Ashley?"

"It's sometimes necessary, to make hypocrisy endurable."

"I'm afraid you can't do it and be a schoolmaster."

Rowles lit the pipe.

"It's arrant nonsense to tell me you're incapable of any more," said Ashley. "You could have gone to the Board."

"The Headmaster is well supported. And, curiously enough, it is my duty to support him. But I don't expect *you* to understand that."

"Not when duty conflicts with your own honor, no. Never."

"You're beginning to make me extremely angry, Ashley."

"Good. Just tell me what you think. Just tell me. I'd be very interested."

"You don't give an arsehole what I think."

Ashley crossed his legs and tensed his nostrils, and seemed to the Doctor more mad than drunk.

"You believe these are the aberrations of a sickly, shuttered community."

"I believe nothing of the kind. My life is the evidence of that."

"You believe they're aberrations."

"I believe they're childish."

"Juliet was fourteen. Romeo of an age with these people. Can you not conceive of the possibility of present passion and present poetry?"

"Oh, for God's sake, man. Go away and sober up. And don't raise your voice at me, like a good fellow. At any rate, not when talking balderdash."

They looked at each other directly for some moments. The Doctor sighed.

"They must be led, Ashley, in this as in mathematics. They must grow. That's all. They must grow. That is our duty."

"Grow? Grow? But you're still Rowles of the sixth!" shouted Ashley, hitting the arm of his chair.

There was an unpleasant silence.

"You'd better take that back."

"Very well. It was unkind. But. . . ."

"Growing up is your problem, Ashley, not mine. If you go on the way you're going you'll find yourself marrying a young barmaid when you're fifty."

Rowles was shocked by his own words. Ashley sensed it.

"Ah, that's better. I like that. I like a little spite. Against an old friend. At least it's open. No hypocrisy. At least it shows feeling."

"That's true," said Rowles heatedly. "You like all feelings, good or bad. You gave yourself up to the sewer of the emotions some years ago, and you haven't grown out of it. Indeed, it's destroying you."

Each silence was the more painful.

"Will you have a cup of tea?" the Doctor said.

"No. Listen, Rowles, I didn't come here to discuss you or me, but others. . . ."

"I think you *do* care about others, Ashley, I'll grant you that. Even too much. It's one of the most dangerous of all the emotions. It's not only conceit and self-indulgence. It is falsely based. You are apt to suffer more than the so-called victim. Because you cannot possibly experience what the other experiences."

"But I can, I can! I was here, blast you!"

"Perhaps you should not have been. At any rate, you speak for a minuscule minority."

"How can you know that? How can you possibly know that?"

"By observation."

"Pah!" Ashley said. "I know your observation. Evasion is the right word. Just let's get back to what's being done. Let's not evade that. I'll tell you what's being done. Tenderness is being turned into shame. The mystery of another presence is being written out as sin. War is being declared upon imagination. And this villainy, this probably irreparable harm, is being done by a pugilist with a cast-iron ego. And you are permitting it."

The Doctor leaned forward and knocked his pipe out on an ashtray. His hand was shaking a little.

"The capacity to love and dream is being decreed a loathsome thing," Ashley said. "Perhaps for someone's lifetime. And you are permitting it."

"You come of a theatrical family . . ."

"Christ, Rowles, is that all you have to say? Is that all you have to say?"

"I'm afraid so."

"Then damn you!"

Ashley jumped up and moved to the door.

"There is a treasure of infinite worth, Ashley, and it's called detachment."

"Oh no. No, please. Don't make me sick."

"By the way, this damn thing has been lying in the common room for the past three days."

He took the envelope from his pocket and handed it to Ashley, who saw the Italian stamp.

"Find your own garden and cultivate it, man, for God's sake," said Rowles. "And find it soon."

Ashley went out and slammed the door.

Rowles sat unhappily for some minutes. The most unlikely fact was suddenly revealed to him: he was fond of this extraordinary bird. He tried, and could think of no one else, except the Old Man, who was dead, for whom he felt this feeling.

But he had never been given to analyzing others, or himself, much below the surface. And he was soon contentedly at work again on his problem.

Ashley was glad that they were all immured: he was aware that he was not walking steadily, and he banged against one of the lockers in the corridor. He went out into the streaming rain without being aware of it; and along to the new buildings and up to his room, with a dark and alarmingly strong sense of apartness and desolation. He sat on the bed, and saw that the soaking envelope was still in his hand. He opened it and took out a wet, flimsy piece of paper. On it was written, "Dear old friend, It seems strange to me, but my sixth sense tells me that you are not well or that you are in difficulties. Please let me know as soon as possible if I am wrong. Yours very affectionately, Paolo."

He lowered the letter and felt tears mixing with the rain on his cheeks.

"Jolly good," said the Beatle. "That'll come along nicely." Carleton relaxed a little and moved away from the piano, surprised that he had been able to sing at all on this dreadful, unforgettable day.

It was cold in the large end room of the Music Building. It seemed to be all windows, lashed by wind and rain. Only the Beatle's good cheer kept them going. The twelve stood behind him, looking over his shoulder at words and music in his illegible hand. His black hair was thick and long over his coat collar. It was the only reason for his nickname. His music was of another sort: a sort that the school had always loved. A few of Clinton's artists had tried to introduce guitars and modern noises, but nobody cared for it.

Nicky had moved in beside him. Their arms had touched. Nobody knew. McIver was there, looking terrible. Naylor was there too. Without the Beatle it would have been intolerable.

"Now that we're all here," said the Beatle, spinning around on his piano stool and putting his hands up to his mouth, together, as if in prayer. "I'd better sketch out for you what *Peter Piper* is all about. We haven't time for much more today, I'm afraid. Well, let's see. . . . We're at Little Dingley-on-the-Marsh. Rousing opening Chorus—'At Little Dingley-on-the-Marsh, where days are fair, and never harsh. . . .' A village . . . in the Oxford area. Our vicar, the Reverend Arthur Cecil Sinclair—you, Naylor—is a widower with a daughter, Alice— you, Allen—who is engaged to an Oxford undergraduate named Percy Fenwick—you, Caldicott.

"Percy arrives to stay at the vicarage—we have a nice little croquet scene, with real balls—bringing his mother, a widow named Matilda—you, McIver, and a fellow undergraduate, on a scholarship from Canada, called Peter Piper—you, Carleton.

"Peter is a kind of clean, outdoor, healthy specimen—the sort of chap we'd all like to be. Alice gradually falls in love with him. You have this rather lovely thing with Allen, Carleton. Would you like to try it with me? Sorry to put you on the mat again, but you do have the leading role."

Carleton leaned over the Beatle's head, which moved from side to side as the Beatle sang with enthusiasm:

"Come with me—to Canada.
Come and see the magic of a prairie sky.
See the snowflakes fall,
Hear the coyotes call.
Come with me—to Canada.

When you fill your lungs with air—in Canada,
You will feel a millionaire—in Canada.
So let us not delay,
Let us make our way.
Come with me—to Canada,
Today!

"Well done. I'm afraid my writing is abominable. I'm having twelve copies printed. However, Alice doesn't go yet," said the Beatle, spinning around. "Oh dear me, no. We have Percy to worry about. Well, it so happens that in our fête scene . . . rather fun this. . . ." The Beatle swung back and was playing and singing with verve:

"Though it rain,
Though it pour,
Though the lightning flash and thunder roar,
Our English fêtes are fun.
Yes, fun!
An Englishman's fête is fun.

The pram race may not be decorous,

"And so on and so on. As I was saying, it happens that a young lady arrives called the Honorable Priscilla Wainwright—you, Stoddart Major. She has known Percy at Oxford and she means trouble. Well, to cut to the end, she gets her man. And all is happy there.

"But the vicar still thinks it's his daughter, Alice, that Percy loves. And you have this catchy one, Naylor. Come along. Vicar to Percy:

"Feminine society,
Conducive to sobriety,

275

Leads men straight to the al-tar.
So beware,
Take good care,
Choose the one beyond compare,
And never, ne-ver fal-ter.

"Good, good! Again!"
Yes, Naylor was singing well. Nothing was troubling him.
Carleton moved close and whispered to McIver, "What happened?"
"I said what you told me."
"Did he believe you?"
"I don't know."
Carelton glanced at Nicky. "Did you get it?"
(McIver was listening, but it didn't seem to matter now.)
"Yes."
"Has he sent for you?"
"No."
"Splendid!" the Beatle said. "However, our vicar is not so safe himself. Matilda Fenwick, Percy's mother, has this. . . . Where are you, McIver?"
"Here, sir."
"Come along then:

"I'm in love with a clergyman,
Named Arthur Cecil Sinclair.
And my little gray-headed clergyman
Is in love with me, I declare.
If he should ask me to marry him,
I'd be delighted to go.

Arthur Cecil, will you be mine?
Will you be mine? Will you be mine?
Arthur Cecil, will you be mine?
My little gray-headed bo-oy,
My little gray-headed boy.

"Well done. We'll have to powder your hair, Naylor. My wife, by the way, is hard at work on the costumes. The ladies among you will have some really pretty dresses. She'll be asking you to come to the bungalow for fittings. Which reminds me, Allen, you have a reprise on our Canada song. Here we are. You're singing to Carleton, don't forget. . . ."

Nicky's neck was red, and his voice very faint.

"How I'd love to go with you—to Canada.
How I dream of just we two—in Canada.
So let us not delay,
Let us make our way,
Let us go today,
To Canada!"

"That's it. Don't be nervous. It'll come easier as we go along. Da-da-da-dee-dum-da-da-dadadada. . . . Now then, that's all of us, except your chorus. And don't you worry, you've plenty to do. So we have three weddings at the end, before Alice and Peter set sail. We have a wedding reception on the croquet lawn. A marquee. We can use a tent. The vicar is a little sad to see his daughter go so far, but then he's happy with Matilda Fenwick, now Mrs. Sinclair. The three couples embrace. We have our final number. Chorus of guests. I think they'll like this one. They always used to. I think we might have the whole school singing it. Come on!

"We dreamed that we might be together,
And now our dream has come to pass,
We dreamed we'd come through stormy weather,
And here we are, at last.

"All together!" shouted the Beatle, striking the piano hard, with his head tossing.

"Our dream is ending now,
Our life begins with the dawn.
Our day is starting now,
Though the stars linger on.

The happy days that lie ahead,
Are beckoning so clear.
We must be wending now,
Our life is starting anew.
And now it's time to go to bed,
My darling . . . my . . . dear."

"Our couples kiss. Final curtain."

The Beatle turned around more slowly, beaming with satisfaction.

"By the way, you chaps, this is going to be a real treat for our new Head," he said. "He doesn't know our talents. He is in for a big surprise."

"Well, dear children, we have not long to go now," said the chaplain, at his private tea. He smiled, more benignly than wickedly, assuming that the end of term meant freedom from the persecutors to all of them. But added, perversely, "Humphrey is looking forward to Gleneagles."

"Serve him right for eating all the chocolate biscuits."

"Now, now, Robert. Charity. Charity."

It was a full house of Starlings. They entirely covered the carpet. The rain had stopped everything. Farming included. It had even stopped the run, which was normally enforced in all conditions: the Cod had decided that there really was a danger of pneumonia.

The green satin had been pulled by Philomena against the deluge—as it had been against the sun. The chaplain avoided all extremes, except the one Extreme. The fire blazed. Without it, the room would have been dark. As it was, it was dim. An atmosphere that tempted one to confession. They could scarcely see his face.

"What would you say if I were to tell you that this is my last orange?"

They were absolutely silent. It was mildly satisfying.

"How do you mean, sir?"

"I mean, dear Charles, that I shall no longer need protection from the curious scents you bring me from the farm—and otherwise."

They stopped munching.

"I am going to the Hebrides," the chaplain said.

"You mean, for the hol?"

"No, Humphrey, not for the hol, as you so quaintly term it. Forever."

The silence was remarkable. He almost permitted himself the thought that they cared.

"Under the circumstances, a brief period," he added.

Aghast faces were looking up at him from the floor. They did care, though presumably less for him than for their own skins. No more tea. No more flag of NO SURRENDER. No more safety and refuge. They would be at sea, with no shore to swim to; buffeted, without hope of consolation. They would even have no name.

Thinking of this, and feeling sad now, though mildly amused, the chaplain said: "There will be a cuckoo in our nest."

"How do you mean?" a voice appealed anxiously out of the gloom.

"A new chaplain."

There were sounds of surprise and distress.

"And I am afraid we cannot rely on him to provide chocolate cake, my dear Robert."

Having played with their feelings, he found that he had touched his own. He could not rely on a remotely situated home for decaying clergy to provide a circle of dirty boys of infinite charm to be spread about his feet in the afternoons.

Everyone was losing.

No one spoke. The fire flamed. The chaplain gazed down into it.

"But *why*, sir? *Why* are you going?"

They all watched, while he continued to stare at the fire. It was like dusk; like an evening in autumn. The square white head came slowly round; a glint of inky hair, and black eyes.

"Because, my dear Adrian, I am dying."

They had heard that this was something people did. The chaplain gave it a dark resonance. He made it awesome and entirely personal. They might have guessed that he would do it in a different way from everyone else.

"Oh don't alarm yourselves, children," he said, and his smile flashed, and so did his ring. "It is a matter for rejoicing. Humphrey, give everyone some more tea. Come along, you heard me, my dear fellow. And let us all cheer up."

They were unable to make this leap.

"But you seem . . . well."

"They said I would be, Adrian, if they used the knife. I find it amusingly mistaken of them. And I am bold enough to believe that God's view is identical."

It had never been easy to coax them into the flash and flame of conversation. Now they were more mute than ever. He was alone on stage.

"*You* are the subject of proper concern," he said. "We can only trust that you will find another friend in the spirit. With my knowledge of fellow clergy, I can hardly promise that it will be the same. There is an asceticism abroad. . . . But we may hope."

"It'll never be the same."

"No. It won't."

"No. It never will."

"Ssh," he said, raising a hand.

He was touched, perhaps for the first time.

"You are young. You are children. You know nothing of what will be."

"I bet he won't even give us tea."

"No. You bet your life he won't!"

"Ssh, Robert . . . I have one little piece of good news for you. A little surprise. I am altering my end-of-term sermon."

They waited, almost invisible in the gloom. The rain made sudden rushes against the window, as if it wanted to come in and share this sad occasion.

"As you know, at the beginning of term I have always spoken of Our Lord as the burning fire of love," he said. "It puts us on our toes."

"Yes, and at the . . ."

"Allow me, my dear Robert. And at the end I speak . . . it is a time of parting, and of release . . . of feelings, paradoxical ones . . . I speak, more gently, of Christ as the shepherd."

"We know."

"Yes, we know."

"This has been a curious term—to describe it as mildly as I feel compatible with truth. And, in addition, it is a curious time for myself. I am delivering an entirely new sermon!"

There was silence. Normally unaware of any inadequacy in themselves, they knew, each and all of them, that they could not come near appreciating the immensity of this decision.

What happened next was rapid, bewildering, and more than mildly alarming. The chaplain didn't grasp it fully, but the door had opened and his young friend, Beauchamp, was there, looking unrecognizable and shouting in his direction, in a new voice, "You might like to know that the filthy little shits have told me to go—now! And my father's coming and I don't care. I wish I'd never been to this filthy dirty little shit school. And I'll get that dirty bastard later on, you'll see if I don't. I'll come and kick in his dirty little backside. I'll smash his filthy little red face, you'll see. . . ."

Beauchamp's voice had broken and he had evidently gone, because the door had slammed and there were no more sounds.

"Cripes."

They heard a deep breath from the chaplain.

"I think you had better leave, if you don't mind. It's not . . . the best of days. Tomorrow."

They were rising and half-heartedly gathering everything from the floor.

"Run along. Please."

They filtered out, and someone closed the door.

The chaplain watched the fire. He was mildly surprised to find that his mind was empty. At last a thought appeared. He leaned back and pressed the bell by the fireplace. And waited.

There was a knock. Philomena entered. Troubled immediately, she looked down through her hair at the litter on the floor. Near where she stood, Beauchamp had walked on a cup and saucer. She was bending.

"Leave that," the chaplain said. "I want a tossed green salad."

"Righto," said Philomena, and she went quietly out.

As she descended the stairs into the hall and slipped away to the kitchens, she heard Dr. Boucher saying, "Tomorrow then. At the same time. I think that should see us through."

He was putting on a porkpie hat which looked sportive and accorded with his boxing reputation. The Head, watching, felt a vague unease: the hat had a flippancy which did not accord with the dreadful seriousness of what they had just achieved. His wife, who was standing politely in the sitting-room doorway, experienced—such was their present closeness—an identical reaction.

"And may I say, Headmaster, your promptness and decision have all my admiration."

"Not at all, Doctor, it was plain there was no other way of

dealing with this evil. Our thanks go to you. We have now to complete the day, as it were."

"The parents you mean? I don't envy you."

"No, it'll not be an agreeable evening, Doctor. But my wife is an ever present help in time of trouble."

"I've no doubt of it," said the Butcher, instinctively touching his hat toward the doorway. "Well, I'll say good-bye."

The Head went out with him on to the top step, and, scarcely noticing that they stood in a downpour, said: "Do you contemplate that there will be many more?"

Anxiety had crept in, although he had tried to keep it away.

"No, no. There are just a very few cases that still worry me. I want to bring 'em into the ring. Sound 'em out."

"I see."

"Good-bye."

The Butcher sprang away down the stairs with remarkable agility for his age, and seemed to jump into his ancient dusty Vauxhall and drive it off, all in one instant. He left the Head staring blankly out over the lake, the great trees, and the pink roofs of Marston, all sad and subdued under a wet colorless sky. His spirits were very low.

In vain, he scanned the view for a sign of Lucretia, his own alien, incomprehensible daughter. She was late. The poor child was going to be soaked through on her bicycle, even in her heavy uniform.

But Cecilia was waiting within. He turned and walked toward the sitting room, knowing that assurance was there: the certainty that they were doing the right thing for this noble but ailing academy.

Carleton was keeping quiet on the old armchair in the corner, with a plate of burned toast and strawberry jam in his lap.

"It's pretty good going," Rogers said, through mouthfuls. "Four in one day."

He and Pryde were seated at the table, eating voraciously off the rug.

"Serve the bastards right," said Pryde. "Ruddy pansies."

If only one had the courage to say, "What do you mean exactly? Enlarge upon and justify this glib, inhuman thought." Where was his one-time ally? He was there, beyond them, on the ottoman, reading his film book, which seemed to be taking him the entire term. Perhaps he was memorizing it.

Do they know that I am silent—and afraid?

No. Not the second part, thank goodness.

He had never disliked them so much: two brutes hogging toast under a bare light bulb with a filthy white shade. It was on because the gray rain was still falling heavily outside the little window. Rogers' great black glasses like an American lawyer's flashed in the light each time he turned slowly around to throw a piece of sliced bread onto the hotplate of the cooker —or to take it off, too late. And each time he turned, Carleton saw the little snowflakes of dandruff on his collar.

Pryde, on the other hand, had his back to him so that his poxy face could not be seen. Carleton noted that the red boil, or whatever it was, had gone from his neck. He had been in a permanent bad temper ever since Matron's departure and had given up reading the Bible. There seemed to be a controlled ferocity in the movement of his great shoulders, in the bookie's check coat, whenever he speared the jampot with his knife.

"There'll be more tomorrow," said Rogers, settling his glasses with his right hand—which was a kind of nervous tic with him. "He's coming back. Did you see Henderson?"

"Looked as if he'd swallowed a bloody ghost," said Pryde. "Better than Finch Minor, bawling in front of everybody."

You once put cough mixture down his throat, Carleton thought.

"Steele says they've had it a long time coming," Pryde went on. "The Head saw them himself on the first day of term. Good riddance."

Carleton realized what was different: the uproar of the last seniors going to bed, the slamming of the shower door; it was missing. Everyone was chastened.

"Beauchamp was spitting and puking about the place," said Rogers. "That's the one I'm most pleased about. Though why they let Sinnott off the hook I'll never know."

"Steele says the Butcher found nothing on him," said Pryde. "But the Head's had it in for Beauchamp ever since Gillingham and the shambles."

Carleton had finished his toast and was trying to think of an excuse to get out. It was too early for their shower. What was

Johns thinking? Did he know that this conversation was making him feel sick and weak in the stomach?

"I don't know about Peters, but his hair was too bloody long," said Rogers. "That trip to the woods with Fitzmaurice was his little idea—though the Beard was in on it. Steele says the Beard's had a ticking off."

"Is that all?"

"He's a master."

"And what about Fitzmaurice? He's no angel."

"He's an Honorable."

"Yeh. . . . That won't save his backside next time I get the chance."

"Nor me."

There was no sound except the munching of toast and the turning of pages by Johns, who suddenly said: "Aren't you two a little overenjoying this?"

Carleton sat very still, wondering, "Is this some kind of defense of me?"—and then, "Is Johns braver than me—or is he just detached from every blessed thing?"

"What?" said Pryde.

"This rash of expulsions. Aren't you both being a bit sadistic about it? It's giving you kicks, is it?"

"Ah, read your blasted book," said Rogers, settling his glasses agitatedly.

"And mind your own bloody business," said Pryde.

"That was more or less going to be my advice to you," said Johns.

This was the best of Johns for a long time, Carleton thought. It was the person he had once known—before Nicky appeared.

They were quiet, but there was something seething at the table.

"Carleton's not saying much," said Rogers at last. "What's eating your pal, Ashley?"

"How do you mean?" Carleton said faintly.

"He cut both classes this afternoon. Steele went to look for him, and found him in his room, stinking drunk."

"Pissed as a newt," said Pryde, turning his poxy face around.

"I wouldn't know," said Carleton.

"Guilty conscience, I expect," Rogers remarked.

But all at once they seemed curiously uninterested.

"I have a ginger cake," Pryde announced. "Want some?"

"O.K.," said Rogers.

Pryde rose and took down a can from the shelf below the Bible, and placed it on the table, having trouble removing the lid.

His knobbly face was a marvel of facuity as he stared down into the can.

"It's gone," he mumbled stupidly.

Rogers had leaned forward and was peering through his spectacles.

Oh glorious Gower! Carleton was thinking. An enemy had become an ally in this moment of absolute elation. He even wanted to laugh out loud at the glint in Johns' eye as he turned slowly from his book—and somewhere far off was the thought of Roly in the shower, waiting for a proper encumbrance.

"The bastard!" said Pryde, gazing into the empty can. "That bloody little bastard."

CHAPTER TWENTY-FOUR

Next morning the Butcher had to move his car away from the front steps.

A tripod was placed there instead, surmounted by a black cloth.

Percy T. Fothergill—as he signed all his works—had come to take his annual photograph.

When everyone turned up at the start of the break, they found this curious visitor standing there alone, as if it had dropped out of the sky. Old Fothergill was indoors, paying his respects. The sky was good—blue, with fat white clouds. A bit breezy, but bright. Percy T. had notorious luck. He resembled an aged sorcerer, and it was a headmasters' jest that he could arrange his fine days by casting spells.

Under the black gaze of the new arrival, pandemonium raged on the steps.

Dr. Rowles, to whom punctuality was sacred, was already seated on his chair, with his hands over his ears.

This had been for years the Pedant's self-appointed pigeon. His voice was testily snapping out instructions. His bony forefinger stabbed. His frown seemed to express agony: "Not there, Merryman, you blasted idiot! On the table!"

The steps didn't rise sharply enough, even though the boys rose in height. So tables were placed on the wide top step and chairs on the tables. The rougher senior element mounted this shaky edifice by chosen right, their heads as high as the lintel over the hall door. Not having been made prefects, in this way they staked their own claim to superiority. Gentler spirits jostled for position beneath them, spurred on by the Pedant's "Get in there, you people. Don't stand round like the young woman of Rome. We want you in this blasted picture. We have no option."

The prefects stood behind the row of masters' chairs; Steele behind the Head's throne; Carleton behind Rowles, who was seated on the lesser throne used by Ma Crab at lunch. (Ladies were omitted from this memorial.)

"Take your fat head out of our light, Seaton-Scott!"

"Watch it, for Christ's sake, or we've all had it!"

"Ouch, damn you!"

"Clear off, Gower. You stink."

"We want Percy T.!"

"We want Percy T.!"

"We want Percy T.!"

"You people, get down on your arses, we haven't all day," the Pedant shouted at the juniors. They subsided onto the bottom step, under the masters, and the lowest row onto the gravel itself.

Old Mr. Wall came edging his way along behind junior backs, and sat, by right of longevity, beside Rowles. Looking down, Carleton noted with a fascinated distaste that his white hair was curiously streaked with yellow, like tobacco stains.

"Well, he's brought the sun again, Wall."

"What was that, Rowles?"

"Ah, never mind. It's impossible to communicate in this unearthly din."

The chaplain, at his most benign, was seated beside Wall.

He smiled with almost total amusement. Every year he was taken thus, by the place pretending communion and posing for a portrait with no approximation to truth. The smile darkened a little, but with pity for mankind, when the Beatle sat beside him and to the chaplain's near disbelief remarked: "I say, what fun!"

"We want Percy T.!"

"We want Percy T.!"

Ashley moved in beside the Beatle. He felt dazed, distant, and curiously elated. He was unexperienced, and it was only the sudden swoops in which the earth seemed to disappear beneath him that told him it was a hangover. He found himself hypnotized by the black specter on three legs.

"We want Percy T.!"

The truth was, the Head had overdone his attentions to Fothergill—a well-known figure in public-school circles—and when they came out into the hall they found the door blockaded by the backs of the student body, rising up out of sight. Accompanied by the Butcher, they had to retreat, proceed out along the cloisters, up the steps toward the chapel, and around the front of the house.

Until then, everyone, for want of anything else except the tripod, had been looking out onto a magnificent view of Buckinghamshire. The outer world; occupied, so it was said, but as blank as Mars as far as they were concerned. The seniors on the top of the pyramid could even see, miles away beyond the trees, the roofs of Henley and the winding river.

But this remarkable trio turned the corner. The customary cheer for Percy T. broke, and rapidly faded. The Butcher was there.

He took an end seat, and the Head, with mortarboard to his chest, edged between the two rows and assumed the throne.

Percy T. held the stage, gripping his shoulder-length gray hair with both hands to prevent its flying about in the breeze, and running his intent, half-closed eyes up to the highest point of the human pyramid, on which he focused, awestruck, with open mouth, as if this absolute commonplace of his existence were a supreme achievement.

"Bravo," he said, releasing one arm into the air, so that his hair flew about.

"Bravo," several voices instantly responded.

He didn't hear. He leaped forward at the front row, calling out, "Legs crossed, children. Legs crossed, if you please. . . ." Passing down the line, like a huge bird, in a long black all-year coat, tapping them on the knees. His fine head was all nose and chin, surmounting a high wing collar, and a cravat with mother-of-pearl pin.

Back in place, he surveyed them again.

He knew them not, Percy T. He portrayed them as one happy family, and assumed them to be so. Everyone smiled, more or less, from his pictures—as one. School. Strangers saw them as such. You had to have been there to realize that the serried ranks, the compact group, the one smile, seethed with difference, with loves and hates.

It was not his concern; nor had it ever occurred to him. He went about England photgraphing schools and he knew exactly what they were. They were jolly groups. It was very agreeable, paying his calls, though the work was nervously exacting. He had no preference among these cheery places, though there were a few at which he was given a dry sherry before leaving.

Nobody was likely to inform Percy T. that four had been removed from his picture the previous night, being quietly shunted away, in extreme distress, like coffins from a hospital. Their absence was regretted by Carleton. It made the most important photograph ever, not 100 percent complete. It was a pity, too, about Jimmy Rich, though he had him in last year's photo. Otherwise, what a memento!

Nicky had cunningly maneuvered himself to a place on the steps just above, so that he would be looking over his shoulder. He would have this framed. It would hang in his bedroom all his life. It would be the one absolute possession to be saved when the house caught fire.

"There are three handsome fellows up there who won't see my birdie," Percy T. shouted out in a tremendous voice. "They won't see the cuckoo. Could we have you forward a little, please. Make room there. . . ."

There were shouts, catcalls, giggles, whistles, and "Cuckoo! Cuckoo!"

All the same, Carleton thought, it means we're soon leaving. Strange, but it had not struck him before. He had felt that this golden term would last forever. But in a few weeks it was only going to be a memory. All the more reason why they *must* find a way of meeting. True, they would meet afterward. But it had happened here, and here it was especially sweet. Besides, he couldn't wait. Every day without a private meeting would be empty.

"Yes. Yes. But such frowns, my dear people. That will never do. Oh no. Let us see some smiles. That's it. Come along. That's better. Now everyone will watch for the cuckoo. . . ."

What are you doing, you old actor, thought Ashley. You are framing in admiration a portrait of an establishment that can put four children through terror. "You come of a theatrical family," Rowles had said. Had that really any relevance? Players and painted stage took all my love. . . . Now that my ladder's gone, I must lie down where all the ladders start, in the foul rag-and-bone shop of the heart.

It was extraordinary: he was not yet sober.

Striking at Carleton with his gown. Years ago. Years. Does one never know anything at the time of its occurrence?

And now Percy T. moves toward his strange black friend, his life's companion, with a last "All smiling at the birdie. That's the way our mammies and pappies want to see us. They don't want to see us looking down in the dumps, do they? Certainly not. . . ."

And, yes, this is us. This is how it was. This was our two hundred. Cast together by chance, certainly, but deviously united. Masters apart, here we were when thick hair covered our heads and all our eyes were alive. Shoulder to shoulder. In one place. In our life which you cannot know, though every day was vivid beyond remembering. Mind you, there is, if you look carefully, more joy in the junior rows at the bottom. As the pyramid rises, the smile visibly diminishes—while Gower and the chaplain, of course, have their own. But this must merely reflect the childish appeal of Percy T.'s humors. Surely this was us— all of us—when it was simple. And Percy T. is establishing it forever. Yes, the noble head has ducked down and gone quickly in under the black garment, and a hand like a claw is excitedly searching the air for the black bulb. It is discovered. It is held tenderly for a moment. Then the fingers squeeze. In the total silence of the two hundred, there is a sharp click. There you are. That was us; in our spring.

Knowing this, and while Percy T. twice more disappeared, Rowles sat and brooded. It was the same for him always on this occasion: it provoked a slight sadness.

They would soon be going now. Quite an interesting crowd. That was to say, the seniors of the past two years. (In the first two, they scarcely developed.) Carleton—less cynical than of yore, but still complacent; and yet at the same time, curiously naïve. Johns—wry bird, Johns. No flies on *him*. Four or five others. . . .

Still, it was the right age to say good-bye to them, and there would be other crowds. They cropped up at intervals. About eight years ago there was a very good crowd indeed; a chance collection of talented, baffling fellows; extraordinary really. None of them had made a mark; though it was true that one was evidently doing something in the B.B.C.

This was the funny thing. Chaps came back, sometimes up to his room at night for tea and biscuits, and one could sense a disappointment. They found *him* old, limited, unaltering, parochial. . . . They were all profoundly unaware of the fact that *they* had been remarkably curious young birds, filled with unexpectedness, humor, vitality and promise, and were now ordinary, domesticated young men and, by comparison with their former selves, cracking bores.

CHAPTER TWENTY-FIVE

I'm only starting this again because of what Eric Ashley said this morning.

It's silly really, because if it's my memories of school —and that was my idea—there is only one thing worth recording now.

We haven't been alone together.

* * *

The purge is over. There were no more cases, though I think they said something to Sinnott. He's gone very quiet, and very white. Thank goodness, Nicky wasn't questioned, I don't know why.

But the point is, for us, it isn't over. We're scared to meet—by the san, in the gorse, even at Little Hammerton. They're all risky. Nicky said in one note it would kill his mother if anything happened.

We're writing more notes than ever. The natural result, I suppose. And even that is very tricky. It's hard to believe no one's seen me going behind the chapel.

We meet at rehearsals. I can't make up my mind. At one moment it's infinitely better than nothing. At the next it's agony: it makes me yearn all the more, with no way of doing anything.

The parts we play make it all the worse. It's funny—we're not embarrassed any more, I suppose because the Beatle's story is so unreal. Yet, in another way, for us it *is* real.

I don't understand this, but I feel an urgency. I feel there is some deeper reason why we must meet before we break up.

I don't understand that.

But it's why everything, for me, underlines the fact that the term is ending.

I had my last Sunday exeat. They must have thought me awful. I was dying to get back here and see him in chapel.

We had our last match. We were beaten by 5 wickets. I made 16 and Nicky 27. But my average is higher because of that century not out—52. It's my best. My father seemed pleased.

Everyone is doing exams, except those of us who are leaving. They let us read books. It ought to be perfect.

Percy T.'s photos were pinned up on the board, and we wrote down our names. He is looking over my shoulder. In the best one, we're both smiling.

Beside it was a neat little notice by the Pedant asking for all library books to be handed in.

So it goes.

This has nothing to do with Nicky. At least I don't think so. I'm a bit scared.

I suppose it is made very easy for us here. I'm a bit frightened about going out.

Anyhow one must be thankful—and I do thank goodness that I came here. Imagine going to a school, like Lucretia, where you return home very day! Or even—horrors!—a school with girls as well.

He came on me very suddenly, Ashley, I mean. I was standing by the war memorial, looking down into the Quad. I was far off. I was thinking about Nicky, I suppose.

He startled me.

He said, "Any news of the story?"

"No."

"It always takes awhile."

He was staring into my eyes and didn't seem to be concerned with what we were saying. I couldn't make it out. I was uncomfortable.

"Have you been writing?"

"Uh . . . no."

"You must. All the time. If you ever stop you will turn into me. That will be the end of you. I think you'll be all right. The only danger is in your material. You are now in danger of ceasing at eighteen."

"How do you mean?"

"I mean, I know why you're not writing. You're not free. Freedom comes when the relationship is ended. If it ever ends."

I was baffled, but if he meant Nicky, of course it will never end—and of course I'm free.

"You've come through," he said. "I always said you were agile."

I didn't answer.

Then he went on, something like this: "The requirement is alarming. That's to say, there are two requirements. You're not only required to be a writer—which you are. You are also required to have an insight into people that is beyond the ordinary. That's something you have yet to prove. To do it, you will need to have grown out of this."

It was nonsense, I thought, and it was the first time I felt I knew better than him. In fact, I felt I *was* growing—though not out of "this." (Again, I supposed he meant Nicky.)

Then he turned away, very abruptly, and said, "At least keep that diary going," and strode off.

It's odd. Even though he does make me uncomfortable, I have felt closer to him than with any other grown-up.

All the same, I'm not going on with this. There is nothing to say, except that we don't meet.

CHAPTER TWENTY-SIX

He woke in the night. Something wild and strange was happening. A noise. What was it? He had always slept the sleep of the young, and never awoke before the morning bell. The wind was clattering the windows, which Roly insisted on leaving open. But it was not that. It was a bell —but a different one. Deep, mournful, and yet agitated at the same time. It gave an alarm. It called for action. Gosh, yes, it was the chapel bell! This meant fire.

The dorm was stirring in the dark. They were under his command, and in spite of past fire practices he was not sure what he was supposed to do. There were shouts and mutters in the blackness. "Jesus, we're on fire!" from Sinnott. His bare feet were on the cold wood floor. What did one do? Did one dress? The lights all clacked on. Blinding and bleak. Rowles was in the doorway, barking. "Come on! Come on! Up and out, the lot of you. Carleton, get them moving there. Down to the Quad. On the double!" He was in some kind of an old dressing gown. "Do we dress, sir?"

"This is a fire, Carleton, not a circus. Put on your dressing gowns and get out of here. I'll have the arse off anyone who's still here in two minutes. Come on. On the double!"

There was a rattle of lockers and a clatter of slippers on wood, and some of them, still blinded by the unearthly light, banged into the ends of beds. They were dashing out past

Rowles, who stood in the doorway whacking at an occasional behind, and seemingly enjoying himself. Down the stone steps they tangled with the crowd from the other two dormitories, and all broke into the Big Schoolroom in a rush, crashing against the Ping-Pong table and meeting in confusion at the narrow door onto the Chapel Square. Someone was hit and cried out. Others tumbled through the door and fell on the gravel. Everyone from the other houses was pouring into the Quad, shouting with excitement. All the lights had gone on, throwing beams from a distance on the vivid green grass, and making it just possible for them to identify each other. A half moon looked mad behind the chapel. The wind lashed the trees up on the wood. The bell had stopped. When? They hadn't noticed. It had been rung. That was enough.

Steele was roaring down at them. He was standing up by the war memorial with a pocket torch and the roll call in his hands. Rowles was also shouting, "Shut your mouth!" and the Pedant, in a dressing gown to his ankles, "Be quiet, damn you!' Carleton peered about in the dark. Marvelous confusion. Extraordinary sights. De Vere Clinton in a striped kimono. The skivvies giggling in the illuminated cloisters, in floral gowns, with Lloyd, fully dressed, standing amid them, in shame.

Order had won. Steele was shouting down:

"Allen."

"Present."

(Where? Where are you?)

"Andrews."

"Present."

A hand fell on Carleton's shoulder.

"Where are the flames?"

Ashley in profile, breathing tensely through his pointed nose; in his smart suit, with no tie.

"I don't know."

The fingers massaged the bone of his shoulder. Gosh. Why? Were they equals or something? Friends? It was incredible. It stopped. Thank goodness.

"Hamilton Minor."

"Present."

"Hargreaves."

"Present."

The Crabtrees had come blustering into the crowd: all three dressed; and the fire squad—of four seniors and McCaffrey—was with them. Gumboots over their pajamas. A scarlet extinguisher. A drum with reams of hosepipe around it. The Crab calling out, "Where is it, you people?"

"We don't know, sir."

"McIver."

"Present."

"Metcalfe."

"Present."

Carleton saw the enigmatic smile of the chaplain in the light from a lower window: a black, amused figure, removed from them all.

The Crab: "But this is ridiculous, Rowles. Where is the fire?"

"No idea, Headmaster."

"Wallace."

"Present."

"Young."

"Present."

Silence. Only the wind tossing the trees in the moonlight.

"Who rang the bell?" asked the Head.

It was a good question. No one had thought of it except McCaffrey—who was in some kind of overalls. "I ran straight to the chapel, sir. There was no one there. The squad and I have searched the school."

The Head hesitated, and then shouted up the bank, "Come with me, Steele."

He pushed through the crowd, with Rowles shouting. "Make way there!" and joined Steele up on the square. They crossed it together by the light of the torch, and disappeared into the dark doorway of the chapel. Lights went on, illuminating the stained-glass windows. The chaplain smiled more sourly. Everyone watched. They were peculiarly silent now. The wind. The moon. The mystery. The fun was over. Something different was emerging. What did it mean? Was some sinister bell-ringer hiding in the chapel? A hunchback, maybe. Had he been caught?

At last the lights went out, and the two figures and the torch came across the square. The suspense was terrible. They stopped. The Head called out, "There's no sign of anyone."

Ashley was the most keenly aware of what happened next. It was not pleasant. He sensed it even in the first few moments of silence. Then the voices began, from here and there. "It's a hoax." "We've been hoaxed." "Lousy joke." "Rotten trick." They had had many lessons in corporate pride. Now they were hurt. Someone had spat on the team spirit. They were angry and vengeful. No, they had not tumbled, and run, and shouted with excitement. That was forgotten. There was merely indignity—and revenge. "We'll get him." "Let's get him." "Let's crucify him." Rowles, who did not like it, but was not so disgusted as Ashley, was again roaring for silence; and so was the Pedant.

They realized that the Head was addressing them from on high. He had his hands up in the air. He was evidently incensed.

"It is two o'clock in the morning. It is a cold night. Some of you may well be ill as a result of this outrage. We will not let it rest. We will punish whoever is responsible for this wicked, stupid act!"

There was a mild cheer. Never had he been anything like as popular as now.

"It's you who have been tricked. And I'm asking you to help us find the culprit. Anyone who heard anything before the bell went, anyone who has any ideas at all, should come forward tomorrow. Do you understand?"

"Yes, sir!"

"Very well. Go quietly to your beds now, and try and get some sleep."

Ashley woke at six. A faint light through the curtains. There was something different. There was no terror, and no dread.

Still drowsy, he lay looking at the ceiling, and feeling this lightness, and wondering why. He had put himself to sleep with whisky, which should have made awakening even more dreadful. But no. It had fallen away from him.

Suddenly, he remembered. Another being existed in the world.

That was it. The world was made more gracious by the mere existence of Carleton. What was his first name? Life was sweetened. Angst was gone. The terror was displaced by poetry. Living was entirely different.

How strange that someone's mere existence—even without meeting—should work this magic!

Light in heart, he threw back the bedclothes and crossed the room in bare feet and pulled the curtains aside. There was a hazy sun just above the wood. The wind had gone. It was very still. It was going to be a hot day.

He went back to bed, and lay there with his hands behind his head.

But they *had* met. And they would meet. Within the walls of this dominant, indestructible place.

Yes, it was not to be evaded: there was now a quite new burden; better than emptiness and fear, but agonizing too.

He had been astonished by his own spontaneity, in placing his hand on that shoulder; and, finding it there, had dared more, out of love. Had it been received? It had certainly not been rejected. But had it been received? Surely, yes. The young man was no childish innocent, thank God.

And if so. . . .

All at once, the magic was a mockery. The other's mere existence had set up a hollow in his heart. There was no more solitude, but there was a need instead; and it was absolutely hopeless. Not only that, but he was revealed, finally and forever. His own nature abolished hope. He detested himself. He closed his eyes and longed, and tried not to long, and knew that the trying and the longing were both hopeless.

The room lightened without his awareness. The sun rose, and an hour later, after the rude and insistent clanging of the usual bell, found one person in the whole school still profoundly asleep. What was wrong with Gower?

Gower's face was positively yellow with Oriental dirt and mystery. The slanted eyes opened and closed again. The blue and white pajamas of thick material had somehow missed the weekly laundry. They were like old sacking in Carleton's fingers, as he shook him by the shoulder, shouting, "Wake *up*, Gower!" supported similarly by a chorus standing around the bed, like medical students reckless of the victim. Until at last the patient woke, saying, "What's wrong?"

"I'll give you two minutes to get in the shower," said Carleton, remembering Roly in the night.

"That's not fair," said Gower, in his whine.

"Up!" said Carleton. "Out!"

It was bad luck: Rogers, almost blind without his glasses, characterless without the dandruff, was in there behind the sliding door, and he was one of those who relished the icy downpour, and even turned red and warm under it. Three or four others were also lingerers, out of choice. Gower had no choice. He had to edge up to one of the douches, his arms across his shivering chest, the truncheon slightly diminished by the arctic conditions. And Rogers shouted against the thunder and splash of the showers, "Overslept, Gower? A bit late, aren't you?"

The jet hit Gower's face, taking away his breath and speech. Someone had slammed in, shouting, "Wonder why Gower's so tired this morning."

"How do you mean?" from Rogers.

"Carleton had to shake him out of bed."

They were calling out to each other, in the midst of the flood.

"Funny. Gower sleeps next to the door."

"Yeh. That's right."

"Gower could easily have got out."

"Yeh. While we were asleep."

"And," said Rogers, "Gower's just the sort of little shit who'd do it."

They were getting loud and excited.

"What do you mean?" Gower whined, stepping out of the torture, and rubbing his eyes. "I was there when Dr. Rowles told us all to get up."

"Who knows that, Gower?"

"Yes. We don't know that, do we, Gower?"

"It was very easy to slip into the crowd in the Quad."

"Yes. Wasn't it, Gower? Nobody was noticing."

"I was in the dorm. Everyone there saw me," Gower whined.

"Nobody remembers that, Gower."

He had backed to the sliding door and was trying to pull it, in confusion and alarm.

"You're all crazy."

That did it.

"Listen to me, Gower," Rogers was shouting in his face. "You'd better come and see me first thing after breakfast."

And first thing after breakfast the four prefects were discussing it in the common room.

"Roly thinks it's definitely in the cards," said Rogers excitedly. "It's in character. And he can't remember whether he was there in bed or not."

"Of course he wasn't," said Pryde. "We've got him this time. We've got him at last. Oh boy!"

"If he did do it," said Johns, who was flat on the ottoman, reading a new film book all about Eisenstein, "he deserves a medal."

"I'm getting bloody sick of you and your ideas, do you know that?" said Rogers, feverishly fingering his glasses. "They make me sick."

"Too bad," said Johns, reading.

"He only does it to annoy," said Pryde. "It's best not to listen."

Carleton, who had feared a fight, was in two minds. Johns had said it because he thought the place "a prison." It was not. All the same, it was true that they had enjoyed themselves. What had Gower done that was so terribly wrong? It had taken nerve, imagination, maybe even humor. . . .

There was a gentle knock, and Gower came in, faintly smiling: taunting, and fear too.

"Ah," said Rogers, "shut the door, would you. Now then, Gower, I'm afraid the game is up. You've had it this time. It's all over—you little sod!"

"What game?" asked Gower, looking at all four of them, and overacting innocence.

"You rang that bell last night, Gower," said Pryde, who had gone very red and poxy. "And I'll tell you why. Because you're mad, Gower. You're cuckoo. You should be locked up!"

"Me? I *never*. . . ."

"Cut that out, Gower!" Rogers shouted. "Admit it and let's have done with it. You're not getting out of here until you do."

"But I didn't. Carelton knows I didn't."

Carleton heard the whining appeal and saw the sly look. Gower and the note. Was this blackmail?

"And how do I know that?"

"Because you got us up. You and Dr. Rowles. Don't you remember?"

"No, I don't. Were you really there, Gower?"

"Of course he wasn't," said Rogers. "Listen, Gower, you

299

stupid little swine, don't you realize that by not admitting this and all the other things, you're only making matters worse for yourself?"

"What other things?" asked Gower.

"Your filthy thefts," roared Pryde. "Your stealing from us here, and from the lockers. You should be flayed alive."

"My pocketknife, Gower," said Rogers. "Where is my pocketknife?"

"And what about my chocolate cake?" shouted Pryde.

Gower smiled. "I don't know what you're talking about," he said.

It was flawlessly done. Carleton thought he had better exert control.

"Gower, did you or did you not ring that bell?"

"I didn't," said Gower. "Honest, Carleton. I've never heard of such an idea."

"Oh yes, you did," said Rogers, hitting the rug on the table.

"You'd better prove it," murmured Johns, and Gower smiled again.

"We don't have to," said Pryde. "Gower is going to admit it, or bleed."

"But you can't. . . . I haven't. . . ."

It was true. Carleton interrupted.

"You may go for the present, Gower. But you'll hear more of this."

"What the deuce?" said Rogers.

"We'll collect the proof," said Carleton. "Someone must have heard him. Hop it, Gower."

"Thanks awfully," said Gower, opening the door.

"You're crazy," said Pryde.

"No, I'm not," said Carleton.

It was the first time he had controlled them, as head.

Gower went out. He left them to quarrel. But they had insulted him. It was an injustice. He was bitter. He would hit back. He had scanned the room and seen little. But there was another possibility. During the break maybe. Pity it had to be Carleton.

There were these awful stupid exams. Two papers before the break. He made ink blotches on both. One of them, set by Ashley, was last year's, though Gower did not perceive it.

During the break, conditions were good. They were playing Cloister Cricket, and a number of people were rushing about in the Quad after the tennis ball that came flying through the arches. Up on the Chapel Square, McCaffrey was drilling juniors in detested P.T.: they were jumping up and down and waving their arms. They were sweating too: it was now a broiling summer morning. In short, there was noise and confusion, and no one saw him go up in the long grass; no one except Lucretia. Her school term had ended. She was brooding over her rabbit hutches higher up in the wood.

He edged around the corner of the chapel, and so toward the buttress. Oh, yes, he knew! He had seen. He had seen for weeks. Keeping a watching brief on the entire demesne, Gower had seen everything possible outdoors.

What luck! A piece of paper sticking out above the nettles. Was it any good? Yes, it was first-rate. It was not in the previous writing, so it must be Carleton's: "Surely behind the san would be all right now? There are so few days left. What can possibly go wrong? *Please.* I *must* see you before we break up. You say when, and I'll be there."

These activities were incomprehensible to Gower, but one could tell that it was good copy. Slyly, he went farther up through the trees, and then crosswise in the direction of Lucretia, on whose face he saw, to his satisfaction, a look of unaccustomed bemusement.

"What's that?" she called out.

But he turned his back and descended toward the square, where the gymnasts were still jumping up and down. Allen was standing there pretending to watch them, getting ready to nip around behind the chapel. Oh, yes, very satisfactory. He skirted the lower dormitory windows and went in past the washroom and up the stairs. No reason why he shouldn't be visiting the upper dorm. He looked into it: vast and empty. He nerved himself and ventured all for the second time: he knelt at Roly's keyhole. No one there. The handle turned softly. He was in. It was done.

A shout from the bottom of the stairs: "Lower your voices, damn you!"

Roly was coming up.

He hurried into the dorm and was quickly behind a locker.

It wasn't his own, which would be hard to explain. But it was all right. Rowles had gone into his room.

Swift results indeed!

But more was to come. There was the sound of Roly's door flying open, and a shout down the stairs: "Come up here, one of you!"

Gower's pulses were actually putting on speed.

"Ah, you! Find Gower for me, will you! I want him, and I want him now!"

"Yes, sir."

The door slammed.

Gower's heart had jumped into his mouth. This was not what he had anticipated.

But there was no future in being undiscoverable. He tiptoed over the bare wood, down the stairs and into the Big School-room, where all was uproar: and at once that beastly Metcalfe shouted, "You're wanted, Gower! Roly's on the warpath. You're for it."

"Oh," Gower whined. And he went upstairs and knocked on the door.

"Come in!"

Rowles was holding the note. The sun blazed through the window. It was all happening with horrible speed and naked-ness.

Rowles was boiling.

"Thank you for this," he said.

"How do you mean, sir?"

"Cut that out, Gower! It's high time for plainness. I've had enough. Where did you get this?"

"Um. . . ."

"Answer me!"

"Behind the chapel, sir."

"Well, I don't in fact thank you for it. But it gives us an opportunity to clear things up."

"What things, sir?"

Rowles had cultivated the rare gift of cooling from white heat. He took up the pipe and the pouch.

"I'm afraid the game's up, old man."

"What game, sir? I don't know any game, sir."

"I'm afraid you do. You've been stealing from my prefects,

302

and my chaps, all term. I've been foolishly lenient. But I've done now."

"Stealing, sir? Stealing what?"

"I'll grant you may just be loopy enough not to know it. But it's immaterial. I'm no longer concerned with proof. I'm afraid you'll have to go, old chap."

"Go, sir?"

"Yes. I'm writing your father. You needn't worry. I'll explain, so that you'll have no trouble. You're not well, my dear fellow, you see. You need attention."

"I don't know what you mean, sir."

"Ah, don't, Gower, don't."

The Doctor sighed. Gower looked ashen, as well as dirty.

"Since it won't make any difference one way or the other, you may as well tell me. Did you ring that bell?"

"Me? No, sir."

"God knows whether that's true or not."

He sighed again and turned to the note.

"This you certainly do know about, and I don't know what you think you're doing to these wretched people. The curious thing is you could have done much more harm in handing them elsewhere; and I can't decide whether this is some vestige of generosity in you or mere stupidity."

"But I don't even know what it is, sir."

"Ah, cut that out! I've done now. You understand the position. I'm sorry, but that's it. Would you send Carleton to me, please. Straight away. Run along now."

"But, sir. . . ."

"Get out! Hop it! Off with you!"

Gower went wanly out. He was not smiling.

The Doctor put his head in his hands. The blasted sun was back. He felt drowsy. A knock on the door brought him alive.

"Come in, Carleton!"

"Sorry to disappoint you."

Ashley entered. He shut the door and stood there, brooding and tense, and running a finger through his hair.

"Oh God," said Rowles, putting his hands over his head.

"You may be able to give me some advice—even help."

Rowles, embarrassed, scratched his forehead with a delicate thumbnail. "This is a school, Ashley. Not a sanatorium."

"That's it. Tell me more about that. These schools of yours. These public schools of yours."

"Mine?"

"Yes, one-sexed and presided over by benighted bachelor Old Boys. What is their purpose? What are they producing? Homosexually experienced persons who believe themselves superior, but are, in fact, pitifully limited. You really can't. . . ."

"Stop it, man!" Rowles banged the back of his fat pipe on a cigarette box on the desk. "You make the mistake, Ashley, of thinking you are representative. You represent nothing except yourself. I did my best with you. It was no use."

"There are thousands like me."

"There is no one like you, Ashley," said Rowles, calming himself again. "In my opinion"—he blew a cloud out into the sunshine—"you are a quite extraordinary bird."

"Yes, indeed!" said Ashley, excitedly. "Yes, indeed! Because you're at the heart of the system, Rowles. You need all involved to be extraordinary. You need it. You don't give a damn whether they're benighted or not. Misery doesn't interest you. Eccentricity is all. Staff and school must be as dotty as possible for your entertainment—no, even so that the blood should continue to flow in your veins. Two people who weren't benightedly, interestingly, lost, were dispatched. There was no place for Rich and Matron here. You said so yourself. There is no place for any simple man here. And certainly for no woman—because they are anathema to you. This is a public school. It is all wrong. And you are in it—up to the neck!"

Rowles puffed his pipe. His hand trembled a little. But otherwise he had gained calm. "Ashley, this is a place where people learn to behave with decency toward each other, and where they receive an absolutely first-class education—probably the best in the world. Far from being all wrong, it is ninety-nine percent right. If extraordinary birds like you choose to come here and misbehave, it is not my fault. It is not the system's fault. I should have got you out and kept you out. That is my failure."

"Rowles, I really believe you're as blind as you seem. Can you not see that I am a relative of everyone in this factory—including yourself?"

"I certainly can not. You are Ashley, and always were. We are not concerned with sausages."

"People, people, people! And, by God, Rowles, you bear responsibility. For me, for Dotterel, Clinton, Starr, and for all the superior children who walk out with undeveloped hearts and souls. . . ."

"Oh dry up, Ashley!" Rowles was flushed. His voice was raised. "And leave Forster out of it. I'm sick of your interminable complaints. Your indulgence in your own little self has reached a nauseating—'

"I know!"

Rowles raised his pale blue eyes and studied this very curious bird. "What's that?"

"I know it has. Help me."

"What did you say?"

"Help me."

"Ah, help yourself, man!"

Rowles put his head in his hands again, and the pipe nearly burned the top of his right ear.

There was a knock.

"Come in!"

Carleton was surprised to find Ashley there, looking so odd. Something had been happening.

"You wanted me, sir?"

"Yes. Stay, Ashley. You may be able to advise," said the Doctor in a funny voice.

He picked up the piece of paper and threw it along the desk toward Carleton.

He felt sick and stupid as he saw his writing, and couldn't even think of Gower.

Ashley put a finger on it and drew it across and looked down on it.

In the silence, even though it was the worst moment of his life, Carleton felt himself struck with the extraneous thought that it was the first time the three of them had been in one room together.

"When I saw you at Glen Court, Carleton," the Doctor said, "and accepted you for my House, I had no idea you were a person who would go in for all this muck."

"This isn't muck," Ashley said. "This is public-school life."

"That's right," said Carleton loudly, desperation having given him courage. A sense of injustice at his fate was making him react to Rowles in a quite new way. "That's right. And Glen Court is right too. At that time I was being courted *night and day* by a master called Mr. Brownlow. Prep schools are just the same!"

The Doctor dropped his mouth open.

Ashley gave a kind of laugh.

"Ah, stop your complaints!" Rowles said, meaning them both.

"I'm not complaining," Carleton said. "I'm glad."

Everyone was astonished.

"Have you looked at Mr. Ashley lately?" said Rowles.

Carleton looked and replied, "I'm not him."

"Show me that thing." Rowles groped for the note. "You're glad of this?"

"Yes."

Rowles read it. Carleton watched, and felt his confidence ebbing.

"Frankly, Carleton," the Doctor said, "it is inconceivable to me that it matters a damn in hell whether you meet this creature or not. You don't realize it now, but this is merely childish emotion—skin deep. It is of no interest whatever to adult people, and of no real seriousness." He looked up. "Candidly, Carleton, that's how it strikes me."

"But you're not me," Carleton said.

"Answer that," said Ashley.

The bell began ringing.

"I don't have to answer either of you," said Rowles, who was now very angry. "I have an exam to take." He stood up and went to collect his gown, which was hanging in a corner. "Put that in the waste paper. It's all it is. Remember this, Carleton —allow the emotions to rule you, and you turn into diseased rubbish."

"You wouldn't have your Shakespeare to read without them."

It was extremely impertinent, and Rowles looked as if he might hit him. "You stay here and explain it to him, Ashley. God knows, you're well equipped. Do one thing of value in your misbegotten life." He hoisted the gown around his shoulders. It fell to his ankles. "Oh," he said, remembering something and putting a hand in his pocket, "I read this one. It's been there a week."

He stepped out and banged the door behind him.

The postcard to Ashley said: "Wedding next month. Counting on you. How are you, you old so-and-so? Will discuss further on last night of term. We're coming up to embarrass the shellfish. The new job is great and pays double. You should try it. Marriage too. Be seeing you. Love, Jimmy and Nancy."

He threw it away on the desk.

They faced each other. Carleton didn't know what to do. Ashley was looking at him in a different way. Admiration? Yes—and tenderly too. It made him nearly as uncomfortable as the more usual sneer.

"There's a slight truth in what he says," he said. "But I shouldn't worry. You're leaving. That's the end of it."

"It isn't."

"What?"

"It isn't. He's coming to Oxford. We'll go on the same."

Ashley made a mad noise, a kind of laugh. His old expression was back.

"The same? My dear fellow. You poor creature, you haven't an idea what you're talking about."

"Yes, I have."

Ashley picked up the note and threw it in the waste-paper basket. He perched himself on the end of the desk with his legs dangling.

"You haven't the faintest idea what the world's like outside here. Not the faintest. Have you considered it for a single moment? Do you know what you'd have to endure every single day of your life from other people—spoken and unspoken?"

Things seemed easier suddenly: almost a conversation between friends. Carleton said: "I suppose I haven't really had to think about it. But let them if they want. It'd be a thousand times worth it!"

Ashley actually smiled—like he used to do, though maybe more sadly.

"Would it?" he said. "Would it? Dear friend, you've no notion what you're saying. Condemnation by majority decision. Living a prison offense. . . . You cannot conceive how these things would eat into you."

"They seem to eat into you," Carleton said, knowing his daring. "But we're different."

Ashley didn't appear to be angry.

Carleton went on, "*You* seem to think and worry a terrible lot."

Ashley smiled. It was very strange.

"Damn your impertinence," he said quietly. "Every single day it would occupy and trouble a part of your mind. Every day. Writing would certainly be your only hope—at least you have that. I wish I did. Must you meet?"

"Um . . . oh . . . yes. Yes."

Ashley looked down at his brown handmade shoes as he swung them above the carpet.

"I thought of going for a long walk this afternoon. Here you are. This is the key of my room. Lock the door. If anyone knocks, don't answer. If they send the police, there's always a way into the dispensary."

"But. . . ."

"Take it."

Carleton took it.

"But . . . this . . . it's mad."

"No, it's not."

"But why? Why would you risk . . . ?"

"Because I detest them, and their beliefs," said Ashley quietly. "Because I understand your need. Because you have changed and grown, or else I was blind before. Because you have beautiful ears. . . ."

"Oh . . . gosh . . . no."

Ashley laughed.

"And because you make me laugh. And ten minutes ago I came here in despair."

Carelton had turned white.

"Take this back," he said faintly.

"Don't be a fool. If you arrive and leave separately, nobody can possibly know. I'm sorry about the ears. I won't do that again. Don't you want to meet?"

"Yes. . . . Yes. . . . But I don't know if he'll do it."

"Of course he will. Ask him. If he won't, he won't. I'll be out all afternoon. Go away now."

Carelton hesitated. What had this man said?

But they might meet.

As against this, what did it matter what had been spoken? "O.K.," he said. "Thanks."

He went out.

Ashley remained seated on the Doctor's desk. Amazing: the company of another brought happiness out of the air. The greatest trick of all.

It had disappeared with equal magic. Almost instantly there was loss and longing.

But wait . . . had Master Carleton really been so shocked, so revolted, or even so surprised? Hope is strong. Ashley thought not.

CHAPTER TWENTY-SEVEN

He was beside the Head at lunch—for the last time. Though this was normally the source of dull dread all morning, today it was not; simply because of that "last time." It was a little sad. Still, when Carleton came to take his place he was thinking of something else.

The Beatle had managed to fit in the twenty minutes before lunch, in helping them put the final polish on their "Canada" song. And Nicky had whispered, "There was nothing there."

"I know. It's all right. Eric Ashley has lent me the key to his room. He's out for the day. I'll be there at four. Come at ten past. It's dead safe. No one could guess."

"You're crazy."

"No."

"But why?"

"He's on our side. I'll explain. Will you do it? Please."

"Um . . . all right."

Thinking of this in expectation, delight and alarm, Carleton hadn't noticed that the Head was talking to them all, even before Lloyd had served the soup. The prefects were leaning forward around the silver cups and trying to hear against the din down the hall. On the other side of the Head, Ma Crab was looking at the ceiling with a nasty smile of satisfaction.

"Yes," said the Head, "I'm glad to say the culprit—or culprits, as it happens—have been detected."

They waited tensely. No one dared ask bluntly who. Instead, Steele said, around a silver cup, "How, sir?"

"They came from outside. They are no longer one of us. Which to my mind makes it even more offensive to the school. When old Gregory heard the bell ring he came out of the Gate Lodge and walked up the drive, looking for the fire. He found something else." The Crab pulled down the corners of his mouth.

"What, sir?" from Steele.

"His torch fell on two bicycles propped against a tree. He was shrewd enough to hide them in the farmyard and he himself hid behind the wall. Shortly, two youths came running down. They found their bicycles gone, searched for a while, and then became afraid, and vanished down the drive."

"Did he know them, sir?" asked Pryde.

"Yes."

The tension was terrific.

"Who?" said Steele.

"Bond and Tyson," said the Crab, tightening his lips.

The high table was silent.

"I've telephoned Bond," the Crab added. "They're both returning for their bicycles on the quarter-to-four bus. It will be their last visit, you may be sure of that."

Everyone was wondering at this strange news. Everyone except the Crabtrees knew Bond and Tyson. They had only left at the end of the previous term. They had been Starlings. They had been despised. They had been no good at work and no good at games. They did not wash. They kept a jackdaw and other filthy creatures up in the wood. They had lived their own lives, and never joined in. Never.

Some of them were whispering. Not Carleton. He was merely feeling sorry toward Gower, in spite of Gower's vengeance on himself. But others were roused. The unspeakable indignity was now changed to something even worse: a deliberate act of mockery and revenge by two ex-Starlings.

Finally, Steele said, "Sir, we do feel that these people should be told what we think of them."

"Well, Steele," replied the Head, "I can only repeat to you what I have just said to the staff in the common room. It is the school that has been outraged, and if the school sees fit to pull together in this matter, it is no concern of ours."

"I see, sir."

Ma Crab spoke, dropping her eyes down to the tablecloth. "The Headmaster has, in fact, advised the staff to remain indoors," she said.

"That is so," the Head agreed.

"Oh boy," said Pryde, rubbing his hands, "I can hardly wait."

"Yeh," said Rogers, "this is going to be good."

"Pity about Gower, though, wasn't it?" said Johns.

"Oh, we don't care a fig about that now," said Pryde. "We've got bigger fish to fry."

They were in the common room after rest. The news had spread fast, and nobody had rested much; agog for the return of Bond and Tyson. Some juniors didn't understand, and the Starlings only with alarm; but in general the wrath of the seniors had infected everyone.

"But what's the idea?" Carleton asked. "What's to be done?"

"Steele is working it out," Rogers replied. "We're to meet later."

"I'm not," said Johns. "I can tell you that."

"You wouldn't!" said Pryde.

"I don't think I will either," Carleton ventured. "I don't see any point in making a business of this."

"You'll have to," said Rogers. "You're second prefect."

"Yeh, you'll have to be with us," said Pryde.

"Balls," Johns declared.

"But I don't understand what you're so worked up about," said Carleton.

"Oh come off it!" said Rogers. "You know what the sods did."

"That's it," said Pryde. "Oh boy, this is going to be good. I always hated that brave pair."

"That is surely not relevant," said Johns.

*   *   *

The others who had to do the two afternoon end-of-term exams were perhaps not as well concentrated as they might have been.

After that, many juniors were occupied in cricket, which was all to the good. And the prefects had gone about ordering everyone else except the privileged few to stay away from the farmyard, where a surprise was planned.

Shortly before the time of arrival, a select group of about a dozen was hurrying down the main drive.

Carleton walked reluctantly in the rear, irritated by the company of Sinnott, who kept on talking about "kicking them up the arse." The square military head of Steele marched on in front. The checked coat of Pryde and the dandruffed shoulders of Rogers were close beside him. Carleton had thought it advisable to be seen before slipping away to Ashley's room. In other circumstances he might have risked their animosity and opted out.

It was a glorious afternoon. The junior cricketers were already out on the field down below. Senior cricket had waned, as there were no more matches. Yes, the last match was over.

It was far too nice a day, Carleton thought, for the grim arrangements of Steele and his associates. But he was really thinking about Nicky.

A stony lane led off the drive, alongside the high stucco wall of the farm—and ultimately up to the hills of gorse. A wooden gate interrupted the wall. Steele opened it, and the party followed him into the farm. Two inquisitive pigs appeared, and he shooed them away.

The dozen were now standing behind an old stone wall—about chest high—which looked onto the drive. Across on the other side, the two muddy bicycles had been propped against a tree. Over the wall they could see the line of splendid trees running all the way down to the main gate and Gregory's lodge.

"As soon as we hear the bus I want everybody to duck down," said Steele.

"Yeh, that's right," said Pryde. "Everybody must get down."

"Nobody must be seen," said Rogers.

They were very excited, and unpleasantly so. That oaf Merryman, Carleton thought, was the only one who looked a bit uncertain.

They all watched the cars rushing continually past the open gates. No bus. They were quiet. Hearts were beating faster. Carleton watched Rogers fiddling with his glasses like a lunatic. They seemed to be waiting, waiting. . . . Steele kept looking at his watch. It was just a quarter to four.

Suddenly, the top of a green single-decker bus appeared, moving slowly along, just above the wall.

"This is it," said Steele solemnly from his place in the front-line trench.

Mesmerized, they watched it move. Then the whole bus appeared between the gate pillars. They waited the necessary moment to see the two figures step out. Yes, it was them! "Down, everyone!" said Steele, and they all went down.

The general in command, after a moment, raised his eyes just above the wall. So did Pryde and Rogers. So, briefly, did Carleton. It was Bond and Tyson all right! Old Boys, it was true, but looking just the same, and maybe even dirtier. Bond was short and round, with fairish hair, flabby cheeks and a blubbery mouth. Tyson was stringy, with a bony pale face and black hair slicked back with hair oil and sticking out in spikes on his neck. They wore the same brown coats and gray flannels that everyone remembered, with additional stains. They were walking very slowly and appeared apprehensive. But suddenly Tyson pointed. They had seen the bicycles. They hurried forward.

Obviously, they must have wondered why no one was about. But now they were at ease, and as they came up to the bicycles, Tyson was smiling. They took hold of these old familiars and were about to mount them when Steele, standing erect, said: "Good afternoon."

Bond and Tyson turned and saw the line of faces above the wall. They took some time to react: long enough for Steele to step quickly out of the yard and onto the drive, followed by his party.

Bond looked aghast. But Tyson smiled a sly, peculiar smile.

"Welcome back," said Pryde.

"Thank you," said Tyson.

"Cut that out!" Steele shouted.

Tyson gazed back at him, pale and surprised. Bond looked at Tyson, who eventually met his look and said, "Come on," attempting to mount his bicycle.

"Oh no, you don't," Steele said, moving forward. "We want you on foot. And there are twelve of us."

Tyson paused and evidently assented, because he began to turn his bicycle around to go down the drive.

"No, not that way," Rogers said. "The other way."

Before Bond and Tyson had taken this in, several of them had rushed forward and grabbed the handlebars of the two bicycles.

"Here, what are you doing?" said Bond, as he and Tyson tried to hold on.

"Shut up, Bond, you little rat!"

"Clear off," shouted someone, pushing at Tyson.

"All right, all right!" said Steele. "Let go. Let them do the work. They've got the message."

The bicycles were released.

"All right, Tyson, quick march!" said Pryde. "Up to the school."

Tyson waited and sized them up, and was persuaded. He began to walk with his bicycle. Bond, obviously frightened now, followed. The group walked on either side of them.

"What about ringing the bell tonight, eh?"

"Yeh, good idea. Hell of a joke!"

"Yeh, get everyone out of bed."

"Damn funny."

"You dirty sods!"

The parade moved slowly. Carleton lingered behind. It was pointless. It was nasty. He was doing nothing to stop it. What could he do?

"What's the idea, Steele?" said Tyson. "You can't touch us. We're not school kids, you know."

"We'll see about that," said Steele.

"Yeh. Shut your mouth, Tyson."

"They thought they'd get away with it, fellows."

"Yeh, that's what you thought, Bond, you fat little runt."

They were coming up in front of the Head's House. Tyson glanced upward, as if for assistance. Ma Crab and Lucretia, who were unknown to him, were seated in a window. They didn't look helpful. Suddenly, he pulled out a scout knife from his hip, looking fierce and afraid. Some of them gasped and

backed away, but it was in his left hand, and there was a rush
from behind, and he was trying to hold onto the bicycle as
well, and it was being pulled at and kicked, and Pryde had him
by the wrist. His arm was bent up behind his back. His head
fell forward, showing his spiky hairs. Pryde was terribly strong.
The knife was wrenched from him. They were incensed. He
stood there, white and breathless, as someone hit him in the
face. Sinnott, who was in the rear, rushed at Bond and kicked
him fiercely, and Bond cried out. Pryde shoved the knife into
Tyson's face.

"All right, all right!" roared Steele. "Steady on! You've had
it now, Tyson, you dirty swine. Get their bikes! Get on with the
plan!"

The bikes were torn from them and thrown to the ground.
They were seized with their arms behind their backs and
marched forward up the steps toward the chapel.

Carleton followed, hating it, and thinking, I'm doing nothing about it, nothing.

Up the steps they forced them, and toward the chapel door.
There were tears in Bond's eyes. Tyson was a ghastly color.

Steele and his commanders led them in through the open
door. Everyone crowded outside. Carleton hung back, looking
over their heads. It was almost four o'clock, and here was a
chance to escape. The bell-rope hung just inside, extending to
the red flagstone floor, on which it lay in a single coil.

"What are you doing?" gasped Tyson.

"Shut up, Tyson!" someone shouted.

He and Bond were stood back to back, and Steele tied the
rope jointly about their necks. Since Bond was much shorter, it
strained tight under his chin. He raised a hand to loosen it, and
someone said, "Leave that alone, Bond."

"Yeh, unless you want your face smashed in."

Bond lowered his hand. There were tears on his cheeks. A
crowd was unexpectedly collecting behind Carleton, which was
a help. Boys appeared from the cloisters, the Big Schoolroom,
everywhere. The school was pulling together.

"Bond's blubbing."

"Boo-hoo!"

"Ugly sods, aren't they?"

315

"Look at Tyson, he'll throw up in a minute."

"They might have washed for the occasion. Look at Bond's neck."

"And Tyson's hair. Ugh!"

"We can't do both at once, Steele," said Rogers. "Who'll we do first?"

"Tyson!" said several voices.

"Yeh. Besides, Bond will enjoy the wait."

Carleton quietly moved away, across the square. No one appeared to be looking. It was a planned charade. It would be over shortly. Even so, he had been revolted and ashamed at his own incapacity. No one about on the hot and dusty square. Why had the masters accepted? Rowles up there, secure in his room, letting it happen! Loyalty to the Head, he would call it.

He ducked past the common-room window, in case Johns was on the ottoman. Nicky must be hiding somewhere, waiting for the time. Ashley's room. They had never met in a room before. He was nervous and uncertain. A bedroom. Somehow, the out-doors seemed more natural. If Clinton and Dotterel had obeyed the rules, they might spot him from their own windows. But the sun glinted back, and there seemed to be no sign of life. Somewhere or other, the staff had all gone to ground.

Coming down the wood, Ashley saw him going into the new buildings. Why have I done this? he wondered. Is this true sympathy and understanding, or is it some vicarious self-deception?

It was not the reason for his sudden return. Heading up the hills, through the gorse, he had been nagged at by Crabree's declaration to the common room: "I'm asking you, gentlemen, to remain out of the way, and allow the school to act as it sees fit." It had smelled then. It still did. They had two mass emotions, these young creatures, Ashley thought: sentimentality and savagery. There was no doubt which would be put to use today. He heard shouts and began to hurry down through the long grass.

The rope had been untied; the pretense of separate hangings was over; and Bond and Tyson were being bundled out of the chapel, surrounded by a dense crowd. The addition of these younger admirers had revivified Steele, Pryde, Rogers and the others in their desire for blood. The hangings had faded into anticlimax. It was ending without satisfaction. Tyson, who had regained his battered bicycle, was even wearing a half-grin. And though insults were being delivered with much shoving, there was no doubt that the two victims, who were pushing their bikes at the center of the parade, were on their way down the drive again, and so toward freedom.

Tyson solved the problem for them. He murmured, "Dirty little cowards," and after a moment's surprised silence Pryde stepped in and hit him hard on the teeth with his fist. Tyson fell back, with his hand to his mouth. Bond dropped his bicycle and rushed bravely at Pryde. Two boys jumped on him, and the three crashed down on top of the bicycle. Tyson aimed a blow at Pryde, and both Steele and Rogers went for him. All control was gone; Bond and Tyson were on the ground, grunting with pain as the others lashed out at them. Someone was shouting at them to stop, but no one heard; until Pryde found himself pulled back, saw a flash of Ashley's fair hair, and Ashley's fist coming at his jaw. Even in the melee it took only a moment for everyone to realize that a master had struck a boy. The two heaps were slowly unraveling, though Bond and Tyson were still on the ground.

"Filthy little swine, all of you!" Ashley shouted.

"You can't do this," Steele said.

"Hold your tongue, you ugly bully!" said Ashley.

Bond and Tyson were getting up. They were covered with gravel. Bond had filthy marks of tears and dirt on his face, and at the corner of Tyson's mouth there was bright red blood. He wiped it with the back of his hand, and it smeared across his cheek.

"Get on your bicycles and go!" said Ashley. "And the rest of you, bow your rotten little heads in shame."

"You hit Pryde," said Steele. "I saw it. You can't do that. I'm going to the Head."

"I'm coming with you," said Ashley.

It was silent in the sunny room.

Will I pull the curtains? No, no, that would be too daring, and embarrassing. Besides, there was not a soul outside, not even Lucretia. Just sunshine and silence. It was stuffy. He opened the window, and a wasp immediately buzzed in and out again.

The long grass of the wood looked cool. He was leaning over the desk in the window and a photo of a handsome woman in some play. She was probably Ashley's mother. Imagine him having one!

What was it he had said about the story, and the mother? There was no need for her—and he had sounded odd for a moment.

If so, why was she on his desk?

He turned back again into the room. On the mantelpiece, under a round mirror, there was a small clock in a leather case, ticking away fast and softly in the silence. It was just ten past four. Where was Nicky? Surely he was coming? He must be. Why did small clocks seem to tick faster than large clocks?

He realized he had been trying not to look at the bed, but he didn't like to think why, and suddenly he saw the wooden crucifix over the end of it on the wall. He had the alarming thought that this might make Nicky become religious and remote, and even moved across the room with the mad idea of taking it down and hiding it under the bed. But it was fixed there with a large rusty nail.

No, it wasn't so mad, he thought. Because this is terribly important. Dr. Rowles said it wasn't—it was just childish. But Rowles wasn't waiting here, aglow with love and excitement; impatient, frightened, with his heart banging in his chest.

He went back agitatedly toward the window, and his eyes fell on a row of shoes under bookshelves. They were highly polished, and nearly all had little holes in them—whatever that was called. There was also a gray coat on the chair at the desk. And for a moment he had the disconcerting thought: This is someone else's room; this is no good; we don't want to be concerned with anyone else. Yes, there was something new, a personal something, about the room: aspects of a private life, of a more human and ordinary Ashley than the one who presented himself. A person like oneself; just another person, that was all. Someone who needed shoes too. Funny, there was something sad about people's belongings when the person wasn't there. Yes, even the striped rug over the dispensary door. They were deserted. Deprived of any meaning. Waiting.

Like Carleton.

But there was a definite sound in the corridor, and he became tense. He had locked the door. He saw the handle turn. He didn't dare call out, but a voice whispered, "It's me."

He unlocked it, and Nicky slipped in, and he locked it again. The cool, the unconcerned Nicky was trembling slightly! He gave Carleton his hand, as if for help. It was quite cold. "Hey, what's up? It's all right. It's all right. This is safe as houses. Here—let's sit down."

Carleton led him across and pulled the chair around and sat on it, taking Nicky onto his knees. He was much shyer than usual. It was warming to feel oneself the leader, the older, for a change.

"Sorry I'm wearing this old coat," Nicky said, looking at the floor.

It wasn't his brown one. It was a faded dark blue, with a red line in it.

"Oh, for heaven's sake, what does it matter! Anyhow, I like it. You look marvelous."

It was true. Carleton lifted Nicky's chin with a finger and turned his head, and they gazed at each other and smiled.

"You're all right now, aren't you?"

"Yes."

They didn't need to speak. But at length Carleton heard himself saying, "You're a bit high up there. Someone might see. Let's . . . lie down."

"What?"

"Over there. More comfortable."

Nicky hesitated. "O.K.," he said, and slipped off Carleton's lap.

Carleton led him across. They lay face to face and found themselves almost laughing with happiness.

"Oh I do love you," Carleton said, and he had moved impulsively over on top of Nicky, putting his arms around him. "I love you, I love you, I love you." He bent his head to kiss, and Nicky turned away, saying "Tch, tch"—exactly like Naylor. Though, unlike Naylor, he blushed crimson, while Carleton kissed him on the cheek and the eyebrow. And the most appalling, unbelievable, terrible thing began to happen; and he could not stop it. He tried, but he could not stop it. And the worst part was that it was wonderful too, and yet it was awful. Thus the shame was doubled. The disgrace and horror were absolute. It was profane. It was ruin. It was done now. It could not be undone. He lay still. He was paralyzed. And Nicky smiled up at him. He didn't even know! He didn't even seem to know! "What's up?" Nicky whispered. He couldn't speak. He looked down into Nicky's face, in despair. But there was no response. Only a query. Nicky was innocent. Yes, entirely innocent. Though it made no difference. All was defamed and finished. He moved off and sat on the edge of the bed with his back to Nicky, trembling with shock.

"What is it?" Nicky said, putting a hand on his shoulder. "What on earth's up?"

"Don't."

Nicky took his hand away. There was a coldness in the room. Carleton had to move out of reach. He stood up and went over toward the window. His legs were shaking. Everything, everything lovely, their whole past, was contaminated. He had sinned and profaned; as with Naylor, but this was with Nicky!

"You'd better go," he said, gazing blindly out of the window.

"What? Go?"

"Yes. Go now."

He turned. Nicky was standing up, looking pale and confused.

"It's best. I don't feel. . . . Somebody may come up. You'd best go . . . really."

Nicky stared back into his eyes, surprised, miserable, and then, just as he had begun to look like crying, angry. "I told you, didn't I?" he said calmly.

"What?"

"I told you. I told you."

"No. No. . . ."

"I told you, I told you." Nicky went to the door. "Blast you, blast you, blast you. . . ."

There were tears in his voice, and he was turning the key. Carleton stared at his back. He couldn't move. There was nothing to be done.

Nicky threw the door open and went out, and slammed it, and was gone from his life—just like Naylor.

He didn't realize what he was doing. He felt powerless to leave the room and go out into the sun. What did it matter now whether he was here or not? He could not face anybody outside.

Rowles had been right. Rowles had advised, and he hadn't listened. Diseased rubbish. The emotions—they just led to horror and disgust. But what about this school, yes, this school? He'd been sent here. Not his fault. Thank goodness he was going. If only today, yes, today, he had been already gone!

He didn't remember moving there, but he was standing against the mantelpiece, with his bent head on his arm, when he heard the door open and shut.

Ashley had come in, breathing heavily, and looking almost unrecognizable.

After a long stare he slowly turned his head and glanced down at the bed. There was a depression along the center, in the dark green cover. Carleton had not thought of rearranging it.

Ashley looked along the bed in a deliberate way, and addressed him finally with that sneering expression: "Satisfactory?"

Carleton was numb, and afraid, and couldn't reply.

"Evidently not. I'm not surprised. You should stick to your elders."

"I don't understand."

"We're in the same boat now. I have been requested to leave at the end of this delightful term. So you see—we haven't much time."

"Oh gosh . . . I'm sorry. . . . But what do you mean?"

"You know perfectly well what I mean," said Ashley, taking a pace forward. "You've worked hard, and I grant you your success. I love you."

"What?!"

"Stop pretending," said Ashley, in a most peculiar voice; and he was coming toward him. His arms were out. His hands were coming at him. There was a moaning noise. It was like some animal. It wasn't him. It was vile. His hands had clutched Carleton's arms, and his mad face was pushing forward, and it was incredible but it must be that he was trying to kiss him. Carleton moved his head aside and banged back against the mantelpiece, fighting against the fierce grip on his arms. In silence they struggled until Carleton managed to dodge aside, pushing Ashley across the room. The clock had fallen face down on the tiles, and he bent to pick it up, though Ashley was shouting from somewhere, "Never mind the clock!" The glass was broken. He put it back on the mantelpiece, panting and shivering and not daring to look. Ashley said, from out of the blinding light in the window, "You blow neither hot nor cold. I spew you out of my mouth!" Carleton couldn't move or speak. He couldn't see the figure there against the light. The voice became calmer. "*Je m'égare, Seigneur, ma folle ardeur malgré moi se déclare.*" It was *Phèdre* or something. The only thing was to escape. He managed to get to the door, and going out heard a cry behind him: "This is what will happen to *you!*" Then he ran away down the corridor with the words ringing in his head.

CHAPTER TWENTY-EIGHT

At tea he was at the end of the table no longer dominated by the departed Beauchamp, nor even by Sinnott, who had grown very quiet. The others chattered. The whole dining hall seethed with the drama of the afternoon. The Cod was on duty, marching up and down and saying, "Hush, hush," now and then. Carleton ate nothing, and sat in a daze of confusion and shame. He gathered that Ashley had entered the fray, struck Pryde and been asked to leave. So he must have been in a terrible state. Never mind; it excused none of the horror that had happened.

At last the Cod released them, and he wandered out, avoiding Nicky and not knowing what to do. Someone had grabbed the old bat and they were playing cloister cricket already in the break before prep. The tennis ball appeared at his feet as he crossed the Quad, and someone called out to him to chuck it back. He paid no attention and went up the steps toward the war memorial. There was no prep for him. He couldn't face the others in the common room. He wandered across the Chapel Square and into the wood, which looked inviting on this still, warm, marvelous summer evening. There were midges under the trees, and he had to scratch his itching head. Where the sun came through, it was surprisingly bright for this hour of day. He would rather it had retired by now. His own mood was not sunny at all. He felt wretched and terribly alone.

He strolled up the wood. The sound of voices behind faded. It was strangely quiet. It was mysterious, with a brooding life of its own. Lucretia's rabbits in the wire cage hurried about and nibbled, on silent feet. Their activity seemed an intrusion. They were impostors and should have been placed elsewhere. He passed them and went on higher, wondering, What has happened? What really has happened? How wrong was it, how final? Who in the world was there to ask? What about mothers and fathers? Weren't they supposed to help sometimes? But they were a thousand miles away. For eight years of his young life he had been put out on his own, to decide everything for himself.

More voices were heard in the distance now. When he came out of the wood, into the far too brilliant sunshine, he saw that there were people in the pool, way up on top of the grassy hill. The hooligans had come over the wall again and were disporting themselves, their filthy clothes piled in heaps around the pool. He had better avoid them and go around behind the gorse bushes. They didn't interest him anymore; and besides, he was unlikely to be able to disperse them on his own.

And had he ever decided anything? No, he seemed to have always merely done what others had moved him to do. Except for getting out of things. Was he doing that now? But he had to, surely? Surely?

There was that sweet smell from the great clumps of gorse under a pale blue sky. He knew every foot of this, every one of the pathways between them. And it was nearly all gone. One could be sad in bright sunshine. The far-off shouts from the hooligans sounded mournful.

"Slipping through with agility." That was fine from Ashley, who had turned into a disgusting animal!

Getting out of things? Was it possible? Like senior prefect? Showing no charity to others? Being a cynic? But surely he was respecting Nicky, and admitting his own shame?

An old dried-up tree stump. He had once sat on it and smoked a cigarette, until he heard someone coming. His past. Every-thing was dusty and dried-up and comfortless. But it felt cooler. The sun was beginning to descend. Would a cigarette ever be so good again?

He was above the pool now. It was way up at the end of this alleyway, where the view appeared, that they used to meet.

"You go your own sweet way and they can go to hell. . . . I've *got* to see you. *Please* meet me, if only once. . . ."

Well, he had met. And now?

At the memory of that first note he was nearly in tears.

Was it really over? Muck and carry-on, Rowles called it. Was that right? All term the Crab had been trying to part everyone, and Rowles said he'd begun to agree. Contentment is to be found in solitude. In yourself. Was it true? Was it really true?

After the last great clump, the view struck him like a blow. Here they had met. The fields swept away to the far horizon, with the winding Thames in the middle distance. And straight down below was the school itself.

"Well, just now he talked mostly about temptation."

Was there any point in going to see the chaplain? No, there was none.

He lay down on the grass on his elbow. Their favorite place. The sun was going behind the hill.

"You'll get tired of me."

"Never, never, never."

"Oh yes. You will. Even before the term is over."

But he hadn't!

That was not it at all. Nicky thought it was. But it wasn't.

Two people were coming slowly up through the wood. Surely everyone was in prep. It must be prefects. No, it was a man and a woman. They emerged. My gosh, it was the Pedant and that girl, and he had his arm around her waist. It was hor-rible. But why? Well, it was so unbelievable. They stopped— and my goodness he was kissing her! For quite a long time. And then they walked on, disappearing behind the gorse.

What was one to make of it? What was right?

The light was fading, and it was becoming quite cool.

"Do you know what I'm going to tell you? We're in love, lads, and we're going to be married. And I only hope you'll be as happy in later life."

Why was that right? I want to be happy now, and it's gone, and I've made it go.

It was almost unbearable being in this same place. Never again. I haven't even got his photo, except in the school photo —though Sherriff has. Nicky has mine. He will tear it up. He'll throw it away. He's strong like that.

There were distant shouts. The Pedant was at the pool. "Out of there, the lot of you! You wretched creatures, you won't get away with it! I'm setting the police on you this time!"

The Pedant might come this way. In any case, the memories here were intolerable. He rose and started down between the gorse, walking more quickly as he reached the wood. Nothing was resolved; nothing was clear. There was no one to advise. He felt he was fleeing from these hills forever.

There were sounds from the chapel. Music. They had stood beside the buttress, in silence.

He went quietly in past the oaken doors and the bell rope. It was dusk in here: no, thanks to the stained glass it was almost dark. The Beatle had his little light on, as he sat up there on his perch; and Carleton saw his feet dancing about on the pedals. He had just begun the D Minor Toccata and Fugue—a glorious sound.

Almost impossible to see who was there as he tiptoed down the aisle. About ten people seated alone and apart, like dark statues. The great rumbling announcement of the toccata made him feel small. He was looking for a place with no one near, and eventually settled on the front pew up near the pulpit and glanced back.

Johns was closest to him—which was nearly enough to put one off! The suspicion that Johns found something dry, remote and superior and Johns-like in Bach. Never mind. Each found himself, and he found other things.

Naylor—another puzzling fellow. Several artists. Way at the end, against the antechapel screen, Rowles was seated in his customary throne, shrunken into it, with its flat wooden arms jutting out. And Ashley was up at the back on the far side, under some old tattered regimental banners—still here, still alive! That didn't matter either: Carleton merely felt distance and disgust.

One couldn't spoil this. Such nights. Never again. The center of school life: yes, there was something warm and touching and memorable about the chapel—and the Beatle playing. Reading lessons here he had loved too. He had always rehearsed them out loud, here alone in the semidarkness. The others never bothered. They got names and everything wrong. But he was ready, assured and clear. The whole school listening. If he wasn't going to be a writer, he'd like to be an actor.

But the Beatle had begun the fugue, and Carleton, who was sensitive to music, was stirred at once. A clear, laughing stream of notes. . . . Chills of delight up his arms and round the back of his neck.

Rowles, who had spotted him, was listening more calmly—to church music by a master. Church music was the only music he knew; it was the only noise that was tolerable; and this, of course, was supreme. It was not a resolution of anything. It didn't dabble in disturbance. It was without trouble, thank God. It was religious, and mercifully sane. Old Bach was a bit like himself, though of course a quite extraordinary and remarkable fellow. Sixteen brats, wasn't it? Poor chap, how on earth did he manage? Shut himself up—the only thing to do.

Still, it was difficult to attend with Ashley sitting over there. What a damned fool! What a wretchedly upsetting case! Why didn't he go? What was one to do? Help? There was no help. He had tried, God knows.

Ashley sat immune to these reflections. Numb. He didn't know why he had wandered in here. The music was comfortless, meaningless, scuttling around in circles. It was certainly not Beethoven. There was nothing here to break down the reliable walls of youth. No goblins here to walk quietly over the universe. No acknowledgment at all of panic and emptiness.

Or of shame. How squalid! It had been distress . . . urgency. . . . He really loved the youth with tenderness. But that was equally without hope. And that creature's poxy face as he hit it. And the other's scarlet face shouting at him: "This is the end! This is the last interference." Yes, everything ends in this damn place—where it all began.

What alternative? His mother's flat. Theatrical society. Players and painted stage. . . . A pity it was not an inherited talent. Othello's occupation's gone, along with everything else. As a child he had sat in the stalls of every theater in London, watching his mother pour tea gracefully. With no result. No temptation whatever to parade: though it didn't seem so far from schoolmastering.

Why hang on? What else to do? Besides, Carleton was here—and there were only three more days.

I am simply a person like other persons. How is it that I find myself empty, perverted, without hope, dead inside, dark inside . . . with that sense of futility near to panic? Why? When did it happen? Here?

Once, and once only, he suddenly remembered, he had met J.L.M. away from here. In the holidays. He was not yet a Cambridge man: two children . . . two young people. Two people? In a cinema in London's West End. What had they seen? He had no recollection. It was winter. He had put his brown overcoat over their knees. Under it, they touched legs, held hands. . . . An usherette shone a torch, requesting them to stand up for new arrivals. It seemed to shine with disapproval . . . disgust? Could she have known? He had put his coat under a seat. They sat close, but more tense. And afterward, having tea upstairs in a terrible place, on wicker chairs, with violins playing. J.L.M. had said: "Supposing someone from school sees us?" School—which seemed a thousand miles away! But it frightened them both. And, more important, the meeting now seemed unreal. They had not tried it again. They were very young.

What had they done in his room? Had they really done something? Carleton with bowed head.

A nice future, God help him.

Carleton was needing no help. He listened in delight. The stream of notes was slowly gaining a ground bass of strength, melding in patterns too swift to follow into a great tapestry. For a while, urgent questions were asked, and were responded to with deep resounding certain answers. And then gradually the whole chapel became one marvelous, thundering bell of triumphant certainty and joy.

Then silence.

It seemed to leave the stone walls trembling.

Silence.

How small are my troubles!

A strange sharp little sound. Ashley's shoes on the pink flags.

He was walking out. The ten dark figures watched. On the slender step down into the antechapel he nearly fell. My God, he's been drinking again, thought Rowles. Then he was gone.

Oblivious of this, the Beatle, who had been taking a breather, began again.

It was the Fantasia and Fugue in G Minor.

Carleton was not interested in Ashley. This was quieter. It was more reflective. The noble sound of organs. In chapels, churches, yes cathedrals. . . . What are my troubles! Profound . . . peace. Sitting beside someone you loved. The love made more pure and yet more intense. Two fingers gently interlocked on the pew. His and Nicky's eyes raised to the great golden organ pipes, to the vast height above. Together as never before. Blissfully humbled into two simple souls made for each other, chosen and found by marvelous fortune out of the whole world. So simple, and perfect. Us, and something greater which unites us all the more. . . .

Stop dreaming.

For something was wrong. The Beatle had commenced the fugue, and there was a disconcerting memory. What was it?

Yes, the Beatle had once sung them, with delight, a rhyme to this fugue, about some old arranger:

> "Old Ebenezer Prout.
> Oh, what a funny man!
> He plays Bach fugues
> As quickly as he can.
> He-ee plays Bach fugues
> As quickly as he can.
> Old Ebenezer Prout,
> Oh, what a. . . ."

Very hard to listen properly with this nonsense running in one's head. The Beatle's feet leaped and plunged: What a funny man! and again, What a funny man! His head tossed. His hands danced. As quickly as he can. Oh, what a funny man!

Yet wait. . . . It gradually swept you in, as did the toccata. It persuaded, and overwhelmed. Funny, yes, happy, yes. And why not? Happiness. Laughter. Fun. How terrible to forget such things. The Beatle knew his Bach. They must be main-

tained, enjoyed . . . never forgotten. How easy to lose them!
And mope about the hills. And yet how valuable beyond meas-
ure.

They had smiled often, with this kind of happiness. They
had smiled on the pillow. And then. . . .

A complete surprise, and shock. That was all.

How simple. Just love.

Again, all was resolved: serenely this time. Not so thunder-
ously. The world and life were to be properly enjoyed. It was
all there. It was up to oneself. This was what it sounded like
when you achieved it. Serenity after. . . .

Silence again. And his guilt was washed away. Nothing was
crushed.

The others began to drift out. He sat there, remembering
how music leaves you with wonders which promptly vanish.

But not this time. Not this time.

CHAPTER TWENTY-NINE

 But how?
The days were few. One could count it in hours now.
And they were rushing past.

In the morning he wrote a pleading, begging note and left it
in the buttress, and saw Nicky on the way to lunch—the second-
last lunch—and put his hand in his pocket.

Nicky promptly turned his head away.

In the afternoon the Big Schoolroom was out of bounds to
everyone else. It was their dress rehearsal for the following
night.

He came in from the Chapel Square and stood for a moment,
dazed by the noise, the footlights, the excitement and confusion. Someone was hammering like the devil up at the back of
the stage, which blazed with a backcloth of Little Dingley-on-
the-Marsh, done by Clinton's artists: church tower, village

green, post office, pub, and so on: The sunny afternoon was obliterated by curtains and sacking across the high-up windows; though thin beams came through, alive with dust. In the wings, the Beatle was trying to run over points on the upright piano, against the bangs of the hammer. His tall, gray-headed wife sat at a desk in front of a pile of clothes. The chaplain—surprisingly, for he emerged seldom—was seated at a desk near where Carleton stood, smiling to himself. And across the blinding stage wandered Nicky.

Nicky wore a red velvet frock with a double string of pearls. He looked amazing!

My gosh. Shiny black high-heeled shoes.

"Ah," said the Beatle's wife, "I've been waiting for you."

She held up a marvelous kind of fancy-dress summer suit. It was black and white stripes.

"This may not fit."

She plonked a straw hat on his head. It covered his eyes.

"It doesn't. Never mind."

She wiped it off again.

"Go and change at the back of the stage."

The Beatle's wife was older than her husband, with gray hair going straight up and cut short at the back. But there was something young and easy about her. A breeziness like the Beatle's, with an extra commanding "No nonsense" which the boys respected.

Carleton climbed onto the stage, past McCaffrey, who was fiddling about with one of the big aluminum plates that covered the footlights, and went around the back of Little Dingley. There was an exciting smell . . . greasepaint, old clothes. Desks in a row with mirrors on them. The Old Crone was putting stuff on Stoddart Major, who wore a frock with big red roses; a job that Nancy had always done so well, but this Matron seemed irritable and uncertain, and Stoddart was wincing. Nicky had been called over to the piano by the Beatle. Almost unrecognizable people were milling about: Naylor, with his crinkly hair all powdered, in a clergyman's collar; McIver, rolling his eyes, in a black lace dress down to his ankles. But no mockery, no embarrassment. Serious, and exciting. A job to be done. They were going to slay them. A true team spirit. We will astonish them together. How to get off his trousers without Matron seeing? Maybe she should be used to it, but after all she was an old spinster.

The suit was great!

It was all stripey.

"Do *I* need anything, Matron?"

She was still painting Stoddart.

"A moment, please! One at a time. I'm doing this now," she added, blacking Stoddart's eyelids, "so that I'll remember to-morrow night. I can't remember if you interrupt."

He moved over toward the piano.

The chorus was standing about, brightly dressed as villagers of both sexes; and Nicky was beside the Beatle, finishing:

"Come with me to Canada.
Today!"

Strange, and disconcerting. His brown cheeks were slightly rouged. But when you got used to it, he was even more beautiful than ever. Carleton's heart felt like a balloon.

"Good!" the Beatle said.

Nicky came out through the group.

I wonder how I look in this, Carleton thought. Surely I look rather dashing. He's marvelous, but maybe it's not fair that I'm allowed to be a man. My goodness, I can just see the tops of two tennis balls inside his red dress. "I'm terribly sorry," he whispered, looking into those dark eyes. "It was all a mis—"

"I'm not interested," Nicky said. And he walked past.

It was unbelievable. It wasn't him at all. It opened up a sudden emptiness that was impossible, unbearable. . . .

"All right, everybody!" the Beatle called out. "Are you there, Milner?"

"Yes, yes."

The Pedant was somewhere out front. He always came in at the end to help: because the Beatle had to play the piano. The Pedant was surprisingly good at it: it was the Jack Buchanan in him; and the need to get everything neat and tidy, and in the right declensions, and so on.

"Now let's see if that wretched curtain will come across."

McCaffrey pulled a string. The two old red curtains joined. The Beatle began playing a medley of all his tunes. The chaplain—which was unlike him—closed his eyes. The schoolroom was stifling. The pain had, of late, turned into a constant grinding, accompanied by nausea; and only the green salad was tenable.

But the curtains clattered aside, and someone was beating a bell, and there was the devil of a din, and his eyes opened. Villagers of both sexes were strolling arm in arm in the sunshine, with the gentlemen raising straw hats and bowing. There were only two Starlings, and both of them, to his mild disgust, in summer frocks. Remarkable how it obliterated all attraction. There was a sudden outburst:

"At Little-Dingley-in-the-Marsh,
Where days are fair, and never harsh. . . ."

The chaplain was almost dozing.

Naylor had walked on, altered by gray hair and a dog collar.

"Good morning, dear people."

"Good morning, Vicar!"

"Well, well, what a day, eh! I believe I quote the immortal Wodehouse correctly when he takes his metaphor from the golf course: 'It was a day when all nature shouted "Fore!" ' "

"Yes, indeed, Vicar! Very true. . . . Quite right. . . ."

"But to our onions," said Naylor. "Since I have but five minutes till morning service. We *all* have only ten days now till our Little-Dingley fête. Firstly, may I address myself to you ladies. . . . Ah, but here comes my daughter, Alice, who is better equipped than I. . . ."

At the sight of Allen in red velvet, the chaplain felt iller and chose darkness. The disease, he knew, was not improving his nature. They have expelled my friends, he thought. They have committed brutality on Bond and Tyson. The place is now cleansed, they imagine. As if people can be cleansed! Only by the fire. Next term will be no different. No term will. The naïveté of fools. Ignorance is the only crime. In its name all sins are committed. Allen was singing, and the chaplain actually smiled.

It seemed his fiancé, Percy, was on the way from Oxford.

"Percy,
Waiting for Percy.
Will he bring me the love that I require?
Will he bring me the life that I desire?
Surely,
But surely,
Yes he'll. . . ."

He was old. That was it. Never before had he really appreciated it, but it was so. They were in their springtime. How strong were their feelings? Were they truly a blueprint? That quaint fellow, Proust, whose mother had omitted to kiss him. Childish things that are not put away. Unless one became a man. Whatever that meant. As far as he was concerned, all men were children: God's. And there was only one strong feeling. He could recall bringing no one to it, save a lady who had poked his fire; and this, regrettably, had proved to be a testimony—transitory, thank God—to his own personal charms. Ashley had slipped in and was leaning back against the far wall. An odd, remote, troubled looking fellow. The chaplain had never communicated with any of the staff. Had this been a mistake? Adults were so childish.

Caldicott, who wore a monocle, Carleton, in stripes, and McIver, in black lace, had come laboring on with suitcases.

McIver said, with nice humor, rolling his eyes, "A short walk from the station, indeed! You young men have no respect for age. Let us rest here awhile, or I shall expire in this heat. Where is everyone?"

"I think they're all in church, Mamma," Caldicott replied.

"I am glad to hear it," McIver said. "People should always have an occupation of some kind. You look somewhat *fatigué* too, my son. But as for your friend, Peter, he seems horribly fresh. These Canadians! The wide-open spaces, they call them, do they not?"

Carleton said, "That's right, ma'am. Why, sometimes we'll walk fifty miles in one day."

"Gracious!" McIver exclaimed.

"You're joking," said Caldicott.

"I'm not," said Carleton.

"Well. . . . Well, well!" said McIver. "I do think that Alice as your fiancée, Percy—might at least have met us at the station with some conveyance."

"Well, her father is the vicar, Mamma," Caldicott explained. "And he does like her in church, you know. She did say so in her letter."

"If *I* may say so," Carleton interposed, "it seems mighty reasonable to me, ma'am."

"Well, I suppose so," McIver conceded. "A vicarage. It's many years since I stayed at a vicarage. The vicarages of England."

"They mean a lot, Mamma," said Caldicott.

"Shall we tell him?" McIver suggested coyly.

"I'd be mighty obliged if you would, ma'am," said Carleton. They sang.

McIver: "Oh, they may be somewhat drafty,"
Caldicott: "And *some* rooms in bad repair,"
McIver: "But England needs her vicars."
Caldicott: "To stay and prosper there."
McIver: "The plumbing may be risky,"
Caldicott: "The roof—"

"Just a moment, just a moment!" The Pedant was irritated. The Beatle was silent at the piano. "It's far too static. We'd better have you swapping places on each line. Now then. . . ."

Carleton was dazzling in that suit, Ashley thought. Dazzling. But there is something wrong. My hands. They're apart. Separate entities. Bring them together, and they will not have it. They seem wise. But what's to be done? Now, apart, they feel dead. My feet too. The body needs to love. But there is no action to be taken. A cloud passed over him. But it departed. He had not fainted. The body gives in, but it recovers. Optimist. It needs to be taught a lesson. This cannot continue. The hands —if they were chopped off, would they be missed? Yes. Odd. Alarming. . . . Definitely. Dimly he saw Allen run on, with his tennis balls bobbing:

"I thought I heard singing, and I slipped out. . . . Percy!" He rushed into Caldicott's arms and kissed him on the cheek.

"Mrs. Fenwick, how nice! Oh?"

"Ah, yes, uh, darling," said Caldicott, "this is my great friend at Oxford, Peter Piper."

"How do you do?"

"How do you do?"

The Pedant shouted out, "Well, for heaven's sake, Allen, do at least look at the fellow! And look closely. You're about to fall in love. Do that again."

"How do you do?"

"How do you do?"

Allen looked briefly and coldly. Carleton looked with desire and without shame, his heart thumping. How to disguise it? Had the Pedant seen? Dreadful of Nicky. Hellish. What was it? "I don't want ever again to turn away whenever I see somebody. Never again."

Very well, the chaplain thought, I shall give them a taste of the refiner's fire. I shall enter their hearts. I shall tear out the distresses. I shall show them, for their own good, and whether it be true or not, that the distresses are garbage in the eye of heaven. The greater love, yes, but not this red velvet. . . .

His right hand felt empty. He had come without the orange.

"That was worse," the Pedant said. "But we haven't time. By the way, can you hear us back there, chaplain? Are we loud enough?"

The chaplain was asleep.

"Damn the man," said the Pedant. "Very well, then. Get on with it!"

CHAPTER THIRTY

My last day. My last rest in the dorm—ever.
I will do this once more, just to finish it.
It's hard to believe things end, but they do.
A funny mixture of sadness and excitement.

The dorm is all littered with trunks, with an odd, old smell. Some people have great boxes with big clamps on them. Clothes are strewn about. Everybody is a bit hysterical. It took us about ten minutes to get silence. Gower was extremely cheeky to me.

He seems quite content to be chucked out. I wonder what he's got in his trunk!

The Doctor said last night, "There's a kettle on if you happen to be passing," and for the first time I didn't feel like it. I felt we've no more to say. And we hadn't really. He kept on mumbling things like "So you're leaving us," and there were awful silences. He didn't mention the subject. It seems I'm forgiven. Not that I care.

After tea I had gone around behind the chapel with some crazy hope: and there *was* a note sticking out of the buttress, and I was ready to shout out with happiness and joy. But it was my own. He hadn't even touched it.

As for singing with him, I could scarcely control myself, and he could scarcely look at me. The Pedant congratulated me, and told Nicky off. My hand around his waist at the end was shaking. But he was like a cold fish. He wouldn't kiss. He turned his head away when I tried. What on earth will happen tonight?

My greatest night.

It's not a Sunday, but of course we have a full-dress chapel— early. Cyril Starr's last sermon. He's going. It seems he was really ill all the time. You never know. And we'll sing, "Lord, dismiss us, with Thy blessing." I've been moved enough before, when I wasn't even leaving. What will it be like now?

Afterward, everyone troops into the schoolroom for our performance. I'm scared.

Then we all line up and go into the common room and say good-bye to the masters. (Ashley is still here. Why? He looks a bit bonkers to me.)

Pryde said that later there was a plan for cigarettes and beer somewhere up in the wood, and he even asked me to join the group—which surprised me.

But there's only one person I want to meet in the dark.

I know that Nicky will have been "Weatherhill." And yet it was only one term. How strange.

What can I do? How can I save it?

I mustn't forget to tip the skivvies. Philomena looks tearful. She really liked old Starr. There's a warmth in people. They're amazing really. Muck, the Doctor calls it. I'm tired of hearing that.

Tomorrow morning—will I sleep at all tonight?—Father with the car . . . and all the other cars on the drive. Except for fellows who live farther away. They're all going on the early train to London. *We* can sleep later. I said not to come too early. I've never slept late here. Breakfast lingers on—which is fun. Not that I'll be able to eat much.

I must know his address. I must do it. I must see him. I can't go out into the world without him. I know now that it's absolutely impossible.

I was finishing like that, but there's a question I've never admitted to, and I feel I must set it down.

Who *is* Nicky? Who is he? Love is blind, they say, but must he remain quite such a mystery? Is he really better than me . . . than us all? Petty piped up about Dante not knowing Beatrice, but for gosh sakes he has been in my arms and I still don't know who he is. Can it be, he's too young to be anyone? No, he doesn't seem young. Not a bit. He's perfect, yes. Is he too perfect? Must we not risk things, risk being wrong, a little? Should I move him? He didn't say yes. He didn't say no. He blows neither . . . what was it? Hot nor cold.

Gosh, that was Ashley.

CHAPTER THIRTY-ONE

317. Carleton slotted the number of the third hymn into the board. "Lord dismiss us" in the end-of-term section of the public-school hymnbook.

He was hanging the board up on the hook when he heard Naylor, who was doing something with the gold plate away near the altar, say quietly down the length of the deserted chapel: "You don't seem to be having much success."

He had remembered. Naylor, of all people! Or had he?

"How do you mean?"

"Hadn't you better patch it up, whatever it is, or this show tonight's going to go for a burton?"

"I don't know what you're talking about." What he wanted to say was, Yes, yes, but how, Naylor, how, damn you?"

"Everybody else does," said Naylor.

"Boo!" Seaton-Scott jumped out from behind the screen to the antechapel.

"Oh, go to hell, Seaton-Scott," said Carleton.

"I thought I'd visit you guys for the last time," Seaton-Scott said humbly, with his glasses flashing.

All three of them were wearing white surplices—a garment to be discarded for the rest of one's life. They were like specters in the dusk.

"We're not flattered," said Carleton, "but you can make yourself useful and switch on the lights. I can't see where to hang this."

"Oh. Right."

There were a lot of clicks, and the place was ablaze.

"Where the devil is Metcalfe?" said Carleton, who was experiencing the old, old fear that he might have to try and ring the bell himself.

"At your service, my lord."

Metcalfe had appeared, bowing in his white sheet, in the antechapel. He had evidently polished his black shoes with the hem of his surplice.

"Is the time nigh?"

"Yes, get going. And you, Seaton-Scott, buzz off, you're supposed to be at roll call."

"Not till the bell stops. I know why you want to get rid—"

"Scram!"

"All right. All right. Keep your hair on."

Metcalfe was pulling the rope, and there was a light clanging at first, and then the great boom ringing out.

Carleton felt nervous and excited. Everything . . . everything that mattered . . . was now about to happen.

Rowles and the Pedant, in gowns and hoods, had already been the first to assemble in the oak-paneled common room. Rowles was knocking out his pipe against the fireplace and saying, "Has it occurred to you, Milner, that this performance you're conducting on the stage may not exactly meet with approval?"

"Oh, for heaven's sake, Rowles, you're becoming quite preposterously prim of late. We've been putting on the precentor's works for thirty years."

Milner was examining *The Times* crossword—which was irritating.

"I know, but *he* is unacquainted, Milner. And his attitude could scarcely be plainer. I foresee ructions, I don't mind telling you."

Milner sniffed, and said nothing.

"I wish someone would tell me why this wretched Ashley is hanging on here and haunting us like some damn ghost," said the Doctor, blowing out smoke. "Why hasn't he the decency to clear off?"

"Don't ask me, Rowles. I thought you had his ear. I thought you had some understanding of that particular gentleman."

"You did, did you?"

"Certainly. I'll even go so far as to say I thought you liked him."

Rowles was silenced. The bell continued to boom out over Weatherhill. He scratched his forehead with his pipe stem.

"My God, what can one do, Milner? There's nothing to be done."

"Where will he go?"

"How in arsehole would I know? I don't see what there is for him if he won't grow."

"You sound concerned."

"I'm not. Not a bit. Not a bit."

"I see."

"His mother will be . . . much upset. Well, there it is."

He was thinking that he, personally, was going—but only for the holidays—to the usual hotel in the hinterland of Eastbourne, where he would enjoy a vast intake of mathematical reading. Milner would decamp into the bungalow in the field, an unnecessary and preposterous victim of the emotions.

"I . . . uh . . . read a postcard. You may expect Rich and our former Matron among your audience."

"You don't say?" Milner was interested at last.

"I do. Our unfortunate Head is surrounded by embarrassments."

"He has caused a few himself."

"Really, Milner!"

"The term has borne a notable resemblance to the Spanish Inquisition."

"Come, come, man! I'm inclined to think he has done well. Showed a firm hand. We'll be better for it. There was too much muck altogether."

"You know what the old man of Nepal said about muck?"

"No, I don't. And I don't care to. I'm not in the mood."

Yes, that sadness was still there. They were almost bores already. Carleton—last night. Their many talks about literature and life and school might never have been. Scarcely an intelligent word had fallen. One scented that the quest was over . . . and this was one of those dreadful creatures called a young man. Reasonably, school meant nothing any more. But the mind retired from *all* matters. Literature ceased to be an adventure. Life was not discussable as a mystery. They were out in it already. Plodding about. Educated bores. The child extinguished. He had thought that the creature would never go to bed. This being their last cup of tea, it had seemed harsh to hustle him out.

An expectant silence. The bell had stopped.

"Allen," shouted Steele for the last time.

"Present."

"Andrews."

"Present."

"Beauchamp . . . oh . . . sorry. Bewick."

"Present."

The evening sun came through the arches upon the angels in white, lining the cloisters below.

"The comedy is almost ended," murmured Johns, beside Carleton in the alcove.

It was best not to reply, though the answer was, "Oh no, it's not—and it's not a comedy either."

Yet the dark and beautiful one, halfway along the outer

line, was resolutely turning his head away and looking out onto the Quad.

Goodness, what can I do, and what's going to happen?

A sudden terror struck him. I can't remember a word I say! How do I start, how do I start? Oh, yes. . . . "That's right, ma'am. Why, sometimes we'll walk fifty miles in one day." Could that be right? Wasn't it odd? No, it was correct, and his Canadian accent was fine. But what on earth came next? It's gone!

To go blank! And my songs. What order are they in?

I can't remember!

Stop it. It'll all come back. Have faith. There's nothing else to be done.

"Hamilton Minor."

"Present."

"Hargreaves."

"Present."

Philip Crabtree rejoined his wife and daughter in the sitting room, having said farewell to Lord Mountheath and Sir Charles at the front door. He was still holding a brandy glass. They had dined above, served by the supernatural Lloyd. His wife had been enigmatic, and his daughter in a silent sulk, but benevolence had carried the day. The two new governors were satisfied without reservations. Laughing, and no longer sober, they had tactfully departed, because the last service was for the school alone; a time of private group emotion and divine dismissal.

Seeing him so rosy and benign, when he rebuked her Lucretia thought: Will I tell him he's called the Crab?

"Don't do that, dear, there's a good child."

She had been striking haphazard notes on the piano.

"Well, well, that was most satisfactory."

"One would seem to have found favor in their sight," Ma Crab agreed. She stood, as so often, with her back to the fireplace studying the ceiling and wearing a new costume for the evening, a suit of thick brown tweed.

"*We* have, my dear. *We* have."

"Let us hope the rest of the night is equally comforting," she said, and jerked downward.

For once, he had scarcely heard. He was beyond alarms. He warmed the brandy glass and drank. Only three months now till the Headmasters' Conference. The news would go around. Weatherhill was batting again. He was captain. He knew the whole team now: all two hundred names, gleaned over Scripture. And those unwanted had been erased.

He spoke automatically: "How do you mean?"

"Our chaplain grows gaunt," she replied. "I fear some upheaval."

"Ah. Have no qualms about that. I've made inquiries. It seems his end-of-term sermon is of a modest and wholesome nature."

She faintly smiled—which at other times had been unnerving—and studied the miniature chandelier.

"One hopes so. He looks as if he might bring us news from the underworld."

"Now, now, not before. . . ." said the Crab, and Lucretia gave a grunt.

"Have you also inquired into the night's entertainment?"

"I've not had time. I gather it's some harmless stuff that they've enjoyed for years."

"Let us hope that too," she said.

"And now my lace, Philomena, my finest lace," said the chaplain.

He stood at the center of the room, already billowing in white and speaking almost through the orange. The room temperature this summer evening, with the logs ablaze, brought an extra pungency to her black-frocked armpits. Inches taller than himself, thin as a stick, and perspiring miserably, she was searching among linen shelves behind a corner curtain.

"Hold on a minute. I'm looking."

Her voice lacked its usual certainty. It was faint. With her back to him, and behind her hair, she was weeping. His present appearance, the last robing, the coming departure of which he had informed her, had altered mere love into passionate despair. Dare she turn around?

She decided to trust to her hair.

"I think this is it."

He was examining his own hair in a silver hand mirror and was, as ever, oblivious of her state.

He lowered the mirror as the attendant approached and from her immense height allowed the lacework to descend over his head, without ruffling his careful design. She considered him lovely as a lady in a lace blouse and yet with this tremendous man's head. There was a gorgeous smell of perfume.

But suddenly she thought, It's like doing up a corpse. His cheeks had sunk right in: he was white as death. But the black eyes still flashed and twinkled.

"Are you sure you'll be all right?"

"I'll be more than all right," he said, swirling around like a ballerina and crossing the room with a magnificent squeaking of the buckled shoes.

Through her fringe she watched him lift up a golden throat spray and give three terrific squirts into his cavernous mouth.

She thought she was going to swoon. With terrible difficulty she said, "But where you're goin', after? Will you be all right there?"

"Ah, my dear Philomena," he replied, with the eyes wickedly laughing at her over the orange, "none of us can tell *that* in advance."

The second bell was ringing. Ashley came striding past Lady Jane Grey's chest, his sweeping gown brushing against a grand-father clock, his outward-turning brown feet resounding on the gray stone flags of the Head's Hall. His face was tense, his hair uncombed. Reaching the white door of the common room, he seized the porcelain handle and flung the door open, announcing loudly, "Good even, homosexuals all!"

Male faces gazed back in sudden total silence from every part of the hallowed room. They were hazy, undefinable . . . though he did note Clinton's black beard. From somewhere came Rowles' familiar bark, "Look here, Ashley . . . !"

But there was another voice behind him. He turned and found the detested red face and purple lips close to his own. The eyes evaded his and looked past him into the room. The Head's voice said brightly: "Ready, gentlemen? Let us proceed."

CHAPTER THIRTY-TWO

"All praise and thanks to God
The Father now be given,"

Heedlessly, Carleton sang the words of the second hymn, trying all the while to make his darling, over the way, raise his eyes from his hymnbook. But the black wavy head remained down. He can't do this. He can't turn it all into emptiness. I will take him and shake him and force him to admit that this is pretense. How *can* he have altered overnight? I will take him in my arms and say, Stop it, admit, give in, you are breaking both our hearts.

"The Son, and Him who reigns"

The whole chapel was aglow. There was sadness and excitement: everyone sharing this emotional night. Everyone waiting for that final hymn and—less so—for the chaplain.
And the two of us are parted!

"With them in highest heaven;"

On the other hand, Ashley, up in the back row, directly behind Nicky, was looking straight at him. So that he himself had to lower his head; because it was painful.

"The one eternal God,"

Maybe I'm being just as cruel as Nicky, he thought suddenly. Maybe he really feels just as I do. It seemed incredible, for a grown man, but perhaps it was just possible. There had been another boy, Roly said. A clergyman now. Nicky was going

344

to be one. Ought I not, of all people, to have been more understanding? Outside of this, he had been the best of all the staff.
He made for me the marvelous discovery of writing. He has
made learning for each of us a delight, made us think, made us
laugh, treated us as equals. He stepped in on behalf of Nicky,
of Jimmy Rich, of Bond and Tyson. And he is sacked and must
be miserable. It is horrible that he should want to hold and persuade me, but isn't that exactly what I want to do with Nicky?

"Whom earth and heaven adore,"

Carleton raised his eyes, but could not meet that puzzling,
frightening stare.
All the same, he had forgiven.

"For thus it was, is now,"

That's the sort of glance, Ashley thought, that I took for flirtation. But it's merely embarrassment. I am finished now. I
stand here as a sickly outcast. I have insulted them finally.
Thinking man, and child. Emotional immaturity. Yes, I know
what it's called. I know what it's *all* called. It is not popular in
the world outside, and it is terrifyingly real and utterly hopeless
here. Not to be needed. His mother, yes, but that was all mothers. Joan, only under a delusion. But no one, no one at all,
with need *and* comprehension.

"And shall be evermore.
Amen."

The chaplain had arrived at his central position, and his
burning eyes seemed to hypnotize them into sitting down. He
waited, motionless, for absolute silence. He looked horribly impressive and unwell.
"The Second Book of Samuel, Verse Twenty-six," he said;
and only Ma Crab knew what was coming. " 'I am distressed
for thee, my brother Jonathan: very pleasant hast thou been
unto me: thy love to me was wonderful, passing the love of
women.' "
A sudden final emphasis had assured an even deeper silence.

The Head, beginning to redden, tried quickly to gauge his wife's expectations but saw only a tilted nose and chin.

"Tonight is a time of parting. We say good-bye to acquaintances, friends . . . loved ones. I myself am saying good-bye to you all, forever. I am going away to die."

An indescribable smile, as he let the deeply satisfying word fall into the arena. The Head, startled, really did look at Ma Crab to see if she had prior information. But nothing was revealed except a pallor comparable to the speaker's.

"I go, I trust, if I may say so, to a more agreeable place than this. I leave no David in distress. Hush, Humphrey, hush." With pain and a curious pleasure, he had heard the astonishing sound of Watson-Wyatt uttering a sob. "Earthly love has not been to my taste. It *has* been, however, to many of you. This is as it should be. I hold no brief for the criminally ignorant activities of our rulers in the course of this remarkable and pitiful term."

As all eyes slowly turned his way, the Head cleared his throat loudly, in a vain attempt at warning: being unable to think of anything else to do.

"This remarkable and pitiful term," the chaplain repeated, putting out a supporting hand against the side of the pulpit. Something had happened: the grinding had become more painful, and everything had grown hazy. He could distinguish no single face. He felt himself sway a little. And worst of all, it had gone. Something about feeling the earthly love too deeply. Something about embracing the heavenly. But it had all gone. There were no words.

He waited. Gradually, distinctness returned. Yes, he held them rapt.

But still it was all gone.

He felt cold sweat on his skeleton face. How long had he paused? How long had they waited?

The solution came as if from heaven.

"It is my office to remind you . . . and to remind you forcibly. . . ."

Amazed, marveling, they were sitting up on their pews. Right out of the blue, it was coming at them . . . like an unexpected catch at cricket.

". . . that such persons are, in their blindness, in their ignorance, and in their folly. . . ."

Down it came, and they nearly cheered.

"CRUCIFYING CHRIST FOR THE SECOND TIME."

Yes, his voice had regained full strength. His right hand was
already up.

"No! No! No! This is not Christianity! This is the vapid
spawn of misguided blasphemers. This comes not from Christ,
but from small men too ignorant . . . nay, too cowardly . . .
to embrace the true message. Cast your eyes upon the windows
of this very *building!*"

No one turned. Not one. They could not leave him for a second.

Now he was the great white bird with both wings outstretched.

"Look what they have done to him!"

They looked, but only at the Reverend Cyril Starr.

"This pale, weak . . . *effeminate* . . . creature. This is
their Christ! And fittingly so. For only such a one could tell us
to accept the pattern . . . to become ciphers . . . to embrace
. . . respectability."

He spat it out and folded his wings. He was all right now.
He was more than all right. He was playing the concerto as
never before. What folly to have been tempted to play a new
one! Divine providence had guided him sharply back.

"But this is not Christ. This is *not* Christianity. This is not
. . . love. What . . . you may well ask yourselves . . ." (And
they did. To a man.) "What is love to these people? I will tell
you. . . . It is some faint, wishy-washy anemic little regard
for playing the game . . . for doing honor to these premises in
which we reside. But this is not love. . . ."

He saw them leaning forward, gaping, restraining themselves with the utmost difficulty from leaping into the air and
shouting.

"No, no, no! Christ is love . . . And Christ . . . is a BURN-
ING FIRE!"

It was hot gas; it was molten lava; it roared forth and burst
like an atomic weapon. And he rushed in after it.

"Yes! Yes! Christ is a scorching flame of love! Such love that ravages the heart and soul of those who truly know him. A love that burns its way to our very innards—reducing to dust and ashes our sackcloth—our pettiness, our pride, our ambition—all the vile balderdash of creed, class and society . . . and leaving us naked and alone and free, and *joyful,* before Him. No, no, I tell you! Christ is not a milkmaid! Christ is not a bearded lady! Christ is not even a schoolmaster . . . or a rural dean. Christ . . . is a BURNING FIRE!"

The long glance, to his deep satisfaction, took in staring face after staring face. He spun. "And-now-to-God-the-Father. . . ."

He spun back, gathered up his skirt, and swept down and away, squeaking to shattering effect; stumbled suddenly on the steps up to his place, thrust away the helping hands that reached out; regained his position, announced, "Hymn Number Three Hundred and Seventeen," and sank down with his head in his hands, in prayer.

Immediately, Ma Crab did the same.

Comprehensive though the sermon had seemed to him, it had been abbreviated to one of the shortest ever delivered. Dazed by the speed and passion of it, no one moved. The Beatle himself, blinking through his glasses, was facing the wrong way around on the organ bench.

But it was as well that they had time to recover. For this was the moment. And as the Beatle began the first loved notes, they rose, even better equipped emotionally, after these transports from a dying man. Another Starling—Robert—was crying. The sad melody was coming forth in a lingering, tempting manner. The Beatle knew that they liked it this way. They liked to give it everything.

> "Lord . . . dis-miss us . . . with thy . . . bless-ing;
> Thanks for . . . mercies past . . . re-ceive,
> Pardon all . . . their faults confess-ing;
> Time that's lost . . . may all re-trieve."

He *must* look at me now, Carleton thought. Surely he can't help it?

> "May thy chil-dren
> Ne'er again . . . thy spi-ir-it grieve."

348

The chaplain's head was still in his hands. Also Ma Crab's. What were they praying? It was sad. Ashley, with no hymn-book, was looking down at nothing. The wrong sadness, each of them. The right sadness swelled up, fortissimo, from every other voice: the Beard quavering, the Head doing bravely under the circumstances, even Lucretia piping high, Rowles and the Pedant giving forth close at hand. . . . And those who were really saying good-bye making the stoutest effort of all. Carleton fought against tears in his eyes and a catch in his throat. It all seemed to have been right and good now; everything, even cold showers, even geometry; everything, every day and hour of it; and all about to be lost forever.

> "Bless then . . . all our . . . days of leis-ure;
> Help us . . . selfish lures . . . to flee;"

Nicky glanced up, and down again!

It was very quick, but there was no doubt about it. He looked at me. He's relented. He will, he will. Oh, why have we wasted this time! Never mind, never mind, we have all time!

The last verse. A mass intake of breath. And then they gave it forth.

> "Let thy . . . Fa-ther . . . hand be . . . shield-ing
> All who here . . . shall meet . . . no more;"

Yes, it was true. They had all time, but never here again. Not on these hills. How sweet it has been; how sad and happy and rich; my boyhood at Weatherhill!

> "May their . . . seed-time . . . past be yield-ing
> Year by year . . . a richer store:"

The Beatle paused, for the last deep breath; and out they gave them—the final, thunderous, heartrending lines!

> "Those re-turn-ing
> Make more . . . faith-ful . . . tha-an . . . be-fore."

CHAPTER THIRTY-THREE

"Chuck us over the lipstick, would you, Carleton?" said Stoddart Major.

A big fellow, he looked enormous in red roses on a white ground.

Carleton picked up the lipstick from the hollowed-out pencil rack on an inky desk and threw it across. Backstage was alive with people and noise. It was almost impossible to move.

"I'm darn well doing it myself this time," said Stoddart eagerly reddening his lips. "She made a balls of it yesterday."

Carleton could only just hear. From the other side of the Little Dingley backdrop, behind which they prepared the mysteries of their art, there was additional uproar. Everyone had dashed into the Big Schoolroom, fighting for places. Several of the chairs up on tables at the far end had crashed to the floor. Only the three front rows were now untenanted: waiting for the Crabtrees, parents and staff. There were catcalls and whistles, and objects flew about. It was almost over now. No more Latin, no more French, no more sitting on the hard old bench.

"Want some?"

Naylor, amazingly enough, had produced a half-bottle of brandy from under his cassock.

"Have it. It's good for the nerves."

Carleton took a swig. He had never tasted it before. It was like fire.

"Thanks."

It was all very well, but was he now going to reel on and fall down on his face?

No, he seemed to be all right: except for the one terror that he was pushing aside—his part. The only memory at the moment was "That's right, ma'am. Why, sometimes we'll walk fifty miles in one day." Then absolute blankness.

"Have you patched it up?"

"What?"

Naylor nodded toward Nicky, who was separated from them by about fifteen people in various kinds of dress and undress. The Beatle's wife was on her knees, doing something to the back of his red velvet. She had a huge safety pin in her mouth.

"What chance have I had?" said Carleton, thinking, I'm being terribly open with Naylor, but after all it's not the first time. We both revealed ourselves once.

"Well, I only hope he acts up, or he'll ruin the show."

They found Ashley in his room.

He had been lying on his bed, drinking whisky as a cure for alarm. It had not been working well. The chaplain's collapse had been very disturbing. When he opened the door, he was dismayed to realize that he had no wish to see either of them.

Rich said: "Found you out, me boy!"

His smile seemed offensive, his teeth enormous, the swoops of his hair and his purple-orange coat vulgar in the extreme. Nancy, beside him, appeared to have shrunken over the months, diminished in stature and person.

"Well, well."

"Are you going to ask us in?" she said. She had been smiling too, but her Matronly scrutiny evidently told her that there was nothing to smile about.

"Yes, yes, of course. Enter."

"We had to come and see how you poor devils have been lasting the . . ." Rich began. "What's this, what's this? I didn't know you went in for the hard stuff, Eric."

"No? Uh . . . sit down, sit down. Yes, my seedtime past is yielding, year by year, a richer store."

"Ah, ha, you've just been singing that old number. Don't tell me you fell for it?"

"Only that line."

They sat in silence for a moment, surprised by the awkwardness of the meeting. He wondered how he had ever associated with such common, ordinary people. Who had changed? It must be him. They, in turn, were shocked by his altered appearance.

"I'm sorry . . . I've . . . only one glass."

"That's O.K., old man, you go ahead."

When he raised the glass, his hand was not steady. What right had they to come here and inspect him?

"Some of us have *not* been lasting, as you can see."

"What is it, Eric; what's wrong?" Nancy asked.

"Yes, you're looking a bit down, old chap."

"A number of things. One of them will appeal to you. I'm being removed from office. This is my last night."

"Oh no!" she said.

"That bastard!" said Jimmy Rich. And after a moment, "What reason has he cooked up this time?"

Ashley downed his drink.

"Disturbing, once too often, the correct functioning of the team spirit. I saved two wretches from being beaten to a pulp. They came and rang our bell in the middle of the night."

"Sounds like quite a wheeze," said Rich.

"I enjoyed it."

"Oh dear," said Nancy. "But you can do much better outside, Eric. Jimmy's making a mint."

"As what?"

"Golf club secretary," said Rich. "The salary's nearly double."

"Can you see me as a golf club secretary?"

"No," said Nancy. "But there must be something else."

"Must there?"

They were silent. He found them inadequate, and in this particular case they knew themselves to be.

"Well, let's cheer up, for the Lord's sake," said Jimmy Rich. "Come on, are you coming to the show?"

"Yes, do, Eric."

"Very well."

"We'll have to stay at the back," said Rich. "We want to be in evidence, but not too much."

"That suits me."

How on earth had he ever endured—indeed, enjoyed—their company? Plainly, they had not changed. How much, then, had *he* altered in a brief time? Plainly, as they say, out of all recognition.

The schoolroom was full now, with everyone except the Crabtrees and the parents. There were shouts and cheers at the back as Jimmy Rich and Nancy came in through the door from the Chapel Square. Dr. Rowles and other masters were up in front.

It was the moment for action. Gower slipped out of the other door, into the corridor, and up the stone steps to Roly's room. It was done in a trice.

Cunning and long practice told him that the objects selected must be such that their absence would not be noted until at least the following day. First, a random selection from the bookshelves: one Dickens, one Scott, one Meredith, one Thackeray, and one Jane Austen; something about Shakespeare by somebody called Bentley, something about geometry, something about algebra, *A Passage to India* by E. M. Forster, and something about Bach by Albert Schweitzer. He piled them on the desk, leaving his hands free for filling his pockets. Subtly, he restricted himself to only one pipe from a rack holding four, six biscuits from the can, and a thick wad of incomprehensible papers from the very bottom drawer. The kettle proved a ridiculous temptation, but he resisted it. Seizing the books again, he tiptoed rapidly out of the room and into the upper dorm.

Totally deserted.

On top of his trunk was a half-empty tuck box which had served to conceal many a social indiscretion before now. He unlocked the clasp, raised the lid, and emptied the entire hoard into it, on top of three slices of stale bread and a pot of raspberry jam, abstracted that very afternoon from their beastly common room.

He closed and locked it.

He smiled. No fear of any kind. Entirely taunting.

"He's here, he's here, the Head's here," said McCaffrey, who had been keeping watch through the crack in the curtains.

"All right, all right, calm down, man," snapped the Pedant. "Now then, I want you all in line, and be smart about it."

The din in the auditorium had diminished, more out of curiosity than respect. With the Crabtrees in the middle, the front two rows were filled by strange men and women, parents of the dear knew who. Strangers were a rare sight. Everyone had a good, critical look.

With bony fingers, the Pedant pushed and pulled the people of Little Dingley into line for their opening entrance.

"Are you all right there with the curtains, McCaffrey?"

"Yes, sir."

"Ready, Kingsley?"

"Right you be," said the Beatle, and he suddenly started to bang out the opening number on the piano. McCaffrey pulled a cord and the curtains parted, and the villagers poured onto the stage, singing at the tops of their voices.

The Head, who had been chatting with the mother of somebody in the seat behind him, turned back contentedly to view the stage and in a moment of frozen disbelief saw four boys, dressed and painted as young women, holding onto the arms of four other boys. Someone had instructed them to walk in a mincing manner that was assumed to be ladylike. Someone, it seemed to him, in an undisguised and blinding light, was throwing his life's achievement straight back in his face. The violence of the chaplain's insane hostility was as nothing to this.

"I can't believe it," he said, "I can't believe it."

"It seems it's customary," murmured Ma Crab.

"You knew about it?"

"Well, no. But I gathered some form of disguise was assumed."

"I would have banned it on the spot."

"I'm afraid there's no option now but to endure."

He sat there, scarlet, as they roared "At Little-Dingley-in-the-Marsh" for the fourth time, gazing flirtatiously into each other's eyes.

The exodus had suddenly left a vacant space backstage. Carleton approached Nicky, who turned his head away. In his rouge and lipstick he was breathtaking. The Beatle's wife had produced a pink brassiere to contain the tennis balls.

"This is madness. Stop it. I love you. I'll explain. I can't explain now. Meet me afterward behind the chapel."

"Leave me alone."

"Stop it, you must give me a chance. I'll be there anyhow. But you've got to pretend now. You've got to act."

Nicky said nothing.

Naylor came over and butted in. "Do what he says. Don't be a damn fool. You'll mess up the whole thing."

There was loud applause for the end of the song. They were winning already! Naylor walked away and onto the stage, and they heard him say, "Good morning, dear people," and a shout of "Good morning, Vicar!"

"Have you patched it up?" that fool Naylor had said. He thought he was talking about something small. He didn't know that he was talking about everything.

Nicky had turned his back to him. They were both looking onto the stage. Naylor was doing it very well. But Carleton could only look at Nicky's black wavy hair going down to the pearls. He wanted to hold him. "Ah, but here comes my daughter, Alice, who is better equipped than I. . . ." Nicky strode away, on his high heels. Carleton saw the Head, in the middle of the row, utter some exclamation and sharply turn his head toward Ma Crab, who continued to gaze at the stage. Then Nicky was standing out in front, immediately above them, and singing confidently, "Percy, Waiting for Percy, Will he bring me the love that I require?"

Everyone was doing terribly well. His legs felt weak and he had an awful fear that he was going to have to go to the lavatory. Where the devil was his group? They were there. They came shuffling over, and the three stood together; Caldicott with his monocle, and McIver in black lace. "You forgot your case, you clot," whispered McIver, handing it to him.

To be called a clot by McIver, whom he had recently beaten! This was the last night and no mistake! Still, how awful to have forgotten the suitcase. Was it an omen? What on earth was it he had to say?

No time to think. Everyone went off the other side, and they labored on, wiping their brows.

"A short walk from the station, indeed!" said McIver, and he rolled his eyes, and the audience roared.

And suddenly it was easy; it was wonderful; out there all dressed up, with a disguised face, in the hot, dazzling light, which threw the adversary into impenetrable darkness; with nothing to do but let oneself go and let them admire. He sat down on his case—which the Pedant had never told him to do, but it seemed absolutely right. And it was coming now. He had the strange illusion that McIver was personally concocting it and throwing it at him as a challenge, and, at the same time,

355

paradoxically, he sensed a sympathetic alarm in McIver's face that he was not going to be able to answer.

"The wide-open spaces, they call them, do they not?"

It came out frightfully North American and with a terrific emphasis that he had never thought to use before.

"That's right, ma'am. Why, sometimes we'll walk *fifty miles* in *one day.*"

"Gracious!"

McIver threw both hands in the air, and simpered, and there was a roar of laughter. He did it brilliantly, and Carleton had difficulty in keeping a straight face. How incredible to have beaten this gifted fellow!

"You're joking," said Caldicott.

"I'm not," said Carleton, for the first time lingering on it and shaking his head from side to side; so that there was another laugh, and someone in the audience actually gave an admiring imitation, "I'm naht."

"Well . . . well, well!" McIver for the first time sat on his own suitcase, crossed his legs, remembered roguishly, and delicately pulled his skirt over his knee, using two fingers. And there were screams from the auditorium.

It seemed to be nearly all from the back. There was a curious patch of silence just beyond the footlights.

But now Nicky was under discussion. Caldicott's fiancée. What on earth was Nicky going to do? He came rushing into Caldicott's arms, very nearly losing one of his shoes. Carleton felt a ridiculous pang of jealousy. Acting this was not very difficult. They were well cast.

But now the introduction.

". . . great friend at Oxford, Peter Piper."

"How do you do?"

"How do you do?"

Nicky looked him straight in the eyes. To Carleton it was cold and even hostile. But to the audience it must have seemed meaningful.

In fact, someone whistled!

All was well. At least Nicky was trying.

Far removed from the crowd, the chaplain lay in red silk pajamas which clashed a little with his pink sheets and pillowcases.

He had been asleep, with the bedside lamp still on. It illuminated a room more ascetic than the adjoining salon: white, with purple curtains; no fireplace; few decorations—a nature photograph of a boy standing by a lily pond; a figurine of beautiful Perseus, holding up the bleeding head of Medusa who, he liked to think, bore such a striking resemblance to the headmaster's wife. He could remember nothing except praying for the peace that passeth all understanding. He didn't even remember how he got into bed, and vaguely wondered, with mild alarm, if Philomena had been in attendance.

It was her knock that had awakened him. Though only half her face was visible, she was plainly in distress.

"I don't know," she said. "I don't know how to say it."

"You're trembling. Are you unwell?"

"No, no, not a bit. It's . . . the Doctor's here."

"Doctor? What Doctor?"

"Dr. Boucher. It seems Herself phoned him to come up at once."

"Herself? Ah, God, will no one rid me . . . ?" His eyes fell instinctively upon Medusa. He felt himself being turned to stone. "Tell the man to go home, Philomena."

"Oh, Lord, he's just out on the landing."

"I don't see why that—"

"Ah, chaplain," said the Butcher, pushing past her in a very peppery suit, carrying the porkpie hat and a black bag. "Sorry for barging in like this, but Mrs. Crabtree sounded concerned. . . ."

He paused, startled, even in his professional capacity, by the white skull and black eyes on the pink pillow.

"How dare you," the chaplain said quietly, closing the eyes and opening them again. "Tell me something before you go— what exactly have I delivered?"

"I beg your pardon?" said the Butcher, who had the curious and instantaneous notion that he had been attending at an accouchement.

"What did I come out with?" the chaplain asked.

"When, chaplain? When?"

"Oh God," the chaplain said. "Would you be kind enough to hand me that orange?"

"Just a moment, chaplain. I'm not so sure that you should be eating. . . ."

"I don't intend to eat it, you preposterous creature," said the chaplain. "Just hand it to me, would you? There is an odor of hospitals. . . . Thank you. Now you may go."

"Go?!"

"Yes, there is nothing for either of us to learn. I am afflicted with cancer of the abdomen, my dear ass."

The Butcher was only just controlling the temper which had won him many a bout. "If that is so, there are remedies."

"A carving knife," the chaplain said. "No thank you. I have had life as abundantly as was within me. I may not have warmed both hands, but I am unquestionably ready to depart. I suggest you follow my example. At any rate, I am now going to sleep."

"Might I have a look?"

"Certainly not, you obscene creature," said the chaplain, closing his eyes.

The Butcher was boiling. He clenched his hat. "It is contrary to my Hippocratic Oath for me to leave you in this condition."

"I am fully acquainted with your morality. You may well have destroyed four young lives. Go home."

"I did my duty," said the Butcher.

"You did mine."

"Only because you refused to do it."

"Your oath is to attend the sick who request it. Not to enter uninvited and weary them with specious argument."

"Good night!"

The Butcher banged the door.

The chaplain felt nauseated, and very faint indeed, having eaten only lettuce for a week. But it didn't matter. Not to him or anyone else. Not, certainly, to the sister with three children in Los Angeles. Absolutely nothing mattered. It was an ideal state for sleeping. Philomena tiptoed in and stole a long, tearful, secret look.

Exulting in the heat of the lights, his own dashing costume, and the roars of the audience, Carleton made an emphatic ges-

358

ture of the hands as he told Nicky, "Gee, I'm just crazy about you, Alice. You know that, don't you?"

"Yes, Peter, darling," Nicky solemnly replied, giving him an overwhelming glance. He had been acting properly, spurred on by the competition, yet retaining, to Carleton's knowledge alone, a distance and coldness. The combination was maddening.

"But, dearest, what about Percy?" Nicky inquired.

"Nothing to worry about there, Alice, darling. Anyone can see Percy is just crazy about the Honorable Priscilla. That gal sure got her hooks into him mighty fast."

There was a shout of laughter at the recollection of Stoddart Major going to work. He had been rivaling McIver as chief comic. The farthest spectators were becoming increasingly noisy, though the leading lovers had hitherto been treated with silent respect. Jimmy Rich, seated between Ashley and Nancy, could be heard above everyone. They were perched high, on chairs, on tables, and everything shook when he laughed. The noise had started when a real croquet ball, loosely struck, had landed in Ma Crab's lap and Rich had called out to his neighbors, "It's a goal, lads!"

"Same with your dad," Carleton continued. "He's starry-eyed about Matilda. That just leaves us, honey. Whaddya say, sweetheart?"

"What are you suggesting, Peter?" asked Nicky, with a shattering glance.

Carleton moved near and as instructed by the Pedant put his arm round Nicky's waist and his cheek beside Nicky's. The Beatle was playing. They swayed slightly to the music. Carleton sang

"Come with me—to Canada."

Rich suddenly shouted, "That's it, Carleton boy! That's a nice little bit of stuff you've got there!"

There was a guffaw from the rougher element.

It filled Ashley with disgust.

Carleton was too engrossed to hear, and it came from too far. Surely now, he thought, I can win him back. He must feel more in my touch now. We have been too delicate. He must feel that I really mean him to be mine.

"Come and see the magic of a prairie sky."

"I simply can't believe it," the Head said. "The precentor is out of his mind."

"See the snowflakes fall,
Hear the coyotes call."

"Better than the Crabs any day," Rich addressed his admirers, who were in transports.

Ashley sat frozen beside his boorish, uncomprehending, vulgar, former associate, thinking, My God, you in your striped suit, with your blasted little darling, what a blazing nerve! How you must be in heaven. You are nearly my age. It would seem nearly possible. Yet it is fatally impossible.

Nicky's cheek was hot, and soft. Carleton held him more tightly around the waist.

"When you fill your lungs with air—in Canada,
You will feel a millionaire—in Canada."

"Not too near the footlights, lads! You're making someone jealous."

It was just audible in front, and the Head's scarlet face flashed around. Several parents turned. Ma Crab remained motionless.

"Ssh, Jimmy," said Nancy.

"Yes, shut up," said Ashley.

"So let us not delay,
Let us make our way.
Come with me—to Canada,
Today!"

In the midst of the applause there was a shouting of—"That's it, Carleton, boy, clear off out of harm's way! Let them stew in their own juice!"

It came to Carleton as incomprehensible uproar, somewhere beyond the lights.

There was a sense of loss as Nicky moved out of his arms. The whole cast was slowly gathering. The parishioners of Little Dingley showed their approval as McIver sang, "I'm in love with a clergyman, named Arthur Cecil Sinclair." The audience cheered. Weddings were in the air. Carleton's heart felt like exploding as Nicky sang, "How I'd love to go with you to Canada," and again he put his arm around Nicky's waist. Three couples were thus joined. "Hurrah's!" were given by the people of Little Dingley. And then all together they began the Beatle's most haunting melody. First the introduction from the three couples—"We dreamed that we might be together. . . ." And then the whole cast gave it out:

> "Our dream is ending now,
> Our life begins with the dawn. . . ."

Just right, it was, for the last night: the audience was silenced; touched, saddened.

> "Our day is starting now,
> Though the stars linger on.
> The happy days that lie ahead
> Are beckoning so clear. . . ."

Ashley felt sickened. In the mass they were either savage or sentimental.

An increased outpouring of emotion:

> "We must be wending now,
> Our life is starting anew.
> And now it's time to go to bed,
> My darling . . . my . . . *dear!*"

He turned Nicky toward him and kissed him hard on his warm cheek. All three couples kissed. A roar from the audience. Cheers. And McCaffrey pulled the curtains, and it was over. Nicky broke away. The curtains parted again, and they bowed. Tumult. The Crabtrees were on their feet, pushing their way out in protest. No one was interested. The Pedant, uplifted by his triumph, had leaped to a corner of the stage, and was shouting, "All together everybody!"

The Beatle struck up again. The cast gave forth. The audience joined them. The Pedant conducted.

"Our dream is ending now," sang Weatherhill School, "Our life begins with the dawn. . . ."

Ashley jumped down from where he was seated and went out into the Chapel Square and the purity of the night.

The huge dark bulk of the Big Schoolroom pursued him with song, as he strode away:

> "We must be wending now,
> Our life is starting anew. . . ."

CHAPTER THIRTY-FOUR

The scene was confused in the Head's Hall, as the school shuffled along in double file on the way to the common room, and the handshakes and good-byes with the assembled masters. The chandelier threw a dim light. It had not been dusted for twenty-odd years.

The Beatle came past, in a flurry, with his gown flapping, knocked on the door of the Head's study, across the hall, and entered.

"You wish to see me, Headmaster?"

The Head's face looked purple above the green table-lamp.

"Close the door, if you please. Dr. Kingsly, we are outraged and appalled by this repulsive contribution of yours."

"I beg your pardon?" said the Beatle, coming eagerly forward with his glasses shining and the black fringe nodding on his forehead.

"This obscene dressing up of . . . this pantomime of indecencies. . . ."

362

"Are you referring to *Peter Piper*?" said the Beatle, turning white with astonishment and shock.

"I refer to the unspeakable scandal you have perpetrated tonight."

"Scandal?" said the Beatle. "Gracious me!"

"You have done your utmost to destroy our entire term's achievement at Weatherhill!" the Head shouted.

The Beatle held onto the desk. "My dear Headmaster . . ."

"How dare you address me in that way! My wife and I have had to sit through a personal and vile insult. How your own wife, not to mention Mr. Milner, have lent themselves to it, I don't know, but I intend to find out."

"My dear fellow, you can't be referring to our little show?"

The Head had lost the gift of speech. The blood pounded in his brain.

"*Peter Piper* is an old favorite," said the Beatle. "I have a dozen others. We perform them regularly."

"You will never perform them again!" shouted the Head.

Across the way, the queue moved in, around the great polished table and out again. Masters' faces passed quickly by. Roly, the Pedant, the Cod. . . . "Good-bye, sir." "Good-bye." "Good-bye, sir." "Good-bye." A slightly altered relationship. They were almost free—at least for the holiday. They were on more level terms. Dotty and the Beard gave an extra special squeeze of the hand to their associates. There was no sign of Ashley.

Carleton and Naylor came hurrying past Lady Jane's chest. They had been changing into their suits. Nicky was already there. He was in the queue, beside Hamilton Minor. He was in his Sunday suit, but still wore makeup. So did Carleton. They would have to wash before bed. Meanwhile, he felt important and exhilarated; a star, for the watching queue.

They were headed for the sitting room next to the study. Here there was always coffee and biscuits for those who were leaving. But something was wrong. The door was open and a group, including Johns and Pryde and Steele, was standing uncertainly just inside. Carleton peered around Johns' beaky profile and saw Ma Crab before the fireplace, her hands behind her back, her eyes on the ceiling. "I repeat," she said, "there *is* no coffee."

"We don't quite understand, Mrs. Crabtree," said Johns.

"I should have thought it was perfectly clear," said Ma Crab. "The Headmaster and I are deeply distressed and repelled by the lesson in the less wholesome facts of life to which Dr. Kingsly subjected us tonight. My daughter is prostrate. We are in no mood for entertaining. You may go."

While they hesitated, she added, "And you might ask them to reduce the sound in the hall. Our chaplain has taken to his bed. He is extremely unwell."

They moved out, and Johns closed the door, saying: "I just can't believe it, I can't believe it! How does it feel to be unwholesome?"

"I don't know what she's talking about," Carleton said. He was entirely bewildered. He didn't feel like a star anymore. Had they seen through his performance with Nicky? It was baffling.

"Less noise there, you people," said Steele, who had suffered his final, surprising, loss of esteem as senior prefect.

The group wandered away, but Naylor was still there, murmuring, "Since he's apparently safely in bed, why don't we have a final libation?"

Carleton hesitated. Nicky was still nowhere near the common-room door. Was he coming behind the chapel? He must be, he must be. But there was time; and, besides, the wine might help.

"O.K."

They went quickly up the stairs, with members of the queue watching inquisitively. The landing light was on. The wooden grapes gleamed on the front of the huge cupboard. Naylor had done everything by himself after chapel, as Carleton had to be on stage, and he had kept the key. He lifted out the bottle, which was three-quarters full.

"After you," Carleton said.

They passed it back and forth. It was warm, red, sweet, and delicious.

"We may as well have the lot," said Naylor, tilting the bottle and drinking deep. "Never again."

He looked middle-aged and different. His hair was still powdered.

"O.K. Steady on."

"The poor old sod," said Naylor, in a funny voice. "Do you think he's really dying in there?"

Carleton giggled—which was shocking, but he couldn't help it. This was delightful. His face, which was already slightly pained, felt warm and flushed.

"So he said. *He* ought to know."

They both giggled, and Naylor biffed him on the shoulder.

"Imagine him falling into the burning fire," said Naylor. "I don't think he meant to at all."

"'Course not," said Carleton. "It was super, though. His mind must have gone, poor man."

"The mind has boggled," Naylor said, choking.

"Ssh. . . . There's only about two swigs more."

"You can finish it. I had some before. . . . Listen, there's a crowd going up the wood. Pryde and some other sods. We've beer and cigarettes. Are you coming?"

It wasn't just his powdered head. Naylor had changed, almost alarmingly. He wasn't at all the silent fellow who said "Tch, tch" and nothing much more.

"I know . . . I can't."

The last swig in Carleton's mouth was most peculiar. Little grains between his teeth.

"Oh, ho," said Naylor, too loudly. "A final bid. O.K. But use your head, for God's sake."

"How do you mean?"

"You know what was wrong, don't you?"

"No."

"We both wanted to be boss. No good. You have it made. Christ, I'm tight. It was the brandy. Can you get this damn key in?"

Carleton locked the cupboard. He was taken aback and thought he should be shocked. But he felt too well. They crept down the stairs, trying not to laugh. The hallway was deserted. They must have stayed above longer than he realized. My goodness, had Nicky already gone to the buttress and found no one there?

They tiptoed down to the back of the hall. The grandfather clock began to strike ten and gave them both a fright. In the cloisters Carleton said, "You go ahead." There were people scampering about in the dark. No one was bothering to play cloister cricket: it was over; next term was football. "All right, all right," said Naylor, "I'm not nosey. Come and join us if it doesn't work out. We'll be up near the pool."

"O.K. Thanks."

Naylor took the stone steps in several bounds and nearly fell on his face, and then disappeared across the Chapel Square. Carleton followed. It was very dark: a starless night.

Someone shouted, "A burning fah!" and someone else was whistling the tune of "We Must Be Wending Now." A night of freedom, release. Nothing punishable now. The long grass brushed his trousers. In a faint light through the stained glass he could just see the dark slope of the buttress. He was intensely excited and also full of confidence from the wine. Approaching the buttress, he spoke the one word in the world for the first time in his life, "Nicky?"

No reply. Well, he hadn't arrived yet; that was all.

I'll wait.

Yes.

And when he does arrive I'll waste no more time. I'll show him what we've been missing. I'll be what Naylor calls boss. I'll embrace him up against the buttress. Our mouths kissing. I'll bend over him. I'll open his trousers, because when one really loves someone, one must know all of them, and the rest is just agonizing and stupid flirtation, and I'm a fool to have let it go on so long, so that it's darn nearly died on me . . . on the two of us.

Carleton was aching, and warm, and not entirely sober.

Something white in the buttress appeared like an hallucination. But it was real.

It was a note!

He held it up high, so that reddish-purple light fell dimly on it from the window, making it seem evil and hellish: "I saw you go up, so don't think I expected to meet you here. I'm not meeting you in the dark. I'll give you a few minutes to say good-bye in the morning, though you don't deserve it. After breakfast, down by the farmyard."

It was unsigned.

Carleton felt blank and empty for a moment, and then tears rushed out of his eyes. He indulged them. There was something wretchedly sweet about giving way to emotion now, of whatever kind. Until he heard himself sob out loud and was afraid of being discovered. He brushed his face with the back of his hand, controlled himself, and stepped away from the buttress. He didn't know where to go. He couldn't face the group up at the pond. The light was still on in the chapel. It came between the narrow crack in the oaken doors. It had always been peaceful in there. The handle was a round black ring. He gently turned it and opened one of the two doors.

There was, at once, the echoing, unearthly sound of a single voice.

He couldn't distinguish the words.

Curious, he stepped in, and closed the door behind him, and tiptoed across the antechapel to where he could look down the aisle.

Ashley was standing at the lectern, reading at the top of his voice.

Carleton felt afraid. He didn't know why. The empty chapel. The lectern light just revealing the great strained forehead under unruly blond hair. But most of all the angry, defiant, almost crazy tone of voice . . . and the crazy words. It was Ecclesiastes. He had read it before himself, but never like this.

> "And the grinders cease because they are few,
> And those that look out of the windows be darkened,
> And the doors shall be shut in the street;"

I have deserted him, as Nicky has deserted me. And there's nothing I can do.

> "When the sound of the grinding is low,
> And one shall rise up at the voice of a bird,
> And all the daughters of music shall be brought low;
> Yea, they shall be afraid of that which is high,
> And *terrors* . . ."

The chapel reverberated. Ashley had—by chance?—raised his head.

They stared at each other down the length of the chapel.

Carleton couldn't speak. The silence went on and on.

> "... shall be in the way;
> And the almond tree shall blossom,
> And the grasshopper shall be a burden,
> And desire . . . shall . . . *fail.*"

Ashley raised his head again. He said quietly but in a horrible tone, "Go away. You painted, pampered, jade."

Carleton hesitated. Ashley stared at him. He didn't even run his fingers through his hair. He was calm, in a crazy way. He seemed to hate. It was terrible.

"Leave!"

Carleton tried to murmur "Sorry" but couldn't. He walked to the door.

> "Because man goeth to his long home,
> And the mourners go about in the streets."

He opened the door and went out. The voice seemed to stay with him. He could scarcely see his way across the Chapel Square. There were no lights. What time was it? He went through the Big Schoolroom, stumbling between two rows of chairs, along the corridor and into the washroom, to remove his makeup. Rowles was polishing his shoes. He turned with one foot up on the bench, and roared, "Where in tarnation have *you* been, Carleton?"

"Um . . ."

"And where are the others? There's not one living prefect in the whole house."

"I don't know, sir. I didn't know it was so late, sir."

"Late! I've had to put out all the blasted lights myself. Take that muck off your face!"

Rowles went on polishing. Carleton washed off the makeup.

"Just because it's the last night, you people think you can make merry hell. I may tell you I've given six on the arse on the last night before now. And I've given it to prefects too!"

"Yes, sir."

You even polish your shoes, Carleton thought. Rowles hadn't spoken to him like this for years. It was a sad way to end things, but he couldn't see any escape. Where was Johns? Surely he hadn't joined the others. He must be having some private celebration of his prison release.

"The Head is beside himself. I warned Milner, but it was no use. You certainly overdid it with your inamorata. I've never seen such infernal and disgusting cheek!"

"We were . . . supposed to be acting, sir."

"Acting my arsehole," said Rowles, starting on the other foot. "And another thing . . . what's Ashley getting up to? Rich has been here with that female, pestering me about him. *I* don't know where he is."

"He's . . . um . . . reading out loud in the chapel. Ecclesiastes."

The Doctor's mouth dropped open. He hurled his materials into the box. "I'd rather work in an asylum," he said. "Get on up to bed."

"Yes, sir. Good night, sir."

There was no reply. Carleton went up in the dark. He bumped his knee against the end of Gower's bed, and groped his way toward his own. McIver's torch was out. His acting must have exhausted him. Nicky was away in a corner. Tomorrow morning—good-bye? A deep silence. They were tired out. They were young, after all. He was the old one.

As he lay there for the last time in his life, strange recollections of Ashley ran through his head. What did they mean? Art before life. Art is solitude. The way back to isolation. Substitute. . . . Natural defense. . . . Owen with his cars, until life refuse to be rejected. . . . Freedom comes when the relationship is ended. If you stop you will turn into me. This is what will happen to *you*. And the almond tree shall blossom, and the grasshopper shall be a burden. And the almond tree shall blossom. . . .

Unexpectedly, and with benefit of communion wine, he was asleep.

CHAPTER THIRTY-FIVE

Ashley woke in a cold sweat. He had heard no bells, but it must be late: the room was warmed by brilliant sunshine. His hands and feet seemed totally dead, and he tried to move them. A strange tingling, and something swept over him. He managed to raise a hand to his face and found it as wet as if he had been out in a rainstorm. Then the thought of the coming day produced its customary alarm, but terrifyingly intensified. "I will show you fear in a handful of dust" took hold of his mind and went on repeating itself. He was afraid to look at his watch to see whether the day was, or was not, truly launched. He pulled the clothes around him: he was shivering in the hot room. He tried to sleep, but unconsciousness would not come; only these passing waves of faintness and fright.

At last he decided to pick up the watch. His fingers were almost uncontrollable. It was twenty past nine. The train left at ten five. There was only just time. He was not going to be left alone in this deathly place. He stood out of bed and was seized with an agonizing cramp in his right leg, so that he had to sit down. Then he limped toward the curtains.

Yes, it was a dazzling morning. The sycamore tree . . . the wood beyond . . . it all seemed hostile and desolate. Panic and emptiness. Oo-boum. He wiped his face and chest with a towel and washed, but decided not to shave, because his hands were fluttering preposterously. He had to use them both, to drink from the tooth mug and relieve his dead dry mouth. He put the toothbrush and his pajamas and slippers in the briefcase and dressed with great difficulty. His face in the mirror was puffed and mottled and belonged to a stranger. When he raised his hand to comb his hair, it went dead again; so he abandoned the idea.

And now he was afraid to go out, to be seen. The troubled contemptuous scrutiny of others. How would he buy his ticket with these hands? Would he even be able to complete the walk without fainting?

And was there anywhere to go to?

His mother's scrutiny?

There seemed to be nothing except this place which had been so monstrously fateful to him. Nothing.

He decided he would not stay sane if he remained in this room and suffered a fresh onrush of fear. He opened the door. On the outside he had, last night, pinned his favorite motto in order to avert a return visit by Rich and his lady. He left it there—it was true this time—and set off shakily along the corridor.

Safe, so far.

It was eerily deserted as he made his way between the borders and under the arch of the vine. An odd reflection came from somewhere—no one had replaced the PEDANT'S PALACE sign. The sun was brilliant. It was an insult to the day to feel this weakness, this darkness. He held on tight to the thin green railing at the top of the steep concrete steps. Parents' cars were pulling up on the drive, under the oak trees. There was a group of boys piling the last load of trunks onto the open gray van which McCaffrey was about to drive to the station. Their faces were indistinct. The one face was not there. He seemed safe from attention and descended, willing himself not to fall. The thing to do, he decided, was to walk very quickly. A woman, seated passively in the front of her car waiting for her off-spring, gazed at him curiously, turning her head. A cloud of dust came up from the back of McCaffrey's van, as it bucketed away on the ill-laid concrete. The distance to the Gate Lodge suddenly seemed immense and impossible. He felt that there was nothing to do now but to lie down on the grassy verge and sleep. But he stumbled on. Somewhere behind was his love, and his perversion. No, the latter went with him—inescapably. Who else was there? J.L.M., the forerunner, the ideal, the prime cause, the forever, was gone—out in the world; denying, obliterating, smiling down from the pulpit at ladies in flowered frocks. And Rowles? Rowles was a schoolmaster. Paolo, in Assisi. Dear old friend, my sixth sense tells me. . . . There was

371

something remote about him now, something artificial and protected; as if he had only a sixth sense. The Old Man was dead. What would he have said? There was nothing to say.

Mother. Would she really care if he lay down and slept forever? Would it not be a relief? Would it not spare her the future, *his* future?

No sign of old Gregory, thank God. A saloon car very nearly hit him as he stepped out of the gate. The world outside. He retreated to the grass border. There seemed to be an endless openness under the blue sky of Buckinghamshire, on a path leading nowhere: with cars roaring past, roaring in his head. But red houses appeared, and oh God that hotel, that scene of pity and misery and infantilism. Where had *she* gone? Not that it mattered.

I am not going to be able to ask for the ticket, he thought, nor handle the change to pay for it. The only alternative was to wait and try to do it on the train. A car hooted at him and he staggered stupidly aside. They were assembling in number up against the long low red-brick Victorian building. McCaffrey and a fresh group were unloading trunks.

He went dazedly through the little gate. On the opposite platform was a long line of boys and several masters, some standing, some sitting on trunks and tuck boxes; none of them ever to be seen again. That was the side for London. One had to climb up the covered-in bridge and down to join them. But a glider was mesmerizing him. It went around and around, very slowly, up in the blue. Just around and around, nowhere, nothingness . . . silence, emptiness and panic. There was a sound to his left, from behind the curve of the trees. Directly ahead of him was the stretch of wooden planks, for the convenience of railway workers. And suddenly it was perfectly simple. This was the nonstop train going the other way. As he stepped forward, a kindly face—two big rectangular glass eyes, with a number written underneath them, in yellow—approached, as it seemed, gently, remarkably slowly. He closed his eyes. He closed his mind. He was thinking about nothing at all when someone on the platform let out a shout and the train bore down on him at full speed.

He was not conscious. He felt nothing.

He may have been at peace. At any rate, he was dead.

He had set a bad example. One of the boys on the platform had fainted, and another was being sick.

CHAPTER THIRTY-SIX

What a strange luxury, a breakfast to be eaten whenever one liked: no classes, nothing to follow. The dining hall was only half full. The rest had gone to the train. No one bothered to sit as previously ordained. They slipped onto the nearest bench by the oily wood tables with their jampot stains. Miss Bull was ladling out sausages in a lethargic way as if the term had exhausted her. Carleton walked away with his plate, feeling too nervous to eat, avoiding Nicky, who was in a corner with Hamilton Minor. There was a hubbub of excited noises. So this was how it ended . . . faded out. How could they rejoice so brashly! The mended window was just above his head. The beginning. Ages ago. A stranger in a brown jacket dangling in the sunshine.

Was there hope? Surely there must be. Yes, yes, away from here would be different. Nicky was going to say, "I'm terribly sorry, when can we meet?"

"Wonderful, I'll ask my parents when you can come and stay. They'll be delighted. We'll do some sailing."

Otherwise? Just two objects, two memories. His diary and the school photo. He had packed them last. Fags had taken his trunk down to the drive, where his father or mother would soon be arriving. The farmyard was adjacent and convenient. Nicky as organizer had always been a little disconcerting. He was now eating a hunk of bread and jam, whereas Carleton couldn't even face the two shiny brown greasy sausages. Someone had been murmuring beside him. The beak of Johns in profile. Why sit here?

"Sorry. What did you say?"

"I might give you a ring sometime."

"Oh. Oh yes, do."

Yes, there would always be a Johns hanging around.

"Might take in a flick."

"Yes. Yes, fine."

Having to go to a flick with Johns! Was it possible Johns actually liked him? If so, it had been well camouflaged.

"It wasn't Margaret Rutherford, by the way."

"What wasn't?"

"In *The Lady Vanishes*. I looked it up. It was Dame May Whitty."

Imagine being able to think of such a thing at the last breakfast!

" 'Bye, Carleton."

McIver had stopped at the end of the table with a camera hanging from his shoulder. A nice, funny fellow. He would never see him again. Someone he once beat.

" 'Bye, McIver."

"Sorry I never took that photo." McIver rolled his eyes. "But you won't want it now. 'Bye."

" 'Bye."

McIver was gone. But McIver would still be here to take it . . . for anyone who wanted it. Nearly all these fellows would still be here with him.

"You won't want it now!" Why not?

"What's your cure for hangovers?" said Johns.

"I've never had one."

"No . . . no, I suppose you wouldn't. You were missing from our little rout last night. You should have come and observed the Philistines. It was extremely sordid."

"So I gather," said Carleton. "Sinnott was sick all over the washroom."

"Rowles has confined himself to his room. I fear we're leaving in bad order . . . or odor."

Something he had never properly realized—Johns was a deathly bore.

Nicky and several others at his table were getting up.

"I hope you said your good-byes nicely."

"What?"

"Last night."

"I don't know what you mean."

Nicky had gone out.

"You're well rid of that particular episode. It was not exactly bringing out the best in you."

Carleton felt tempted to pour the cluster of jampots over Johns.

"I must go; the car's probably waiting for me."

"I'll give you a ring."

"Right. 'Bye."

" 'Bye."

There was a black cluster of skivvies in the doorway, towered over by Philomena, their self-appointed leader and collector of funds. Carleton handed her two pounds—from the departing second prefect—and said, "Good-bye, Philomena."

"Thanks very much. Good-bye now."

"Is the . . . chaplain all right?"

"He's gone."

Philomena's voice sounded odd. But her eyes were secure behind her hair.

"Gone?!"

"He went off in a great car with a whole crowd of priests . . . I mean clergy. Off to some airport . . . for Scotland."

"Good heavens."

"All his lovely pictures went after in a van. And the little statues."

"Really!"

"He was a good man," said one of his supporters. "Poor soul." Philomena was silent.

"His soul has nothing to fear."

Ma Crab came through the black bevy, in her crossword-puzzle suit. She was pale and angry, but she spoke as slowly and precisely as ever, with her head nodding up and down. "I will not have you all standing here like a Greek chorus in mourning. See to these tables. They're a disgrace."

Dazed by these curious words, they slowly began to move away.

"I'll say good-bye, Mrs. Crabtree."

She gave him a cold, lifeless hand and addressing a spot somewhere above his head said, "You are bound for my old university, I believe?"

"Uh . . . Oxford?"

"We must hope that it leads you to maturity and more acceptable forms of behavior."

He had not realized she could be so alarming.

"If you ever care to come back to us, you will find things much changed. Not least our theatrical entertainments."

Come back! Would they let him see Nicky here if he came back? Yes. Why not? He'd be a senior.

There was the sound of Lloyd clearing his throat. The gaunt ghost in a tailcoat filled the doorway.

"Excuse me, madam, but the Marston stationmaster is on the phone. The Headmaster is indisposed. A matter of some importance, I understand."

"How curious! Let us hope the trains still run. Good-bye, Mr. Carleton."

"Good-bye."

He was a "Mr." now. That was fine.

They departed, and he hurried out after them into the bright morning. What a term of sunshine it had been! Strangely vivid. Never to be forgotten. He couldn't go to the farmyard via the drive, because his mother or father might already be sitting there, but Nicky had said there was a way out at the end of the other yard. Rushing down the steep steps, he found himself impeded, to his annoyance, by Gower. He was laboring with a tuck box, being assisted, astonishingly enough, by Lucretia, who was in front. As they reached the bottom, she said, "It's blasted heavy. What have you got in it?"

Gower's reply was inaudible. What a fine marital pair they would make, thought Carleton, and he congratulated himself on this grown-up reflection. Cars lined the drive, but he couldn't see the family Rover. He went into the cobbled yard, past the photographic room, thinking. What am I going to say? Does he regard me as being on trial? If so, what will I do? Will I tell him everything? Actions speak louder. Take him in your arms.

Oh my God, to have my arms around him again!

Weirdly silent and deserted, it was. The photographic room was closed. So was the printing room.

What makes it difficult is that he has always been, curiously, a stranger. Why? Is it our ages? Only two years? Or is it Nicky?

Not so deserted. The Honorable Fitzmaurice came out of the

senior Ping-Pong room with a prefect named Scott. They were hand in hand. They looked odd; quiet, self-absorbed, unhappy. They didn't even notice him. It was a surprise to be reminded that there were others parting today. Dozens of couples. Love either temporarily or forever interrupted.

Funny—one is sent to a place selected for no particular reason. It's called "going to school." They think—even people who've gone to school themselves—you learn lessons and depart.

This is not what happens at all.

He had been given only one lesson.

Poor Ashley. It's not fair to have blamed him because he's a man. I'm a man myself now. And I love too. It matters nothing who one loves, as long as one loves. But why should Ashley be so desperate? Yes, he'd been sacked. That was true. That was terrible.

It's also true that Ashley needs to be the boss. Bad luck. So do I. Let him search.

Suiting this reflection neatly, the way out presented itself. There was a green wooden door in the high stone wall. He stepped out and found himself in the sunny lane that led down to the farmyard and the drive. One figure stood there, some ten yards away. A simple vision that would last forever. Nicky against the stone wall, which was bright gray—almost white—in the morning sunshine. In the brown coat and gray flannels that always seemed so clean and new and freshly pressed. Black-haired, sunburned, astonishingly beautiful, and strangely calm and complete. Emerging from the coat cuff, the slim and surprisingly strong hand which had once slipped into his. Even though it was brown you could see the white bone of the fore-finger. Eyes that overwhelmed, whether he wished them to or not. Not just their beauty, but their openness, a giving and needing of love.

A soft snuffling of the pigs could be heard now and then from behind the wall. Otherwise they were surrounded by silence. Just the two of them in the sunshine. Which was all that mattered in the world. This was bliss. The devil with solitude!

But Nicky was saying, "I've only a few minutes. My mother's waiting. It was just to say good-bye . . . though you don't deserve it."

Impossible to believe that this hard, hostile person was the same Nicky who had lain and kissed with him in the summer fields.

"Why, why? What have I done? What do you mean 'Good-bye'? Do you mean you won't see me?"

"Oh, don't be so stupid. It's over. Long ago. It was *you* who said so. . . ."

"No!"

"Now it seems you want to change your mind. I'm to jump whenever you say. . . . Whenever you change your mind. Well, I won't."

"Listen, Nicky . . ."

"Don't say that."

"Why not, you let everybody else call you that? Listen . . . something upset me, for the moment, but I was all wrong . . ."

"I don't know what you're talking about. I've got to go. . . ."

"Wait! I'll explain."

"I don't want to hear. You can't play with people like this. I'll tell you one thing."

"What?"

"You're no Christian."

This extraordinary remark, though it had no meaning for Carleton, hurt more than any other possible, because he knew what it meant to Nicky.

"You should never say that to anyone. *You*, of all people!"

" 'You' is the word for it. You've always been full of yourself. You, you, you. Hamilton Minor agrees. . . ."

"What?!"

They stared coldly at each other.

"I can't believe it! So that's it. But he's your junior by miles."

"You should know about that."

"Nicky . . . Nicky, that's not you. So that's it. You're setting up for next term, are you?"

"It's not like that at all. He's very intelligent."

"Hamilton Minor?! But he wants to be an *accountant!*"

"Why not? You don't understand. We've had talks. He's a Christian. He believes."

"You're crazy."

"He needs someone older to talk to."

"You?"

"Yes."

"And so it goes on."

"For those of us still here," Nicky said, very calmly. "Now I must go. . . ."

"I can't believe this. It's just impossible. I can't believe it's all to be wiped out as if it had never been. All our wonderful time together."

Carleton was trying not to cry. It would be shameful if his junior saw him cry.

"I always told you it would happen. I told you what you'd do."

"But I haven't done it!"

"Yes, you have. You have. You're different already."

"I'm NOT."

"You are. Don't touch me! You are. You don't know it, but you are. You want everything your way. You think you're grown-up. Good luck. Go on. Leave us alone here."

"Do you mean to say you'll never see me—or ever write to me?"

"Yes."

"I couldn't stand it! Listen, did you think I did something wrong? Is that it?"

"I don't know what you mean. You got tired of me. I knew you would. Now you think you can change your mind, just like that. Well, you can't. It's done. You'd only change it again. It's you who did it—not me."

"You don't seem much upset."

"I'd have been ruined if I hadn't expected it."

"I'll never understand."

"Well, that's how it is. I'm going . . ."

"In twenty years I won't understand. I'll still wonder. All my life I'll wonder."

"That's silly; that's the sin of pride. There are things much greater than us."

"But I don't believe in them! I believed in *this*. I'll never forget it, never understand. I'll always wonder."

"Good-bye. Don't come near me!"

"And I'll never have complete trust in anyone again. I'll always be afraid of this. Because I don't understand it. *You* got tired of me—is that it? Say no. Help me. Now."

"I can't. You can only help yourself—with the help of God."

"Oh stop that—stop it. . . . You're pretending, Nicky. You *must* be. I know you feel as I do. But you're stronger. Or else you're weaker and you're afraid to go on with it. I don't know . . . I don't know. . . ."

"Good-bye."

Nicky walked smartly away.

Carleton watched his retreating back with disbelief. It was impossible. It couldn't have happened. The last time he would ever see him. He stood there paralyzed with tears in his eyes. The sunny day was a mockery.

How could he face anyone in this state?

But it had to be done. He went apprehensively down to the drive and back up toward the school. Nicky gone. No one in the world now. More and more cars were arriving. No sign of Nicky. Yes, the Rover was there, outside the Music Building. His father sat placidly at the wheel, with a pipe in his mouth. Parents were marching about, with haughty voices, helping to heave trunks, which were piled beside the drive. "Derek" . . . "John" . . . Christian names one had never heard. He reached the window and said, "Hello. My trunks's across the way."

"Right."

Tall, distinguished, graying, in a brown tweed suit. Very nearly a stranger. He followed his son over the drive, and they lifted the trunk on which Mother had painted "T.P.C." in large black letters, and carried it over to the boot.

His father dusted off his hands and said, "You seem to be taking it badly, old fellow. Sorry to leave?"

"No, no. It's . . . nothing."

They got in the car and his father took an envelope out of the dashboard, saying, "Oh, by the way, your mother thought you might be anxious to see this. It came yesterday."

On the back of the envelope was printed *New Arts Review*.

His heart began to beat faster. He tore it open. His father put his hand on the ignition key. Carleton said, "Wait! Just a minute!" The letter read—

380

DEAR MR. CARLETON,

Thank you for sending us the ms of "Carter and Mc-Cracken," which we are indeed anxious to publish at the earliest possible date. We both considered it a delightful little story. We gather from Eric Ashley's accompanying letter that you are still at school. In which case you show rare promise.

As you may know, unfortunately literary magazines are not gold mines. We wonder if you would be content with a fee of 15 guineas?

Congratulations.

ANGUS DAVIDSON⎫
FRANK SALMON ⎬ JOINT EDITORS

P.S. We particularly liked your ending. It comes off beautifully.

"Gosh! Look."

His father read it in a considered manner, moving his pipe between his teeth.

"That's good work. I didn't know you were going in for writing. Of course, you can't expect these people to come up with much more these days. They've got their printing costs and . . ."

But Carleton wasn't there. Carleton was sitting up somewhere on a bright cloud in the sky.

"Look, could you wait five minutes? I've got to tell Eric Ashley about this. It's all due to him. I've got to tell him. I'll run. I'll be back in a minute."

"Oh, no, write him . . ."

"No, no, I must tell him, and thank him. I'll be back in a second."

Carleton jumped out and closed the door. His father looked resigned again. He felt he was several feet above the ground. He wanted to dance, sing, shout. . . . He was a writer. He wanted to tell them all, though he didn't really see anyone as he dodged between the parents and trunks and ran up the stone steps. Eric was the only person worth seeing. Yes, he was Eric now. They were both men, equals, writers. And out in the adult world. Yes, he had the curious feeling as he ran that this little faded place was already nothing, had diminished; the tight little garden, the lawns, the mulberry tree, all tiny, tiny, past and over.

The Quad—a few square yards of green. The buildings—small and gray. For goodness sake, how had he ever bothered? . . . shrunken . . . and, blast it, old Rowles came out of the Big Schoolroom door, right in his way, and *he* was totally different already. An old, limited, parochial fogey, stuck in this place. Small, stale, frightened of adventure; not understanding anything when people reached eighteen. The same pitiful polished shoes. Content to stick, unable to do anything else. Old and half alive and pathetic and a waste of one's time when the real world began.

"Sorry, I'm in a terrible hurry."

"He didn't need to do it, Carleton! He didn't need to do it!"

Carleton paused for a second, thought He's still on about the Pedant, he must be going off his rocker, said, "Sorry, my father's waiting," and dodged past him round the corner of the schoolroom. But, gosh, hadn't there been tears in those pale blue eyes, and hadn't his voice sounded almost desperate. Why? Why? Was the poor old fellow giving up? End-of-term and no strength to go on with the farce? Never mind, he would work it out later. He was going to work out *all* these things. Know and contain them all. Eric said he had to. He had to have an insight into people as well as be a writer.

Exuberant, deeply happy, he plunged into the new buildings and up the stairs, ready to wave the letter, ready to shout, "Look at this! The story!—It's taken!"

He was about to knock on Eric's door when he saw something pinned there: a small piece of paper and two drawing pins. On it were written in a complete circle the words "The birde has flowne."

Puzzled and disappointed, he tried the handle. The door opened. The rather too familiar room was deserted.

Ah well, he thought, departing, it can't be helped. I'll write to him.

He hurried out of the building and along between the borders. The room had recalled to him the amazing fact that in all this excitement Nicky had passed from mind. That was it. It was over. He was cured. What had Eric said? "Freedom comes when the relationship is over." It was a memory. A nice one— not like Mr. Brownlow. A sweet, gentle, nostalgic one: perhaps he'd see Nicky's name from time to time in the Old Boys' magazine. Meanwhile, he was free. He was walking out into the world, unharmed: it was simply something that was over, and childish. It had left no mark at all. None whatever. Far more important, he was going to write Eric a very special letter of gratitude. He had already begun composing it as he went down the steps and crossed the drive and joined his father in the car.

"Sorry. He wasn't even there."

"Do you know where to find him?"

"No. But if I write they'll send it on."

His father started up the engine and drove slowly out between fathers and mothers, and sons who already belonged to Carleton's past.

DEAR ERIC,
    The most marvelous thing has happened, and it's all due to you. . . .

Down the rippled concrete, between the oak trees, for the last, last time.

DEAR ERIC,
    We've brought it off! . . .

"What was your final average?"

"What?"

"Batting."

"Oh . . . uh . . . fifty-two . . . I think."

"You sound rather casual about it. I presume you'll keep it up at Oxford?"

"Um . . . I suppose so. I don't really know."

Out past the Gate Lodge, onto the main road.

They were humming along in Buckinghamshire, in a new existence.

"Well . . . it's over. What does it feel like, knowing that the basis of your life has been formed?"

"Oh, fine," Carleton replied. But he was scarcely listening. He was thinking about that letter.

"You'll discover it will all stand you in good stead," his father said. "Our boarding-school system is still the best in the world."

383

He didn't hear this. He was trying to get that first sentence correct. The letter must be good. It must be absolutely the best he could do.

After all, he was a writer.